Stern Alan

SO-ACH-616

HENRIK IBSEN

GHOSTS
AN ENEMY OF THE PEOPLE
THE WILD DUCK
HEDDA GABLER

HENRIK IBSEN

Introduction by Benfield Pressey

SECOND EDITION

Holt, Rinehart and Winston, Inc.

NEW YORK · CHICAGO · SAN FRANCISCO · ATLANTA · DALLAS
MONTREAL · TORONTO · LONDON · SYDNEY

CREDITS:

Hedda Gabler was taken from *Hedda Gabler and
Three Other Plays* by Henrik Ibsen, translated by
Michael Meyer. Copyright © 1961 by Michael
Meyer. Reprinted by permission of Doubleday
& Company, Inc.

*Introduction and notes copyright, 1948, © 1970,
by Benfield Pressey
Typography by Stefan Salter
SBN: 03-080805-7
Library of Congress Catalog Card Number: 76-119104
Printed in the United States of America.
01234   68   987654321*

GHOSTS

AN ENEMY OF THE PEOPLE

THE WILD DUCK

HEDDA GABLER

These four plays should be known by every educated man and woman in the Western world because the attitudes and ideas they represent have entered the body of thought and feeling which makes our "culture" and remains there, affecting how we live. Possibly you may not like them, as you may not like the shape of your face, but you had best learn to get along with it and them. And since they are plays and were written to entertain, you probably will like them. Producers, directors, and actors have repeatedly chosen these plays for performance during the last seventy-five years of their existence, and critics and cultural historians have constantly discussed them.

They all appeared in the decade 1880–1890 when Ibsen was between the ages of fifty-three and sixty-two. To later times the decade appears quiet because it was not disturbed by a major war. But it did not seem quiet to those who lived through it, and Ibsen seemed to be a disturber during it, and even more so in the following decades.

He had already established his importance in the drama by the time the earliest of these four plays appeared. Unlike an American dramatist of today, Ibsen wrote his plays to be read and to have the pressure for performance come from readers. He came from a small and unimportant country and wrote in a language not widely known. His living was precarious; he had to time his plays to appear in the bookstores in November so that they would be sold to Christmas bookbuyers, and such sales provided him with the bulk of his income until late in his life. He had begun as a dramatist in verse and continued to write in verse, or verse and prose together, in seven out of his first eleven plays. Then in 1869 he tried his hand at prose realism with *The League of Youth*.

Even a writer more committed to poetry than Ibsen would have found it hard to resist the cultural currents which made bourgeois manners and fashions of living increasingly the favorite objects of social scrutiny. In France, which set the standards for the rest of Europe, such a novelist as Flaubert, and before him Balzac, had converted the reading public's taste toward interest in middle-class people and their problems. Ibsen was not prone to follow literary fashion, but he could not help sharing this interest and responding to it in his creative life.

The League of Youth rather lacks distinction, and Ibsen devoted his energies for the four years after its publication to *Emperor and Galilean*, the epic philosophical play in ten acts. But the change in subject and writing mode signaled in *The League of Youth* became permanent with *Pillars of Society* in 1877. In addition, a kind of topicality first appearing in *The League of Youth* reappeared in *Pillars of Society* and the plays that followed. Ibsen became a reformer.

We are so accustomed to the idea that works of art can be created with the deliberate purpose of changing our values and therefore our ways of life that Ibsen's originality has lost its brilliance. But plays like his had not been written before. He wished to make men new, and in the attempt he made a new drama.

He seemed to ask a new dedication to Truth in society: in politics, in business, in the family. In *A Doll's House* (1879), for instance, the latest play before *Ghosts*, Ibsen asserted what seems commonplace today but what shocked the 1880s; that since a wife has a moral responsibility as serious as her husband's she should have the same freedoms and the same dignity. Out of her demand for freedom and dignity, Nora leaves her husband's doll's house, risking the ostracism which such conduct invited then.

Ibsen's support of the emancipation of women in *A Doll's House* was powerful and sympathetic enough to turn him from a read playwright to a seen one. Within very few years, *A Doll's House* was staged all over Europe and even in America. It aroused controversy, but only a teacup storm compared with the furore over *Ghosts*, the first play in this volume.

In *A Doll's House* appeared Dr. Rank, whose life had been spoiled through inherited weakness. Dr. Rank says, "My poor innocent spine must do penance for my father's wild oats," and "you can trace in every family some such inexorable retribution." Ibsen, the reformer, was not content with showing that wives should be free; he wished to show in *Ghosts* how the family itself, the nucleus of society, might imprison the spirits of both husband and wife and might exact the most terrible penalties from the children. Oswald, in *Ghosts*, is a younger Dr. Rank; Mrs. Alving is an older Nora, who ran away but came back without freedom or dignity; Pastor Manders is the voice of society, the mind that settles all questions by rule.

Venereal disease is really only incidental to the theme of *Ghosts*, though it is hard to imagine how Ibsen could have said what he wanted to say in this play if venereal disease had not existed. But the abuse heaped on the play (for samples see Shaw's *The Quintessense of Ibsenism*, pp. 99–102 of the 1913 edition), the sensationalism that made it the banner play it became over at least two decades for all the groups of rebels and reformers, arose in great measure because in it the disease was contemplated. On the other hand, Ibsen could justly feel that criticism of *Ghosts* misrepresented him. He knew he was, in a sense, an enemy of society as at present constituted, but he was not merely that. He was also an earnest seeker after the good, though not, to be sure, an impeccable one. He was very like Dr. Stockmann, the character he created in his next play, *An Enemy of the People*, the second play in this volume. In Dr. Stockmann's willful assertion of his rightness and in his angry defiance of the majority he mirrors Ibsen's response to the criticism and rejection of *Ghosts*.

For *Ghosts* was almost completely rejected by the theatre. Even in Scandinavia no manager would touch it. It had its world premiere in Chicago by a group of Norwegians acting in their own language in 1882. In 1883 an actor who very much wanted to play Oswald succeeded over heavy opposition in presenting it in Stockholm, but it made its way in the ordinary theatres very slowly. In book form the play was so harshly reviewed that the first printing did not sell out until after thirteen years. Then in the late 1880s the Free Theatre movement, led by Antoine in Paris, quickly followed in Berlin under Brahm and in London under Grein, took *Ghosts* as the play which above all other plays must be seen by audiences of the forward-looking. *An Enemy of the People* naturally followed *Ghosts* into Free Theatre repertories. "Ibsenism," meaning not only the emancipation of women, but also emancipation from familial and societal tyrannies, rallied the young and ardent. But by the time this happened Ibsen had ceased to care about Ibsenism.

Probably Ibsen would have written *An Enemy of the People* much as it appears here even if *Ghosts* had been better received. He had begun writing *An Enemy of the People* even before any work was done on *Ghosts*, and the attacks on majority and "liberal" opinion made by Dr. Stockmann had been privately expressed by Ibsen for years. He laid *An Enemy of the People* aside in order to write *Ghosts* and went back to it afterward with enthusiasm heightened, no doubt, by the dismay and horror with which *Ghosts* was greeted. But *An Enemy of the People* is not satisfactorily accounted for as an artist's scolding reaction to public disapproval. It seems instead a necessary stage in the growth of Ibsen's creative life.

In *An Enemy of the People* Ibsen shows a man giving society a shock and shows also the effect on the shock-giver. Society is even onstage in the fourth act and appears immovable and narrow-minded. It does not gain from the presence in its midst of the scientist who can discover its ills, but the scientist does not gain either. A cheery, hospitable man of good will is changed by society's narrowness and immovability into a violent enemy of the people, ready to "let the whole country perish, let all these people be exterminated" if they do not accept the same "truths" he accepts. Was Ibsen suggesting this punishment for the rejectors of *Ghosts?*

Dr. Stockmann arouses a powerful sympathy early in the play, but it begins to weaken when he seems more eager to establish his superior foresight than the truth of his case. When we equate Ibsen with Dr. Stockmann and *Ghosts* with the case against the Baths, we are led to wonder if the boycott of *Ghosts* was so unreasonable. But even more we are led, if we are sensitive to Ibsen's creative process, to see that he is making Dr. Stockmann into a character, a character with shadows and highlights, not a shining knight possessed of complete truth, or a brain that foresees clearly, but a life among the rest of us with as many faults. Dr. Stockmann goes on responding to the pressures that his society puts on him, but responding more and more wildly. He insists on a confrontation, which he cannot manipulate as he wishes, which in fact boomerangs. His response now becomes brave and high-hearted, and we give him almost the same degree of sympathy as in the beginning, but we know now what kind of man he is and we cannot give him unqualified admiration.

We have been shown a character artistically created. And we may take it that the process of creation has changed Ibsen. Perhaps he came to like Dr. Stockmann and his truths less and less, and even to question truth's value for human beings in all cases. Might a lie make a good life?

The Wild Duck is a much more complicated play than *An Enemy of the People*, and Ibsen enjoyed writing it more. When he sent it to his publishers he said that he had stopped writing about these characters with regret. Certainly he works very differently with the prime movers of the action in *The Wild Duck*, Gregers Werle and Hialmar Ekdal. The first act runs the risk of leaving the audience uninterested. Neither Gregers nor his father arouse us by their quarrel; Hialmar snubs his father, talks with complacency which Gregers does not share. We are left indifferent. But when we move to the Ekdal home and meet Gina and Hedvig, we know for whom we must feel. The two loving women await their disappointing man, Gina by this time inured to him, but Hedvig still full of illusion and hope. A father who promises his daughter dainties from the rich man's table and instead produces only the dinner menu is wryly comic, but he carries the threat of tragedy. A son who thinks his mission in life is to correct wrongs done by his father even when the wronged feel no pain and have in fact based their happiness on those wrongs, threatens tragedy too. The coming together of these two tragedy-bearers, harmless enough separately, makes the play.

But the development is slow. After a second act which shows mainly how happy the Ekdal family is, despite the selfishness and laziness of Hialmar, the dark mania of Gregers goes to work on them. He identifies them with the wild duck, himself with the rescuing dog, an identification which is itself a masterstroke of characterization as well as plot-direction. He manipulates the mind and imagination of Hedvig with extraordinary skill through taking advantage of an accidental similarity in the language they use, another illustration of Ibsen's artistry.

The eleventh edition of *The Encyclopedia Britannica* describes Hialmar Ekdal as "the meanest scoundrel in all drama," but surely he is not that. Even the sentences that induce Hedvig to turn the pistol on herself: "Hedvig, are you willing to renounce that life for me? No, thank you!" are not worse than blindly unimaginative. Hialmar is posing for himself and others, pitying himself without justi- fication, the happiest way to pity oneself. "The meanest scoundrel in all drama" is surely sterner stuff than Hialmar. He has not planned or worked for his easy self-indulgent life; he is even incapable of resenting with vigor wrongs done him; he is so ordinary and so well described that no character in the play seems more real. Gregers' little intrigue, to have the wild duck killed in order to reconcile Hialmar, works marvelously to show the pervertedness of Gregers' imagina- tion, the childish, trusting faith of Hedvig, and, as we should expect it, the callous indifference of Hialmar. For if the

wild duck had been killed, we can be certain that Hialmar
would have felt deprived, not gratified. He has benefited so
much from the real sacrifice of others that a symbolic
sacrifice would seem meaningless to him.

The sacrifice that Hedda Gabler demands—no less than
Eilert Loevborg's life—mocks her as Gregers' demand on
Hedvig mocks him. Hedda wants Loevborg to die only
according to her specifications, as a Dionysiac rebel against
a confining code of behavior, but he leaves life and her only
in confusion. Did he kill himself at all? What was going
on when the mortal bullet entered his body and why at that
spot in his body? Did he love Hedda enough to die for her?
Or did he die with shame for his betrayal of Thea? Only
one thing is clear: that he has left Hedda implicated if all
is known.

Hedda Gabler differs from the other three plays in the
emphasis on love. This may have come from Ibsen's
acquaintance, when he was sixty-one years old, with a
Viennese girl of eighteen, Emilie Bardach. They met at a
summer resort; Emilie tried hard to impress and please
him, and for a time they saw each other frequently and at
length. Ibsen was undoubtedly impressed by her, but he
did not allow the relationship to become too intimate and
eventually he broke it off sharply, just as he was starting to
write *Hedda Gabler*. It has been supposed that she con-
tributed to his conception of Hedda, though she seems to
have recognized herself more in Hilda Wangel of his following play, *The Master Builder*. Traits and attitudes in
Emilie are paralleled in both characters. But it is unlikely
that Ibsen set himself to draw a portrait of Emilie in either.
There seems to be no real parallel between Hedda's feeling
for Eilert and Emilie's for Ibsen. However, Ibsen may have
begun contemplating more intensely sex relationships as
they might exist between certain kinds of characters through
his acquaintance with Emilie.

In *Hedda Gabler* we see Ibsen at last applying his powers wholly to character. He is not lecturing his audience about truth or the usefulness of illusions or any other problem. Hedda, Eilert, Tesman are people created as carefully and completely as a powerful imagination can create them. From the first entrance of Miss Tesman and Bertha with the flowers to Hedda's death, every move, every speech, every light-change, every placement of furniture is designed to make these people vivid. Ibsen's power is felt at its mightiest.

Ibsen is repeatedly called the Father of the Modern Drama, and his influence can be readily seen in all the later drama of the Western world. First, he brought to the theatre a new and higher standard of intelligence; his plays have a richer and deeper thought-content than his predecessors'. Second, he improved technique; his plays move without that artificiality which haunts the drama and makes it more subject to being dated than any other literary form. He gave his characters lives rooted in a developed past, so that what appears in the play arises out of their histories. Technical study of how he accomplished this is always rewarding; no playwright is more masterly. Through this mastery his plays are full of great roles. Since Ibsen the drama has flowered; the contemporary period in Western drama is as rich as the Elizabethan or the Greek, perhaps richer, because Ibsen showed that the theatre need not be dedicated to empty entertainment but could be intellectually respectable. Since Ibsen, criticism acclaims only those modern plays which show his mixture of intensity and thought.

BENFIELD PRESSEY

Hanover, New Hampshire
April 1948, October 1969

LIST OF IBSEN'S PLAYS

(Dated by first appearance, print or performance)

1850 Catiline

1850 The Viking's Barrow

1853 St. John's Night

1855 Lady Inger of Östraat

1856 The Feast at Solhaug

1857 Olaf Liljekrans

1858 The Vikings at Helgeland

1862 Love's Comedy

1863 The Pretenders

1866 Brand

1867 Peer Gynt

1869 The League of Youth

1873 Emperor and Galilean

1877 Pillars of Society

1879 A Doll's House

1881 Ghosts

1882 An Enemy of the People

1884 The Wild Duck

1886 Rosmersholm

1888 The Lady from the Sea

1890 Hedda Gabler

1892 The Master Builder

1894 Little Eyolf

1896 John Gabriel Borkman

1899 When We Dead Awaken

BIOGRAPHICAL NOTE

Henrik Ibsen was born at Skien, Norway, March 20, 1828. When he was eight, his father became bankrupt, and when he was sixteen, he was apprenticed to an apothecary in Grimstad. He began to write poetry at nineteen, and at twenty-one he finished his first play. At twenty-two he left the apothecary and was admitted conditionally to the University of Christiania (Oslo), where he studied and wrote for a year and a half. He had no later formal education. In 1851 he was appointed playwright-producer at the Bergen theatre. He stayed in Bergen five years and there wrote or revised five plays. Then he became director of a theatre at Oslo, which failed after five years. Thereafter Ibsen depended for his livelihood on his pen or on grants

from the university or the state.   While living in Oslo, he
married and had one son.

In 1864 he left Norway, alienated by the intellectual and
moral climate as he judged it, especially by Norway's
refusal to fight on Denmark's side in the Prusso-Danish
War.   He did not return to live in Norway until 1890.   All
of his plays of international reputation were written after
1864.   He lived at various times in Rome, Dresden, and
Munich, and his work became steadily more known.   His
prosperity increased, but his life remained uneventful.   He
wrote twelve plays during the twenty-six years away from
Norway and four after he returned.   In 1900 he suffered a
stroke which left him almost helpless, and in 1906 he died.

BIBLIOGRAPHICAL NOTE

No book dealing solely with Ibsen's whole life is in print
in English, but F. L. Lucas's *The Drama of Ibsen and
Strindberg*(1962) mixes biography and criticism chattily
yet with scholarship for 300 pages on Ibsen.   *Henrik Ibsen:
the Making of a Dramatist, 1828–1864*(1967) by Michael
Meyer, the translator of *Hedda Gabler* in this volume, will be
the definitive biography if it is continued to the life's end.
Volumes V(1961), VI(1960) and VII(1966) of the Oxford
Ibsen, edited by James Walter Macfarlane, give thorough
background material along with translations of the plays.
John Northam's *Ibsen's Dramatic Method*(1953) analyzes the
plays from *A Doll's House* on and teaches admirably how
they should be read.   P. F. D. Tennant's *Ibsen's Dramatic
Technique*(1948) is valuable though occasionally erratic in
the analysis implied by its title.   It is most detailed on
The Wild Duck.   Maurice Valency's *The Flower and the*

Castle(1963) deals with both Ibsen and Strindberg and describes Ibsen's plays as poetic, autobiographical, and visionary rather than realistic. Bernard Shaw's *The Quintessence of Ibsenism*, a famous book (rev. ed. 1913), regards Ibsen as a reformer and polemicist, and Robert Brustein, in *The Theatre of Revolt*(1964), chap. II, emphasizes Ibsen's revolutionary and antiauthoritarian stance. Hermann J. Weigand subjects the plays beginning with *Pillars of Society* to the closest and most detailed examination in *The Modern Ibsen*(1925), but he somewhat overemphasizes their ironic humor.

CONTENTS

GHOSTS

[1881]

CHARACTERS

MRS. HELEN ALVING, *widow of Captain and Chamberlain**
  Alving.
OSWALD ALVING, *her son, an artist.*
MANDERS, *the Pastor of the parish.*
JACOB ENGSTRAND, *a carpenter.*
REGINA ENGSTRAND, *his daughter, in Mrs. Alving's service.*

The action takes place at MRS. ALVING'S *house on one of the larger fjords of western Norway.*

---

* Non-hereditary title conferred by the King upon men of wealth and attainment.

GHOSTS

ACT ONE

A large room looking upon a garden. A door in the left-hand wall, and two in the right.* In the middle of the room, a round table with chairs set about it, and books, magazines, and newspapers upon it. In the foreground on the left, a window, by which is a small sofa with a work-table in front of it. At the back the room opens into a conservatory rather smaller than the room. From the right-hand side of this a door leads to the garden. Through the large panes of glass that form the outer wall of the conservatory, a gloomy fjord landscape can be discerned, half obscured by steady rain.

*[*ENGSTRAND *is standing close up to the garden door. His left leg is slightly deformed, and he wears a boot with a clump of wood under the sole.* REGINA, *with an empty garden-syringe in her hand, is trying to prevent his coming in.]*

REGINA (*below her breath*). What is it you want? Stay where you are. The rain is dripping off you.

ENGSTRAND. God's good rain, my girl.

REGINA. The Devil's own rain, that's what it is!

ENGSTRAND. Lord, how you talk, Regina. (*Takes a few limping steps forward.*) What I wanted to tell you was this——

REGINA. Don't clump about like that, stupid! The young master is lying asleep upstairs.

ENGSTRAND. Asleep still? In the middle of the day?

REGINA. Well, it's no business of yours.

ENGSTRAND. I was out on the spree last night——

---

* Ibsen described all settings from the point of view of the audience, not the actor.

REGINA. I don't doubt it.

ENGSTRAND. Yes, we are poor weak mortals, my girl——

REGINA. We are indeed.

ENGSTRAND. —and the temptations of the world are manifold, you know—but, for all that, here I was at my work at half-past five this morning.

REGINA. Yes, yes, but make yourself scarce now. I am not going to stand here as if I had a *rendezvous* with you.

ENGSTRAND. As if you had a what?

REGINA. I am not going to have any one find you here: so now you know, and you can go.

ENGSTRAND (*coming a few steps nearer*). Not a bit of it! Not before we have had a little chat. This afternoon I shall have finished my job down at the school house, and I shall be off home to town by to-night's boat.

REGINA (*mutters*). Pleasant journey to you!

ENGSTRAND. Thanks, my girl. To-morrow is the opening of the Orphanage, and I expect there will be a fine kick-up here and plenty of good strong drink, don't you know. And no one shall say of Jacob Engstrand that he can't hold off when temptation comes in his way.

REGINA. Oho!

ENGSTRAND. Yes, because there will be a lot of fine folk here to-morrow. Parson Manders is expected from town, too.

REGINA. What is more, he's coming to-day.

ENGSTRAND. There you are! And I'm going to be precious careful he doesn't have anything to say against me, do you see?

REGINA. Oh, that's your game, is it?

ENGSTRAND. What do you mean?

REGINA (*with a significant look at him*). What is it you want to humbug Mr. Manders out of, this time?

ENGSTRAND. Sh! Sh! Are you crazy? Do you suppose *I* would want to humbug Mr. Manders? No, no—. Mr.

Manders has always been too kind a friend for me to do
that. But what I wanted to talk to you about, was my going
back home to-night.

REGINA. The sooner you go, the better I shall be pleased.

ENGSTRAND. Yes, only I want to take you with me,
Regina.

REGINA (*open-mouthed*). You want to take me——? What
did you say?

ENGSTRAND. I want to take you home with me, I said.

REGINA (*contemptuously*). You will never get me home
with you.

ENGSTRAND. Ah, we shall see about that.

REGINA. Yes, you can be quite certain we *shall* see about
that. I, who have been brought up by a lady like Mrs.
Alving?—I, who have been treated almost as if I were her
own child?—do you suppose I am going home with *you?*—
to such a house as yours? Not likely!

ENGSTRAND. What the devil do you mean? Are you
setting yourself up against your father, you hussy?

REGINA (*mutters, without looking at him*). You have often
told me I was none of yours.

ENGSTRAND. Bah!—why do you want to pay any attention to that?

REGINA. Haven't you many and many a time abused me
and called me a——? *Fidonc!*

ENGSTRAND. I'll swear I never used such an ugly word.

REGINA. Oh, it doesn't matter what word you used.

ENGSTRAND. Besides, that was only when I was a bit
fuddled—hm! Temptations are manifold in this world,
Regina.

REGINA. Ugh!

ENGSTRAND. And it was when your mother was in a
nasty temper. I had to find some way of getting my knife
into her, my girl. She was always so precious genteel.

(*Mimicking her*.) "Let go, Jacob! Let me be! Please to remember that I was three years with the Alvings at Rosenvold, and they were people who went to Court!" (*Laughs*.) Bless my soul, she never could forget that Captain Alving got a Court appointment while she was in service here.

REGINA. Poor mother—you worried her into her grave pretty soon.

ENGSTRAND (*shrugging his shoulders*). Of course, of course; I have got to take the blame for everything.

REGINA (*beneath her breath, as she turns away*). Ugh— that leg, too!

ENGSTRAND. What are you saying, my girl?

REGINA. *Pied de mouton.*

ENGSTRAND. Is that English?

REGINA. Yes.

ENGSTRAND. You have had a good education out here, and no mistake; and it may stand you in good stead now, Regina.

REGINA (*after a short silence*). And what was it you wanted me to come to town for?

ENGSTRAND. Need you ask why a father wants his only child? Ain't I a poor lonely widower?

REGINA. Oh, don't come to me with that tale. Why do you want me to go?

ENGSTRAND. Well, I must tell you I am thinking of taking up a new line now.

REGINA (*whistles*). You have tried that so often—but it has always proved a fool's errand.

ENGSTRAND. Ah, but this time you will just see, Regina! Strike me dead if——

REGINA (*stamping her feet*). Stop swearing!

ENGSTRAND. Sh! Sh!—you're quite right, my girl, quite right! What I wanted to say was only this, that I have put by a tidy penny out of what I have made by working at this new Orphanage up here.

REGINA. Have you? All the better for you.

ENGSTRAND. What is there for a man to spend his money on, out here in the country?

REGINA. Well, what then?

ENGSTRAND. Well, you see, I thought of putting the money into something that would pay. I thought of some kind of an eating-house for seafaring folk——

REGINA. Heavens!

ENGSTRAND. Oh, a high-class eating-house, of course,— not a pigsty for common sailors. Damn it, no; it would be a place ships' captains and first mates would come to; really good sort of people, you know.

REGINA. And what should I——?

ENGSTRAND. You would help there. But only to make a show, you know. You wouldn't find it hard work, I can promise you, my girl. You should do exactly as you liked.

REGINA. Oh, yes, quite so!

ENGSTRAND. But we must have some women in the house; that is as clear as daylight. Because in the evening we must make the place a little attractive—some singing and dancing, and that sort of thing. Remember they are sea-folk—wayfarers on the waters of life! (*Coming nearer to her.*) Now don't be a fool and stand in your own way, Regina. What good are you going to do here? Will this education, that your mistress has paid for, be of any use? You are to look after the children in the new Home, I hear. Is that the sort of work for you? Are you so frightfully anxious to go and wear out your health and strength for the sake of these dirty brats?

REGINA. No, if things were to go as I want them to, then——. Well, it may happen; who knows? It may happen!

ENGSTRAND. What may happen?

REGINA. Never you mind. Is it much that you have put by, up here?

ENGSTRAND. Taking it all round, I should say about seven or eight hundred crowns.

REGINA. That's not so bad.

ENGSTRAND. It's enough to make a start with, my girl.

REGINA. Don't you mean to give me any of the money?

ENGSTRAND. No, I'm hanged if I do.

REGINA. Don't you mean to send me as much as a dress-length of stuff, just for once?

ENGSTRAND. Come and live in the town with me and you shall have plenty of dresses.

REGINA. Pooh!—I can get that much for myself, if I have a mind to.

ENGSTRAND. But it's far better to have a father's guiding hand, Regina. Just now I can get a nice house in Little Harbor Street. They don't want much money down for it—and we could make it like a sort of seamen's home, don't you know.

REGINA. But I have no intention of living with you! I have nothing whatever to do with you. So now, be off!

ENGSTRAND. You wouldn't be living with me long, my girl. No such luck—not if you knew how to play your cards. Such a fine wench as you have grown this last year or two——

REGINA. Well——?

ENGSTRAND. It wouldn't be very long before some first mate came along—or perhaps a captain.

REGINA. I don't mean to marry a man of that sort. Sailors have no *savoir-vivre*.

ENGSTRAND. What haven't they got?

REGINA. I know what sailors are, I tell you. They aren't the sort of people to marry.

ENGSTRAND. Well, don't bother about marrying them. You can make it pay just as well. (*More confidentially.*)

That fellow—the Englishman—the one with the yacht—he gave three hundred dollars, he did; and she wasn't a bit prettier than you.

REGINA (*advancing towards him*). Get out!

ENGSTRAND (*stepping back*). Here! here!—you're not going to hit me, I suppose?

REGINA. Yes! If you talk like that of mother, I *will* hit you. Get out, I tell you! (*Pushes him up to the garden door.*) And don't bang the doors. Young Mr. Alving——

ENGSTRAND. Is asleep—I know. It's funny how anxious you are about young Mr. Alving. (*In a lower tone.*) Oho! is it possible that it is *he* that——?

REGINA. Get out, and be quick about it! Your wits are wandering, my good man. No, don't go that way: Mr. Manders is just coming along. Be off down the kitchen stairs.

ENGSTRAND (*moving towards the right*). Yes, yes—all right. But have a bit of a chat with him that's coming along. He's the chap to tell you what a child owes to its father. For I am your father, anyway, you know. I can prove it by the Register.

[*He goes out through the farther door which* REGINA *has opened. She shuts it after him, looks hastily at herself in the mirror, fans herself with her handkerchief and sets her collar straight, then busies herself with the flowers.* MANDERS *enters the conservatory through the garden door. He wears an overcoat, carries an umbrella and has a small travelling-bag slung over his shoulder on a strap.*]

MANDERS. Good morning, Miss Engstrand.

REGINA (*turning round with a look of pleased surprise*). Oh, Mr. Manders, good morning. The boat is in, then?

MANDERS. Just in. (*Comes into the room.*) It is most tiresome, this rain every day.

REGINA (*following him in*). It's a splendid rain for the farmers, Mr. Manders.

MANDERS. Yes, you are quite right. We town-folk think so little about that. [*Begins to take off his overcoat.*]

REGINA. Oh, let me help you. That's it. Why, how wet it is. I will hang it up in the hall. Give me your umbrella, too; I will leave it open, so that it will dry.

[*She goes out with the things by the farther door on the right.* MANDERS *lays his bag and his hat down on a chair.* REGINA *re-enters.*]

MANDERS. Ah, it's very pleasant to get indoors. Well, is everything going on well here?

REGINA. Yes, thanks.

MANDERS. Properly busy, though, I expect, getting ready for to-morrow?

REGINA. Oh, yes, there is plenty to do.

MANDERS. And Mrs. Alving is at home, I hope?

REGINA. Yes, she is. She has just gone upstairs to take the young master his chocolate.

MANDERS. Tell me—I heard down at the pier that Oswald had come back.

REGINA. Yes, he came the day before yesterday. We didn't expect him till to-day.

MANDERS. Strong and well, I hope?

REGINA. Yes, thank you, well enough. But dreadfully tired after his journey. He came straight from Paris without a stop—I mean, he came all the way without breaking his journey. I fancy he is having a sleep now, so we must talk a little bit more quietly, if you don't mind.

MANDERS. All right, we will be very quiet.

REGINA (*while she moves an armchair up to the table*). Please sit down, Mr. Manders, and make yourself at home. (*He sits down; she puts a footstool under his feet.*) There! Is that comfortable?

MANDERS. Thank you, thank you. That is most comfortable. (*Looks at her.*) I'll tell you what, Miss Engstrand, I certainly think you have grown since I saw you last.

REGINA. Do you think so? Mrs. Alving says, too, that I have developed.

MANDERS. Developed? Well, perhaps a little—just suitably.   [*A short pause.*]

REGINA. Shall I tell Mrs. Alving you are here?

MANDERS. Thanks, there is no hurry, my dear child.— Now tell me, Regina my dear, how has your father been getting on here?

REGINA. Thank you, Mr. Manders, he is getting on pretty well.

MANDERS. He came to see me, the last time he was in town.

REGINA. Did he? He is always so glad when he can have a chat with you.

MANDERS. And I suppose you have seen him pretty regularly every day?

REGINA. I? Oh, yes, I do—whenever I have time, that is to say.

MANDERS. Your father has not a very strong character, Miss Engstrand. He sadly needs a guiding hand.

REGINA. Yes, I can quite believe that.

MANDERS. He needs someone with him that he can cling to, someone whose judgment he can rely on. He acknowledged that freely himself, the last time he came up to see me.

REGINA. Yes, he has said something of the same sort to me. But I don't know whether Mrs. Alving could do without me—most of all just now, when we have the new Orphanage to see about. And I should be dreadfully unwilling to leave Mrs. Alving, too; she has always been so good to me.

MANDERS. But a daughter's duty, my good child——. Naturally we should have to get your mistress' consent first.

REGINA. Still I don't know whether it would be quite the thing, at my age, to keep house for a single man.

MANDERS. What!! My dear Miss Engstrand, it is your own father we are speaking of!

REGINA. Yes, I dare say, but still——. Now, if it were in a good house and with a real gentleman——

MANDERS. But, my dear Regina——

REGINA. ——one whom I could feel an affection for, and really feel in the position of a daughter to——

MANDERS. Come, come—my dear good child——

REGINA. I should like very much to live in town. Out here it is terribly lonely; and you know yourself, Mr. Manders, what it is to be alone in the world. And, though I say it, I really am both capable and willing. Don't you know any place that would be suitable for me, Mr. Manders?

MANDERS. I? No, indeed I don't.

REGINA. But, dear Mr. Manders—at any rate don't forget me, in case——

MANDERS (*getting up*). No, I won't forget you, Miss Engstrand.

REGINA. Because, if I——

MANDERS. Perhaps you will be so kind as to let Mrs. Alving know I am here?

REGINA. I will fetch her at once, Mr. Manders.

[*Goes out to the left.* MANDERS *walks up and down the room once or twice, stands for a moment at the farther end of the room with his hands behind his back and looks out into the garden. Then he comes back to the table, takes up a book and looks at the title page, gives a start and looks at some of the others.*]

MANDERS. Hm!—Really!

[MRS. ALVING *comes in by the door on the left. She is followed by* REGINA, *who goes out again at once through the nearer door on the right.*]

MRS. ALVING (*holding out her hand*). I am very glad to see you, Mr. Manders.

MANDERS. How do you do, Mrs. Alving? Here I am, as I promised.

MRS. ALVING. Always punctual!

MANDERS. Indeed, I was hard put to it to get away. What with vestry meetings and committees——

MRS. ALVING. It was all the kinder of you to come in such good time; we can settle our business before dinner. But where is your luggage?

MANDERS (*quickly*). My things are down at the village shop. I am going to sleep there to-night.

MRS. ALVING (*repressing a smile*). Can't I really persuade you to stay the night here this time?

MANDERS. No, no; many thanks all the same; I will put up there, as usual. It is so handy for getting on board the boat again.

MRS. ALVING. Of course you shall do as you please. But it seems to me quite another thing, now we are two old people——

MANDERS. Ha! ha! You will have your joke! And it's natural you should be in high spirits today—first of all there is the great event to-morrow, and also you have got Oswald home.

MRS. ALVING. Yes, am I not a lucky woman? It is more than two years since he was home last, and he has promised to stay the whole winter with me.

MANDERS. Has he, really? That is very nice and filial of him, because there must be many more attractions in his life in Rome or in Paris, I should think.

MRS. ALVING. Yes, but he has his mother here, you see. Bless the dear boy, he has got a corner in his heart for his mother still.

MANDERS. Oh, it would be very sad if absence and preoccupation with such a thing as Art were to dull the natural affections.

MRS. ALVING. It would, indeed. But there is no fear of that with him, I am glad to say. I am quite curious to see if you recognize him again. He will be down directly; he is just lying down for a little on the sofa upstairs. But do sit down, my dear friend.

MANDERS. Thank you. You are sure I am not disturbing you?

MRS. ALVING. Of course not. [*She sits down at the table.*]

MANDERS. Good. Then I will show you——. (*He goes to the chair where his bag is lying and takes a packet of papers from it, then sits down at the opposite side of the table and looks for a clear space to put the papers down.*) Now first of all, here is—(*breaks off*). Tell me, Mrs. Alving, what are these books doing here?

MRS. ALVING. These books? I am reading them.

MANDERS. Do you read this sort of thing?

MRS. ALVING. Certainly I do.

MANDERS. Do you feel any the better or the happier for reading books of this kind?

MRS. ALVING. I think it makes me, as it were, more self-reliant.

MANDERS. That is remarkable. But why?

MRS. ALVING. Well, they give me an explanation or a confirmation of lots of different ideas that have come into my own mind. But what surprises me, Mr. Manders, is that, properly speaking, there is nothing at all new in these books. There is nothing more in them than what most people think and believe. The only thing is that most people either take no account of it or won't admit it to themselves.

MANDERS. But, good heavens, do you seriously think that most people——?

MRS. ALVING. Yes, indeed, I do.

MANDERS. But not here in the country at any rate? Not here amongst people like ourselves?

MRS. ALVING. Yes, amongst people like ourselves too.

MANDERS. Well, really, I must say——!

MRS. ALVING. But what is the particular objection that you have to these books?

MANDERS. What objection? You surely don't suppose that I take any particular interest in such productions?

MRS. ALVING. In fact, you don't know anything about what you are denouncing?

MANDERS. I have read quite enough about these books to disapprove of them.

MRS. ALVING. Yes, but your own opinion——

MANDERS. My dear Mrs. Alving, there are many occasions in life when one has to rely on the opinion of others. That is the way in this world, and it is quite right that it should be so. What would become of society otherwise?

MRS. ALVING. Well, you may be right.

MANDERS. Apart from that, naturally I don't deny that literature of this kind may have a considerable attraction. And I cannot blame you, either, for wishing to make yourself acquainted with the intellectual tendencies which I am told are at work in the wider world in which you have allowed your son to wander for so long. But——

MRS. ALVING. But——?

MANDERS (lowering his voice). But one doesn't talk about it, Mrs. Alving. One certainly is not called upon to account to every one for what one reads or thinks in the privacy of one's own room.

MRS. ALVING. Certainly not. I quite agree with you.

MANDERS. Just think of the consideration you owe to this Orphanage, which you decided to build at a time when your thoughts on such subjects were very different from what they are now—as far as I am able to judge.

MRS. ALVING. Yes, I freely admit that. But it was about the Orphanage——

MANDERS. It was about the Orphanage we were going to talk; quite so. Well—walk warily, dear Mrs. Alving! And now let us turn to the business in hand. (*Opens an envelope and takes out some papers.*) You see these?

MRS. ALVING. The deeds?

MANDERS. Yes, the whole lot—and everything in order. I can tell you it has been no easy matter to get them in time. I had positively to put pressure on the authorities; they are almost painfully conscientious when it is a question of settling property. But here they are at last. (*Turns over the papers.*) Here is the deed of conveyance of that part of the Rosenvold estate known as the Solvik property, together with the buildings newly erected thereon—the school, the masters' houses, and the chapel. And here is the legal sanction for the statutes of the institution. Here, you see— (*reads*) "Statutes for the Captain Alving Orphanage."

MRS. ALVING (*after a long look at the papers*). That seems all in order.

MANDERS. I thought "Captain" was the better title to use, rather than your husband's Court title of "Chamberlain." "Captain" seems less ostentatious.

MRS. ALVING. Yes, yes; just as you think best.

MANDERS. And here is the certificate for the investment of the capital in the bank, the interest being earmarked for the current expenses of the Orphanage.

MRS. ALVING. Many thanks; but I think it will be most convenient if you will kindly take charge of them.

MANDERS. With pleasure. I think it will be best to leave the money in the bank for the present. The interest is not very high, it is true; four per cent at six months' call. Later on, if we can find some good mortgage—of course it must be a first mortgage and on unexceptionable security—we can consider the matter further.

MRS. ALVING. Yes, yes, my dear Mr. Manders, you know best about all that.

MANDERS. I will keep my eye on it, anyway. But there is one thing in connection with it that I have often meant to ask you about.

MRS. ALVING. What is that?

MANDERS. Shall we insure the buildings, or not?

MRS. ALVING. Of course we must insure them.

MANDERS. Ah, but wait a moment, dear lady. Let us look into the matter a little more closely.

MRS. ALVING. Everything of mine is insured—the house and its contents, my livestock—everything.

MANDERS. Naturally. They are your own property. I do exactly the same, of course. But this, you see, is quite a different case. The Orphanage is, so to speak, dedicated to higher uses.

MRS. ALVING. Certainly, but——

MANDERS. As far as I am personally concerned, I can conscientiously say that I don't see the smallest objection to our insuring ourselves against all risks.

MRS. ALVING. That is exactly what I think.

MANDERS. But what about the opinion of the people here-abouts?

MRS. ALVING. Their opinion——?

MANDERS. Is there any considerable body of opinion here—opinion of some account, I mean—that might take exception to it?

MRS. ALVING. What, exactly, do you mean by opinion of some account?

MANDERS. Well, I was thinking particularly of persons of such independent and influential position that one could hardly refuse to attach weight to their opinion.

MRS. ALVING. There are a certain number of such people here, who might perhaps take exception to it if we——

MANDERS. That's just it, you see. In town there are lots

of them. All my fellow-clergymen's congregations, for instance! It would be so extremely easy for them to interpret
it as meaning that neither you nor I had a proper reliance
on Divine protection.

MRS. ALVING. But as far as you are concerned, my dear
friend, you have at all events the consciousness that——

MANDERS. Yes, I know, I know; my own mind is quite
easy about it, it is true. But we should not be able to prevent a wrong and injurious interpretation of our action.
And that sort of thing, moreover, might very easily end in
exercising a hampering influence on the work of the Orphanage.

MRS. ALVING. Oh, well, if that is likely to be the effect of
it——

MANDERS. Nor can I entirely overlook the difficult—indeed, I may say, painful—position I might possibly be
placed in. In the best circles in town the matter of this
Orphanage is attracting a great deal of attention. Indeed
the Orphanage is to some extent built for the benefit of the
town too, and it is to be hoped that it may result in the
lowering of our welfare taxes by a considerable amount.
But as I have been your adviser in the matter and have
taken charge of the business side of it, I should be afraid
that it would be I that spiteful persons would attack first
of all——
that.

MANDERS. Not to mention the attacks that would undoubtedly be made upon me in certain newspapers and re-
views——

MRS. ALVING. Say no more about it, dear Mr. Manders;
that quite decides it.

MANDERS. Then you don't wish it to be insured?

MRS. ALVING. No, we will give up the idea.

MANDERS (*leaning back in his chair*). But suppose, now, that some accident happened—one can never tell—would you be prepared to make good the damage?

MRS. ALVING. No; I tell you quite plainly I would not do so under any circumstances.

MANDERS. Still, you know, Mrs. Alving—after all, it is a serious responsibility that we are taking upon ourselves.

MRS. ALVING. But do you think we can do otherwise?

MANDERS. No, that's just it. We really can't do otherwise. We ought not to expose ourselves to a mistaken judgment; and we have no right to do anything that will scandalize the community.

MRS. ALVING. You ought not to, as a clergyman, at any rate.

MANDERS. And, what is more, I certainly think that we may count upon our enterprise being attended by good fortune—indeed, that it will be under a special protection.

MRS. ALVING. Let us hope so, Mr. Manders.

MANDERS. Then we will leave it alone?

MRS. ALVING. Certainly.

MANDERS. Very good. As you wish. (*Makes a note.*) No insurance, then.

MRS. ALVING. It's a funny thing that you should just have happened to speak about that to-day——

MANDERS. I have often meant to ask you about it——

MRS. ALVING. ——because yesterday we very nearly had a fire up there.

MANDERS. Do you mean it?

MRS. ALVING. Oh, as a matter of fact it was nothing of any consequence. Some shavings in the carpenter's shop caught fire.

MANDERS. Where Engstrand works?

MRS. ALVING. Yes. They say he is often so careless with matches.

MANDERS. He has so many things on his mind, poor fellow—so many anxieties. Heaven be thanked, I am told he is really making an effort to live a blameless life.

MRS. ALVING. Really? Who told you so?

MANDERS. He assured me himself that it is so. He's a good workman, too.

MRS. ALVING. Oh, yes, when he is sober.

MANDERS. Ah, that sad weakness of his! But the pain in his poor leg often drives him to it, he tells me. The last time he was in town, I was really quite touched by him. He came to my house and thanked me so gratefully for getting him work here, where he could have the chance of being with Regina.

MRS. ALVING. He doesn't see very much of her.

MANDERS. But he assured me that he saw her every day.

MRS. ALVING. Oh well, perhaps he does.

MANDERS. He feels so strongly that he needs some one who can keep a hold on him when temptations assail him. That is the most winning thing about Jacob Engstrand; he comes to one like a helpless child and accuses himself and confesses his frailty. The last time he came and had a talk with me——. Suppose now, Mrs. Alving, that it were really a necessity of his existence to have Regina at home with him again——

MRS. ALVING (standing up suddenly). Regina!

MANDERS. ——you ought not to set yourself against him.

MRS. ALVING. Indeed, I set myself very definitely against that. And, besides, you know Regina is to have a post in the Orphanage.

MANDERS. But consider, after all he is her father——

MRS. ALVING. I know best what sort of father he has been to her. No, she shall never go to him with my consent.

MANDERS (getting up). My dear lady, don't judge so

hastily. It is very sad how you misjudge poor Engstrand. One would really think you were afraid——

MRS. ALVING (*more calmly*). That is not the question. I have taken Regina into my charge, and in my charge she remains. (*Listens.*) Hush, dear Mr. Manders, don't say any more about it. (*Her face brightens with pleasure.*) Listen! Oswald is coming downstairs. We will only think about him now.

[OSWALD ALVING, *in a light overcoat, hat in hand and smoking a big meerschaum pipe, comes in by the door on the left.*]

OSWALD (*standing in the doorway*). Oh, I beg your pardon, I thought you were in the office. (*Comes in.*) Good morning, Mr. Manders.

MANDERS (*staring at him*). Well! It's most extraordinary——

MRS. ALVING. Yes, what do you think of him, Mr. Manders?

MANDERS. I—I—no, can it possibly be——?

OSWALD. Yes, it really is the prodigal son, Mr. Manders.

MANDERS. Oh, my dear young friend——

OSWALD. Well, the son come home, then.

MRS. ALVING. Oswald is thinking of the time when you were so opposed to the idea of his being a painter.

MANDERS. We are only fallible, and many steps seem to us hazardous at first, that afterwards—(*grasps his hand*): Welcome, welcome! Really, my dear Oswald—may I still call you Oswald?

OSWALD. What else would you think of calling me?

MANDERS. Thank you. What I mean, my dear Oswald, is that you must not imagine that I have any unqualified disapproval of the artist's life. I admit that there are many who, even in that career, can keep the inner man free from harm.

OSWALD. Let us hope so.

MRS. ALVING (*beaming with pleasure*). I know one who
has kept both the inner and the outer man free from harm.
Just take a look at him, Mr. Manders.

OSWALD (*walks across the room*). Yes, yes, mother dear,
of course.

MANDERS. Undoubtedly—no one can deny it. And I
hear you have begun to make a name for ·yourself. I have
often seen mention of you in the papers—and extremely
favorable mention, too. Although, I must admit, latterly
I have not seen your name so often.

OSWALD (*going towards the conservatory*). I haven't done
so much painting just lately.

MRS. ALVING. An artist must take a rest sometimes, like
other people.

MANDERS. Of course, of course. At those times the artist
is preparing and strengthening himself for a greater effort.

OSWALD. Yes. Mother, will dinner soon be ready?

MRS. ALVING. In half an hour. He has a fine appetite,
thank goodness.

MANDERS. And a liking for tobacco too.

OSWALD. I found father's pipe in the room upstairs, and

——

MANDERS. Ah, that is what it was!

MRS. ALVING. What?

MANDERS. When Oswald came in at that door with the
pipe in his mouth, I thought for the moment it was his father
in the flesh.

OSWALD. Really?

MRS. ALVING. How can you say so? Oswald takes after me.

MANDERS. Yes, but there is an expression about the corners of his mouth—something about the lips—that reminds
me so exactly of Mr. Alving—especially when he smokes.

MRS. ALVING. I don't think so at all. To my mind, Oswald has much more of a clergyman's mouth.

MANDERS.   Well, yes—a good many of my colleagues in the church have a similar expression.

MRS. ALVING.   But put your pipe down, my dear boy. I don't allow any smoking in here.

OSWALD (*puts down his pipe*). All right, I only wanted to try it, because I smoked it once when I was a child.

MRS. ALVING.   You?

OSWALD.   Yes; it was when I was quite a little chap. And I can remember going upstairs to father's room one evening when he was in very good spirits.

MRS. ALVING.   Oh, you can't remember anything about those days.

OSWALD.   Yes, I remember plainly that he took me on his knee and let me smoke his pipe. "Smoke, my boy," he said, "have a good smoke, boy!" And I smoked as hard as I could, until I felt I was turning quite pale, and the perspiration was standing in great drops on my forehead. Then he laughed—such a hearty laugh——

MANDERS.   It was an extremely odd thing to do.

MRS. ALVING.   Dear Mr. Manders, Oswald only dreamt it.

OSWALD.   No indeed, mother, it was no dream. Because —don't you remember—you came into the room and carried me off to the nursery, where I was sick, and I saw that you were crying. Did father often play such tricks?

MANDERS.   In his young days he was full of fun——

OSWALD.   And, for all that, he did so much with his life—so much that was good and useful, I mean—short as his life was.

MANDERS.   Yes, my dear Oswald Alving, you have inherited the name of a man who undoubtedly was both energetic and worthy. Let us hope it will be a spur to your energies——

OSWALD.   It ought to be, certainly.

MANDERS.   In any case it was nice of you to come home for the day that is to honor his memory.

OSWALD. I could do no less for my father.

MRS. ALVING. And to let me keep him so long here—that's the nicest part of what he has done.

MANDERS. Yes, I hear you are going to spend the winter at home.

OSWALD. I am here for an indefinite time, Mr. Manders. —Oh, it's good to be at home again!

MRS. ALVING (*beaming*). Yes, isn't it?

MANDERS (*looking sympathetically at him*). You went out into the world very young, my dear Oswald.

OSWALD. I did. Sometimes I wonder if I wasn't too young.

MRS. ALVING. Not a bit of it. It is the best thing for an active boy, and especially for an only child. It's a pity when they are kept at home with their parents and get spoilt.

MANDERS. That is a very debatable question, Mrs. Alving. A child's own home is, and always must be, his proper place.

OSWALD. There I agree entirely with Mr. Manders.

MANDERS. Take the case of your own son. Oh yes, we can talk about it before him. What has the result been in his case? He is six or seven and twenty, and has never yet had the opportunity of learning what a well-regulated home means.

OSWALD. Excuse me, Mr. Manders, you are quite wrong there.

MANDERS. Indeed? I imagined that your life abroad had practically been spent entirely in artistic circles.

OSWALD. So it has.

MANDERS. And chiefly amongst the younger artists.

OSWALD. Certainly.

MANDERS. But I imagined that those gentry, as a rule, had not the means necessary for family life and the support of a home.

OSWALD. There are a considerable number of them who have not the means to marry, Mr. Manders.

MANDERS. That is exactly my point.

OSWALD. But they can have a home of their own, all the same; a good many of them have. And they are very well-regulated and very comfortable homes, too.

[MRS. ALVING, *who has listened to him attentively, nods assent, but says nothing.*]

MANDERS. Oh, but I am not talking of bachelor establishments. By a home I mean family life—the life a man lives with his wife and children.

OSWALD. Exactly, or with his children and his children's mother.

MANDERS (*starts and clasps his hands*). Good heavens!

OSWALD. What is the matter?

MANDERS. Lives with—with—his children's mother!

OSWALD. Well, would you rather he should repudiate his children's mother?

MANDERS. Then what you are speaking of are those unprincipled conditions known as irregular unions!

OSWALD. I have never noticed anything particularly unprincipled about these people's lives.

MANDERS. But do you mean to say that it is possible for a man of any sort of bringing-up, and a young woman, to reconcile themselves to such a way of living—and to make no secret of it, either?

OSWALD. What else are they to do? A poor artist, and a poor girl—it costs a good deal to get married. What else are they to do?

MANDERS. What are they to do? Well, Mr. Alving, I will tell you what they ought to do. They ought to keep away from each other from the very beginning—that is what they ought to do!

OSWALD. That advice wouldn't have much effect upon hot-blooded young folk who are in love.

MRS. ALVING. No, indeed it wouldn't.

MANDERS (*persistently*). And to think that the authorities tolerate such things! That they are allowed to go on, openly! (*Turns to* MRS. ALVING.) Had I so little reason, then, to be sadly concerned about your son? In circles where open immorality is rampant—where, one may say, it is honored——

OSWALD. Let me tell you this, Mr. Manders. I have been a constant Sunday guest at one or two of these "irregular" households——

MANDERS. On Sunday, too!

OSWALD. Yes, that is the day of leisure. But never have I heard one objectionable word there; still less have I ever seen anything that could be called immoral. No; but do you know when and where I *have* met with immorality in artists' circles?

MANDERS. No, thank heaven, I don't!

OSWALD. Well, then, I shall have the pleasure of telling you. I have met with it when some one or other of your model husbands and fathers have come out there to have a bit of a look round on their own account, and have done the artists the honor of looking them up in their humble quarters. Then we had a chance of learning something, I can tell you. These gentlemen were able to instruct us about places and things that we had never so much as dreamt of.

MANDERS. What? Do you want me to believe that honorable men when they get away from home will——

OSWALD. Have you never, when these same honorable men come home again, heard them deliver themselves on the subject of the prevalence of immorality abroad?

MANDERS. Yes, of course, but——

MRS. ALVING. I have heard them, too.

OSWALD. Well, you can take their word for it, unhesitatingly. Some of them are experts in the matter. (*Put-*

ting his hands to his head.) To think that the glorious freedom of the beautiful life over there should be so besmirched!

MRS. ALVING. You mustn't get too heated, Oswald; you gain nothing by that.

OSWALD. No, you are quite right, mother. Besides, it isn't good for me. It's because I am so infernally tired, you know. I will go out and take a turn before dinner. I beg your pardon, Mr. Manders. It is impossible for you to realize the feeling; but it takes me that way.

[*Goes out by the farther door on the right.*]

MRS. ALVING. My poor boy!

MANDERS. You may well say so. This is what it has brought him to! (MRS. ALVING *looks at him, but does not speak.*) He called himself the prodigal son. It's only too true, alas—only too true! (MRS. ALVING *looks steadily at him.*) And what do you say to all this?

MRS. ALVING. I say that Oswald was right in every single word he said.

MANDERS. Right? Right? To hold such principles as that?

MRS. ALVING. In my loneliness here I have come to just the same opinions as he, Mr. Manders. But I have never presumed to venture upon such topics in conversation. Now there is no need; my boy shall speak for me.

MANDERS. You deserve the deepest pity, Mrs. Alving. It is my duty to say an earnest word to you. It is no longer your business man and adviser, no longer your old friend and your dead husband's old friend, that stands before you now. It is your priest that stands before you, just as he did once at the most critical moment of your life.

MRS. ALVING. And what has mv priest to say to me?

MANDERS. First of all I must stir your memory. The moment is well chosen. To-morrow is the tenth anniversary of your husband's death; to-morrow the memorial to the departed will be unveiled; to-morrow I shall speak to the whole assembly that will be met together. But today I want to speak to you alone.

MRS. ALVING. Very well, Mr. Manders, speak!

MANDERS. Have you forgotten that after barely a year of married life you were standing at the very edge of a precipice?—that you forsook your house and home?—that you ran away from your husband—yes, Mrs. Alving, ran away, ran away—and refused to return to him in spite of his requests and entreaties?

MRS. ALVING. Have you forgotten how unspeakably unhappy I was during that first year?

MANDERS. To crave for happiness in this world is simply to be possessed by a spirit of revolt. What right have we to happiness? No! we must do our duty, Mrs. Alving. And your duty was to cleave to the man you had chosen and to whom you were bound by a sacred bond.

MRS. ALVING. You know quite well what sort of life my husband was living at that time—what excesses he was guilty of.

MANDERS. I know only too well what rumor used to say of him; and I should be the last person to approve of his conduct as a young man, supposing that rumor spoke the truth. But it is not a wife's part to be her husband's judge. You should have considered it your bounden duty humbly to have borne the cross that a higher will had laid upon you. But, instead of that, you rebelliously cast off your cross; you deserted the man whose stumbling footsteps you should have supported; you did what was bound to imperil your good name and reputation, and came very near to imperilling the reputation of others into the bargain.

MRS. ALVING. Of others? Of one other, you mean.

MANDERS. It was the height of imprudence, your seeking refuge with me.

MRS. ALVING. With our priest? With our intimate friend?

MANDERS. All the more on that account. You should thank God that I possessed the necessary strength of mind —that I was able to turn you from your outrageous intention, and that it was vouchsafed to me to succeed in leading you back into the path of duty and back to your lawful husband.

MRS. ALVING. Yes, Mr. Manders, that certainly was your doing.

MANDERS. I was but the humble instrument of a higher power. And is it not true that my having been able to bring you again under the yoke of duty and obedience sowed the seeds of a rich blessing on all the rest of your life? Did things not turn out as I foretold to you? Did not your husband turn from straying in the wrong path as a man should? Did he not, after all, live a life of love and good report with you all his days? Did he not become a benefactor to the neighborhood? Did he not so raise you up to his level, so that by degrees you became his fellow-worker in all his undertakings—and a noble fellow-worker, too, I know, Mrs. Alving; that praise I will give you.—But now I come to the second serious false step in your life.

MRS. ALVING. What do you mean?

MANDERS. Just as once you forsook your duty as a wife, so, since then, you have forsaken your duty as a mother.

MRS. ALVING. Oh——!

MANDERS. You have been overmastered all your life by a disastrous spirit of wilfulness. All your impulses have led you towards what is undisciplined and lawless. You have never been willing to submit to any restraint. Anything in life that has seemed irksome to you, you have thrown aside recklessly and unscrupulously, as if it were a burden that you were free to rid yourself of if you would. It did not please you to be a wife any longer, and so you left your

husband. Your duties as a mother were irksome to you, so
you sent your child away among strangers.

MRS. ALVING. Yes, that is true; I did that.

MANDERS. And that is why you have become a stranger to
him.

MRS. ALVING. No, no, I am not that!

MANDERS. You are; you must be. And what sort of
son is it that you have got back? Think over it seriously,
Mrs. Alving. You erred grievously in your husband's case
—you acknowledge as much, by erecting this memorial to
him. Now you are bound to acknowledge how much you
have erred in your son's case; possibly there may still be
time to reclaim him from the paths of wickedness. Turn
over a new leaf, and set yourself to reform what there may
still be that is capable of reformation in him. Because
(*with uplifted forefinger*) in very truth, Mrs. Alving, you
are a guilty mother!—That is what I have thought it my
duty to say to you.

[*A short silence.*]

MRS. ALVING (*speaking slowly and with self-control*). You
have had your say, Mr. Manders, and to-morrow you will
be making a public speech in memory of my husband. I shall
not speak to-morrow. But now I wish to speak to you for
a little, just as you have been speaking to me.

MANDERS. By all means; no doubt you wish to bring forward some excuses for your behavior——

MRS. ALVING. No. I only want to tell you something.

MANDERS. Well?

MRS. ALVING. In all that you said just now about me and
my husband, and about our life together after you had, as
you put it, led me back into the path of duty—there was
nothing that you knew at first hand. From that moment
you never again set foot in our house—you, who had been
our daily companion before that.

MANDERS. Remember that you and your husband moved out of town immediately afterwards.

MRS. ALVING. Yes, and you never once came out here to see us in my husband's lifetime. It was only the business in connection with the Orphanage that obliged you to come and see me.

MANDERS (*in a low and uncertain voice*). Helen—if that is a reproach, I can only beg you to consider——

MRS. ALVING. ——the respect you owed to your calling? —yes. All the more as I was a wife who had tried to run away from her husband. One can never be too careful to have nothing to do with such reckless women.

MANDERS. My dear—Mrs. Alving, you are exaggerating dreadfully——

MRS. ALVING. Yes, yes,—very well. What I mean is this, that when you condemn my conduct as a wife you have nothing more to go upon than ordinary public opinion.

MANDERS. I admit it. What then?

MRS. ALVING. Well—now, Mr. Manders, now I am going to tell you the truth. I had sworn to myself that you should know it one day—you, and you only!

MANDERS. And what may the truth be?

MRS. ALVING. The truth is this, that my husband died just as great a profligate as he had been all his life.

MANDERS (*feeling for a chair*). What are you saying?

MRS. ALVING. After nineteen years of married life, just as profligate—in his desires at all events— as he was before you married us.

MANDERS. And can you talk of his youthful indiscretions —his irregularities—his excesses, if you like—as a profligate life?

MRS. ALVING. That was what the doctor who attended him called it.

MANDERS. I don't understand what you mean.

MRS. ALVING. It is not necessary you should.

MANDERS. It makes my brain reel. To think that your marriage—all the years of wedded life you spent with your husband—were nothing but a hidden abyss of misery.

MRS. ALVING. That and nothing else. Now you know.

MANDERS. This—this bewilders me. I can't understand it! I can't grasp it! How in the world was it possible——? How could such a state of things remain concealed?

MRS. ALVING. That was just what I had to fight for incessantly, day after day. When Oswald was born, I thought I saw a slight improvement. But it didn't last long. And after that I had to fight doubly hard—fight a desperate fight so that no one should know what sort of man my child's father was. You know quite well what an attractive manner he had; it seemed as if people could believe nothing but good of him. He was one of those men whose mode of life seems to have no effect upon their reputations. But at last, Mr. Manders—you must hear this too—at last something happened more abominable than everything else.

MANDERS. More abominable than what you have told me?

MRS. ALVING. I had borne with it all, though I knew only too well what he indulged in in secret, when he was out of the house. But when it came to the point of the scandal coming within our four walls——

MANDERS. Can you mean it? Here?

MRS. ALVING. Yes, here, in our own home. It was in there (*pointing to the nearer door on the right*) in the dining-room that I got the first hint of it. I had something to do in there and the door was standing ajar. I heard our maid come up from the garden with water for the flowers in the conservatory.

MANDERS. Well——?

MRS. ALVING. Shortly afterwards I heard my husband come in too. I heard him say something to her in a low voice. And then I heard—(*with a short laugh*)—oh, it rings in my ears still, with its mixture of what was heartbreaking and what was so ridiculous—I heard my own servant whisper: "Let me go, Mr. Alving! Let me be!"

MANDERS. What unseemly levity on his part! But surely nothing more than levity, Mrs. Alving, believe me.

MRS. ALVING. I soon knew what to believe. My husband had his will of the girl—and that intimacy had consequences, Mr. Manders.

MANDERS (*as if turned to stone*). And all that in this house! In this house!

MRS. ALVING. I have suffered a good deal in this house. To keep him at home in the evening—and at night—I have had to play the part of boon companion in his secret drinking-bouts in his room up there. I have had to sit there alone with him, have had to hobnob and drink with him, have had to listen to his ribald senseless talk, have had to fight with brute force to get him to bed——

MANDERS (*trembling*). And you were able to endure all this!

MRS. ALVING. I had my little boy, and endured it for his sake. But when the crowning insult came—when my own servant—then I made up my mind that there should be an end of it. I took the upper hand in the house, absolutely—both with him and all the others. I had a weapon to use against him, you see; he didn't dare to speak. It was then that Oswald was sent away. He was about seven then, and was beginning to notice things and ask questions as children will. I could endure all that, my friend. It seemed to me that the child would be poisoned if he breathed the air of this polluted house. That was why I sent him away. And now you understand, too, why he never set foot here as long as his father was alive. No one knows what it meant to me.

MANDERS. You have indeed had a pitiable experience.

MRS. ALVING. I could never have gone through with it, if I had not had my work. Indeed, I can boast that I have worked. All the increase in the value of the property, all the improvements, all the useful arrangements that my husband got the honor and glory of—do you suppose that he troubled himself about any of them? He, who used to lie the whole day on the sofa reading old Official Lists! No, you may as well know that too. It was I that kept him up to the mark when he had his lucid intervals; it was I that had to bear the whole burden of it when he began his excesses again or took to whining about his miserable condition.

MANDERS. And this is the man you are building a memorial to!

MRS. ALVING. There you see the power of an uneasy conscience.

MANDERS. An uneasy conscience? What do you mean?

MRS. ALVING. I had always before me the fear that it was impossible that the truth should not come out and be believed. That is why the Orphanage is to exist, to silence all rumors and clear away all doubt.

MANDERS. You certainly have not fallen short of the mark in that, Mrs. Alving.

MRS. ALVING. I had another very good reason. I did not wish Oswald, my own son, to inherit a penny that belonged to his father.

MANDERS. Then it is with Mr. Alving's property——

MRS. ALVING. Yes. The sums of money that, year after year, I have given towards this Orphanage make up the amount of property—I have reckoned it carefully—which in the old days made Lieutenant Alving a catch.

MANDERS. I understand.

MRS. ALVING. That was my purchase money. I don't wish it to pass into Oswald's hands. My son shall have everything from me, I am determined.

[OSWALD *comes in by the farther door on the right. He has* *left his hat and coat outside.*]

MRS. ALVING. Back again, my own dear boy?

OSWALD. Yes, what can one do outside in this everlasting rain? I hear dinner is nearly ready. That's good!

[REGINA *comes in from the dining-room, carrying a parcel.*]

REGINA. This parcel has come for you, ma'am.

[*Gives it to her.*]

MRS. ALVING (*glancing at* MANDERS). The ode to be sung to-morrow, I expect.

MANDERS. Hm——!

REGINA. And dinner is ready.

MRS. ALVING. Good. We will come in a moment. I will just—(*begins to open the parcel*).

REGINA (*to* OSWALD). Will you drink white or red wine, sir?

OSWALD. Both, Miss Engstrand.

REGINA. *Bien*—very good, Mr. Alving.

[*Goes into the dining-room.*]

OSWALD. I may as well help you to uncork it——

[*Follows her into the dining-room; the door swings ajar after him.*]

MRS. ALVING. Yes, I thought so. Here is the ode, Mr. Manders.

MANDERS (*clasping his hands*). How shall I ever have the courage to-morrow to speak the address that——

MRS. ALVING. Oh, you will get through it.

MANDERS (*in a low voice, fearing to be heard in the dining-room*). Yes, we must raise no suspicions.

MRS. ALVING (*quietly but firmly*). No; and then this long dreadful comedy will be at an end. After to-morrow, I shall feel as if my dead husband had never lived in this house. There will be no one else here then but my boy and his mother.

[*From the dining-room is heard the noise of a chair falling; then* REGINA'S *voice is heard in a loud whisper:* Oswald! Are you mad! Let me go!]

MRS. ALVING (*starting in horror*). Oh——!

[*She stares wildly at the half-open door.* OSWALD *is heard coughing and humming, then the sound of a bottle being uncorked.*]

MANDERS (*in an agitated manner*). What's the matter? What is it, Mrs. Alving?

MRS. ALVING (*hoarsely*). Ghosts. The couple in the conservatory—over again.

MANDERS. What are you saying? Regina——? Is she ——?

MRS. ALVING. Yes. Come. Not a word——!

[*Grips* MANDERS *by the arm and walks unsteadily with him into the dining-room.*]

CURTAIN

A C T   T W O

[*The same scene. The landscape is still obscured by mist.* MANDERS *and* MRS. ALVING *come in from the dining-room.*]

MRS. ALVING (*calls into the dining-room from the doorway*). Aren't you coming in here, Oswald?

OSWALD. No, thanks; I think I will go out for a bit.

MRS. ALVING. Yes, do; the weather is clearing a little. (*She shuts the dining-room door, then goes to the hall door and calls.*) Regina!

REGINA (*from without*). Yes, ma'am?

MRS. ALVING. Go down into the laundry and help with the garlands.

REGINA. Yes, ma'am.

[MRS. ALVING *satisfies herself that she has gone, then shuts the door.*]

MANDERS. I suppose he can't hear us?

MRS. ALVING. Not when the door is shut. Besides, he is going out.

MANDERS. I am still quite bewildered. I don't know how I managed to swallow a mouthful of your excellent dinner.

MRS. ALVING (*walking up and down, and trying to control her agitation*). Nor I. But what are we to do?

MANDERS. Yes, what are we to do? Upon my word I don't know; I am so completely unaccustomed to things of this kind.

MRS. ALVING. I am convinced that nothing serious has happened yet.

MANDERS. Heaven forbid! But it is most unseemly behavior, for all that.

MRS. ALVING. It is nothing more than a foolish jest of Oswald's, you may be sure.

MANDERS. Well, of course, as I said, I am quite inexperienced in such matters; but it certainly seems to me——

MRS. ALVING. Out of the house she shall go—and at once. That part of it is as clear as daylight——

MANDERS. Yes, that is quite clear.

MRS. ALVING. But where is she to go? We should not be justified in——

MANDERS. Where to? Home to her father, of course.

MRS. ALVING. To whom, did you say?

MANDERS. To her——. No, of course Engstrand isn't ——. But, great heavens, Mrs. Alving, how is such a thing possible? You surely may have been mistaken, in spite of everything.

MRS. ALVING. There was no chance of mistake, more's the pity. Joanna was obliged to confess it to me—and my hus-

band couldn't deny it. So there was nothing else to do but
to hush it up.

MANDERS. No, that was the only thing to do.

MRS. ALVING. The girl was sent away at once, and was
given a tolerably liberal sum to hold her tongue. She looked
after the rest herself when she got to town. She renewed
an old acquaintance with the carpenter Engstrand; gave him
a hint, I suppose, of how much money she had got, and told
him some fairy tale about a foreigner who had been here in
his yacht in the summer. So she and Engstrand were married in a great hurry. Why, you married them yourself!

MANDERS. I can't understand it——. I remember clearly
Engstrand's coming to arrange about the marriage. He was
full of contrition, and accused himself bitterly for the light
conduct he and his fiancée had been guilty of.

MRS. ALVING. Of course he had to take the blame on himself.

MANDERS. But the deceitfulness of it! And with me,
too! I positively would not have believed it of Jacob Engstrand. I shall most certainly give him a serious talking
to.—And the immorality of such a marriage! Simply for the
sake of the money——! What sum was it that the girl had?

MRS. ALVING. It was three hundred dollars.

MANDERS. Just think of it—for a paltry three hundred
dollars to let himself be bound in marriage to a fallen woman!

MRS. ALVING. What about myself, then?—I let myself be
bound in marriage to a fallen man.

MANDERS. Heaven forgive you! what are you saying? A
fallen man?

MRS. ALVING. Do you suppose my husband was any
purer, when I went with him to the altar, than Joanna was
when Engstrand agreed to marry her?

MANDERS. The two cases are as different as day from
night——

MRS. ALVING. Not so very different, after all. It is true there was a great difference in the price paid, between a paltry three hundred dollars and a whole fortune.

MANDERS. How can you compare such totally different things? I presume you consulted your own heart—and your relations.

MRS. ALVING (*looking away from him*). I thought you understood where what you call my heart had strayed to at that time.

MANDERS (*in a constrained voice*). If I had understood anything of the kind, I would not have been a daily guest in your husband's house.

MRS. ALVING. Well, at any rate this much is certain, that I didn't consult myself in the matter at all.

MANDERS. Still you consulted those nearest to you, as was only right—your mother, your two aunts.

MRS. ALVING. Yes, that is true. The three of them settled the whole matter for me. It seems incredible to me now, how clearly they made out that it would be sheer folly to reject such an offer. If my mother could only see what all that fine prospect has led to!

MANDERS. No one can be responsible for the result of it. Anyway, there is this to be said, that the match was made in complete conformity with law and order.

MRS. ALVING (*going to the window*). Oh, law and order! I often think it is that that is at the bottom of all the misery in the world.

MANDERS. Mrs. Alving, it is very wicked of you to say that.

MRS. ALVING. That may be so; but I don't attach importance to those obligations and considerations any longer. I cannot! I must struggle for my freedom.

MANDERS. What do you mean?

MRS. ALVING (*tapping on the window panes*). I ought

never to have concealed what sort of life my husband led. But I had not the courage to do otherwise then—for my own sake, either. I was too much of a coward.

MANDERS. A coward?

MRS. ALVING. If others had known anything of what happened, they would have said: "Poor man, it is natural enough that he should go astray when he has a wife that has run away from him."

MANDERS. They would have had a certain amount of justification for saying so.

MRS. ALVING (looking fixedly at him). If I were the woman I ought to be, I would take Oswald into my confidence and say to him: "Listen, my son, your father was a dissolute man"——

MANDERS. Miserable woman——

MRS. ALVING. ——and I would tell him all I have told you, from beginning to end.

MANDERS. I am almost shocked at you, Mrs. Alving.

MRS. ALVING. I know. I know quite well! I am shocked at myself when I think of it. (Comes away from the window.) I am coward enough for that.

MANDERS. Can you call it cowardice that you simply did your duty? Have you forgotten that a child should love and honor his father and mother?

MRS. ALVING. Don't let us talk in such general terms. Suppose we say: "Ought Oswald to love and honor Mr. Alving?"

MANDERS. You are a mother—isn't there a voice in your heart that forbids you to shatter your son's ideals?

MRS. ALVING. And what about the truth?

MANDERS. What about his ideals?

MRS. ALVING. Oh—ideals, ideals! If only I were not such a coward as I am!

MANDERS. Do not spurn ideals, Mrs. Alving—they have

a way of avenging themselves cruelly. Take Oswald's own case, now. He hasn't many ideals, more's the pity. But this much I have seen, that his father is something of an ideal to him.

MRS. ALVING. You are right there.

MANDERS. And his conception of his father is what you inspired and encouraged by your letters.

MRS. ALVING. Yes, I was swayed by duty and consideration for others; that was why I lied to my son, year in and year out. Oh, what a coward—what a coward I have been!

MANDERS. You have built up a happy illusion in your son's mind, Mrs. Alving—and that is a thing you certainly ought not to undervalue.

MRS. ALVING. Ah, who knows if that is such a desirable thing after all! — But anyway I don't intend to put up with any goings on with Regina. I am not going to let him get the poor girl into trouble.

MANDERS. Good heavens, no—that would be a frightful thing!

MRS. ALVING. If only I knew whether he meant it seriously, and whether it would mean happiness for him——

MANDERS. In what way? I don't understand.

MRS. ALVING. But that is impossible; Regina is not equal to it, unfortunately.

MANDERS. I don't understand. What do you mean?

MRS. ALVING. If I were not such a miserable coward, I would say to him: "Marry her, or make any arrangement you like with her—only let there be no deceit in the matter."

MANDERS. Heaven forgive you! Are you actually suggesting anything so abominable, so unheard of, as a marriage between them?

MRS. ALVING. Unheard of, do you call it? Tell me honestly, Mr. Manders, don't you suppose there are plenty of married couples out here in the country that are just as nearly related as they are?

MANDERS. I am sure I don't understand you.

MRS. ALVING. Indeed you do.

MANDERS. I suppose you are thinking of cases where possibly——. It is only too true, unfortunately, that family life is not always as stainless as it should be. But as for the sort of thing you hint at—well, it's impossible to tell, at all events with any certainty. Here, on the other hand— for you, a mother, to be willing to allow your——

MRS. ALVING. But I am not willing to allow it. I would not allow it for anything in the world; that is just what I was saying.

MANDERS. No, because you are a coward, as you put it. But, supposing you were not a coward——! Great heavens —such a revolting union!

MRS. ALVING. Well, for the matter of that, we are all descended from a union of that description, so we are told. And who was responsible for this state of things, Mr. Manders?

MANDERS. I can't discuss such questions with you, Mrs. Alving: you are by no means in the right frame of mind for that. But for you to dare to say that it is cowardly of you——!

MRS. ALVING. I will tell you what I mean by that. I am frightened and timid, because I am obsessed by the presence of ghosts that I never can get rid of.

MANDERS. The presence of what?

MRS. ALVING. Ghosts. When I heard Regina and Oswald in there, it was just like seeing ghosts before my eyes. I am half inclined to think we are all ghosts, Mr. Manders. It is not only what we have inherited from our fathers and mothers that exists again in us, but all sorts of old dead ideas and all kinds of old dead beliefs and things of that kind. They are not actually alive in us; but there they are dormant, all the same, and we can never be rid of them. Whenever I take up a newspaper and read it, I fancy I see ghosts creeping between the lines. There must be ghosts all over the world. They must be as countless as the grains of the sands, it seems to me. And we are so miserably afraid of the light, all of us.

MANDERS. Ah!—there we have the outcome of your reading. Fine fruit it has borne—this abominable, subversive, free-thinking literature!

MRS. ALVING. You are wrong there, my friend. You are the one who made me begin to think; and I owe you my best thanks for it.

MANDERS. I?

MRS. ALVING. Yes, by forcing me to submit to what you called my duty and my obligations, by praising as right and just what my whole soul revolted against, as it would against something abominable. That was what led me to examine your teachings critically. I only wanted to unravel one point in them; but as soon as I had got that unravelled, the whole fabric came to pieces. And then I realized that it was only machine-made.

MANDERS (*softly, and with emotion*). Is that all I accomplished by the hardest struggle of my life?

MRS. ALVING. Call it rather the most ignominious defeat of your life.

MANDERS. It was the greatest victory of my life, Helen; victory over myself.

MRS. ALVING. It was a wrong done to both of us.

MANDERS. A wrong?—wrong for me to entreat you as a wife to go back to your lawful husband, when you came to me half distracted and crying: "Here I am, take me!" Was that a wrong?

MRS. ALVING. I think it was.

MANDERS. We two do not understand one another.

MRS. ALVING. Not now, at all events.

MANDERS. Never—even in my most secret thoughts have I for a moment regarded you as anything but the wife of another.

MRS. ALVING. Do you believe what you say?

MANDERS. Helen——!

MRS. ALVING. One so easily forgets one's own feelings.

MANDERS. Not I. I am the same as I always was.

MRS. ALVING. Yes, yes—don't let us talk any more about the old days. You are buried up to your eyes now in committees and all sorts of business; and I am here, fighting with ghosts both without and within me.

MANDERS. I can at all events help you to get the better of those without you. After all that I have been horrified to hear from you to-day, I cannot conscientiously allow a young defenceless girl to remain in your house.

MRS. ALVING. Don't you think it would be best if we could get her settled?—by some suitable marriage, I mean.

MANDERS. Undoubtedly. I think, in any case, it would have been desirable for her. Regina is at an age now that —well, I don't know much about these things, but—

MRS. ALVING. Regina developed very early.

MANDERS. Yes, didn't she? I fancy I remember thinking she was remarkably well developed, bodily, at the time I prepared her for Confirmation. But, for the time being, she must in any case go home. Under her father's care—no, but of course Engstrand is not——. To think that he, of all men, could so conceal the truth from me!

[A knock is heard at the hall door.]

MRS. ALVING. Who can that be? Come in!

[ENGSTRAND, dressed in his Sunday clothes, appears in the doorway.]

ENGSTRAND. I humbly beg pardon, but——

MANDERS. Aha! Hm!——

MRS. ALVING. Oh, it's you, Engstrand!

ENGSTRAND. There were none of the maids about, so I took the great liberty of knocking.

MRS. ALVING. That's all right. Come in. Do you want to speak to me?

ENGSTRAND (*coming in*). No, thank you very much, ma'am. It was Mr. Manders I wanted to speak to for a moment.

MANDERS (*walking up and down*). Hm!—do you? You want to speak to me, do you?

ENGSTRAND. Yes, sir, I wanted so very much to——

MANDERS (*stopping in front of him*). Well, may I ask what it is you want?

ENGSTRAND. It's this way, Mr. Manders. We are being paid off now. And many thanks to you, Mrs. Alving. And now the work is quite finished, I thought it would be so nice and suitable if all of us, who have worked so honestly together all this time, were to finish up with a few prayers this evening.

MANDERS. Prayers? Up at the Orphanage?

ENGSTRAND. Yes, sir, but if it isn't agreeable to you, then——

MANDERS. Oh, certainly——but—hm!——

ENGSTRAND. I have made a practice of saying a few prayers there myself each evening——

MRS. ALVING. Have you?

ENGSTRAND. Yes, ma'am, now and then—just as a little edification, so to speak. But I am only a poor common man, and haven't rightly the gift, alas—and so I thought that as Mr. Manders happened to be here, perhaps——

MANDERS. Look here, Engstrand. First of all I must ask you a question. Are you in a proper frame of mind for such a thing? Is your conscience free and untroubled?

ENGSTRAND. Heaven have mercy on me a sinner! My conscience isn't worth our speaking about, Mr. Manders.

MANDERS. But it is just what we must speak about. What do you say to my question?

ENGSTRAND. My conscience? Well—it's uneasy sometimes, of course.

MANDERS. Ah, you admit that at all events. Now will you tell me, without any concealment—what is your relationship to Regina?

MRS. ALVING (*hastily*). Mr. Manders!

MANDERS (*calming her*). Leave it to me!

ENGSTRAND. With Regina? Good Lord, how you frightened me! (*Looks at* MRS. ALVING.) There is nothing wrong with Regina, is there?

MANDERS. Let us hope not. What I want to know is, what is your relationship to her? You pass as her father, don't you?

ENGSTRAND (*unsteadily*). Well—hm!—you know, sir, what happened between me and my poor Joanna.

MANDERS. No more distortion of the truth! Your late wife made a full confession to Mrs. Alving, before she left her service.

ENGSTRAND. What!—do you mean to say——? Did she do that after all?

MANDERS. You see it has all come out, Engstrand.

ENGSTRAND. Do you mean to say that she, who gave me her promise and solemn oath——

MANDERS. Did she take an oath?

ENGSTRAND. Well, no—she only gave me her word, but as seriously as a woman could.

MANDERS. And all these years you have been hiding the truth from me—from me, who have had such complete and absolute faith in you.

ENGSTRAND. I am sorry to say I have, sir.

MANDERS. Did I deserve that from you, Engstrand? Haven't I been always ready to help you in word and deed as far as lay in my power? Answer me! Is is not so?

ENGSTRAND. Indeed there's many a time I should have been very badly off without you, sir.

MANDERS. And this is the way you repay me—by causing me to make false entries in the church registers, and afterwards keeping back from me for years the information which you owed both to me and to the truth. Your conduct has been absolutely inexcusable, Engstrand, and from to-day everything is at an end between us.

ENGSTRAND (*with a sigh*). Yes, I can see that's what it means.

MANDERS. Yes, because how can you possibly justify what you did?

ENGSTRAND. Was the poor girl to go and increase her load of shame by talking about it? Just suppose, sir, for a moment that your reverence was in the same predicament as my poor Joanna——

MANDERS. I!

ENGSTRAND. Good Lord, sir, I don't mean the same predicament. I mean, suppose there were something your reverence were ashamed of in the eyes of the world, so to speak. We men oughtn't to judge a poor woman too hardly, Mr. Manders.

MANDERS. But I am not doing so at all. It is you I am blaming.

ENGSTRAND. Will your reverence grant me leave to ask you a small question?

MANDERS. Ask away.

ENGSTRAND. Shouldn't you say it was right for a man to raise up the fallen?

MANDERS. Of course it is.

ENGSTRAND. And isn't a man bound to keep his word of honor?

MANDERS. Certainly he is; but——

ENGSTRAND. At the time when Joanna had her misfortune with this Englishman—or maybe he was an American or a Russian, as they call 'em—well, sir, then she came to town. Poor thing, she had refused me once or twice before; she only had eyes for good-looking men in those days, and I had this crooked leg then. Your reverence will remember how I had ventured up into a dancing-saloon where seafaring men were revelling in drunkenness and intoxication, as they say. And when I tried to exhort them to turn from their evil ways——

MRS. ALVING (*coughs from the window*). Ahem!

MANDERS. I know, Engstrand, I know—the rough brutes threw you downstairs. You have told me about that incident before. The affliction to your leg is a credit to you.

ENGSTRAND. I don't want to claim credit for it, your reverence. But what I wanted to tell you was that she came then and confided in me with tears and gnashing of teeth. I can tell you, sir, it went to my heart to hear her.

MANDERS. Did it, indeed, Engstrand? Well, what then?

ENGSTRAND. Well, then I said to her: "The American is roaming about on the high seas, he is. And you, Joanna," I said, "you have committed a sin and are a fallen woman. But here stands Jacob Engstrand," I said, "on two strong legs"—of course that was only speaking in a kind of metaphor, as it were, your reverence.

MANDERS. I quite understand. Go on.

ENGSTRAND. Well, sir, that was how I rescued her and made her my lawful wife, so that no one should know how recklessly she had carried on with the stranger.

MANDERS. That was all very kindly done. The only

thing I cannot justify was your bringing yourself to accept the money——

ENGSTRAND. Money? I? Not a cent.

MANDERS (*to* MRS. ALVING, *in a questioning tone*). But——

ENGSTRAND. Ah, yes!—wait a bit; I remember now. Joanna did have a trifle of money, you are quite right. But I didn't want to know anything about that. "Fie," I said, "on the mammon of unrighteousness, it's the price of your sin; as for this tainted gold"—or notes, or whatever it was —"we will throw it back in the American's face," I said. But he had gone away and disappeared on the stormy seas, your reverence.

MANDERS. Was that how it was, my good fellow?

ENGSTRAND. It was, sir. So then Joanna and I decided that the money should go towards the child's bringing-up, and that's what became of it; and I can give a faithful account of every single penny of it.

MANDERS. This alters the complexion of the affair very considerably.

ENGSTRAND. That's how it was, your reverence. And I make bold to say that I have been a good father to Regina —as far as was in my power—for I am a poor erring mortal, alas!

MANDERS. There, there, my dear Engstrand——

ENGSTRAND. Yes, I do make bold to say that I brought up the child, and made my poor Joanna a loving and careful husband, as the Bible says we ought. But it never occurred to me to go to your reverence and claim credit for it or boast about it because I had done one good deed in this world. No; when Jacob Engstrand does a thing like that, he holds his tongue about it. Unfortunately it doesn't often happen; I know that only too well. And whenever I do come to see your reverence, I never seem to have anything but trouble and wickedness to talk about. Because, as I said just now—and I say it again—conscience can be very hard on us sometimes.

MANDERS. Give me your hand, Jacob Engstrand.

ENGSTRAND. Oh, sir, I don't like——

MANDERS. No nonsense. (*Grasps his hand.*) That's it!

ENGSTRAND. And may I make bold humbly to beg your reverence's pardon——

MANDERS. You? On the contrary it is for me to beg your pardon——

ENGSTRAND. Oh no, sir.

MANDERS. Yes, certainly it is, and I do it with my whole heart. Forgive me for having so much misjudged you. And I assure you that if I can do anything for you to prove my sincere regret and my goodwill towards you——

ENGSTRAND. Do you mean it, sir?

MANDERS. It would give me the greatest pleasure.

ENGSTRAND. As a matter of fact, sir, you could do it now. I am thinking of using the honest money I have put away out of my wages up here in establishing a sort of Sailors' Home in the town.

MRS. ALVING. You?

ENGSTRAND. Yes, to be a sort of Refuge, as it were. There are such manifold temptations lying in wait for sailor men when they are roaming about on shore. But my idea is that in this house of mine they should have a sort of parental care looking after them.

MANDERS. What do you say to that, Mrs. Alving?

ENGSTRAND. I haven't much to begin such a work with, I know; but Heaven might prosper it, and if I found any helping hand stretched out to me, then——

MANDERS. Quite so; we will talk over the matter further. Your project attracts me enormously. But in the meantime go back to the Orphanage and put everything tidy and light the lights, so that the occasion may seem a little solemn.

And then we will spend a little edifying time together, my dear Engstrand, for now I am sure you are in a suitable frame of mind.

ENGSTRAND. I believe I am, sir, truly. Good-bye, then, Mrs. Alving, and thank you for all your kindness; and take good care of Regina for me. (*Wipes a tear from his eye.*) Poor Joanna's child—it is an extraordinary thing, but she seems to have grown into my life and to hold me by the heartstrings. That's how I feel about it, truly.

[*Bows and goes out.*]

MANDERS. Now then, what do you think of him, Mrs. Alving? That was quite another explanation that he gave us.

MRS. ALVING. It was, indeed.

MANDERS. There, you see how exceedingly careful we ought to be in condemning our fellow-men. But at the same time it gives one genuine pleasure to find that one was mistaken. Don't you think so?

MRS. ALVING. What I think is that you are, and always will remain, a big baby, Mr. Manders.

MANDERS. I?

MRS. ALVING (*laying her hands on his shoulders*). And I think that I should like very much to give you a good hug.

MANDERS (*drawing back hastily*). No, no, good gracious! What an idea!

MRS. ALVING (*with a smile*). Oh, you needn't be afraid of me.

MANDERS (*standing by the table*). You choose such an extravagant way of expressing yourself sometimes. Now I must get these papers together and put them in my bag. (*Does so.*) That's it. And now good-bye, for the present. Keep your eyes open when Oswald comes back. I will come back and see you again presently.

[*He takes his hat and goes out by the hall door.* MRS. AL-VING *sighs, glances out of the window, puts one or two things tidy in the room and turns to go into the dining-room. She stops in the doorway with a stifled cry.*]

MRS. ALVING. Oswald, are you still sitting at table?

OSWALD (*from the dining-room*). I am only finishing my cigar.

MRS. ALVING. I thought you had gone out for a little turn.

OSWALD (*from within the room*). In weather like this? (*A glass is heard clinking.* MRS. ALVING *leaves the door open and sits down with her knitting on the couch by the window.*) Wasn't that Mr. Manders that went out just now?

MRS. ALVING. Yes, he has gone over to the Orphanage.

OSWALD. Oh.

[*The clink of a bottle on a glass is heard again.*]

MRS. ALVING (*with an uneasy expression*). Oswald, dear, you should be careful with that liqueur. It is strong.

OSWALD. It's a good protective against the damp.

MRS. ALVING. Wouldn't you rather come in here?

OSWALD. You know you don't like smoking in there.

MRS. ALVING. You may smoke a cigar in here, certainly.

OSWALD. All right; I will come in, then. Just one drop more. There! (*Comes in, smoking a cigar, and shuts the door after him. A short silence.*) Where has the parson gone?

MRS. ALVING. I told you he had gone over to the Orphanage.

OSWALD. Oh, so you did.

MRS. ALVING. You shouldn't sit so long at table, Oswald.

OSWALD (*holding his cigar behind his back*). But it's so nice and cosy, mother dear. (*Caresses her with one hand.*) Think what it means to me—to have come home, to sit at my mother's own table, in my mother's own room, and to enjoy the charming meals she gives me.

MRS. ALVING. My dear, dear boy!

OSWALD (*a little impatiently, as he walks up and down*

smoking). And what else is there for me to do here? I have no occupation——

MRS. ALVING. No occupation?

OSWALD. Not in this ghastly weather, when there isn't a blink of sunshine all day long. (*Walks up and down the floor.*) Not to be able to work, it's——!

MRS. ALVING. I don't believe you were wise to come home.

OSWALD. Yes, mother; I had to.

MRS. ALVING. Because I would ten times rather give up the happiness of having you with me than that you should——

OSWALD (*standing still by the table*). Tell me, mother— is it really such a great happiness for you to have me at home?

MRS. ALVING. Can you ask?

OSWALD (*crumpling up a newspaper*). I should have thought it would have been pretty much the same to you whether I were here or away.

MRS. ALVING. Have you the heart to say that to your mother, Oswald?

OSWALD. But you have been quite happy living without me so far.

MRS. ALVING. Yes, I have lived without you—that is true.

[*A silence. The dusk falls by degrees.* OSWALD *walks restlessly up and down. He has laid aside his cigar.*]

OSWALD (*stopping beside* MRS. ALVING). Mother, may I sit on the couch beside you?

MRS. ALVING. Of course, my dear boy.

OSWALD (*sitting down*). Now I must tell you something, mother.

MRS. ALVING (*anxiously*). What?

OSWALD (*staring in front of him*). I can't bear it any longer.

MRS. ALVING. Bear what? What do you mean?

OSWALD (*as before*). I couldn't bring myself to write to you about it; and since I have been at home——

MRS. ALVING (*catching him by the arm*). Oswald, what is it?

OSWALD. Both yesterday and to-day I have tried to push my thoughts away from me—to free myself from them. But I can't.

MRS. ALVING (*getting up*). You must speak plainly, Oswald!

OSWALD (*drawing her down to her seat again*). Sit still, and I will try and tell you. I have made a great deal of the fatigue I felt after my journey——

MRS. ALVING. Well, what of that?

OSWALD. But that isn't what is the matter. It is no ordinary fatigue——

MRS. ALVING (*trying to get up*). You are not ill, Oswald!

OSWALD (*pulling her down again*). Sit still, mother. Do take it quietly. I am not exactly ill—not ill in the usual sense. (*Takes his head in his hands.*) Mother, it's my mind that has broken down—gone to pieces—I shall never be able to work any more!

[*Buries his face in his hands and throws himself at her knees in an outburst of sobs.*]

MRS. ALVING (*pale and trembling*). Oswald! Look at me! No, no, it isn't true!

OSWALD (*looking up with a distracted expression*). Never to be able to work any more! Never—never! A living death! Mother, can you imagine anything so horrible?

MRS. ALVING. My poor unhappy boy! How has this terrible thing happened?

OSWALD (*sitting up again*). That is just what I cannot possibly understand. I have never lived recklessly in any sense. You must believe that of me, mother! I have never done that.

MRS. ALVING. I haven't a doubt of it, Oswald.

OSWALD. And yet this comes upon me all the same!—this terrible disaster!

MRS. ALVING. Oh, but it will all come right again, my dear precious boy. It is nothing but overwork. Believe me, that is so.

OSWALD (*dully*). I thought so too, at first; but it isn't so.

MRS. ALVING. Tell me all about it.

OSWALD. Yes, I will.

MRS. ALVING. When did you first feel anything?

OSWALD. It was just after I had been home last time and had got back to Paris. I began to feel the most violent pains in my head—mostly at the back, I think. It was as if a tight band of iron was pressing on me from my neck upwards.

MRS. ALVING. And then?

OSWALD. At first I thought it was nothing but the head-aches I always used to be so much troubled with while I was growing.

MRS. ALVING. Yes, yes——

OSWALD. But it wasn't; I soon saw that. I couldn't work any longer. I would try and start some big new picture; but it seemed as if all my faculties had forsaken me, as if all my strength were paralyzed. I couldn't manage to collect my thoughts; my head seemed to swim—everything went round and round. It was a horrible feeling! At last I sent for a doctor—and from him I learnt the truth.

MRS. ALVING. What do you mean?

OSWALD. He was one of the best doctors there. He made me describe what I felt, and then he began to ask me a whole heap of questions which seemed to me to have nothing to do with the matter. I couldn't see what he was driving at——

MRS. ALVING. Well?

OSWALD. At last he said: "You have had the canker of

disease in you practically from your birth"—the actual word
he used was "*vermoulu*." *

MRS. ALVING (*anxiously*). What did he mean by that?

OSWALD. I couldn't understand, either—and I asked him
for a clearer explanation. And then the old cynic said—
(*clenching his fist.*) Oh!——

MRS. ALVING. What did he say?

OSWALD. He said: "The sins of the fathers are visited on
the children."

MRS. ALVING (*getting up slowly*). The sins of the
fathers——!

OSWALD. I nearly struck him in the face——

MRS. ALVING (*walking across the room*). The sins of the
fathers——!

OSWALD (*smiling sadly*). Yes, just imagine! Naturally
I assured him that what he thought was impossible. But
do you think he paid any heed to me? No, he persisted
in his opinion; and it was only when I got out your letters
and translated to him all the passages that referred to my
father——

MRS. ALVING. Well, and then?

OSWALD. Well, then of course he had to admit that he
was on the wrong tack; and then I learnt the truth—the
incomprehensible truth! I ought to have had nothing to
do with the joyous happy life I had lived with my comrades.
It had been too much for my strength. So it was my own
fault!

MRS. ALVING. No, no, Oswald! Don't believe that!

OSWALD. There was no other explanation of it possible,
he said. That is the most horrible part of it. My whole
life incurably ruined—just because of my own imprudence.
All that I wanted to do in the world—not to dare to think
of it any more—not to be *able* to think of it! Oh! if only

* Literally, "worm-eaten."

I could live my life over again—if only I could undo what I have done!

[*Throws himself on his face on the couch.* MRS. ALVING *wrings her hands and walks up and down silently fighting with herself.*]

OSWALD (*looks up after a while, raising himself on his elbows*). If only it had been something I had inherited—something I could not help. But, instead of that, to have disgracefully, stupidly, thoughtlessly thrown away one's happiness, one's health, everything in the world—one's future, one's life——

MRS. ALVING. No, no, my darling boy; that is impossible! (*Bending over him.*) Things are not so desperate as you think.

OSWALD. Ah, you don't know——. (*Springs up.*) And to think, mother, that I should bring all this sorrow upon you! Many a time I have almost wished and hoped that you really did not care so very much for me.

MRS. ALVING. I, Oswald? My only son! All that I have in the world! The only thing I care about!

OSWALD (*taking hold of her hands and kissing them*). Yes, yes, I know that is so. When I am at home I know that is true. And that is one of the hardest parts of it to me. But now you know all about it; and now we won't talk any more about it today. I can't stand thinking about it long at a time. (*Walks across the room.*) Let me have something to drink, mother!

MRS. ALVING. To drink? What do you want?

OSWALD. Oh, anything you like. I suppose you have got some punch in the house.

MRS. ALVING. Yes, but my dear Oswald——!

OSWALD. Don't tell me I mustn't, mother. Do be nice! I must have something to drown these gnawing thoughts. (*Goes into the conservatory.*) And how—how gloomy it is here! (MRS. ALVING *rings the bell.*) And this incessant rain. It may go on week after week—a whole month. Never a ray of sunshine. I don't remember ever having seen the sun shine once when I have been at home.

MRS. ALVING. Oswald—you are thinking of going away from me!

OSWALD. Hm!—(*sighs deeply.*) I am not thinking about anything. I *can't* think about anything! (*In a low voice.*) I have to let that alone.

REGINA (*coming from the dining-room*). Did you ring, ma'am?

MRS. ALVING. Yes, let us have the lamp in.

REGINA. In a moment, ma'am; it is all ready lit.

[*Goes out.*]

MRS. ALVING (*going up to* OSWALD). Oswald, don't keep anything back from me.

OSWALD. I don't, mother. (*Goes to the table.*) It seems to me I have told you a good lot.

[REGINA *brings the lamp and puts it upon the table.*]

MRS. ALVING. Regina, you might bring us a small bottle of champagne.

REGINA. Yes, ma'am. [*Goes out.*]

OSWALD (*taking hold of his mother's face*). That's right. I knew my mother wouldn't let her son go thirsty.

MRS. ALVING. My poor dear boy, how could I refuse you anything now?

OSWALD (*eagerly*). Is that true, mother? Do you mean it?

MRS. ALVING. Mean what?

OSWALD. That you couldn't deny me anything?

MRS. ALVING. My dear Oswald——

OSWALD. Hush!

[REGINA *brings in a tray with a small bottle of champagne and two glasses, which she puts on the table.*]

REGINA. Shall I open the bottle?

OSWALD. No, thank you, I will do it. [REGINA *goes out.*]

MRS. ALVING (*sitting down at the table*). What did you mean, when you asked if I could refuse you nothing?

OSWALD (*busy opening the bottle*). Let us have a glass first—or two.

[*He draws the cork, fills one glass and is going to fill the other.*]

MRS. ALVING (*holding her hand over the second glass*). No, thanks—not for me.

OSWALD. Oh, well, for me then!

[*He empties his glass, fills it again and empties it; then sits down at the table.*]

MRS. ALVING (*expectantly*). Now, tell me.

OSWALD (*without looking at her*). Tell me this: I thought you and Mr. Manders seemed so strange—so quiet—at dinner.

MRS. ALVING. Did you notice that?

OSWALD. Yes. Ahem! (*After a short pause.*) Tell me— What do you think of Regina?

MRS. ALVING. What do I think of her?

OSWALD. Yes, isn't she splendid?

MRS. ALVING. Dear Oswald, you don't know her as well as I do——

OSWALD. What of that?

MRS. ALVING. Regina was too long at home, unfortunately. I ought to have taken her under my charge sooner.

OSWALD. Yes, but isn't she splendid to look at, mother?
[*Fills his glass.*]

MRS. ALVING. Regina has many serious faults——

OSWALD. Yes, but what of that?   [*Drinks.*]

MRS. ALVING. But I am fond of her, all the same; and I have made myself responsible for her. I wouldn't for the world she should come to any harm.

OSWALD (*jumping up*). Mother, Regina is my only hope of salvation!

MRS. ALVING (*getting up*). What do you mean?

OSWALD. I can't go on bearing all this agony of mind alone.

MRS. ALVING. Haven't you your mother to help you to bear it?

OSWALD. Yes, I thought so; that was why I came home to you. But it is no use; I see that it isn't. I cannot spend my life here.

MRS. ALVING. Oswald!

OSWALD. I must live a different sort of life, mother, so I shall have to go away from you. I don't want you watching it.

MRS. ALVING. My unhappy boy! But, Oswald, as long as you are ill like this——

OSWALD. If it was only a matter of feeling ill, I would stay with you, mother. You are the best friend I have in the world.

MRS. ALVING. Yes, I am that, Oswald, am I not?

OSWALD (*walking restlessly about*). But all this torment —the regret, the remorse—and the deadly fear. Oh—this horrible fear!

MRS. ALVING (*following him*). Fear? Fear of what? What do you mean?

OSWALD. Oh, don't ask me any more about it. I don't know what it is. I can't put it into words. (MRS. ALVING *crosses the room and rings the bell*.) What do you want?

MRS. ALVING. I want my boy to be happy, that's what I want. He mustn't brood over anything. (*To* REGINA, *who has come to the door*.) More champagne—a large bottle.

[REGINA *goes out*.]

OSWALD. Mother!

MRS. ALVING. Do you think we country people don't know how to live?

OSWALD. Isn't she splendid to look at? What a figure! And the picture of health!

MRS. ALVING (*sitting down at the table*). Sit down, Oswald, and let us have a quiet talk.

OSWALD (*sitting down*). You don't know, mother, that I owe Regina a little reparation.

MRS. ALVING. You!

OSWALD. Oh, it was only a little thoughtlessness—call it what you like. Something quite innocent, anyway. The last time I was home——

MRS. ALVING. Yes?

OSWALD. ——she used often to ask me questions about Paris, and I told her one thing and another about the life there. And I remember saying one day: "Wouldn't you like to go there yourself?"

MRS. ALVING. Well?

OSWALD. I saw her blush, and she said: "Yes, I should like to very much." "All right," I said, "I daresay it might be managed"—or something of that sort.

MRS. ALVING. And then?

OSWALD. I naturally had forgotten all about it; but the day before yesterday I happened to ask her if she was glad I was to be so long at home——

MRS. ALVING. Well?

OSWALD. ——and she looked so queerly at me, and asked: "But what is to become of my trip to Paris?"

MRS. ALVING. Her trip!

OSWALD. And then I got it out of her that she had taken the thing seriously, and had been thinking about me all the time, and had set herself to learn French——

MRS. ALVING. So that was why——

OSWALD. Mother—when I saw this fine, splendid, handsome girl standing there in front of me—I had never paid any attention to her before then—but now, when she stood there as if with open arms ready for me to take her to myself——

MRS. ALVING. Oswald!

OSWALD. ——then I realized that my salvation lay in her, for I saw the joy of life in her.

MRS. ALVING (*starting back*). The joy of life——? Is there salvation in that?

REGINA (*coming in from the dining-room with a bottle of champagne*). Excuse me for being so long, but I had to go to the cellar.   [*Puts the bottle down on the table.*]

OSWALD. Bring another glass, too.

REGINA (*looking at him in astonishment*). The mistress's glass is there, sir.

OSWALD. Yes, but fetch one for yourself, Regina. (REGINA *starts, and gives a quick shy glance at* MRS. ALVING.) Well?

REGINA (*in a low and hesitating voice*). Do you wish me to, ma'am?

MRS. ALVING. Fetch the glass, Regina.
                    [REGINA *goes into the dining-room.*]

OSWALD (*looking after her*). Have you noticed how well she walks?—so firmly and confidently!

MRS. ALVING. It cannot be, Oswald.

OSWALD. It is settled. You must see that. It is no use forbidding it. (REGINA *comes in with a glass, which she holds in her hand.*) Sit down, Regina.

                    [REGINA *looks questioningly at* MRS. ALVING.]

MRS. ALVING. Sit down. (REGINA *sits down on a chair near the dining-room door, still holding the glass in her hand.*) Oswald, what was it you were saying about the joy of life?

OSWALD. Ah, mother—the joy of life! You don't know very much about that at home here. I shall never realize it here.

MRS. ALVING. Not even when you are with me?

OSWALD. Never at home. But you can't understand that.

MRS. ALVING. Yes, indeed, I almost think I do understand you—now.

OSWALD. That—and the joy of work. They are really the same thing at bottom. But you don't know anything about that either.

MRS. ALVING. Perhaps you are right. Tell me some more about it, Oswald.

OSWALD. Well, all I mean is that here people are brought up to believe that work is a curse and a punishment for sin, and that life is a state of wretchedness and that the sooner we can get out of it the better.

MRS. ALVING. A vale of tears, yes. And we quite conscientiously make it so.

OSWALD. But the people over there will have none of that. There is no one there who really believes doctrines of that kind any longer. Over there the mere fact of being alive is thought to be a matter for exultant happiness. Mother, have you noticed that everything I have painted has turned upon the joy of life?—always upon the joy of life, unfailingly. Light and sunshine, and a holiday feeling—and people's faces beaming with happiness. That is why I am afraid to stay at home here with you.

MRS. ALVING. Afraid? What are you afraid of here, with me?

OSWALD. I am afraid that all these feelings that are so strong in me would degenerate into something ugly here.

MRS. ALVING (looking steadily at him). Do you think that is what would happen?

OSWALD. I am certain it would. Even if one lived the same life at home here, as over there—it would never really be the same life.

MRS. ALVING (who has listened anxiously to him, gets up with a thoughtful expression and says:) Now I see clearly how it all happened.

OSWALD. What do you see?

MRS. ALVING. I see it now for the first time. And now I can speak.

OSWALD (*getting up*). Mother, I don't understand you.

REGINA (*who has got up also*). Perhaps I had better go.

MRS. ALVING. No, stay here. Now I can speak. Now, my son, you shall know the whole truth. Oswald! Regina!

OSWALD. Hush!—here is the parson——

[MANDERS *comes in by the hall door.*]

MANDERS. Well, my friends, we have been spending an edifying time over there.

OSWALD. So have we.

MANDERS. Engstrand must have help with his Sailors' Home. Regina must go home with him and give him her assistance.

REGINA. No, thank you, Mr. Manders.

MANDERS (*perceiving her for the first time*). What——? you in here?—and with a wineglass in your hand!

REGINA (*putting down the glass hastily*). I beg your pardon——!

OSWALD. Regina is going away with me, Mr. Manders.

MANDERS. Going away! With you!

OSWALD. Yes, as my wife—if she insists on that.

MANDERS. But, good heavens——!

REGINA. It is not my fault, Mr. Manders.

OSWALD. Or else she stays here if I stay.

REGINA (*involuntarily*). Here!

MANDERS. I am amazed at you, Mrs. Alving.

MRS. ALVING. Neither of those things will happen, for now I can speak openly.

MANDERS. But you won't do that! No, no, no!

MRS. ALVING. Yes, I can and I will. And without destroying any one's ideals.

OSWALD. Mother, what is it that is being concealed from me?

REGINA (*listening*). Mrs. Alving! Listen! They are shouting outside. [*Goes into the conservatory and looks out.*]

OSWALD (*going to the window on the left*). What can be the matter? Where does that glare come from?

REGINA (*calls out*). The Orphanage is on fire!

MRS. ALVING (*going to the window*). On fire?

MANDERS. On fire? Impossible. I was there just a moment ago.

OSWALD. Where is my hat? Oh, never mind that. Father's Orphanage——! [*Runs out through the garden door.*]

MRS. ALVING. My shawl, Regina! The whole place is in flames.

MANDERS. How terrible! Mrs. Alving, that fire is a judgment on this house of sin!

MRS. ALVING. Quite so. Come, Regina.

[*She and* REGINA *hurry out.*]

MANDERS (*clasping his hands*). And no insurance!

[*Follows them out.*]

CURTAIN

ACT THREE

The same scene. All the doors are standing open. The lamp is still burning on the table. It is dark outside, except for a faint glimmer of light seen through the windows at the back. [MRS. ALVING, *with a shawl over her head, is standing in the conservatory, looking out.* REGINA, *also wrapped in a shawl, is standing a little behind her.*]

MRS. ALVING. Everything burnt—down to the ground.

REGINA. It is burning still in the basement.

MRS. ALVING. I can't think why Oswald doesn't come back. There is no chance of saving anything.

REGINA. Shall I go and take his hat to him?

MRS. ALVING. Hasn't he even got his hat?

REGINA (*pointing to the hall*). No, there it is, hanging up.

MRS. ALVING. Never mind. He is sure to come back soon. I will go and see what he is doing.

[*Goes out by the garden door.* MANDERS *comes in from the hall.*]

MANDERS. Isn't Mrs. Alving here?

REGINA. She has just this moment gone down into the garden.

MANDERS. I have never spent such a terrible night in my life.

REGINA. Isn't it a shocking misfortune, sir!

MANDERS. Oh, don't speak about it. I scarcely dare to think about it.

REGINA. But how can it have happened?

MANDERS Don't ask me, Miss Engstrand! How should I know? Are you going to suggest too——? Isn't it enough that your father——?

REGINA. What has he done?

MANDERS. He has nearly driven me crazy.

ENGSTRAND (*coming in from the hall*). Mr. Manders——!

MANDERS (*turning round with a start*). Have you even followed me here?

ENGSTRAND. Yes, God help us all——! Great heavens! What a dreadful thing, your reverence!

MANDERS (*walking up and down*). Oh dear, oh dear!

REGINA. What do you mean?

ENGSTRAND. Our little prayer-meeting was the cause of it all, don't you see? (*Aside to* REGINA.) Now we've got the old fool, my girl. (*Aloud.*) And to think it is my fault that Mr. Manders should be the cause of such a thing!

MANDERS. I assure you, Engstrand——

ENGSTRAND. But there was no one else carrying a light there except you, sir.

MANDERS (*standing still*). Yes, so you say. But I have no clear recollection of having had a light in my hand.

ENGSTRAND. But I saw quite distinctly your reverence take a candle and snuff it with your fingers and throw away the burning bit of wick among the shavings.

MANDERS. Did you see that?

ENGSTRAND. Yes, distinctly.

MANDERS. I can't understand it at all. It is never my habit to snuff a candle with my fingers.

ENGSTRAND. Yes, it wasn't like you to do that, sir. But who would have thought it could be such a dangerous thing to do?

MANDERS (*walking restlessly backwards and forwards*). Oh, don't ask me!

ENGSTRAND (*following him about*). And you hadn't insured it either, had you. sir?

MANDERS. No, no, no; you heard me say so.

ENGSTRAND. You hadn't insured it—and then went and set light to the whole place! Good Lord, what bad luck!

MANDERS (*wiping the perspiration from his forehead*). You may well say so, Engstrand.

ENGSTRAND. And that it should happen to a charitable institution that would have been of service both to the town and the country, so to speak! The newspapers won't be very kind to your reverence, I expect.

MANDERS. No, that is just what I am thinking of. It is almost the worst part of the whole thing. The spiteful attacks and accusations—it is horrible to think of!

MRS. ALVING (*coming in from the garden*). I can't get him away from the fire.

MANDERS. Oh, there you are, Mrs. Alving.

MRS. ALVING. You will escape having to make your inaugural address now, at all events, Mr. Manders.

MANDERS. Oh, I would so gladly have——

MRS. ALVING (*in a dull voice*). It is just as well it has happened. This Orphanage would never have come to any good.

MANDERS. Don't you think so?

MRS. ALVING. Do you?

MANDERS. But it is none the less an extraordinary piece of ill luck.

MRS. ALVING. We will discuss it simply as a business matter.—Are you waiting for Mr. Manders, Engstrand?

ENGSTRAND (*at the hall door*). Yes, I am.

MRS. ALVING. Sit down then, while you are waiting.

ENGSTRAND. Thank you, I would rather stand.

MRS. ALVING (*to* MANDERS). I suppose you are going by the boat?

MANDERS. Yes. It goes in about an hour.

MRS. ALVING. Please take all the documents back with you. I don't want to hear another word about the matter. I have something else to think about now——

MANDERS. Mrs. Alving——

MRS. ALVING. Later on I will send you a power of attorney to deal with it exactly as you please.

MANDERS. I shall be most happy to undertake that. I am afraid the original intention of the bequest will have to be entirely altered now.

MRS. ALVING. Of course.

MANDERS. Provisionally, I should suggest this way of disposing of it. Make over the Solvik property to the parish. The land is undoubtedly not without a certain value; it will always be useful for some purpose or another. And as for the interest on the remaining capital that is on deposit in the bank, possibly I might make suitable use of that in support of some undertaking that promises to be of use to the town.

MRS. ALVING. Do exactly as you please. The whole thing is a matter of indifference to me now.

ENGSTRAND. You will think of my Sailors' Home, Mr. Manders?

MANDERS. Yes, certainly, that is a suggestion. But we must consider the matter carefully.

ENGSTRAND (*aside*). Consider!—devil take it! Oh Lord.

MANDERS (*sighing*). And unfortunately I can't tell how much longer I may have anything to do with the matter— whether public opinion may not force me to retire from it altogether. That depends entirely upon the result of the enquiry into the cause of the fire.

MRS. ALVING. What do you say?

MANDERS. And one cannot in any way reckon upon the result beforehand.

ENGSTRAND (*going nearer to him*). Yes, indeed one can, because here stand I, Jacob Engstrand.

MANDERS. Quite so, but——

ENGSTRAND (*lowering his voice*). And Jacob Engstrand isn't the man to desert a worthy benefactor in the hour of need, as the saying is.

MANDERS. Yes, but, my dear fellow—how——?

ENGSTRAND. You might say Jacob Engstrand is an angel of salvation, so to speak, your reverence.

MANDERS. No, no, I couldn't possibly accept that.

ENGSTRAND. That's how it will be, all the same. I know some one who has taken the blame for some one else on his shoulders before now, I do.

MANDERS. Jacob! (*Grasps his hand.*) You are one in a thousand! You shall have assistance in the matter of your Sailors' Home, you may rely upon that.

[ENGSTRAND *tries to thank him, but is prevented by emotion.*]

MANDERS (*hanging his wallet over his shoulder*). Now we must be off. We will travel together.

ENGSTRAND (*by the dining-room door, says aside to* REGINA). Come with me, you hussy! You shall be as cosy as the yolk is an egg!

REGINA (*tossing her head*). *Merci!*

[*She goes out into the hall and brings back* MANDERS' *luggage.*]

MANDERS. Good-bye, Mrs. Alving! And may the spirit of order and of what is lawful speedily enter into this house.

MRS. ALVING. Good-bye, Mr. Manders.

[*She goes into the conservatory, as she sees* OSWALD *coming in by the garden door.*]

ENGSTRAND (*as he and* REGINA *are helping* MANDERS *on with his coat*). Good-bye, my child. And if anything should happen to you, you know where Jacob Engstrand is to be found. (*Lowering his voice.*) Little Harbor Street, ahem ——! (*To* MRS. ALVING *and* OSWALD.) And my house for poor seafaring men shall be called the "Alving Home," it shall. And, if I can carry out my own ideas about it, I shall make bold to hope that it may be worthy of bearing the late Mr. Alving's name.

MANDERS (*at the door*). Ahem—ahem! Come along, my dear Engstrand. Good-bye—good-bye!

[*He and* ENGSTRAND *go out by the hall door.*]

OSWALD (*going to the table*). What house was he speaking about?

MRS. ALVING. I believe it is some sort of Home that he and Mr. Manders want to start.

OSWALD. It will be burnt up just like this one.

MRS. ALVING. What makes you think that?

OSWALD. Everything will be burnt up; nothing will be left that is in memory of my father. Here am I being burnt up, too.   [REGINA *looks at him in alarm.*]

- - -

MRS. ALVING. Oswald! You should not have stayed so long over there, my poor boy.

OSWALD (*sitting down at the table*). I almost believe you are right.

MRS. ALVING. Let me dry your face, Oswald; you are all wet. [*Wipes his face with her handkerchief.*]

OSWALD (*looking straight before him, with no expression in his eyes*). Thank you, mother.

MRS. ALVING. And aren't you tired, Oswald? Don't you want to go to sleep?

OSWALD (*uneasily*). No, no—not to sleep! I never sleep; I only pretend to. (*Gloomily.*) That will come soon enough.

MRS. ALVING (*looking at him anxiously*). Anyhow, you are really ill, my darling boy.

REGINA (*intently*). Is Mr. Alving ill?

OSWALD (*impatiently*). And do shut all the doors! This deadly fear——

MRS. ALVING. Shut the doors, Regina. (REGINA *shuts the doors and remains standing by the hall door.* MRS. ALVING *takes off her shawl;* REGINA *does the same.* MRS. ALVING *draws up a chair near to* OSWALD'S *and sits down beside him.*) That's it! Now I will sit beside you——

OSWALD. Yes, do. And Regina must stay in here too. Regina must always be near me. You must give me a helping hand, you know, Regina. Won't you do that?

REGINA. I don't understand——

MRS. ALVING. A helping hand?

OSWALD. Yes—when there is need for it.

MRS. ALVING. Oswald, have you not your mother to give you a helping hand?

OSWALD. You? (*Smiles.*) No, mother, you will never give me the kind of helping hand I mean. (*Laughs grimly.*) You? Ha, ha! (*Looks gravely at her.*) After all, you have the best right. (*Impetuously.*) Why don't you call me by

my Christian name, Regina? Why don't you say Oswald?

REGINA (*in a low voice*). I did not think Mrs. Alving
would like it.

MRS. ALVING. It will not be long before you have the
right to do it. Sit down here now beside us, too. (REGINA
sits down quietly and hesitatingly at the other side of the table.)
And now, my poor tortured boy, I am going to take the
burden off your mind——

OSWALD. You, mother?

MRS. ALVING. ——all that you call remorse and regret and
self-reproach.

OSWALD. And you think you can do that?

MRS. ALVING. Yes, now I can, Oswald. A little while
ago you were talking about the joy of life, and what you said
seemed to shed a new light upon everything in my whole life.

OSWALD (*shaking his head*). I don't in the least understand what you mean.

MRS. ALVING. You should have known your father in his
young days in the army. He was full of the joy of life, I
can tell you.

OSWALD. Yes, I know.

MRS. ALVING. It gave me a holiday feeling only to look at
him, full of irrepressible energy and exuberant spirits.

OSWALD. What then?

MRS. ALVING. Well, then this boy, full of the joy of life
—for he was just like a boy, then—had to make his home
in a second-rate town which had none of the joy of life to
offer him, but only dissipations. He had to come out here
and live an aimless life; he had only an official post. He
had no work worth devoting his whole mind to; he had nothing more than official routine to attend to. He had not
a single companion capable of appreciating what the joy of
life meant; nothing but idlers and tipplers——

OSWALD. Mother——!

MRS. ALVING. And so the inevitable happened!

OSWALD. What was the inevitable?

MRS. ALVING. You said yourself this evening what would happen in your case if you stayed at home.

OSWALD. Do you mean by that, that father——?

MRS. ALVING. Your poor father never found any outlet for the overmastering joy of life that was in him. And I brought no holiday spirit into his home, either.

OSWALD. You didn't, either?

MRS. ALVING. I had been taught about duty, and the sort of thing that I believed in so long here. Everything seemed to turn upon duty—my duty, or his duty—and I am afraid I made your poor father's home unbearable to him, Oswald.

OSWALD. Why did you never say anything about it to me in your letters?

MRS. ALVING. I never looked at it as a thing I could speak of to you, who were his son.

OSWALD. What way did you look at it, then?

MRS. ALVING. I only saw the one fact, that your father was a lost man before ever you were born.

OSWALD (*in a choking voice*). Ah——!

[*He gets up and goes to the window.*]

MRS. ALVING. And then I had the one thought in my mind, day and night, that Regina in fact had as good a right in this house—as my own boy had.

OSWALD (*turns round suddenly*). Regina——?

REGINA (*gets up and asks in choking tones*). I——?

MRS. ALVING. Yes, now you both know it.

OSWALD. Regina!

REGINA (*to herself*). So mother was one of that sort.

MRS. ALVING. Your mother had many good qualities, Regina.

REGINA. Yes, but she was one of that sort too, all the

same. I have even thought so myself, sometimes, but——.
Then, if you please, Mrs. Alving, may I have permission to
leave at once?

MRS. ALVING. Do you really wish to, Regina?

REGINA. Yes, indeed, I certainly wish to.

MRS. ALVING. Of course you shall do as you like, but——

OSWALD (*going to* REGINA). Leave now? This is your
home.

REGINA. *Merci*, Mr. Alving—oh, of course I may say
Oswald now, but that is not the way I thought it would become allowable.

MRS. ALVING. Regina, I have not been open with you——

REGINA. No, I can't say you have! If I had known
Oswald was ill——. And now that there can never be anything serious between us——. No, I really can't stay here
in the country and wear myself out looking after invalids.

OSWALD. Not even for the sake of one who has so near a
claim on you? .

REGINA. No, indeed I can't. A poor girl must make
some use of her youth; otherwise she may easily find herself
out in the cold before she knows where she is. And I have
got the joy of life in me, too, Mrs. Alving!

MRS. ALVING. Yes, unfortunately; but don't throw yourself away, Regina.

REGINA. Oh, what's going to happen will happen. If
Oswald takes after his father, it is just as likely I take after
my mother, I expect.——May I ask, Mrs. Alving, whether
Mr. Manders knows this about me?

MRS. ALVING. Mr. Manders knows everything.

REGINA (*putting on her shawl*). Oh, well then, the best
thing I can do is to get away by the boat as soon as I can.
Mr. Manders is such a nice gentleman to deal with; and
it certainly seems to me that I have just as much right to
some of that money as he—as that horrid carpenter.

MRS. ALVING. You are quite welcome to it, Regina.

REGINA (*looking at her fixedly*). You might as well have brought me up like a gentleman's daughter; it would have been more suitable. (*Tosses her head.*) Oh, well—never mind! (*With a bitter glance at the unopened bottle.*) I daresay some day I shall be drinking champagne with gentlefolk, after all.

MRS. ALVING. If ever you need a home, Regina, come to me.

REGINA. No, thank you, Mrs. Alving. Mr. Manders takes an interest in me, I know. And if things should go very badly with me, I know one house at any rate where I shall feel at home.

MRS. ALVING. Where is that?

REGINA. In the "Alving Home."

MRS. ALVING. Regina—I can see quite well—you are going to your ruin!

REGINA. Pooh!—*adieu*.

[*She bows to them and goes out through the hall.*]

OSWALD (*standing by the window and looking out*). Has she gone?

MRS. ALVING. Yes.

OSWALD (*muttering to himself*). I think it's all wrong.

MRS. ALVING (*going up to him from behind and putting her hands on his shoulders*). Oswald, my dear boy—has it been a great shock to you?

OSWALD (*turning his face towards her*). All this about father, do you mean?

MRS. ALVING. Yes, about your unhappy father. I am so afraid it may have been too much for you.

OSWALD. What makes you think that? Naturally it has taken me entirely by surprise; but, after all I don't know that it matters much to me.

MRS. ALVING (*drawing back her hands*). Doesn't matter? —that your father's life was such a terrible failure?

OSWALD. Of course I can feel sympathy for him, just as I would for anyone else, but——

MRS. ALVING. No more than that! For your own father!

OSWALD (*impatiently*). Father—father! I never knew anything of my father. I don't remember anything else about him except that he once made me sick.

MRS. ALVING. It is dreadful to think of!—But surely a child should feel some affection for his father, whatever happens!

OSWALD. When the child has nothing to thank his father for? When he has never known him? Do you really cling to that antiquated superstition—you, who are so broad-minded in other things?

MRS. ALVING. You call it nothing but a superstition!

OSWALD. Yes, and you can see that for yourself quite well, mother. It is one of those beliefs that are put into circulation in the world, and——

MRS. ALVING. Ghosts of beliefs!

OSWALD (*walking across the room*). Yes, you might call them ghosts.

MRS. ALVING (*with an outburst of feeling*). Oswald—then you don't love me either.

OSWALD. You I know, at any rate——

MRS. ALVING. You know me, yes; but is that all?

OSWALD. And I know how fond you are of me, and I ought to be grateful to you for that. Besides, you can be so tremendously useful to me, now that I am ill.

MRS. ALVING. Yes, can't I, Oswald? I could almost bless your illness, as it has driven you home to me. For I see quite well that you are not my very own yet; you must be won.

OSWALD (*impatiently*). Yes, yes, yes; all that is just a way of talking. You must remember I am a sick man, mother. I can't concern myself much with anyone else; I have enough to do, thinking about myself.

MRS. ALVING (*gently*). I will be very good and patient.

OSWALD. And cheerful too, mother!

MRS. ALVING. Yes, my dear boy, you are quite right. (*Goes up to him.*) Now have I taken away all your remorse and self-reproach?

OSWALD. Yes, you have done that. But who will take away the fear?

MRS. ALVING. The fear?

OSWALD (*crossing the room*). Regina would have done it for one kind word.

MRS. ALVING. I don't understand you. What fear do you mean—and what has Regina to do with it?

OSWALD. Is it very late, mother?

MRS. ALVING. It is early morning. (*Looks out through the conservatory windows.*) The dawn is breaking already on the heights. And the sky is clear, Oswald. In a little while you will see the sun.

OSWALD. I am glad of that. After all, there may be many things yet for me to be glad of and to live for——

MRS. ALVING. I should hope so!

OSWALD. Even if I am not able to work——

MRS. ALVING. You will soon find you are able to work again now, my dear boy. You have no longer all those painful depressing thoughts to brood over.

OSWALD. No, it is a good thing that you have been able to rid me of those fancies. If only, now, I could overcome this one thing——. (*Sits down on the couch.*) Let us have a little chat, mother.

MRS. ALVING. Yes, let us.

[*Pushes an armchair near to the couch and sits down beside him.*]

OSWALD. The sun is rising—and you know all about it; so I don't feel the fear any longer.

MRS. ALVING. I know all about what?

OSWALD (*without listening to her*). Mother, didn't you say

this evening there was nothing in the world you would not do for me if I asked you?

MRS. ALVING. Yes, certainly I said so.

OSWALD. And will you be as good as your word, mother?

MRS. ALVING. You may rely upon that, my own dear boy. I have nothing else to live for, but you.

OSWALD. Yes, yes; well, listen to me, mother. You are very strong-minded, I know. I want you to sit quite quiet when you hear what I am going to tell you.

MRS. ALVING. But what is this dreadful thing——?

OSWALD. You mustn't scream. Do you hear? Will you promise me that? We are going to sit and talk it over quite quietly. Will you promise me that, mother?

MRS. ALVING. Yes, yes, I promise—only tell me what it is.

OSWALD. Well, then, you must know that this fatigue of mine—and my not being able to think about my work—all that is not really the illness itself——

MRS. ALVING. What is the illness itself?

OSWALD. What I am suffering from is hereditary; it—(*touches his forehead, and speaks very quietly*)—it lies here.

MRS. ALVING (*almost speechless*). Oswald! No—no!

OSWALD. Don't scream; I can't stand it. Yes, I tell you, it lies here, waiting. And any time, any moment, it may break out.

MRS. ALVING. How horrible——!

OSWALD. Do keep quiet. That is the state I am in——

MRS. ALVING (*springing up*). It isn't true, Oswald! It is impossible! It can't be that!

OSWALD. I had one attack while I was abroad. It passed off quickly. But when I learnt the condition I had been in, then this dreadful haunting fear took possession of me.

MRS. ALVING. That was the fear, then——

OSWALD. Yes, it is so indescribably horrible, you know. If only it had been an ordinary mortal disease——. I am not so much afraid of dying, though, of course, I should like to live as long as I can.

MRS. ALVING. Yes, yes, Oswald, you must!

OSWALD. But this is so appallingly horrible. To become like a helpless child again—to have to be fed, to have to be ——. Oh, it's unspeakable!

MRS. ALVING. My child has his mother to tend him.

OSWALD (*jumping up*). No, never; that is just what I won't endure! I dare not think what it would mean to linger on like that for years—to get old and grey like that. And you might die before I did. (*Sits down in* MRS. ALVING'S *chair.*) Because it doesn't necessarily have a fatal end quickly, the doctor said. He called it a kind of softening of the brain—or something of that sort. (*Smiles mournfully.*) I think that expression sounds so nice. It always makes me think of cherry-colored velvet curtains—something that is soft to stroke.

MRS. ALVING (*with a scream*). Oswald!

OSWALD (*jumps up and walks about the room*). And now you have taken Regina from me! If I had only had her! She would have given me a helping hand, I know.

MRS. ALVING (*going up to him*). What do you mean, my darling boy? Is there any help in the world I would not be willing to give you?

OSWALD. When I had recovered from the attack I had abroad, the doctor told me that when it recurred—and it will recur—there would be no more hope.

MRS. ALVING. And he was heartless enough to——

OSWALD. I insisted on knowing. I told him I had arrangements to make——. (*Smiles cunningly.*) And so I had. (*Takes a small box from his inner breast-pocket.*) Mother, do you see this?

MRS. ALVING. What is it?

OSWALD. Morphia powders.

MRS. ALVING (*looking at him in terror*). Oswald—my boy!

OSWALD. I have twelve of them saved up——

MRS. ALVING (*snatching at it*). Give me the box, Oswald!

OSWALD. Not yet, mother.   [*Puts it back in his pocket.*]

MRS. ALVING. I shall never get over this!

OSWALD. You must. If I had had Regina here now, I would have told her quietly how things stand with me—and asked her to give me this last helping hand. She would have helped me, I am certain.

MRS. ALVING. Never!

OSWALD. If this horrible thing had come upon me and she had seen me lying helpless, like a baby, past help, past saving, past hope—with no chance of recovering——

MRS. ALVING. Never in the world would Regina have done it.

OSWALD. Regina would have done it. Regina was so splendidly light-hearted. And she would very soon have tired of looking after an invalid like me.

MRS. ALVING. Then thank heaven Regina is not here!

OSWALD. Well, now you have got to give me that helping hand, mother.

MRS. ALVING (*with a loud scream*). I!

OSWALD. Who has a better right than you?

MRS. ALVING. I? Your mother!

OSWALD. Just for that reason.

MRS. ALVING. I, who gave you your life!

OSWALD. I never asked you for life. And what kind of life was it that you gave me? I don't want it! You shall take it back!

MRS. ALVING. Help! Help!   [*Runs into the hall.*]

OSWALD (*following her*). Don't leave me! Where are you going?

MRS. ALVING (*in the hall*). To fetch the doctor to you, Oswald! Let me out!

oswald (*going into the hall*). You shan't go out. And no one shall come in.   [*Turns the key in the lock.*]

mrs. alving (*coming in again*). Oswald! Oswald!—my child!

oswald (*following her*). Have you a mother's heart— and can bear to see me suffering this unspeakable terror?

mrs. alving (*controlling herself, after a moment's silence*). There is my hand on it.

oswald. Will you——?

mrs. alving. If it becomes necessary. But it shan't become necessary. No, no—it is impossible it should!

oswald. Let us hope so. And let us live together as long as we can. Thank you, mother.

[*He sits down in the armchair, which* mrs. alving *had moved beside the couch. Day is breaking; the lamp is still burning on the table.*]

mrs. alving (*coming cautiously nearer*). Do you feel calmer now?

oswald. Yes.

mrs. alving (*bending over him*). It has only been a dreadful fancy of yours, Oswald. Nothing but fancy. All this upset has been bad for you. But now you will get some rest, at home with your own mother, my darling boy. You shall have everything you want, just as you did when you were a little child.—There, now. The attack is over. You see how easily it passed off! I knew it would.—And look, Oswald, what a lovely day we are going to have? Brilliant sunshine. Now you will be able to see your home properly.

[*She goes to the table and puts out the lamp. It is sunrise. The glaciers and peaks in the distance are seen bathed in bright morning light.*]

oswald (*who has been sitting motionless in the armchair, with his back to the scene outside, suddenly says:*) Mother, give me the sun.

MRS. ALVING (*standing at the table, and looking at him in amazement*). What do you say?

OSWALD (*repeats in a dull, toneless voice*). The sun—the sun.

MRS. ALVING (*going up to him*). Oswald, what is the matter with you? (OSWALD *seems to shrink up in the chair; all his muscles relax; his face loses its expression, and his eyes stare stupidly.* MRS. ALVING *is trembling with terror.*) What is it? (*Screams.*) Oswald! What is the matter with you? (*Throws herself on her knees beside him and shakes him.*) Oswald! Oswald! Look at me! Don't you know me?

OSWALD (*in an expressionless voice, as before*). The sun—the sun.

MRS. ALVING (*jumps up despairingly, beats her head with her hands, and screams*). I can't bear it! (*Whispers as though paralyzed with fear.*) I can't bear it! Never! (*Suddenly.*) Where has he got it? (*Passes her hand quickly over his coat.*) Here! (*Draws back a little way and cries:*) No, no, no!—Yes!—no, no!

[*She stands a few steps from him, her hands thrust into her hair, and stares at him in speechless terror.*]

OSWALD (*sitting motionless, as before*). The sun—the sun.

CURTAIN

AN ENEMY OF THE PEOPLE

[*1882*]

CHARACTERS

DR. THOMAS STOCKMANN, *Medical Officer of the Municipal Baths.*

MRS. STOCKMANN, *his wife.*

PETRA, *their daughter, a teacher.*

EJLIF
MORTEN } *their sons (aged 13 and 10 respectively).*

PETER STOCKMANN, *the Doctor's elder brother; Mayor of the Town and Chief Constable, Chairman of the Baths' Committee, etc., etc.*

MORTEN KIIL, *owner of a tannery* (MRS. STOCKMANN'S *foster father*).

HOVSTAD, *editor of the "People's Messenger."*

BILLING, *sub-editor.*

CAPTAIN HORSTER.

ASLAKSEN, *a printer.*

MEN *of various conditions and occupations, some few women, and a troop of schoolboys—the audience at a public meeting.*

The action takes place in a coast town in southern Norway.

AN ENEMY OF THE PEOPLE

ACT ONE

DR. STOCKMANN'S *sitting-room. It is evening. The room is plainly but neatly appointed and furnished. In the right-hand* wall are two doors; the farther leads out to the hall, the nearer to the doctor's study. In the left-hand wall, opposite the door leading to the hall, is a door leading to the other rooms occupied by the family. In the middle of the same wall stands the stove, and, further forward, a couch with a looking-glass hanging over it and an oval table in front of it. On the table, a lighted lamp, with a lampshade. At the back of the room, an open door leads to the dining-room.* [BILLING *is seen sitting at the dining table, on which a lamp is burning. He has a napkin tucked under his chin, and* MRS. STOCKMANN *is standing by the table handing him a large plate-full of roast beef. The other places at the table are empty, and the table somewhat in disorder, a meal having evidently recently been finished.*]

MRS. STOCKMANN. You see, if you come an hour late, Mr. Billing, you have to put up with cold meat.

BILLING (*as he eats*). It is uncommonly good, thank you— remarkably good.

MRS. STOCKMANN. My husband makes such a point of having his meals punctually, you know——

BILLING. That doesn't affect me a bit. Indeed, I almost think I enjoy a meal all the better when I can sit down and eat all by myself and undisturbed.

MRS. STOCKMANN. Oh well, as long as you are enjoying

* Ibsen described all settings from the point of view of the audience, not the actor.

it——. (*Turns to the hall door, listening.*) I expect that is Mr. Hovstad coming too.

BILLING. Very likely.

[PETER STOCKMANN *comes in. He wears an overcoat and his official hat, and carries a stick.*]

PETER STOCKMANN. Good evening, Katherine.

MRS. STOCKMANN (*coming forward into the sitting-room*). Ah, good evening—is it you? How good of you to come up and see us!

PETER STOCKMANN. I happened to be passing, and so— (*looks into the dining-room.*) But you have company with you, I see.

MRS. STOCKMANN (*a little embarrassed*). Oh, no—it was quite by chance he came in. (*Hurriedly.*) Won't you come in and have something, too?

PETER STOCKMANN. I! No, thank you. Good gracious —hot meat at night! Not with my digestion.

MRS. STOCKMANN. Oh, but just once in a way——

PETER STOCKMANN. No, no, my dear lady; I stick to my tea and bread and butter. It is much more wholesome in the long run—and a little more economical, too.

MRS. STOCKMANN (*smiling*). Now you mustn't think that Thomas and I are spendthrifts.

PETER STOCKMANN. Not you, my dear; I would never think that of you. (*Points to the* DOCTOR'S *study.*) Is he not at home?

MRS. STOCKMANN. No, he went out for a little turn after supper—he and the boys.

PETER STOCKMANN. I doubt if that is a wise thing to do. (*Listens.*) I fancy I hear him coming now.

MRS. STOCKMANN. No, I don't think it is he. (*A knock is heard at the door.*) Come in! (HOVSTAD *comes in from the hall.*) Oh, it is you, Mr. Hovstad!

HOVSTAD. Yes, I hope you will forgive me, but I was delayed at the printer's. Good evening, Mr. Mayor.

PETER STOCKMANN (*bowing a little distantly*). Good evening. You have come on business, no doubt.

HOVSTAD. Partly. It's about an article for the paper.

PETER STOCKMANN. So I imagined. I hear my brother has become a prolific contributor to the "People's Messenger."

HOVSTAD. Yes, he is good enough to write in the "People's Messenger" when he has any home truths to tell.

MRS. STOCKMANN (*to* HOVSTAD). But won't you——?
[*Points to the dining-room.*]

PETER STOCKMANN. Quite so, quite so. I don't blame him in the least, as a writer, for addressing himself to the quarters where he will find the readiest sympathy. And, besides that, I personally have no reason to bear any ill will to your paper, Mr. Hovstad.

HOVSTAD. I quite agree with you.

PETER STOCKMANN. Taking one thing with another, there is an excellent spirit of toleration in the town—an admirable municipal spirit. And it all springs from the fact of our having a great common interest to unite us—an interest that is in an equally high degree the concern of every right-minded citizen——

HOVSTAD. The Baths, yes.

PETER STOCKMANN. Exactly—our fine, new, handsome Baths. Mark my words, Mr. Hovstad—the Baths will become the focus of our municipal life! Not a doubt of it!

MRS. STOCKMANN. That is just what Thomas says.

PETER STOCKMANN. Think how extraordinarily the place has developed within the last year or two! Money has been flowing in, and there is some life and some business doing in the town. Houses and landed property are rising in value every day.

HOVSTAD. And unemployment is diminishing.

PETER STOCKMANN. Yes, that is another thing. The burden of welfare taxes has been lightened, to the great relief of the propertied classes; and that relief will be even greater if only we get a really good summer this year, and lots of visitors—plenty of invalids, who will make the Baths talked about.

HOVSTAD. And there is a good prospect of that, I hear.

PETER STOCKMANN. It looks very promising. Enquiries about apartments and that sort of thing are reaching us every day.

HOVSTAD. Well, the doctor's article will come in very suitably.

PETER STOCKMANN. Has he been writing something just lately?

HOVSTAD. This is something he wrote in the winter, a recommendation of the Baths—an account of the excellent sanitary conditions here. But I held the article over, temporarily.

PETER STOCKMANN. Ah,—some little difficulty about it, I suppose?

HOVSTAD. No, not at all; I thought it would be better to wait till the spring, because it is just at this time that people begin to think seriously about their summer quarters.

PETER STOCKMANN. Quite right; you were perfectly right, Mr. Hovstad.

MRS. STOCKMANN. Yes, Thomas is really indefatigable when it is a question of the Baths.

PETER STOCKMANN. Well—remember, he is the Medical Officer to the Baths.

HOVSTAD. Yes, and what is more, they owe their existence to him.

PETER STOCKMANN. To him? Indeed! It is true I have heard from time to time that some people are of that opinion. At the same time I must say I imagined that I took a modest part in the enterprise.

MRS. STOCKMANN. Yes, that is what Thomas is always saying.

HOVSTAD. But who denies it, Mr. Stockmann? You set the thing going and made a practical concern of it; we all know that. I only meant that the idea of it came first from the doctor.

PETER STOCKMANN. Oh, ideas—yes! My brother has had plenty of them in his time—unfortunately. But when it is a question of putting an idea into practical shape, you have to apply to a man of different mettle, Mr. Hovstad. And I certainly should have thought that in this house at least——

MRS. STOCKMANN. My dear Peter——

HOVSTAD. How can you think that——?

MRS. STOCKMANN. Won't you go in and have something, Mr. Hovstad? My husband is sure to be back directly.

HOVSTAD. Thank you, perhaps just a morsel.

[*Goes into the dining-room.*]

PETER STOCKMANN (*lowering his voice a little*). It is a curious thing that these farmers' sons never seem to lose their want of tact.

MRS. STOCKMANN. Surely it is not worth bothering about! Cannot you and Thomas share the credit as brothers?

PETER STOCKMANN. I should have thought so; but apparently some people are not satisfied with a share.

MRS. STOCKMANN. What nonsense! You and Thomas get on so capitally together. (*Listens.*) There he is at last, I think. [*Goes out and opens the door leading to the hall.*]

DR. STOCKMANN (*laughing and talking outside*). Look here —here is another guest for you, Katherine. Isn't that jolly? Come in, Captain Horster; hang your coat up on this peg. Ah, you don't wear an overcoat. Just think, Katherine; I met him in the street and could hardly persuade him to come up! (CAPTAIN HORSTER *comes into the room and greets* MRS. STOCKMANN. *He is followed by* DR. STOCKMANN.) Come along in, boys. They are ravenously hungry again, you know. Come along, Captain Horster; you must have a slice of beef.

[*Pushes* HORSTER *into the dining-room.* EJLIF *and* MORTEN *go in after them.*]

MRS. STOCKMANN. But, Thomas, don't you see——?

DR. STOCKMANN (*turning in the doorway*). Oh, is it you, Peter? (*Shakes hands with him.*) Now that is very delightful.

PETER STOCKMANN. Unfortunately I must go in a moment——

DR. STOCKMANN. Rubbish! There is some toddy just coming in. You haven't forgotten the toddy, Katherine?

MRS. STOCKMANN. Of course not; the water is boiling now. [*Goes into the dining-room.*]

PETER STOCKMANN. Toddy too!

DR. STOCKMANN. Yes, sit down and we will have it comfortably.

PETER STOCKMANN. Thanks, I never care about an evening's drinking.

DR. STOCKMANN. But this isn't an evening's drinking.

PETER STOCKMANN. It seems to me——. (*Looks towards the dining-room.*) It is extraordinary how they can put away all that food.

DR. STOCKMANN (*rubbing his hands*). Yes, isn't it splendid to see young people eat? They have always got an appetite, you know! That's as it should be. Lots of food—to build up their strength! They are the people who are going to stir up the fermenting forces of the future, Peter.

PETER STOCKMANN. May I ask what they will find here to "stir up," as you put it?

DR. STOCKMANN. Ah, you must ask the young people that—when the time comes. We shan't be able to see it, of course. That stands to reason—two old fogies, like us——

PETER STOCKMANN.   Really, really! I must say that is an extremely odd expression to——

DR. STOCKMANN.   Oh, you mustn't take me too literally, Peter. I am so heartily happy and contented, you know. I think it is such an extraordinary piece of good fortune to be in the middle of all this growing, germinating life. It is a splendid time to live in! It is as if a whole new world were being created around one.

PETER STOCKMANN.   Do you really think so?

DR. STOCKMANN.   Ah, naturally you can't appreciate it as keenly as I. You have lived all your life in these surroundings, and your impressions have got blunted. But I, who have been buried all these years in my little corner up north, almost without ever seeing a stranger who might bring new ideas with him—well, in my case it has just the same effect as if I had been transported into the middle of a crowded city.

PETER STOCKMANN.   Oh, a city——!

DR. STOCKMANN.   I know, I know; it is all cramped enough here, compared with many other places. But there is life here—there is promise—there are innumerable things to work for and fight for; and that is the main thing. (*Calls.*) Katherine, hasn't the postman been here?

MRS. STOCKMANN (*from the dining-room*).   No.

DR. STOCKMANN.   And then to be comfortably off, Peter! That is something one learns to value, when one has been on the brink of starvation, as we have.

PETER STOCKMANN.   Oh, surely——

DR. STOCKMANN.   Indeed I can assure you we have often been very hard put to it, up there. And now to be able to live like a lord! Today, for instance, we had roast beef for dinner—and, what is more, for supper too. Won't you come and have a little bit? Or let me show it to you, at any rate? Come here——

PETER STOCKMANN.   No, no—not for worlds!

DR. STOCKMANN. Well, but just come here then. Do you see, we have got a table-cover?

PETER STOCKMANN. Yes, I noticed it.

DR. STOCKMANN. And we have got a lamp-shade too. Do you see? All out of Katherine's savings! It makes the room so cosy. Don't you think so? Just stand here for a moment—no, no, not there—just here, that's it! Look now, when you get the light on it altogether—I really think it looks very nice, doesn't it?

PETER STOCKMANN. Oh, if you can afford luxuries of this kind——

DR. STOCKMANN. Yes, I can afford it now. Katherine tells me I earn almost as much as we spend.

PETER STOCKMANN. Almost—yes!

DR. STOCKMANN. But a scientific man must live in a little bit of style. I am quite sure an ordinary civil servant spends more in a year than I do.

PETER STOCKMANN. I daresay. A civil servant—a man in a well-paid position——

DR. STOCKMANN. Well, any ordinary merchant, then! A man in that position spends two or three times as much as——

PETER STOCKMANN. It just depends on circumstances.

DR. STOCKMANN. At all events I assure you I don't waste money unprofitably. But I can't find it in my heart to deny myself the pleasure of entertaining my friends. I need that sort of thing, you know. I have lived for so long shut out of it all that it is a necessity of life to me to mix with young, eager, ambitious men, men of liberal and active minds; and that describes every one of those fellows who are enjoying their supper in there. I wish you knew more of Hovstad——

PETER STOCKMANN. By the way, Hovstad was telling me he was going to print another article of yours.

DR. STOCKMANN. An article of mine?

PETER STOCKMANN. Yes, about the Baths. An article you wrote in the winter.

DR. STOCKMANN. Oh, that one! No, I don't intend that to appear just for the present.

PETER STOCKMANN. Why not? It seems to me that this would be the most opportune moment.

DR. STOCKMANN. Yes, very likely—under normal conditions. [*Crosses the room.*]

PETER STOCKMANN (*following him with his eyes*). Is there anything abnormal about the present conditions?

DR. STOCKMANN (*standing still*). To tell you the truth, Peter, I can't say just at this moment—at all events not tonight. There may be much that is very abnormal about the present conditions—and it is possible there may be nothing abnormal about them at all. It is quite possible it may be merely my imagination.

PETER STOCKMANN. I must say it all sounds most mysterious. Is there something going on that I am to be kept in ignorance of? I should have imagined that I, as Chairman of the governing body of the Baths——

DR. STOCKMANN. And I should have imagined that I——. Oh, come, don't let us fly out at one another, Peter.

PETER STOCKMANN. Heaven forbid! I am not in the habit of flying out at people, as you call it. But I am entitled to request most emphatically that all arrangements shall be made in a business-like manner, through the proper channels, and shall be dealt with by the legally constituted authorities. I can allow no going behind our backs by any roundabout means.

DR. STOCKMANN. Have I ever at any time tried to go behind your backs?

PETER STOCKMANN. You have an ingrained tendency to take your own way, at all events; and that is almost equally inadmissible in a well-ordered community. The individual ought undoubtedly to acquiesce in subordinating himself to the community—or, to speak more accurately, to the authorities who have the care of the community's welfare.

DR. STOCKMANN. Very likely. But what the deuce has all this got to do with me?

PETER STOCKMANN. That is exactly what you never appear to be willing to learn, my dear Thomas. But, mark my words, some day you will have to suffer for it—sooner or later. Now I have told you. Good-bye.

DR. STOCKMANN. Have you taken leave of your senses? You are on the wrong scent altogether.

PETER STOCKMANN. I am not usually that. You must excuse me now if I—(calls into the dining-room). Good night, Katherine. Good night, gentlemen.   [Goes out.]

MRS. STOCKMANN (coming from the dining-room). Has he gone?

DR. STOCKMANN. Yes, and in such a bad temper.

MRS. STOCKMANN. But, dear Thomas, what have you been doing to him again?

DR. STOCKMANN. Nothing at all. And, anyhow, he can't oblige me to make my report before the proper time.

MRS. STOCKMANN. What have you got to make a report to him about?

DR. STOCKMANN. Hm! Leave that to me, Katherine. ——It is an extraordinary thing that the postman doesn't come.

[HOVSTAD, BILLING, and HORSTER have got up from the table and come into the sitting-room. EJLIF and MORTEN come in after them.]

BILLING (stretching himself). Ah!—one feels a new man after a meal like that.

HOVSTAD. The mayor wasn't in a very sweet temper tonight, then.

DR. STOCKMANN. It is his stomach; he has a wretched digestion.

HOVSTAD. I rather think it was us two of the "People's Messenger" that he couldn't digest.

MRS. STOCKMANN. I thought you came out of it pretty well with him.

HOVSTAD. Oh yes; but it isn't anything more than a sort of truce.

BILLING. That is just what it is! That word sums up the situation.

DR. STOCKMANN. We must remember that Peter is a lonely man, poor chap. He has no home comforts of any kind; nothing but everlasting business. And all that infernal weak tea that he pours into himself! Now then, my boys, bring chairs up to the table. Aren't we going to have that toddy, Katherine?

MRS. STOCKMANN (*going into the dining-room*). I am just getting it.

DR. STOCKMANN. Sit down here on the couch beside me, Captain Horster. We so seldom see you——. Please sit down, my friends.

[*They sit down at the table.* MRS. STOCKMANN *brings a tray, with a spirit-lamp, glasses, bottles, etc., upon it.*]

MRS. STOCKMANN. There you are! This is arrack, and this is rum, and this one is the brandy. Now every one must help himself.

DR. STOCKMANN (*taking a glass*). We will. (*They all mix themselves some toddy.*) And let us have the cigars. Ejlif, you know where the box is. And you, Morten, can fetch my pipe. (*The two boys go into the room on the right.*) I have a suspicion that Ejlif pockets a cigar now and then!— but I take no notice of it. (*Calls out.*) And my smoking-cap too, Morten. Katherine, you can tell him where I left it. Ah, he has got it. (*The boys bring the various things.*) Now,

my friends. I stick to my pipe, you know. This one has seen
plenty of bad weather with me up north. (*Touches glasses
with them.*) Your good health! Ah! it is good to be sitting
snug and warm here.

MRS. STOCKMANN (*who sits knitting*). Do you sail soon,
Captain Horster?

HORSTER. I expect to be ready to sail next week.

MRS. STOCKMANN. I suppose you are going to America?

HORSTER. Yes, that is the plan.

MRS. STOCKMANN. Then you won't be able to take part
in the coming election.

HORSTER. Is there going to be an election?

BILLING. Didn't you know?

HORSTER. No, I don't mix myself up with those things.

BILLING. But do you not take an interest in public affairs?

HORSTER. No, I don't know anything about politics.

BILLING. All the same, one ought to vote, at any rate.

HORSTER. Even if one doesn't know anything about what
is going on?

BILLING. Doesn't know! What do you mean by that?
A community is like a ship; every one ought to be prepared
to take the helm.

HORSTER. Maybe that is all very well on shore, but on
board ship it wouldn't work.

HOVSTAD. It is astonishing how little most sailors care
about what goes on on shore.

BILLING. Very extraordinary.

DR. STOCKMANN. Sailors are like birds of passage; they
feel equally at home in any latitude. And that is only an
additional reason for our being all the more keen, Hovstad.
Is there to be anything of public interest in tomorrow's
"Messenger"?

HOVSTAD.   Nothing about municipal affairs.   But the day after to-morrow I was thinking of printing your article——

DR. STOCKMANN.   Ah, devil take it—my article!   Look here, that must wait a bit.

HOVSTAD.   Really?   We had just got convenient space for it, and I thought it was just the opportune moment——

DR. STOCKMANN.   Yes, yes, very likely you are right; but it must wait all the same.   I will explain to you later.

[PETRA *comes in from the hall, in hat and cloak and with a bundle of exercise books under her arm.*]

PETRA.   Good evening.

DR. STOCKMANN.   Good evening, Petra; come along.

[*Mutual greetings;* PETRA *takes off her things and puts them down on a chair by the door.*]

PETRA.   And you have all been sitting here enjoying yourselves, while I have been out slaving!

DR. STOCKMANN.   Well, come and enjoy yourself too!

BILLING.   May I mix a glass for you?

PETRA (*coming to the table*).   Thanks, I would rather do it; you always mix it too strong.   But I forgot, father—I have a letter for you.

[*Goes to the chair where she has laid her things.*]

DR. STOCKMANN.   A letter?   From whom?

PETRA (*looking in her coat pocket*).   The postman gave it to me just as I was going out——

DR. STOCKMANN (*getting up and going to her*).   And you only give it to me now!

PETRA.   I really had not time to run up again.   There it is!

DR. STOCKMANN (*seizing the letter*).   Let's see, let's see, child!   (*Looks at the address.*)   Yes, that's all right!

MRS. STOCKMANN.   Is it the one you have been expecting so anxiously, Thomas?

DR. STOCKMANN.   Yes, it is.   I must go to my room now

and——. Where shall I get a light, Katherine? Is there no lamp in my room again?

MRS. STOCKMANN. Yes, your lamp is all ready lit on your desk.

DR. STOCKMANN. Good, good. Excuse me for a moment——. [*Goes into his study.*]

PETRA. What do you suppose it is, mother?

MRS. STOCKMANN. I don't know; for the last day or two he has always been asking if the postman has not been.

BILLING. Probably some country patient.

PETRA. Poor old dad!—he will overwork himself soon. (*Mixes a glass for herself.*) There, that will taste good!

HOVSTAD. Have you been teaching in the evening school again today?

PETRA (*sipping from her glass*). Two hours.

BILLING. And four hours of school in the morning——

PETRA. Five hours.

MRS. STOCKMANN. And you have still got exercises to correct, I see.

PETRA. A whole heap, yes.

HORSTER. You are pretty full up with work too, it seems to me.

PETRA. Yes—but that is good. One is so delightfully tired after it.

BILLING. Do you like that?

PETRA. Yes, because one sleeps so well then.

MORTEN. You must be dreadfully wicked, Petra.

PETRA. Wicked?

MORTEN. Yes, because you work so much. Mr. Rörlund says work is a punishment for our sins.

EJLIF. Pooh, what a duffer you are, to believe a thing like that!

MRS. STOCKMANN. Come, come, Ejlif!

BILLING (*laughing*). That's capital!

HOVSTAD. Don't you want to work as hard as that, Morten?

MORTEN. No, indeed I don't.

HOVSTAD. What do you want to be, then?

MORTEN. I should like best to be a Viking.

EJLIF. You would have to be a pagan then.

MORTEN. Well, I could become a pagan, couldn't I?

BILLING. I agree with you, Morten! My sentiments, exactly.

MRS. STOCKMANN (*signalling to him*). I am sure that is not true, Mr. Billing.

BILLING. Yes, I swear it is! I am a pagan, and I am proud of it. Believe me, before long we shall all be pagans.

MORTEN. And then shall be allowed to do anything we like?

BILLING. Well, you see, Morten——.

MRS. STOCKMANN. You must go to your room now, boys; I am sure you have some lessons to learn for tomorrow.

EJLIF. I should like so much to stay a little longer——

MRS. STOCKMANN. No, no; away you go, both of you.

[*The boys say good-night and go into the room on the left.*]

HOVSTAD. Do you really think it can do the boys any harm to hear such things?

MRS. STOCKMANN. I don't know, but I don't like it.

PETRA. But you know, mother, I think you really are wrong about it.

MRS. STOCKMANN. Maybe, but I don't like it—not in our own home.

PETRA. There is so much falsehood both at home and at school. At home one must not speak, and at school we have to stand and tell lies to the children.

HORSTER. Tell lies?

PETRA. Yes, don't you suppose we have to teach them all sorts of things that we don't believe?

BILLING. That is perfectly true.

PETRA. If only I had the means I would start a school of my own, and it would be conducted on very different lines.

BILLING. Oh, bother the means——!

HORSTER. Well, if you are thinking of that, Miss Stockmann, I shall be delighted to provide you with a school-room. The great big old house my father left me is standing almost empty; there is an immense dining-room downstairs——

PETRA (*laughing*). Thank you very much; but I am afraid nothing will come of it.

HOVSTAD. No, Miss Petra is much more likely to take to journalism, I expect. By the way, have you had time to do anything with that English story you promised to translate for us?

PETRA. No, not yet; but you shall have it in good time.

[DR. STOCKMANN *comes in from his room with an open letter in his hand.*]

DR. STOCKMANN (*waving the letter*). Well, now the town will have something new to talk about, I can tell you!

BILLING. Something new?

MRS. STOCKMANN. What is this?

DR. STOCKMANN. A great discovery, Katherine.

HOVSTAD. Really?

MRS. STOCKMANN. A discovery of yours?

DR. STOCKMANN. A discovery of mine. (*Walks up and down.*) Just let them come saying, as usual, that it is all fancy and a crazy man's imagination! But they will be careful what they say this time, I can tell you!

PETRA. But, father, tell us what it is.

DR. STOCKMANN. Yes, yes—only give me time, and you shall know all about it. If only I had Peter here now! It just shows how we men can go about forming our judgments, when in reality we are as blind as any moles——

HOVSTAD. What are you driving at, Doctor?

DR. STOCKMANN (*standing still by the table*). Isn't it the universal opinion that our town is a healthy spot?

HOVSTAD. Certainly.

DR. STOCKMANN. Quite an unusually healthy spot, in fact—a place that deserves to be recommended in the warmest possible manner either for invalids or for people who are well——

MRS. STOCKMANN. Yes, but my dear Thomas——

DR. STOCKMANN. And we have been recommending it and praising it—I have written and written, both in the "Messenger" and in pamphlets——

HOVSTAD. Well, what then?

DR. STOCKMANN. And the Baths—we have called them the "main artery of the town's life-blood," the "nerve-centre of our town," and the devil knows what else——

BILLING. "The town's pulsating heart" was the expression I once used on an important occasion——

DR. STOCKMANN. Quite so. Well, do you know what they really are, these great, splendid, much praised Baths, that have cost so much money—do you know what they are?

HOVSTAD. No, what are they?

MRS. STOCKMANN. Yes, what are they?

DR. STOCKMANN. The whole place is a pesthouse!

PETRA. The Baths, father?

MRS. STOCKMANN (*at the same time*). Our Baths!

HOVSTAD. But, Doctor——

BILLING. Absolutely incredible!

DR. STOCKMANN. The whole Bath establishment is a whited, poisoned sepulchre, I tell you—the gravest possible danger to the public health! All the nastiness up at Mölledal, all that stinking filth, is infecting the water in the conduit-pipes leading to the reservoir; and the same cursed, filthy poison oozes out on the shore too——

HORSTER. Where the bathing-place is?

DR. STOCKMANN. Just there.

HOVSTAD. How do you come to be so certain of all this, Doctor?

DR. STOCKMANN. I have investigated the matter most conscientiously. For a long time past I have suspected something of the kind. Last year we had some very strange cases of illness among the visitors—typhoid cases, and cases of gastric fever——

MRS. STOCKMANN. Yes, that is quite true.

DR. STOCKMANN. At the time, we supposed the visitors had been infected before they came; but later on, in the winter, I began to have a different opinion; and so I set myself to examine the water, as well as I could.

MRS. STOCKMANN. Then that is what you have been so busy with?

DR. STOCKMANN. Indeed I have been busy, Katherine. But here I had none of the necessary scientific apparatus, so I sent samples, both of the drinking-water and of the sea-water, up to the University, to have an accurate analysis made by a chemist.

HOVSTAD. And have you got that?

DR. STOCKMANN (*showing him the letter*). Here it is! It proves the presence of decomposing organic matter in the water—it is full of bacteria. The water is absolutely dangerous to use, either internally or externally.

MRS. STOCKMANN. What a mercy you discovered it in time.

DR. STOCKMANN. You may well say so.

HOVSTAD. And what do you propose to do now, Doctor?

DR. STOCKMANN. To see the matter put right—naturally.

HOVSTAD. Can that be done?

DR. STOCKMANN. It must be done. Otherwise the Baths will be absolutely useless and wasted. But we need not anticipate that; I have a very clear idea what we shall have to do.

MRS. STOCKMANN. But why have you kept this all so secret, dear?

DR. STOCKMANN. Do you suppose I was going to run about the town gossiping about it, before I had absolute proof? No, thank you. I am not such a fool.

PETRA. Still, you might have told us——

DR. STOCKMANN. Not a living soul. But to-morrow you may run round to the old Badger——

MRS. STOCKMANN. Oh, Thomas! Thomas!

DR. STOCKMANN. Well, to your grandfather, then. The old boy will have something to be astonished at! I know he thinks I am cracked—and there are lots of other people think so too, I have noticed. But now these good folks shall see—they shall just see——! (*Walks about, rubbing his hands.*) There will be a nice upset in the town, Katherine; you can't imagine what it will be. All the conduit-pipes will have to be relaid.

HOVSTAD (*getting up*). All the conduit-pipes——?

DR. STOCKMANN. Yes, of course. The intake is too low down; it will have to be lifted to a position much higher up.

PETRA. Then you were right after all.

DR. STOCKMANN. Ah, you remember, Petra—I wrote opposing the plans before the work was begun. But at that time no one would listen to me. Well, I am going to let them have it, now! Of course I have prepared a report for the Baths Committee; I have had it ready for a week, and was only waiting for this to come. (*Shows the letter.*) Now it shall go off at once. (*Goes into his room and comes back with some papers.*) Look at that! Four closely written sheets!—and the letter shall go with them. Give me a bit of paper, Katherine—something to wrap them up in. That will do! Now give it to—to—(*stamps his foot*)—what the

deuce is her name?—give it to the maid, and tell her to take
it at once to the Mayor.

[MRS. STOCKMANN *takes the packet and goes out through the
dining-room.*]

PETRA. What do you think uncle Peter will say, father?

DR. STOCKMANN. What is there for him to say? I should
think he would be very glad that such an important truth
has been brought to light.

HOVSTAD. Will you let me print a short note about your
discovery in the "Messenger?"

DR. STOCKMANN. I shall be very much obliged if you will.

HOVSTAD. It is very desirable that the public should be
informed of it without delay.

DR. STOCKMANN. Certainly.

MRS. STOCKMANN (*coming back*). She has just gone with it.

BILLING. Upon my soul, Doctor, you are going to be the
foremost man in the town!

DR. STOCKMANN (*walking about happily*). Nonsense! As
a matter of fact I have done nothing more than my duty.
I have only made a lucky find—that's all. Still, all the
same——

BILLING. Hovstad, don't you think the town ought to
give Dr. Stockmann some sort of testimonial?

HOVSTAD. I will suggest it, anyway.

BILLING. And I will speak to Aslaksen about it.

DR. STOCKMANN. No, my good friends, don't let us have
any of that nonsense. I won't hear of anything of the kind.
And if the Baths Committee should think of voting me an
increase of salary, I will not accept it. Do you hear, Katherine?— I won't accept it.

MRS. STOCKMANN. You are quite right, Thomas.

PETRA (*lifting her glass*). Your health, father!

HOVSTAD *and* BILLING. Your health, Doctor! Good
health!

HORSTER (*touches glasses with* DR. STOCKMANN). I hope it will bring you nothing but good luck.

DR. STOCKMANN. Thank you, thank you, my dear fellows! I feel tremendously happy! It is a splendid thing for a man to be able to feel that he has done a service to his native town and to his fellow-citizens. Hurrah, Katherine!

[*He puts his arms round her and whirls her round and round, while she protests with laughing cries. They all laugh, clap their hands and cheer the* DOCTOR. *The boys put their heads in at the door to see what is going on.*]

CURTAIN

ACT TWO

The DOCTOR's *sitting-room. The door into the dining-room is shut. It is morning.* [MRS. STOCKMANN, *with a sealed letter in her hand, comes in from the dining-room, goes to the door of the* DOCTOR's *study and peeps in.*]

MRS. STOCKMANN. Are you in, Thomas?

DR. STOCKMANN (*from within his room*). Yes, I have just come in. (*Comes into the room.*) What is it?

MRS. STOCKMANN. A letter from your brother.

DR. STOCKMANN. Aha, let us see! (*Opens the letter and reads:*) "I return herewith the manuscript you sent me"— (*reads on in a low murmur*) Hm!——

MRS. STOCKMANN. What does he say?

DR. STOCKMANN (*putting the papers in his pocket*). Oh, he only writes that he will come up here himself about midday.

MRS. STOCKMANN. Well, try and remember to be at home this time.

DR. STOCKMANN. That will be all right; I have got through all my morning visits

MRS. STOCKMANN. I am extremely curious to know how he takes it.

DR. STOCKMANN. You will see he won't like it's having been I, and not he, that made the discovery.

MRS. STOCKMANN. Aren't you a little nervous about that?

DR. STOCKMANN. Oh, he really will be pleased enough, you know. But, at the same time, Peter is so confoundedly afraid of anyone's doing any service to the town except himself.

MRS. STOCKMANN. I will tell you what, Thomas—you should be good-natured, and share the credit of this with him. Couldn't you make out that it was he who set you on the scent of this discovery?

DR. STOCKMANN. I am quite willing. If only I can get the thing set right. I——

[MORTEN KIIL *puts his head in through the door leading from the hall, looks round in an enquiring manner and chuckles.*]

MORTEN KIIL (*slyly*). Is it—is it true?

MRS. STOCKMANN· (*going to the door*). Father!—is it you?

DR. STOCKMANN. Ah, Mr. Kiil—good morning, good morning!

MRS. STOCKMANN. But come along in.

MORTEN KIIL. If it is true, I will; if not, I am off.

DR. STOCKMANN. If what is true?

MORTEN KIIL. This tale about the water-supply. Is it true?

DR. STOCKMANN. Certainly it is true. But how did you come to hear it?

MORTEN KIIL (*coming in*). Petra ran in on her way to the school——

DR. STOCKMANN. Did she?

MORTEN KIIL. Yes; and she declares that——. I thought she was only making a fool of me, but it isn't like Petra to do that.

DR. STOCKMANN. Of course not. How could you imagine such a thing?

MORTEN KIIL. Oh well, it is better never to trust anybody; you may find you have been made a fool of before you know where you are. But it is really true, all the same?

DR. STOCKMANN. You can depend upon it that it is true. Won't you sit down? (*Settles him on the couch.*) Isn't it a real bit of luck for the town——

MORTEN KIIL (*suppressing his laughter*). A bit of luck for the town?

DR. STOCKMANN. Yes, that I made the discovery in good time.

MORTEN KIIL (*as before*). Yes, yes, yes!—But I should never have thought you the sort of man to pull your own brother's leg like this!

DR. STOCKMANN. Pull his leg!

MRS. STOCKMANN. Really, father dear——

MORTEN KIIL (*resting his hands and his chin on the handle of his stick and winking slyly at the* DOCTOR). Let me see, what was the story? Some kind of beast that had got into the water-pipes, wasn't it?

DR. STOCKMANN. Bacteria—yes.

MORTEN KIIL. And a lot of these beasts had got in, according to Petra—a tremendous lot.

DR. STOCKMANN. Certainly; hundreds of thousands of them, probably.

MORTEN KIIL. But no one can see them—isn't that so?

DR. STOCKMANN. Yes; you can't see them.

MORTEN KIIL (*with a quiet chuckle*). Damme—it's the finest story I have ever heard!

DR. STOCKMANN. What do you mean?

MORTEN KIIL. But you will never get the Mayor to believe a thing like that.

DR. STOCKMANN. We shall see.

MORTEN KIIL. Do you think he will be fool enough to——?

DR. STOCKMANN. I hope the whole town will be fools enough.

MORTEN KIIL. The whole town! Well, it wouldn't be a bad thing. It would just serve them right, and teach them a lesson. They think themselves so much cleverer than we old fellows. They hounded me out of the council; they did, I tell you—they hounded me out. Now they shall pay for it. You pull their legs too, Thomas!

DR. STOCKMANN. Really, I——

MORTEN KIIL. You pull their legs! (*Gets up.*) If you can work it so that the Mayor and his friends all swallow the same bait, I will give a hundred crowns to a charity—like a shot!

DR. STOCKMANN. That is very kind of you.

MORTEN KIIL. Yes, I haven't got much money to throw away, I can tell you; but if you can work this, I will give fifty crowns to a charity at Christmas.

[HOVSTAD *comes in by the hall door.*]

HOVSTAD. Good morning! (*Stops.*) Oh, I beg your pardon——

DR. STOCKMANN. Not at all; come in.

MORTEN KIIL (*with another chuckle*). Oho!—is he in this too?

HOVSTAD. What do you mean?

DR. STOCKMANN. Certainly he is.

MORTEN KIIL. I might have known it! It must get into the papers. You know how to do it, Thomas! Set your wits to work. Now I must go.

DR. STOCKMANN. Won't you stay a little while?

MORTEN KIIL. No, I must be off now. You keep up this game for all it is worth; you won't repent it, I'm damned if you will!

[*He goes out;* MRS. STOCKMANN *follows him into the hall.*]

DR. STOCKMANN (*laughing*). Just imagine—the old chap doesn't believe a word of all this about the water-supply.

HOVSTAD. Oh, that was it, then?

DR. STOCKMANN. Yes, that was what we were talking about. Perhaps it is the same thing that brings you here?

HOVSTAD. Yes, it is. Can you spare me a few minutes, Doctor?

DR. STOCKMANN. As long as you like, my dear fellow.

HOVSTAD. Have you heard from the Mayor yet?

DR. STOCKMANN. Not yet. He is coming here later.

HOVSTAD. I have given the matter a great deal of thought since last night.

DR. STOCKMANN. Well?

HOVSTAD. From your point of view, as a doctor and a man of science, this affair of the water-supply is an isolated matter. I mean, you do not realise that it involves a great many other things.

DR. STOCKMANN. How do you mean? — Let us sit down, my dear fellow. No, sit here on the couch. (HOVSTAD *sits down on the couch,* DR. STOCKMANN *on a chair on the other side of the table.*) Now then. You mean that——?

HOVSTAD. You said yesterday that the pollution of the water was due to impurities in the soil.

DR. STOCKMANN. Yes, unquestionably it is due to that poisonous morass up at Mölledal.

HOVSTAD. Begging your pardon, doctor, I fancy it is due to quite another morass altogether.

DR. STOCKMANN. What morass?

HOVSTAD. The morass that the whole life of our town is built on and is rotting in.

DR. STOCKMANN. What the deuce are you driving at, Hovstad?

HOVSTAD. The whole of the town's interests have, little by little, got into the hands of a pack of officials.

DR. STOCKMANN. Oh, come!—they are not all officials.

HOVSTAD. No, but those that are not officials are at any rate the officials' friends and adherents; it is the wealthy folk, the old families in the town, that have got us entirely in their hands.

DR. STOCKMANN. Yes, but after all they are men of ability and knowledge.

HOVSTAD. Did they show any ability or knowledge when they laid the conduit-pipes where they are now?

DR. STOCKMANN. No, of course that was a great piece of stupidity on their part. But that is going to be set right now.

HOVSTAD. Do you think that will be all such plain sailing?

DR. STOCKMANN. Plain sailing or no, it has got to be done, anyway.

HOVSTAD. Yes, provided the press takes up the question.

DR. STOCKMANN. I don't think that will be necessary, my dear fellow; I am certain my brother——

HOVSTAD. Excuse me, doctor; I feel bound to tell you I am inclined to take the matter up.

DR. STOCKMANN. In the paper?

HOVSTAD. Yes. When I took over the "People's Messenger," my idea was to break up this ring of self-opinionated old fossils who had got hold of all the influence.

DR. STOCKMANN. But you know you told me yourself what the result had been; you nearly ruined your paper.

HOVSTAD. Yes, at the time we were obliged to climb down a peg or two, it is quite true, because there was a danger of the whole project of the Baths coming to nothing if they failed us. But now the scheme has been carried through, and we can dispense with these grand gentlemen.

DR. STOCKMANN. Dispense with them, yes; but we owe them a great debt of gratitude.

HOVSTAD. That shall be recognised ungrudgingly. But a journalist of my democratic tendencies cannot let such an opportunity as this slip. The bubble of official infallibility must be pricked. The superstition must be destroyed, like any other.

DR. STOCKMANN. I am whole-heartedly with you in that, Mr. Hovstad; if it is a superstition, away with it!

HOVSTAD. I should be very reluctant to bring the Mayor into it, because he is your brother. But I am sure you will agree with me that truth should be the first consideration.

DR. STOCKMANN. That goes without saying. (*With sudden emphasis.*) Yes, but—but——

HOVSTAD. You must not misjudge me. I am neither more self-interested nor more ambitious than most men.

DR. STOCKMANN. My dear fellow—who suggests anything of the kind?

HOVSTAD. I am of humble origin, as you know; and that has given me opportunities of knowing what is the most crying need in the humbler ranks of life. It is that they should be allowed some part in the direction of public affairs, Doctor. That is what will develop their faculties and intelligence and self-respect——

DR. STOCKMANN. I quite appreciate that.

HOVSTAD. Yes—and in my opinion a journalist incurs a heavy responsibility if he neglects a favorable opportunity of emancipating the masses—the humble and oppressed. I know well enough that in exalted circles I shall be called an agitator, and all that sort of thing; but they may call what they like. If only my conscience doesn't reproach me, then——

DR. STOCKMANN. Quite right! Quite right, Mr. Hovstad. But all the same—devil take it! (*A knock is heard at the door.*) Come in!

[ASLAKSEN *appears at the door. He is poorly but decently*

*dressed, in black, with a slightly crumpled white neckcloth; he
wears gloves and has a felt hat in his hand.*]

ASLAKSEN (*bowing*). Excuse my taking the liberty, Doctor——

DR. STOCKMANN (*getting up*). Ah, it is you, Aslaksen!

ASLAKSEN. Yes, Doctor.

HOVSTAD (*standing up*). Is it me you want, Aslaksen?

ASLAKSEN. No; I didn't know I should find you here. No,
it was the Doctor I——

DR. STOCKMANN. I am quite at your service. What is it?

ASLAKSEN. Is what I heard from Mr. Billing true, sir—
that you mean to improve our water-supply?

DR. STOCKMANN. Yes, for the Baths.

ASLAKSEN. Quite so, I understand. Well, I have come to
say that I will back that up by every means in my power.

HOVSTAD (*to the* DOCTOR). You see!

DR. STOCKMANN. I shall be very grateful to you but——

ASLAKSEN. Because it may be no bad thing to have us
small tradesmen at your back. We form, as it were, a compact majority in the town—if we choose. And it is always
a good thing to have the majority with you, Doctor.

DR. STOCKMANN. That is undeniably true; but I confess
I don't see why such unusual precautions should be necessary in this case. It seems to me that such a plain, straightforward thing——

ASLAKSEN. Oh, it may be very desirable, all the same. I
know our local authorities so well; officials are not generally
very ready to act on proposals that come from other people.
That is why I think it would not be at all amiss if we made
a little demonstration.

HOVSTAD. That's right.

DR. STOCKMANN. Demonstration, did you say? What on
earth are you going to make a demonstration about?

ASLAKSEN. We shall proceed with the greatest modera-

tion, Doctor. Moderation is always my aim; it is the greatest virtue in a citizen—at least, I think so.

DR. STOCKMANN. It is well known to be a characteristic
of yours, Mr. Aslaksen.

ASLAKSEN. Yes, I think I may pride myself on that. And
this matter of the water-supply is of the greatest importance
to us small tradesmen. The Baths promise to be a regular
gold-mine for the town. We shall all make our living out of
them, especially those of us who are householders. That is
why we will back up the project as strongly as possible.
And as I am at present Chairman of the Householders' Association——

DR. STOCKMANN. Yes——?

ASLAKSEN. And, what is more, local secretary of the Temperance Society—you know, sir, I suppose, that I am a
worker in the temperance cause?

DR. STOCKMANN. Of course, of course.

ASLAKSEN. Well, you can understand that I come into
contact with a great many people. And as I have the reputation of a temperate and law-abiding citizen—like yourself,
Doctor—I have a certain influence in the town, a little bit
of power, if I may be allowed to say so.

DR. STOCKMANN. I know that quite well, Mr. Aslaksen.

ASLAKSEN. So you see it would be an easy matter for me
to set on foot some testimonial, if necessary.

DR. STOCKMANN. A testimonial?

ASLAKSEN. Yes, some kind of address of thanks from
the townsmen for your share in a matter of such importance
to the community. I need scarcely say that it would have
to be drawn up with the greatest regard to moderation, so
as not to offend the authorities—who, after all, have the
reins in their hands. If we pay strict attention to that, no
one can take it amiss, I should think!

HOVSTAD. Well, and even supposing they didn't like it ——

ASLAKSEN. No, no, no; there must be no discourtesy to
the authorities, Mr. Hovstad. It is no use falling foul of
those upon whom our welfare so closely depends. I have
done that in my time, and no good ever comes of it. But no
one can take exception to a reasonable and frank expression
of a citizen's views.

DR. STOCKMANN (*shaking him by the hand*). I can't tell
you, dear Mr. Aslaksen, how extremely pleased I am to find
such hearty support among my fellow-citizens. I am delighted—delighted! Now, you will take a small glass of
sherry, eh?

ASLAKSEN. No, thank you; I never drink alcohol of that
kind.

DR. STOCKMANN. Well, what do you say to a glass of
beer, then?

ASLAKSEN. Nor that either, thank you, Doctor. I never
drink anything as early as this. I am going into town now
to talk this over with one or two householders, and prepare
the ground.

DR. STOCKMANN. It is tremendously kind of you, Mr. Aslaksen; but I really cannot understand the necessity for all
these precautions. It seems to me that the thing should go
of itself.

ASLAKSEN. The authorities are somewhat slow to move,
Doctor. Far be it from me to seem to blame them——

HOVSTAD. We are going to stir them up in the paper to-
morrow, Aslaksen.

ASLAKSEN. But not violently, I trust, Mr. Hovstad. Proceed with moderation, or you will do nothing with them.
You may take my advice; I have gathered my experience in
the school of life. Well, I must say good-bye, Doctor.
You know now that we small tradesmen are at your back at
all events, like a solid wall. You have the compact majority
on your side, Doctor.

DR. STOCKMANN. I am very much obliged, dear Mr. Aslaksen. (*Shakes hands with him.*) Good-bye, good-bye.

ASLAKSEN. Are you going my way, towards the printing-office, Mr. Hovstad?

HOVSTAD. I will come later; I have something to settle up first.

ASLAKSEN. Very well.

[*Bows and goes out;* STOCKMANN *follows him into the hall.*]

HOVSTAD (*as* STOCKMANN *comes in again*). Well, what do you think of that, Doctor? Don't you think it is high time we stirred a little life into all this slackness and vacillation and cowardice?

DR. STOCKMANN. Are you referring to Aslaksen?

HOVSTAD. Yes, I am. He is one of those who are floundering in a bog—decent enough fellow though he may be, otherwise. And most of the people here are in just the same case—seesawing and edging first to one side and then to the other, so overcome with caution and scruple that they never dare to take any decided step.

DR. STOCKMANN. Yes, but Aslaksen seemed to me so thoroughly well-intentioned.

HOVSTAD. There is one thing I esteem higher than that; and that is for a man to be self-reliant and sure of himself.

DR. STOCKMANN. I think you are perfectly right there.

HOVSTAD. That is why I want to seize this opportunity, and try if I cannot manage to put a little virility into these well-intentioned people for once. The idol of Authority must be shattered in this town. This gross and inexcusable blunder about the water-supply must be brought home to the mind of every municipal voter.

DR. STOCKMANN. Very well; if you are of opinion that it is for the good of the community, so be it. But not until I have had a talk with my brother.

HOVSTAD. Anyway, I will get a leading article ready; and if the Mayor refuses to take the matter up——

DR. STOCKMANN. How can you suppose such a thing possible?

HOVSTAD. It is conceivable. And in that case——

DR. STOCKMANN. In that case I promise you——. Look here, in that case you may print my report—every word of it.

HOVSTAD. May I? Have I your word for it?

DR. STOCKMANN (*giving him the MS.*). Here it is; take it with you. It can do no harm for you to read it through, and you can give it back to me later on.

HOVSTAD. Good, good! That is what I will do. And now good-bye, Doctor.

DR. STOCKMANN. Good-bye, good-bye. You will see everything will run quite smoothly, Mr. Hovstad—quite smoothly.

HOVSTAD. Hm!—we shall see.   [*Bows and goes out.*]

DR. STOCKMANN (*opens the dining-room door and looks in*). Katherine! Oh, you are back, Petra?

PETRA (*coming in*). Yes, I have just come from the school.

MRS. STOCKMANN (*coming in*). Has he not been here yet?

DR. STOCKMANN. Peter? No. But I have had a long talk with Hovstad. He is quite excited about my discovery. I find it has a much wider bearing than I at first imagined. And he has put his paper at my disposal if necessity should arise.

MRS. STOCKMANN. Do you think it will?

DR. STOCKMANN. Not for a moment. But at all events it makes me feel proud to know that I have the liberal-minded independent press on my side. Yes, and—just imagine—I have had a visit from the Chairman of the Householders' Association!

MRS. STOCKMANN. Oh! What did he want?

DR. STOCKMANN. To offer me his support too. They will support me in a body if it should be necessary. Katherine —do you know what I have got behind me?

MRS. STOCKMANN. Behind you? No, what have you got behind you?

DR. STOCKMANN. The compact majority.

MRS. STOCKMANN. Really? Is that a good thing for you, Thomas?

DR. STOCKMANN. I should think it was a good thing. (*Walks up and down rubbing his hands.*) By Jove, it's a fine thing to feel this bond of brotherhood between oneself and one's fellow-citizens!

PETRA. And to be able to do so much that is good and useful, father!

DR. STOCKMANN. And for one's own native town into the bargain, my child!

MRS. STOCKMANN. That was a ring at the bell.

DR. STOCKMANN. It must be he, then. (*A knock is heard at the door.*) Come in!

PETER STOCKMANN (*comes in from the hall*). Good morning.

DR. STOCKMANN. Glad to see you, Peter!

MRS. STOCKMANN. Good morning, Peter. How are you?

PETER STOCKMANN. So so, thank you. (*To* DR. STOCKMANN.) I received from you yesterday, after office-hours, a report dealing with the condition of the water at the Baths.

DR. STOCKMANN. Yes. Have you read it?

PETER STOCKMANN. Yes, I have.

DR. STOCKMANN. And what have you to say to it?

PETER STOCKMANN (*with a sidelong glance*). Hm!——

MRS. STOCKMANN. Come along, Petra.

[*She and* PETRA *go into the room on the left.*]

PETER STOCKMANN (*after a pause*).   Was it necessary to make all these investigations behind my back?

DR. STOCKMANN.   Yes, because until I was absolutely certain about it——

PETER STOCKMANN.   Then you mean that you are absolutely certain now?

DR. STOCKMANN.   Surely you are convinced of that.

PETER STOCKMANN.   Is it your intention to bring this document before the Baths Committee as a sort of official communication?

DR. STOCKMANN.   Certainly.   Something must be done in the matter—and that quickly.

PETER STOCKMANN.   As usual, you employ violent expressions in your report.   You say, amongst other things, that what we offer visitors in our Baths is a permanent supply of poison.

DR. STOCKMANN.   Well, can you describe it any other way, Peter?   Just think—water that is poisonous, whether you drink it or bathe in it!   And this we offer to the poor sick folk who come to us trustfully and pay us at an exorbitant rate to be made well again!

PETER STOCKMANN.   And your reasoning leads you to this conclusion, that we must build a sewer to draw off the alleged impurities from Mölledal and must re-lay the water-conduits.

DR. STOCKMANN.   Yes.   Do you see any other way out of it?   I don't.

PETER STOCKMANN.   I made a pretext this morning to go and see the town engineer, and, as if only half seriously, broached the subject of these proposals as a thing we might perhaps have to take under consideration some time later on.

DR. STOCKMANN.   Some time later on!

PETER STOCKMANN.   He smiled at what he considered to be my extravagance, naturally.   Have you taken the trouble to consider what your proposed alterations would cost? According to the information I obtained, the expenses would probably mount up to several hundred thousand crowns.

DR. STOCKMANN. Would it cost so much?

PETER STOCKMANN. Yes; and the worst part of it would be that the work would take at least two years.

DR. STOCKMANN. Two years? Two whole years?

PETER STOCKMANN. At least. And what are we to do with the Baths in the meantime? Close them? Indeed we should be obliged to. And do you suppose any one would come near the place after it had got about that the water was dangerous?

DR. STOCKMANN. Yes, but, Peter, that is what it is.

PETER STOCKMANN. And all this at this juncture—just as the Baths are beginning to be known. There are other towns in the neighborhood with qualifications to attract visitors for bathing purposes. Don't you suppose they would immediately strain every nerve to divert the entire stream of strangers to themselves? Unquestionably they would; and then where should we be? We should probably have to abandon the whole thing, which has cost us so much money—and then you would have ruined your native town.

DR. STOCKMANN. I—should have ruined——!

PETER STOCKMANN. It is simply and solely through the Baths that the town has before it any future worth mentioning. You know that just as well as I.

DR. STOCKMANN. But what do you think ought to be done, then?

PETER STOCKMANN. Your report has not convinced me that the condition of the water at the Baths is as bad as you represent it to be.

DR. STOCKMANN. I tell you it is even worse!—or at all events it will be in summer, when the warm weather comes.

PETER STOCKMANN. As I said, I believe you exaggerate

the matter considerably. A capable physician ought to
know what measures to take—he ought to be capable of
preventing injurious influences or of remedying them if they
become obviously persistent.

DR. STOCKMANN. Well? What more?

PETER STOCKMANN. The water-supply for the Baths is
now an established fact, and in consequence must be treated
as such. But probably the Committee, at its discretion, will
not be disinclined to consider the question of how far it
might be possible to introduce certain improvements con-
sistent with a reasonable expenditure.

DR. STOCKMANN. And do you suppose that I will have
anything to do with such a piece of trickery as that?

PETER STOCKMANN. Trickery!!

DR. STOCKMANN. Yes, it would be a trick—a fraud, a lie,
a downright crime towards the public, towards the whole
community!

PETER STOCKMANN. I have not, as I remarked before, been
able to convince myself that there is actually any imminent
danger.

DR. STOCKMANN. You have not! It is impossible that you
should not be convinced. I know I have represented the
facts absolutely truthfully and fairly. And you know it
very well, Peter, only you won't acknowledge it. It was
owing to your action that both the Baths and the water-
conduits were built where they are; and that is what you
won't acknowledge—that damnable blunder of yours. Pooh!
—do you suppose I don't see through you?

PETER STOCKMANN. And even if that were true? If I perhaps guard my reputation somewhat anxiously, it is in the
interests of the town. Without moral authority I am pow-
erless to direct public affairs as seems, to my judgment, to be
best for the common good. And on that account—and for
various other reasons, too—it appears to me to be a matter

of importance that your report should not be delivered to the Committee. In the interests of the public, you must withhold it. Then, later on, I will raise the question and we will do our best, privately; but nothing of this unfortunate affair—not a single word of it—must come to the ears of the public.

DR. STOCKMANN. I am afraid you will not be able to prevent that now, my dear Peter.

PETER STOCKMANN. It must and shall be prevented.

DR. STOCKMANN. It is no use, I tell you. There are too many people that know about it.

PETER STOCKMANN. That know about it? Who? Surely you don't mean those fellows on the "People's Messenger"?

DR. STOCKMANN. Yes, they know. The liberal-minded independent press is going to see that you do your duty.

PETER STOCKMANN (*after a short pause*). You are an extraordinarily independent man, Thomas. Have you given no thought to the consequences this may have for yourself?

DR. STOCKMANN. Consequences?—for me?

PETER STOCKMANN. For you and yours, yes.

DR. STOCKMANN. What the deuce do you mean?

PETER STOCKMANN. I believe I have always behaved in a brotherly way to you—have always been ready to oblige or to help you?

DR. STOCKMANN. Yes, you have, and I am grateful to you for it.

PETER STOCKMANN. There is no need. Indeed, to some extent I was forced to do so—for my own sake. I always hoped that, if I helped to improve your financial position, I should be able to keep some check on you.

DR. STOCKMANN. What!! Then it was only for your own sake——!

PETER STOCKMANN. Up to a certain point, yes. It is pain-

ful for a man in an official position to have his nearest rela-
tive compromising himself time after time.

DR. STOCKMANN. And do you consider that I do that?

PETER STOCKMANN. Yes, unfortunately, you do, without
even being aware of it. You have a restless, pugnacious,
rebellious disposition. And then there is that disastrous
propensity of yours to want to write about every sort of possible and impossible thing. The moment an idea comes into
your head, you must needs go and write a newspaper article
or a whole pamphlet about it.

DR. STOCKMANN. Well, but is it not the duty of a citizen
to let the public share in any new ideas he may have?

PETER STOCKMANN. Oh, the public doesn't require any
new ideas. The public is best served by the good, old-
established ideas it already has.

DR. STOCKMANN. And that is your honest opinion?

PETER STOCKMANN. Yes, and for once I must talk frankly
to you. Hitherto I have tried to avoid doing so, because I
know how irritable you are; but now I must tell you the
truth, Thomas. You have no conception what an amount
of harm you do yourself by your impetuosity. You complain of the authorities, you even complain of the government—you are always pulling them to pieces; you insist that
you have been neglected and persecuted. But what else can
such a cantankerous man as you expect?

DR. STOCKMANN. What next! Cantankerous, am I?

PETER STOCKMANN. Yes, Thomas, you are an extremely
cantankerous man to work with—I know that to my cost.
You disregard everything that you ought to have consideration for. You seem completely to forget that it is me you
have to thank for your appointment here as medical officer
to the Baths——

DR. STOCKMANN. I was entitled to it as a matter of
course!—I and nobody else! I was the first person to see

that the town could be made into a flourishing watering-place, and I was the only one who saw it at that time. I had to fight single-handed in support of the idea for many years; and I wrote and wrote——

PETER STOCKMANN. Undoubtedly. But things were not ripe for the scheme then—though, of course, you could not judge of that in your out-of-the-way corner up north. But as soon as the opportune moment came I—and the others—took the matter into our hands——

DR. STOCKMANN. Yes, and made this mess of all my beautiful plan. It is **pretty** obvious now what clever fellows you were!

PETER STOCKMANN. To my mind the whole thing only seems to mean that you are seeking another outlet for your combativeness. You want to pick a quarrel with your superiors—an old habit of yours. You cannot put up with any authority over you. You look askance at anyone who occupies a superior official position; you regard him as a personal enemy, and then any stick is good enough to beat him with. But now I have called your attention to the fact that the town's interests are at stake—and, incidentally, my own too. And therefore I must tell you, Thomas, that you will find me inexorable with regard to what I am about to require you to do.

DR. STOCKMANN. And what is that?

PETER STOCKMANN. As you have been so indiscreet as to speak of this delicate matter to outsiders, despite the fact that you ought to have treated it as entirely official and confidential, it is obviously impossible to hush it up now. All sorts of rumors will get about directly, and everybody who has a grudge against us will take care to embellish these rumors. So it will be necessary for you to refute them publicly.

DR. STOCKMANN. I! How? I don't understand.

PETER STOCKMANN. What we shall expect is that, after making further investigations, you will come to the conclusion that the matter is not by any means as dangerous or as critical as you imagined in the first instance.

DR. STOCKMANN. Oho!—so that is what you expect!

PETER STOCKMANN. And, what is more, we shall expect you to make public profession of your confidence in the Committee and in their readiness to consider fully and conscientiously what steps may be necessary to remedy any possible defects.

DR. STOCKMANN. But you will never be able to do that by patching and tinkering at it—never! Take my word for it, Peter; I mean what I say, as deliberately and emphatically as possible.

PETER STOCKMANN. As an officer under the Committee, you have no right to any individual opinion.

DR. STOCKMANN (amazed). No right?

PETER STOCKMANN. In your official capacity, no. As a private person, it is quite another matter. But as a subordinate member of the staff of the Baths, you have no right to express any opinion which runs contrary to that of your superiors.

DR. STOCKMANN. This is too much! I, a doctor, a man of science, have no right to——!

PETER STOCKMANN. The matter in hand is not simply a scientific one. It is a complicated matter, and has its economic as well as its technical side.

DR. STOCKMANN. I don't care what it is! I intend to be free to express my opinion on any subject under the sun.

PETER STOCKMANN. As you please—but not on any subject concerning the Baths. That we forbid.

DR. STOCKMANN (shouting). You forbid——! You! A pack of——

PETER STOCKMANN. *I* forbid it—I, your chief; and if I forbid it, you have to obey.

DR. STOCKMANN (*controlling himself*). Peter—if you were not my brother——

PETRA (*throwing open the door*). Father, you shan't stand this!

MRS. STOCKMANN (*coming in after her*). Petra, Petra!

PETER STOCKMANN. Oh, so you have been eavesdropping.

MRS. STOCKMANN. You were talking so loud, we couldn't help——

PETRA. Yes, I was listening.

PETER STOCKMANN. Well, after all, I am very glad——

DR. STOCKMANN (*going up to him*). You were saying something about forbidding and obeying?

PETER STOCKMANN. You obliged me to take that tone with you.

DR. STOCKMANN. And so I am to give myself the lie, publicly?

PETER STOCKMANN. We consider it absolutely necessary that you should make some such public statement as I have asked for.

DR. STOCKMANN. And if I do not—obey?

PETER STOCKMANN. Then we shall publish a statement ourselves to reassure the public.

DR. STOCKMANN. Very well; but in that case I shall use my pen against you. I stick to what I have said; I will show that I am right and that you are wrong. And what will you do then?

PETER STOCKMANN. Then I shall not be able to prevent your being dismissed.

DR. STOCKMANN. What——?

PETRA. Father—dismissed!

MRS. STOCKMANN. Dismissed!

PETER STOCKMANN. Dismissed from the staff of the Baths.

I shall be obliged to propose that you shall immediately be given notice, and shall not be allowed any further participation in the Baths' affairs.

DR. STOCKMANN. You would dare to do that!

PETER STOCKMANN. It is you that are playing the daring game.

PETRA. Uncle, that is a shameful way to treat a man like father!

MRS. STOCKMANN. Do hold your tongue, Petra!

PETER STOCKMANN (*looking at* PETRA). Oh, so we volunteer our opinions already, do we? Of course. (*To* MRS. STOCKMANN.) Katherine, I imagine you are the most sensible person in this house. Use any influence you may have over your husband, and make him see what this will entail for his family as well as——

DR. STOCKMANN. My family is my own concern and nobody else's!

PETER STOCKMANN. ——for his own family, as I was saying, as well as for the town he lives in.

DR. STOCKMANN. It is I who have the real good of the town at heart! I want to lay bare the defects that sooner or later must come to the light of day. I will show whether I love my native town.

PETER STOCKMANN. You, who in your blind obstinacy want to cut off the most important source of the town's welfare?

DR. STOCKMANN. The source is poisoned, man! Are you mad? We are making our living by retailing filth and corruption! The whole of our flourishing municipal life derives its sustenance from a lie!

PETER STOCKMANN. All imagination—or something even worse. The man who can throw out such offensive insinuations about his native town must be an enemy of our community.

DR. STOCKMANN (*going up to him*). Do you dare to——!

MRS. STOCKMANN (*throwing herself between them*). Thomas!

PETRA (*catching her father by the arm*). Don't lose your temper, father!

PETER STOCKMANN. I will not expose myself to violence. Now you have had a warning; so reflect on what you owe to yourself and your family. Good-bye. [*Goes out.*]

DR. STOCKMANN (*walking up and down*). Am I to put up with such treatment as this? In my own house, Katherine! What do you think of that!

MRS. STOCKMANN. Indeed it is both shameful and absurd, Thomas——

PETRA. If only I could give uncle a piece of my mind——

DR. STOCKMANN. It is my own fault. I ought to have flown out at him long ago!—shown my teeth!—bitten! To hear him call me an enemy to our community! Me! I shall not take that lying down, upon my soul!

MRS. STOCKMANN. But, dear Thomas, your brother has power on his side——

DR. STOCKMANN. Yes, but I have right on mine, I tell you.

MRS. STOCKMANN. Oh yes, right—right. What is the use of having right on your side if you have not got might?

PETRA. Oh, mother!—how can you say such a thing!

DR. STOCKMANN. Do you imagine that in a free country it is no use having right on your side? You are absurd, Katherine. Besides, haven't I got the liberal-minded, independent press to lead the way, and the compact majority behind me? That is might enough, I should think!

MRS. STOCKMANN. But, good heavens, Thomas, you don't mean to——?

DR. STOCKMANN. Don't mean to what?

MRS. STOCKMANN. To set yourself up in opposition to your brother.

DR. STOCKMANN. In God's name, what else do you suppose I should do but take my stand on right and truth?

PETRA. Yes, I was just going to say that.

MRS. STOCKMANN. But it won't do you any earthly good. If they won't do it, they won't.

DR. STOCKMANN. Oho, Katherine! Just give me time, and you will see how I will carry the war into their camp.

MRS. STOCKMANN. Yes, you carry the war into their camp, and you get your dismissal—that is what you will do.

DR. STOCKMANN. In any case I shall have done my duty towards the public—towards the community. I, who am called its enemy!

MRS. STOCKMANN. But towards your family, Thomas? Towards your own home! Do you think that is doing your duty towards those you have to provide for?

PETRA. Ah, don't think always first of us, mother.

MRS. STOCKMANN. Oh, it is easy for you to talk; you are able to shift for yourself, if need be. But remember the boys, Thomas; and think a little, too, of yourself, and of me——

DR. STOCKMANN. I think you are out of your senses, Katherine! If I were to be such a miserable coward as to go on my knees to Peter and his damned crew, do you suppose I should ever know an hour's peace of mind all my life afterwards?

MRS. STOCKMANN. I don't know anything about that; but God preserve us from the peace of mind we shall have, all the same, if you go on defying him! You will find yourself again without the means of subsistence, with no income to count upon. I should think we had had enough of that in the old days. Remember that, Thomas; think what that means.

DR. STOCKMANN (*collecting himself with a struggle and*

clenching his fists). And this is what this slavery can bring upon a free, honorable man! Isn't it horrible, Katherine?

MRS. STOCKMANN. Yes, it is sinful to treat you so, it is perfectly true. But, good heavens, one has to put up with so much injustice in this world.—There are the boys, Thomas! Look at them! What is to become of them? Oh, no, no, you can never have the heart——.

[EJLIF *and* MORTEN *have come in while she was speaking, with their school books in their hands.*]

DR. STOCKMANN. The boys——! (*Recovers himself suddenly.*) No, even if the whole world goes to pieces, I will never bow my neck to this yoke! [*Goes towards his room.*]

MRS. STOCKMANN (*following him*). Thomas—what are you going to do!

DR. STOCKMANN (*at his door*). I mean to have the right to look my sons in the face when they are grown men.

[*Goes into his room.*]

MRS. STOCKMANN (*bursting into tears*). God help us all!

PETRA. Father is splendid! He will not give in.

[*The boys look on in amazement;* PETRA *signs to them not to speak.*]

CURTAIN

ACT THREE

The editorial office of the "People's Messenger." The entrance door is on the left-hand side of the back wall; on the right-hand side is another door with glass panels through which the printing-room can be seen. Another door in the right-hand wall. In the middle of the room is a large table covered with papers, newspapers, and books. In the foreground on the left a window, before which stand a desk and a high stool. There

*are a couple of easy chairs by the table, and other chairs stand-
ing along the wall.   The room is dingy and uncomfortable;
the furniture is old, the chairs stained and torn.   In the printing-
room the compositors are seen at work, and a printer is working
a hand-press.*   [HOVSTAD *is sitting at the desk, writing.* BILL-
ING *comes in from the right with* DR. STOCKMANN'S *manuscript
in his hand.*]

BILLING. Well, I must say!

HOVSTAD (*still writing*). Have you read it through?

BILLING (*laying the manuscript on the desk*). Yes, indeed
I have.

HOVSTAD. Don't you think the Doctor hits them pretty
hard?

BILLING. Hard? Bless my soul, he's crushing! Every
word falls like—how shall I put it?—like the blow of a
sledgehammer.

HOVSTAD. Yes, but they are not the people to throw up
the sponge at the first blow.

BILLING. That is true; and for that reason we must strike
blow upon blow until the whole of this aristocracy tumbles
to pieces. As I sat in there reading this, I almost seemed to
see a revolution in being.

HOVSTAD (*turning round*). Hush!—Speak so that Aslaksen cannot hear you.

BILLING (*lowering his voice*). Aslaksen is a chicken-hearted
chap, a coward; there is nothing of the man in him. But this
time you will insist on your own way, won't you? You will
put the Doctor's article in?

HOVSTAD. Yes, and if the Mayor doesn't like it——

BILLING. That will be the devil of a nuisance.

HOVSTAD. Well, fortunately we can turn the situation to
good account, whatever happens. If the Mayor will not fall
in with the Doctor's project, he will have all the small trades-

men down on him—the whole of the Householders' Association and the rest of them.   And if he does fall in with it, he will fall out with the whole crowd of large shareholders in the Baths, who up to now have been his most valuable supporters——

BILLING.   Yes, because they will certainly have to fork out a pretty penny——

HOVSTAD.   Yes, you may be sure they will.   And in this way the ring will be broken up, you see, and then in every issue of the paper we will enlighten the public on the Mayor's incapability on one point and another, and make it clear that all the positions of trust in the town, the whole control of municipal affairs, ought to be put in the hands of the Liberals.

BILLING.   That is perfectly true!   I see it coming—I see it coming;   we are on the threshold of a revolution!

[*A knock is heard at the door.*]

HOVSTAD.   Hush!   (*Calls out.*)   Come in!   (DR. STOCKMANN *comes in by the street door.*   HOVSTAD *goes to meet him.*) Ah, it is you, Doctor!   Well?

DR. STOCKMANN.   You may set to work and print it, Mr. Hovstad!

HOVSTAD.   Has it come to that, then?

BILLING.   Hurrah!

DR. STOCKMANN.   Yes, print away.   Undoubtedly it has come to that.   Now they must take what they get.   There is going to be a fight in the town, Mr. Billing!

BILLING.   War to the knife, I hope!   We will get our knives to their throats, Doctor!

DR. STOCKMANN.   This article is only a beginning.   I have already got four or five more sketched out in my head.   Where is Aslaksen?

BILLING (*calls into the printing-room*).   Aslaksen, just come here for a minute!

HOVSTAD. Four or five more articles, did you say? On the same subject?

DR. STOCKMANN. No—far from it, my dear fellow. No, they are about quite another matter. But they all spring from the question of the water-supply and the drainage. One thing leads to another, you know. It is like beginning to pull down an old house, exactly.

BILLING. Upon my soul, it's true; you find you are not done till you have pulled all the old rubbish down.

ASLAKSEN (coming in). Pulled down? You are not thinking of pulling down the Baths surely, Doctor?

HOVSTAD. Far from it; don't be afraid.

DR. STOCKMANN. No, we meant something quite different Well, what do you think of my article, Mr. Hovstad?

HOVSTAD. I think it is simply a masterpiece——

DR. STOCKMANN. Do you really think so? Well, I am very pleased, very pleased.

HOVSTAD. It is so clear and intelligible. One need have no special knowledge to understand the bearing of it. You will have every enlightened man on your side.

ASLAKSEN. And every prudent man too, I hope?

BILLING. The prudent and the imprudent—almost the whole town.

ASLAKSEN. In that case we may venture to print it.

DR. STOCKMANN. I should think so!

HOVSTAD. We will put it in tomorrow morning.

DR. STOCKMANN. Of course—you must not lose a single day. I wanted to ask you, Mr. Aslaksen, if you would supervise the printing of it yourself.

ASLAKSEN. With pleasure.

DR. STOCKMANN. Take care of it as if it were a treasure! No misprints—every word is important. I will look in again a little later; perhaps you will be able to let me see a proof. I can't tell you how eager I am to see it in print, and see it burst upon the public——

BILLING. Burst upon them—yes, like a flash of lightning!

DR. STOCKMANN. ——and to have it submitted to the judgment of my intelligent fellow-townsmen. You cannot imagine what I have gone through today. I have been threatened first with one thing and then with another; they have tried to rob me of my most elementary rights as a man——

BILLING. What! Your rights as a man!

DR. STOCKMANN. ——they have tried to degrade me, to make a coward of me, to force me to put personal interests before my most sacred convictions——

BILLING. That is too much—I'm damned if it isn't.

HOVSTAD. Oh, you mustn't be surprised at anything from that quarter.

DR. STOCKMANN. Well, they will get the worst of it with me; they may assure themselves of that. I shall consider the "People's Messenger" my sheet-anchor now, and every single day I will bombard them with one article after another, like bomb-shells——

ASLAKSEN. Yes, but——

BILLING. Hurrah!—it is war, it is war!

DR. STOCKMANN. I shall smite them to the ground—I shall crush them—I shall break down all their defences, before the eyes of the honest public! That is what I shall do!

ASLAKSEN. Yes, but in moderation, Doctor—proceed with moderation——

BILLING. Not a bit of it, not a bit of it! Don't spare the dynamite!

DR. STOCKMANN. Because it is not merely a question of water-supply and drains now, you know. No—it is the whole of our social life that we have got to purify and disinfect——

BILLING. Spoken like a deliverer!

DR. STOCKMANN. All the incapables must be turned out, you understand—and that in every walk of life! Endless vistas have opened themselves to my mind's eye today. I cannot see it all quite clearly yet, but I shall in time. Young and vigorous standard-bearers—those are what we need and must seek, my friends; we must have new men in command at all our outposts.

BILLING. Hear, hear!

DR. STOCKMANN. We only need to stand by one another, and it will all be perfectly easy. The revolution will be launched like a ship that runs smoothly off the stocks. Don't you think so?

HOVSTAD. For my part I think we have now a prospect of getting the municipal authority into the hands where it should lie.

ASLAKSEN. And if only we proceed with moderation, I cannot imagine that there will be any risk.

DR. STOCKMANN. Who the devil cares whether there is any risk or not? What I am doing, I am doing in the name of truth and for the sake of my conscience.

HOVSTAD. You are a man who deserves to be supported, Doctor.

ASLAKSEN. Yes, there is no denying that the Doctor is a true friend to the town—a real friend to the community, that he is.

BILLING. Take my word for it, Aslaksen, Dr. Stockmann is a friend of the people.

ASLAKSEN. I fancy the Householders' Association will make use of that expression before long.

DR. STOCKMANN (*affected, grasps their hands*).   Thank you, thank you, my dear staunch friends. It is very refreshing to me to hear you say that; my brother called me something quite different. By Jove, he shall have it back, with interest! But now I must be off to see a poor devil ——. I will come back, as I said. Keep a very careful eye on the manuscript, Aslaksen, and don't for worlds leave out any of my exclamation marks! Rather put one or two more in! Capital, capital! Well, good-bye for the present— good-bye, good-bye!

[*They show him to the door, and bow him out.*]

HOVSTAD. He may prove an invaluably useful man to us.

ASLAKSEN. Yes, so long as he confines himself to this matter of the Baths. But if he goes farther afield, I don't think it would be advisable to follow him.

HOVSTAD. Hm!—that all depends——

BILLING. You are so infernally timid, Aslaksen!

ASLAKSEN. Timid? Yes, when it is a question of the local authorities, I am timid, Mr. Billing; it is a lesson I have learnt in the school of experience, let me tell you. But try me in higher politics, in matters that concern the government itself, and then see if I am timid.

BILLING. No, you aren't, I admit. But this is simply contradicting yourself.

ASLAKSEN. I am a man with a conscience, and that is the whole matter. If you attack the government, you don't do the community any harm, anyway; those fellows pay no attention to attacks, you see—they go on just as they are, in spite of them. But *local* authorities are different; they *can* be turned out, and then perhaps you may get an ignorant lot into office who may do irreparable harm to the householders and everybody else.

HOVSTAD. But what of the education of citizens by self-government—don't you attach any importance to that?

ASLAKSEN. When a man has interests of his own to protect, he cannot think of everything, Mr. Hovstad.

HOVSTAD. Then I hope I shall never have interests of my own to protect!

BILLING. Hear, hear!

ASLAKSEN (*with a smile*). Hm! (*Points to the desk.*) Mr.

Sheriff Stensgaard* was your predecessor at that editorial desk.

BILLING (*spitting*). Bah! That turncoat.

HOVSTAD. I am not a weathercock—and never will be.

ASLAKSEN. A politician should never be too certain of anything, Mr. Hovstad. And as for you, Mr. Billing, I should think it is time for you to be taking in a reef or two in your sails, seeing that you are applying for the post of secretary to the Bench.

BILLING. I——!

HOVSTAD. Are you, Billing?

BILLING. Well, yes—but you must clearly understand I am doing it only to annoy the bigwigs.

ASLAKSEN. Anyhow, it is no business of mine. But if I am to be accused of timidity and of inconsistency in my principles, I want to point out: my political past is an open book. I have never changed, except perhaps to become a little more moderate, you see. My heart is still with the people; but I don't deny that my reason has a certain bias towards the authorities—the local ones, I mean.

[*Goes into the printing-room.*]

BILLING. Oughtn't we to try and get rid of him, Hovstad?

HOVSTAD. Do you know anyone else who will advance the money for our paper and printing bill?

BILLING. It is an infernal nuisance that we don't possess some capital to trade on.

HOVSTAD (*sitting down at his desk*). Yes, if we only had that, then——

BILLING. Suppose you were to apply to Dr. Stockmann?

HOVSTAD (*turning over some papers*). What is the use? He has got nothing.

BILLING. No, but he has got a warm man in the background, old Morten Kiil—"the Badger," as they call him.

HOVSTAD (*writing*). Are you so sure *he* has got anything?

*Both Stensgaard and Aslaksen appear as characters in Ibsen's *The League of Youth* (1869).

BILLING. Good Lord, of course he has! And some of it must come to the Stockmanns. Most probably he will do something for the children, at all events.

HOVSTAD (*turning half round*). Are you counting on that?

BILLING. Counting on it? Of course I am not counting on anything.

HOVSTAD. That is right. And I should not count on the secretaryship to the Bench either, if I were you; for I can assure you—you won't get it.

BILLING. Do you think I am not quite aware of that? My object is precisely *not* to get it. A slight of that kind stimulates a man's fighting power—it is like getting a supply of fresh bile—and I am sure one needs that badly enough in a hole-and-corner place like this, where so seldom anything happens to stir one up.

HOVSTAD (*writing*). Quite so, quite so.

BILLING. Ah, I shall be heard of yet!—Now I shall go and write the appeal to the Householders' Association.

[*Goes into the room on the right.*]

HOVSTAD (*sitting at his desk, biting his penholder, says slowly*). Hm!—that's it, is it? (*A knock is heard.*) Come in! (PETRA *comes in by the outer door.* HOVSTAD *gets up.*) What, you!—here?

PETRA. Yes, you must forgive me——

HOVSTAD (*pulling a chair forward*). Won't you sit down?

PETRA. No, thank you; I must go again in a moment.

HOVSTAD. Have you come with a message from your father, by any chance?

PETRA. No, I have come on my own account. (*Takes a book out of her coat pocket.*) Here is the English story.

HOVSTAD. Why have you brought it back?

PETRA. Because I am not going to translate it.

HOVSTAD. But you promised me faithfully——

PETRA. Yes, but then I had not read it. I don't suppose you have read it either?

HOVSTAD. No, you know quite well I don't understand English; but——

PETRA. Quite so. That is why I wanted to tell you that you must find something else. (*Lays the book on the table.*) You can't use this for the "People's Messenger."

HOVSTAD. Why not?

PETRA. Because it conflicts with all your opinions.

HOVSTAD. Oh, for that matter——

PETRA. You don't understand me. The burden of this story is that there is a supernatural power that looks after the so-called good people in this world and makes everything happen for the best in their case—while all the so-called bad people are punished.

HOVSTAD. Well, but that is all right. That is just what our readers want.

PETRA. And are you going to be the one to give it to them? For myself, I do not believe a word of it. You know quite well that things do not happen so in reality.

HOVSTAD. You are perfectly right, but an editor cannot always act as he would prefer. He is often obliged to bow to the wishes of the public in unimportant matters. Politics are the most important thing in life—for a newspaper, anyway; and if I want to carry my public with me on the path that leads to liberty and progress, I must not frighten them away. If they find a moral tale of this sort in the serial at the bottom of the page, they will be all the more ready to read what is printed above it; they feel more secure, as it were.

PETRA. For shame! You would never go and set a snare like that for your readers; you are not a spider!

HOVSTAD (*smiling*). Thank you for having such a good

opinion of me.   No; as a matter of fact that is Billing's idea and not mine.

PETRA. Billing's!

HOVSTAD. Yes; anyway he propounded that theory here one day.   And it is Billing who is so anxious to have that story in the paper; I don't know anything about the book.

PETRA.   But how can Billing, with his emancipated views——

HOVSTAD. Oh, Billing is a many-sided man.   He is applying for the post of secretary to the Bench, too, I hear.

PETRA. I don't believe it, Mr. Hovstad. How could he possibly bring himself to do such a thing?

HOVSTAD. Ah, you must ask him that.

PETRA. I should never have thought it of him.

HOVSTAD (*looking more closely at her*). No? Does it really surprise you so much?

PETRA. Yes. Or perhaps not altogether. Really, I don't quite know——

HOVSTAD. We journalists are not worth much, Miss Stockmann.

PETRA. Do you really mean that?

HOVSTAD. I think so sometimes.

PETRA. Yes, in the ordinary affairs of everyday life, perhaps; I can understand that. But now, when you have taken a weighty matter in hand——

HOVSTAD. This matter of your father's, you mean?

PETRA. Exactly. It seems to me that now you must feel you are a man worth more than most.

HOVSTAD. Yes, today I do feel something of that sort.

PETRA. Of course you do, don't you? It is a splendid vocation you have chosen—to smooth the way for the march of unappreciated truths and new and courageous lines of thought. If it were nothing more than because you stand fearlessly in the open and take up the cause of an injured man——

HOVSTAD. Especially when that injured man is—ahem! —I don't rightly know how to——

PETRA. When that man is so upright and so honest, you mean?

HOVSTAD (*more gently*). Especially when he is your father, I meant.

PETRA (*suddenly checked*). *That?*

HOVSTAD. Yes, Petra—Miss Petra.

PETRA. Is it *that*, that is first and foremost with you? Not the matter itself? Not the truth?—not my father's big generous heart?

HOVSTAD. Certainly—of course—that too.

PETRA. No, thank you; you have betrayed yourself, Mr. Hovstad, and now I shall never trust you again in anything.

HOVSTAD. Can you really take it so amiss in me that it is mostly for your sake——?

PETRA. I am angry with you for not having been honest with my father. You talked to him as if the truth and the good of the community were what lay nearest to your heart. You have made fools of both my father and me. You are not the man you made yourself out to be. And that I shall never forgive you—never!

HOVSTAD. You ought not to speak so bitterly, Miss Petra —least of all now.

PETRA. Why not now, especially?

HOVSTAD. Because your father cannot do without my help.

PETRA (*looking him up and down*). Are you that sort of man too? For shame!

HOVSTAD. No, no, I am not. This came upon me so unexpectedly—you must believe that.

PETRA. I know what to believe. Good-bye.

ASLAKSEN (*coming from the printing-room, hurriedly and with an air of mystery*). Damnation, Hovstad!—(*Sees* PETRA.) Oh, this is awkward——

PETRA. There is the book; you must give it to some one else.   [*Goes towards the door.*]

HOVSTAD (*following her*). But, Miss Stockmann——

PETRA. Good-bye.   [*Goes out.*]

ASLAKSEN. I say—Mr. Hovstad——

HOVSTAD. Well, well!—what is it?

ASLAKSEN. The Mayor is outside in the printing-room.

HOVSTAD. The Mayor, did you say?

ASLAKSEN. Yes, he wants to speak to you. He came in by the back door—didn't want to be seen, you understand.

HOVSTAD. What can he want? Wait a bit—I will go myself. (*Goes to the door of the printing-room, opens it, bows and invites* PETER STOCKMANN *in.*) Just see, Aslaksen, that no one——

ASLAKSEN. Quite so.   [*Goes into the printing-room.*]

PETER STOCKMANN. You did not expect to see me here, Mr. Hovstad?

HOVSTAD. No, I confess I did not.

PETER STOCKMANN (*looking round*). You are very snug in here—very nice indeed.

HOVSTAD. Oh——

PETER STOCKMANN. And here I come, without any notice, to take up your time!

HOVSTAD. By all means, Mr. Mayor. I am at your service. But let me relieve you of your—— (*takes* STOCKMANN's *hat and stick and puts them on a chair.*) Won't you sit down?

PETER STOCKMANN (*sitting down by the table*). Thank you. (HOVSTAD *sits down.*) I have had an extremely annoying experience today, Mr. Hovstad.

HOVSTAD. Really? Ah well, I expect with all the various business you have to attend to——

PETER STOCKMANN. The Medical Officer of the Baths is responsible for what happened today.

HOVSTAD. Indeed? The Doctor?

PETER STOCKMANN. He has addressed a kind of report to the Baths Committee on the subject of certain supposed defects in the Baths.

HOVSTAD. Has he indeed?

PETER STOCKMANN. Yes—has he not told you? I thought he said——

HOVSTAD. Ah, yes—it is true he did mention something about——

ASLAKSEN (*coming from the printing-room*). I ought to have that copy——

HOVSTAD (*angrily*). Ahem!—there it is on the desk.

ASLAKSEN (*taking it*). Right.

PETER STOCKMANN. But look there—that is the thing I was speaking of!

ASLAKSEN. Yes, that is the Doctor's article, Mr. Mayor.

HOVSTAD. Oh, is *that* what you were speaking about?

PETER STOCKMANN. Yes, that is it. What do you think of it?

HOVSTAD. Oh, I am only a layman—and I have only taken a very cursory glance at it.

PETER STOCKMANN. But you are going to print it?

HOVSTAD. I cannot very well refuse a distinguished man——

ASLAKSEN. I have nothing to do with editing the paper, Mr. Mayor——

PETER STOCKMANN. I understand.

ASLAKSEN. I merely print what is put into my hands.

PETER STOCKMANN. Quite so.

ASLAKSEN. And so I must——

[*Moves off towards the printing-room.*]

PETER STOCKMANN. No, but wait a moment, Mr. Aslaksen. You will allow me, Mr. Hovstad?

HOVSTAD. If you please, Mr. Mayor.

PETER STOCKMANN. You are a discreet and thoughtful man, Mr. Aslaksen.

ASLAKSEN. I am delighted to hear you think so, sir.

PETER STOCKMANN. And a man of very considerable influence.

ASLAKSEN. Chiefly among the small tradesmen, sir.

PETER STOCKMANN. The small taxpayers are the majority —here as everywhere else.

ASLAKSEN. That is true.

PETER STOCKMANN. And I have no doubt you know the general trend of opinion among them, don't you?

ASLAKSEN. Yes, I think I may say I do, Mr. Mayor.

PETER STOCKMANN. Yes. Well, since there is such a praiseworthy spirit of self-sacrifice among the less wealthy citizens of our town——

ASLAKSEN. What?

HOVSTAD. Self-sacrifice?

PETER STOCKMANN. It is pleasing evidence of a public-spirited feeling, extremely pleasing evidence. I might almost say I hardly expected it. But you have a closer knowledge of public opinion than I.

ASLAKSEN. But, Mr. Mayor——

PETER STOCKMANN. And indeed it is no small sacrifice that the town is going to make.

HOVSTAD. The town?

ASLAKSEN. But I don't understand. Is it the Baths——?

PETER STOCKMANN. At a provisional estimate, the alterations that the Medical Officer asserts are desirable will cost somewhere about two hundred thousand crowns.

ASLAKSEN. That is a lot of money, but——

PETER STOCKMANN. Of course it will be necessary to raise a municipal loan.

HOVSTAD (*getting up*). Surely you never mean that the town must pay——?

ASLAKSEN.   Do you mean that it must come out of the municipal funds?—out of the ill-filled pockets of the small tradesmen?

PETER STOCKMANN.   Well, my dear Mr. Aslaksen, where else is the money to come from?

ASLAKSEN.   The gentlemen who own the Baths ought to provide that.

PETER STOCKMANN.   The proprietors of the Baths are not in a position to incur any further expense.

ASLAKSEN.   Is that absolutely certain, Mr. Mayor?

PETER STOCKMANN.   I have satisfied myself that it is so. If the town wants these very extensive alterations, it will have to pay for them.

ASLAKSEN.   But, damn it all—I beg your pardon—this is quite another matter, Mr. Hovstad!

HOVSTAD.   It is, indeed.

PETER STOCKMANN.   The most fatal part of it is that we shall be obliged to shut the Baths for a couple of years.

HOVSTAD.   Shut them? Shut them altogether?

ASLAKSEN.   For two years?

PETER STOCKMANN.   Yes, the work will take as long as that—at least.

ASLAKSEN.   I'm damned if we will stand that, Mr. Mayor! What are we householders to live upon in the meantime?

PETER STOCKMANN.   Unfortunately, that is an extremely difficult question to answer, Mr. Aslaksen. But what would you have us do? Do you suppose we shall have a single visitor in the town, if we go about telling stories that our water is polluted, that we are living over a plague spot, that the entire town——

ASLAKSEN.   And the whole thing is merely imagination?

PETER STOCKMANN.   With the best will in the world, I have not been able to come to any other conclusion.

ASLAKSEN.   Well then, I must say it is absolutely unjustifiable of Dr. Stockmann—I beg your pardon, Mr. Mayor——

PETER STOCKMANN.   What you say is lamentably true, Mr. Aslaksen.   My brother has, unfortunately, always been a headstrong man.

ASLAKSEN.   After this, do you mean to give him your support, Mr. Hovstad?

HOVSTAD.   Can you suppose for a moment that I——?

PETER STOCKMANN.   I have drawn up a short *résumé* of the situation as it appears from a reasonable man's point of view. In it I have indicated how certain possible defects might suitably be remedied without outrunning the resources of the Baths Committee.

HOVSTAD.   Have you got it with you, Mr. Mayor?

PETER STOCKMANN (*fumbling in his pocket*).   Yes, I brought it with me in case you should——

ASLAKSEN.   Good Lord, there he is!

PETER STOCKMANN.   Who?   My brother?

HOVSTAD.   Where?   Where?

ASLAKSEN.   He has just gone through the printing-room.

PETER STOCKMANN.   How unlucky!   I don't want to meet him here, and I had still several things to speak to you about.

HOVSTAD (*pointing to the door on the right*).   Go in there for the present.

PETER STOCKMANN.   But——?

HOVSTAD.   You will only find Billing in there.

ASLAKSEN.   Quick, quick, Mr. Mayor—he is just coming.

PETER STOCKMANN.   Yes, very well; but see that you get rid of him quickly.

[*Goes out through the door on the right, which* ASLAKSEN *opens for him and shuts after him.*]

HOVSTAD.   Pretend to be doing something, Aslaksen.

[*Sits down and writes.* ASLAKSEN *begins foraging among a heap of newspapers that are lying on a chair.*]

DR. STOCKMANN (*coming in from the printing-room*). Here I am again.   [*Puts down his hat and stick.*]

HOVSTAD (*writing*). Already, Doctor? Hurry up with what we were speaking about, Aslaksen. We are very pressed for time today.

DR. STOCKMANN (*to* ASLAKSEN). No proof for me to see yet, I hear.

ASLAKSEN (*without turning round*). You couldn't expect it yet, Doctor.

DR. STOCKMANN. No, no; but I am impatient, as you can understand. I shall not know a moment's peace of mind till I see it in print.

HOVSTAD. Hm!—it will take a good while yet, won't it, Aslaksen?

ASLAKSEN. Yes, I am almost afraid it will.

DR. STOCKMANN. All right, my dear friends; I will come back. I do not mind coming back twice if necessary. A matter of such great importance—the welfare of the town at stake—it is no time to shirk trouble. (*Is just going, but stops and comes back.*) Look here—there is one thing more I want to speak to you about.

HOVSTAD. Excuse me, but could it not wait till some other time?

DR. STOCKMANN. I can tell you in half a dozen words. It is only this. When my article is read tomorrow and it is realized that I have been quietly working the whole winter for the welfare of the town——

HOVSTAD. Yes, but, Doctor——

DR. STOCKMANN. I know what you are going to say. You don't see how on earth it was any more than my duty —my obvious duty as a citizen. Of course it wasn't; I know that as well as you. But my fellow-citizens, you know——! Good Lord, think of all the good souls who think so highly of me——!

ASLAKSEN. Yes, our townsfolk have had a very high opinion of you so far, Doctor.

DR. STOCKMANN. Yes, and that is just why I am afraid they——. Well, this is the point; when this reaches them, especially the poorer classes, and sounds in their ears like a summons to take the town's affairs into their own hands for the future——

HOVSTAD (*getting up*). Ahem! Doctor, I won't conceal from you the fact——

DR. STOCKMANN. Ah!—I knew there was something in the wind! But I won't hear a word of it. If anything of that sort is being set on foot——

HOVSTAD. Of what sort?

DR. STOCKMANN. Well, whatever it is—whether it is a demonstration in my honor, or a banquet, or a subscription list for some presentation to me—whatever it is, you must promise me solemnly and faithfully to put a stop to it. You too, Mr. Aslaksen; do you understand?

HOVSTAD. You must forgive me, Doctor, but sooner or later we must tell you the plain truth——

[*He is interrupted by the entrance of* MRS. STOCKMANN, *who comes in from the street door.*]

MRS. STOCKMANN (*seeing her husband*). Just as I thought!

HOVSTAD (*going towards her*). You too, Mrs. Stockmann?

DR. STOCKMANN. What on earth do *you* want here, Katherine?

MRS. STOCKMANN. I should think you know very well what I want.

HOVSTAD. Won't you sit down? Or perhaps——

MRS. STOCKMANN. No, thank you; don't trouble. And you must not be offended at my coming to fetch my husband; I am the mother of three children, you know.

DR. STOCKMANN. Nonsense!—we know all about that.

MRS. STOCKMANN. Well, one would not give you credit for much thought for your wife and children today; if you had had that, you would not have gone and dragged us all into misfortune.

DR. STOCKMANN. Are you out of your senses, Katherine? Because a man has a wife and children, is he not to be allowed to proclaim the truth—is he not to be allowed to be an actively useful citizen—is he not to be allowed to do a service to his native town?

MRS. STOCKMANN. Yes, Thomas—in reason.

ASLAKSEN. Just what I say. Moderation is everything.

MRS. STOCKMANN. And that is why you wrong us, Mr Hovstad, in enticing my husband away from his home and making a dupe of him in all this.

HOVSTAD. I certainly am making a dupe of no one——

DR. STOCKMANN. Making a dupe of me! Do you suppose *I* should allow myself to be duped?

MRS. STOCKMANN. It is just what you do. I know quite well you have more brains than anyone in the town, but you are extremely easily duped, Thomas. (*To* HOVSTAD.) Please realize that he loses his post at the Baths if you print what he has written——

ASLAKSEN. What!

HOVSTAD. Look here, Doctor——

DR. STOCKMANN (*laughing*). Ha—ha!—just let them try! No, no—they will take good care not to. I have got the compact majority behind me, let me tell you!

MRS. STOCKMANN. Yes, that is just the worst of it—your having any such horrid thing behind you.

DR. STOCKMANN. Rubbish, Katherine!—Go home and look after your house and leave me to look after the community. How can you be so afraid, when I am so confident and happy? (*Walks up and down, rubbing his hands.*) Truth and the People will win the fight, you may be certain! I see the whole of the broad-minded middle class marching like a victorious army——! (*Stops beside a chair.*) What the deuce is that lying there?

ASLAKSEN. Good Lord!

HOVSTAD. Ahem!

DR. STOCKMANN. Here we have the topmost pinnacle of authority!

[*Takes the* MAYOR's *official hat carefully between his finger-tips and holds it up in the air.*]

MRS. STOCKMANN. The Mayor's hat!

DR. STOCKMANN. And here is the staff of office too. How in the name of all that's wonderful——?

HOVSTAD. Well, you see——

DR. STOCKMANN. Oh, I understand. He has been here trying to talk you over. Ha—ha!—he made rather a mistake there! And as soon as he caught sight of me in the printing-room——. (*Bursts out laughing.*) Did he run away, Mr. Aslaksen?

ASLAKSEN (*hurriedly*). Yes, he ran away, Doctor.

DR. STOCKMANN. Ran away without his stick or his——. Fiddlesticks! Peter doesn't run away and leave his belongings behind him. But what the deuce have you done with him? Ah!—in there, of course. Now you shall see, Katherine.

MRS. STOCKMANN. Thomas—please don't——!

ASLAKSEN. Don't be rash, Doctor.

[DR. STOCKMANN *has put on the* MAYOR's *hat and taken his stick in his hand. He goes up to the door, opens it and stands with his hand to his hat at the salute.* PETER STOCKMANN *comes in, red with anger.* BILLING *follows him.*]

PETER STOCKMANN. What does this tomfoolery mean?

DR. STOCKMANN. Be respectful, my good Peter. I am the chief authority in the town now. [*Walks up and down.*]

MRS. STOCKMANN (*almost in tears*). Really, Thomas!

PETER STOCKMANN (*following him about*). Give me my hat and stick.

DR. STOCKMANN (*in the same tone as before*). If you are chief constable, let me tell you that I am the Mayor—I am the master of the whole town, please understand!

PETER STOCKMANN. Take off my hat, I tell you. Remember it is part of an official uniform.

DR. STOCKMANN. Pooh! Do you think the newly awakened lion-hearted people are going to be frighened by an official hat? There is going to be a revolution in the town tomorrow, let me tell you. You thought you could turn me out; but now I shall turn you out—turn you out of all your various offices. Do you think I cannot? Listen to me. I have triumphant social forces behind me. Hovstad and Billing will thunder in the "People's Messenger," and Aslaksen will take the field at the head of the whole Householders' Association——

ASLAKSEN. That I won't, Doctor.

DR. STOCKMANN. Of course you will——

PETER STOCKMANN. Ah!—may I ask then if Mr. Hovstad intends to join this agitation?

HOVSTAD. No, Mr. Mayor.

ASLAKSEN. No, Mr. Hovstad is not such a fool as to go and ruin his paper and himself for the sake of an imaginary grievance.

DR. STOCKMANN (*looking round him*). What does this mean?

HOVSTAD. You have represented your case in a false light, Doctor, and therefore I am unable to give you my support.

BILLING. And after what the Mayor was so kind as to tell me just now, I——

DR. STOCKMANN. A false light! Leave that part of it to me. Only print my article; I am quite capable of defending it.

HOVSTAD. I am not going to print it. I cannot and will not and dare not print it.

DR. STOCKMANN. You dare not? What nonsense!—you are the editor; and an editor controls his paper, I suppose!

ASLAKSEN. No, it is the subscribers, Doctor.

PETER STOCKMANN. Fortunately, yes.

ASLAKSEN. It is public opinion—the enlightened public—householders and people of that kind; they control the newspapers.

DR. STOCKMANN (*composedly*). And I have all these influences against me?

ASLAKSEN. Yes, you have. It would mean the absolute ruin of the community if your article were to appear.

DR. STOCKMANN. Indeed.

PETER STOCKMANN. My hat and stick, if you please. (DR. STOCKMANN *takes off the hat and lays it on the table with the stick.* PETER STOCKMANN *takes them up.*) Your authority as mayor has come to an untimely end.

DR. STOCKMANN. We have not got to the end yet. (*To* HOVSTAD.) Then it is quite impossible for you to print my article in the "People's Messenger"?

HOVSTAD. Quite impossible—out of regard for your family as well.

MRS. STOCKMANN. You need not concern yourself about his family, thank you, Mr. Hovstad.

PETER STOCKMANN (*taking a paper from his pocket*). It will be sufficient, for the guidance of the public, if this appears. It is an official statement. May I trouble you?

HOVSTAD (*taking the paper*). Certainly; I will see that it is printed.

DR. STOCKMANN. But not mine. Do you imagine that you can silence me and stifle the truth? You will not find it so easy as you suppose. Mr. Aslaksen, kindly take my manuscript at once and print it as a pamphlet—at my expense. I will have four hundred copies—no, five—six hundred.

ASLAKSEN. If you offered me its weight in gold, I could not lend my press for any such purpose, Doctor. It would be flying in the face of public opinion. You will not get it printed anywhere in the town.

DR. STOCKMANN. Then give it back to me.

HOVSTAD (*giving him the manuscript*). Here it is.

DR. STOCKMANN (*taking his hat and stick*). It shall be made public all the same. I will read it out at a mass meeting of the townspeople. All my fellow-citizens shall hear the voice of truth!

PETER STOCKMANN. You will not find any public body in the town that will give you the use of their hall for such a purpose.

ASLAKSEN. Not a single one, I am certain.

BILLING. No, I'm damned if you will find one.

MRS. STOCKMANN. But this is too shameful! Why should every one turn against you like that?

DR. STOCKMANN (*angrily*). I will tell you why. It is because all the men in this town are old women—like you; they all think of nothing but their families, and never of the community.

MRS. STOCKMANN (*putting her arm into his*). Then I will show them that an—an old woman can be a man for once. I am going to stand by you, Thomas!

DR. STOCKMANN. Bravely said, Katherine! It shall be made public—as I am a living soul! If I can't hire a hall, I shall hire a drum, and parade the town with it and read it at every street corner.

PETER STOCKMANN. You are surely not such an arrant fool as that!

DR. STOCKMANN. Yes, I am.

ASLAKSEN. You won't find a single man in the whole town to go with you.

BILLING. No, I'm damned if you will.

MRS. STOCKMANN. Don't give in, Thomas. I will tell the boys to go with you.

DR. STOCKMANN. That is a splendid idea!

MRS. STOCKMANN. Morten will be delighted; and Ejlif will do whatever he does.

DR. STOCKMANN. Yes, and Petra!—and you too, Katherine!

MRS. STOCKMANN. No, I won't do that; but I will stand at the window and watch you, that's what I will do.

DR. STOCKMANN (*puts his arms round her and kisses her*). Thank you, my dear! Now you and I are going to try a fall, my fine gentlemen! I am going to see whether a pack of cowards can succeed in gagging a patriot who wants to purify society!   [*He and his wife go out by the street door.*]

PETER STOCKMANN (*shaking his head seriously*). Now he has sent *her* out of her senses, too.

CURTAIN

ACT FOUR

SCENE: *A big old-fashioned room in* CAPTAIN HORSTER'S *house. At the back folding-doors, which are standing open, lead to an ante-room. Three windows in the left-hand wall. In the middle of the opposite wall a platform has been erected. On this is a small table with two candles, a water-bottle and glass, and a bell. The room is lit by lamps placed between the windows. In the foreground on the left there is a table with candles and a chair. To the right is a door and some chairs standing near it. The room is nearly filled with a crowd of townspeople of all sorts, a few women and schoolboys being amongst them. People are still streaming in from the back, and the room is soon filled.*

FIRST CITIZEN (*meeting another*). Hullo, Lamstad! You here too?

SECOND CITIZEN. I go to every public meeting, I do.

THIRD CITIZEN. Brought your whistle too, I expect!

SECOND CITIZEN. I should think so. Haven't you?

THIRD CITIZEN. Rather! And old Evensen said he was going to bring a cow-horn, he did.

SECOND CITIZEN. Good old Evensen!

[*Laughter among the crowd.*]

FOURTH CITIZEN (*coming up to them*). I say, tell me what is going on here tonight.

SECOND CITIZEN. Dr. Stockmann is going to deliver an address attacking the Mayor.

FOURTH CITIZEN. But the Mayor is his brother.

FIRST CITIZEN. That doesn't matter; Dr. Stockmann's not the chap to be afraid.

THIRD CITIZEN. But he is in the wrong; it said so in the "People's Messenger."

SECOND CITIZEN. Yes, I expect he must be in the wrong this time, because neither the Householders' Association nor the Citizens' Club would lend him their hall for his meeting.

FIRST CITIZEN. He couldn't even get the loan of the hall at the Baths.

SECOND CITIZEN. No, I should think not.

A MAN IN ANOTHER PART OF THE CROWD. I say—who are we to back up in this?

ANOTHER MAN, BESIDE HIM. Watch Aslaksen, and do as he does.

BILLING (*pushing his way through the crowd, with a writ-*

ing-case under his arm). Excuse me, gentlemen—do you mind letting me through? I am reporting for the "People's Messenger." Thank you very much!

> [*He sits down at the table on the left.*]

A WORKMAN. Who was that?

SECOND WORKMAN. Don't you know him? It's Billing, who writes for Aslaksen's paper.

[CAPTAIN HORSTER *brings in* MRS. STOCKMANN *and* PETRA *through the door on the right.* EJLIF *and* MORTEN *follow them in.*]

HORSTER. I thought you might all sit here; you can slip out easily from here, if things get too lively.

MRS. STOCKMANN. Do you think there will be a disturbance?

HORSTER. One can never tell—with such a crowd. But sit down, and don't be uneasy.

MRS. STOCKMANN (*sitting down*). It was extremely kind of you to offer my husband the room.

HORSTER. Well, if nobody else would——

PETRA (*who has sat down beside her mother*). And it was a plucky thing to do, Captain Horster.

HORSTER. Oh, it is not such a great matter as all that.

[HOVSTAD *and* ASLAKSEN *make their way through the crowd.*]

ASLAKSEN (*going up to* HORSTER). Has the Doctor not come yet?

HORSTER. He is waiting in the next room.

> [*Movement in the crowd by the door at the back.*]

HOVSTAD. Look—here comes the Mayor!

BILLING. Yes, I'm damned if he hasn't come after all!

[PETER STOCKMANN *makes his way gradually through the crowd, bows courteously and takes up a position by the wall on the left. Shortly afterwards* DR. STOCKMANN *comes in by the right-hand door. He is dressed in a black frockcoat, with a white tie. There is a little feeble applause, which is hushed down. Silence is obtained.*]

DR. STOCKMANN (*in an undertone*). How do you feel, Katherine?

MRS. STOCKMANN. All right, thank you. (*Lowering her voice.*) Be sure not to lose your temper, Thomas.

DR. STOCKMANN. Oh, I know how to control myself. (*Looks at his watch, steps on to the platform and bows.*) It is a quarter past—so I will begin.

[*Takes his manuscript out of his pocket.*]

ASLAKSEN. I think we ought to elect a chairman first.

DR. STOCKMANN. No, it is quite unnecessary.

SOME OF THE CROWD. Yes—yes!

PETER STOCKMANN. I certainly think, too, that we ought to have a chairman.

DR. STOCKMANN. But I have called this meeting to deliver a lecture, Peter.

PETER STOCKMANN. Dr. Stockmann's lecture may possibly lead to a considerable conflict of opinion.

VOICES IN THE CROWD. A chairman! A chairman!

HOVSTAD. The general wish of the meeting seems to be that a chairman should be elected.

DR. STOCKMANN (*restraining himself*). Very well—let the meeting have its way.

ASLAKSEN. Will the Mayor be good enough to undertake the task?

THREE MEN (*clapping their hands*). Bravo! Bravo!

PETER STOCKMANN. For various reasons, which you will easily understand, I must beg to be excused. But fortunately we have amongst us a man who I think will be acceptable to you all. I refer to the President of the Householders' Association, Mr. Aslaksen.

SEVERAL VOICES. Yes—Aslaksen! Bravo, Aslaksen!

[DR. STOCKMANN *takes up his manuscript and walks up and down the platform.*]

ASLAKSEN. Since my fellow-citizens choose to entrust me with this duty, I cannot refuse.

[*Loud applause.* ASLAKSEN *mounts the platform.*]

BILLING (*writing*). "Mr. Aslaksen was elected with enthusiasm."

ASLAKSEN. And now, as I am in this position, I should like to say a few brief words. I am a quiet and peaceable man, who believes in discreet moderation, and—and—in moderate discretion. All my friends can bear witness to that.

SEVERAL VOICES. That's right! That's right, Aslaksen!

ASLAKSEN. I have learnt in the school of life and experience that moderation is the most valuable virtue a citizen can possess——

PETER STOCKMANN. Hear, hear!

ASLAKSEN. ——And moreover that discretion and moderation are what enable a man to be of most service to the community. I would therefore suggest to our esteemed fellow-citizen who has called this meeting that he should strive to keep strictly within the bounds of moderation.

A MAN BY THE DOOR. Three cheers for the Moderation Society!

A VOICE. Shame!

SEVERAL VOICES. Sh!—Sh!

ASLAKSEN. No interruptions, gentlemen, please! Does anyone wish to make any remarks?

PETER STOCKMANN. Mr. Chairman.

ASLAKSEN. The Mayor will address the meeting.

PETER STOCKMANN. In consideration of the close relationship in which, as you all know, I stand to the present Medical Officer of the Baths, I should have preferred not to speak this evening. But my official position with regard to the Baths and my solicitude for the vital interests of the town compel me to bring forward a motion. I venture to presume that there is not a single one of our citizens present who considers it desirable that unreliable and exaggerated accounts of the sanitary condition of the Baths and the town should be spread abroad.

SEVERAL VOICES. No, no! Certainly not! We protest against it!

PETER STOCKMANN. Therefore I should like to propose that the meeting should not permit the Medical Officer either to read or to comment on his proposed lecture.

DR. STOCKMANN (*impatiently*). Not permit——! What the devil——!

MRS. STOCKMANN (*coughing*). Ahem!—ahem!

DR. STOCKMANN (*collecting himself*). Very well. Go ahead!

PETER STOCKMANN. In my communication to the "People's Messenger," I have put the essential facts before the public in such a way that every fair-minded citizen can easily form his own opinion. From it you will see that the main result of the Medical Officer's proposals—apart from their constituting a vote of censure on the leading men of the town—would be to saddle the taxpayers with an unnecessary expenditure of at least some thousands of pounds.

[*Sounds of disapproval among the audience, and some cat-calls.*]

ASLAKSEN (*ringing his bell*). Silence, please, gentlemen! I beg to support the Mayor's motion. I quite agree with him that there is something behind this agitation started by the Doctor. He talks about the Baths; but it is a revolution he is aiming at—he wants to get the administration of the town put into new hands. No one doubts the honesty of the Doctor's intentions—no one will suggest that there can be any two opinions as to that. I myself am a believer in self-government for the people, provided it does not fall too heavily on the taxpayers. But that would be the case here; and that is why I will see Dr. Stockmann damned—I beg your pardon—before I go with him in the matter. You can pay too dearly for a thing sometimes; that is my opinion. [*Loud applause on all sides.*]

HOVSTAD. I, too, feel called upon to explain my position. Dr. Stockmann's agitation appeared to be gaining a certain amount of sympathy at first, so I supported it as impartially as I could. But presently we had reason to suspect that we had allowed ourselves to be misled by misrepresentation of the state of affairs——

DR. STOCKMANN. Misrepresentation——!

HOVSTAD. Well, let us say a not entirely trustworthy representation. The Mayor's statement has proved that. I hope no one here has any doubt as to my liberal principles; the attitude of the "People's Messenger" towards important political questions is well known to every one. But the advice of experienced and thoughtful men has convinced me that in purely local matters a newspaper ought to proceed with a certain caution.

ASLAKSEN. I entirely agree with the speaker.

HOVSTAD. And, in the matter before us, it is now an undoubted fact that Dr. Stockmann has public opinion against him. Now, what is an editor's first and most obvious duty, gentlemen? Is it not to work in harmony with his readers? Has he not received a sort of tacit mandate to work persistently and assiduously for the welfare of those whose opinions he represents? Or is it possible I am mistaken in that?

VOICES FROM THE CROWD. No, no! You are quite right!

HOVSTAD. It has cost me a severe struggle to break with a man in whose house I have been lately a frequent guest— a man who till today has been able to pride himself on the undivided goodwill of his fellow-citizens—a man whose only, or at all events whose essential, failing is that he is swayed by his heart rather than his head.

A FEW SCATTERED VOICES. That is true! Bravo, Dr. Stockmann!

HOVSTAD. But my duty to the community obliged me to break with him. And there is another consideration that impels me to oppose him, and, as far as possible, to arrest him on the perilous course he has adopted; that is, consideration for his family——

DR. STOCKMANN. Please stick to the water-supply and drainage!

HOVSTAD. ——consideration, I repeat, for his wife and his children for whom he has made no provision.

MORTEN. Is that us, mother?

MRS. STOCKMANN. Hush!

ASLAKSEN. I will now put the Mayor's proposition to the vote.

DR. STOCKMANN. There is no necessity! Tonight I have no intention of dealing with all that filth down at the Baths. No; I have something quite different to say to you.

PETER STOCKMANN (aside). What is coming now?

A DRUNKEN MAN (by the entrance door). I am a taxpayer! And therefore I have a right to speak too! And my entire— firm—inconceivable opinion is——

A NUMBER OF VOICES. Be quiet at the back there!

OTHERS. He is drunk! Turn him out!

[They turn him out.]

DR. STOCKMANN. Am I allowed to speak?

ASLAKSEN (ringing his bell). Dr. Stockmann will address the meeting.

DR. STOCKMANN. I should like to have seen anyone, a few days ago, dare to attempt to silence me as has been done tonight! I would have defended my sacred rights as a man, like a lion! But now it is all one to me; I have something of even weightier importance to say to you.

[The crowd presses nearer to him, MORTEN KIIL conspicuous among them.]

DR. STOCKMANN (continuing). I have thought and pondered a great deal, these last few days—pondered over such a variety of things that in the end my head seemed too full to hold them——

PETER STOCKMANN (*with a cough*). Ahem!

DR. STOCKMANN. ——but I got them clear in my mind at last, and then I saw the whole situation lucidly. And that is why I am standing here tonight. I have a great revelation to make to you, my fellow-citizens! I will impart to you a discovery of a far wider scope than the trifling matter that our water-supply is poisoned and our medicinal Baths are standing on pestiferous soil.

A NUMBER OF VOICES (*shouting*). Don't talk about the Baths! We won't hear you! None of that!

DR. STOCKMANN. I have already told you that what I want to speak about is the great discovery I have made lately —the discovery that all the sources of our *moral* life are poisoned and that the whole fabric of our civic community is founded on the pestiferous soil of falsehood.

VOICES OF DISCONCERTED CITIZENS. What is that he says?

PETER STOCKMANN. Such an insinuation——!

ASLAKSEN (*with his hand on his bell*). I call upon the speaker to moderate his language.

DR. STOCKMANN. I have always loved my native town as a man only can love the home of his youthful days. I was not old when I went away from here; and exile, longing, and memories cast, as it were, an additional halo over both the town and its inhabitants. (*Some clapping and applause.*) And there I stayed, for many years, in a horrible hole far away up north. When I came into contact with some of the people that lived scattered about among the rocks, I often thought it would have been more service to the poor half-starved creatures if a veterinary doctor had been sent up there, instead of a man like me.

[*Murmurs among the crowd.*]

BILLING (*laying down his pen*). I'm damned if I have ever heard——!

HOVSTAD. It is an insult to a respectable population!

DR. STOCKMANN. Wait a bit! I do not think anyone will charge me with having forgotten my native town up there. I was like one of the eider-ducks brooding on its nest, and what I hatched was—the plans for these Baths. (*Applause and protests.*) And then when fate at last decreed for me the great happiness of coming home again—I assure you, gentlemen, I thought I had nothing more in the world to wish for. Or rather, there was one thing I wished for— eagerly, untiringly, ardently—and that was to be able to be of service to my native town and the good of the community.

PETER STOCKMANN (*looking at the ceiling*). You chose a strange way of doing it—ahem!

DR. STOCKMANN. And so, with my eyes blinded to the real facts, I revelled in happiness. But yesterday morning—no, to be precise, it was yesterday afternoon—the eyes of my mind were opened wide, and the first thing I realized was the colossal stupidity of the authorities——.

[*Uproar, shouts, and laughter.* MRS. STOCKMANN *coughs persistently.*]

PETER STOCKMANN. Mr. Chairman!

ASLAKSEN (*ringing his bell*). By virtue of my authority——!

DR. STOCKMANN. It is a petty thing to catch me up on a word, Mr. Aslaksen. What I mean is only that I got scent of the unbelievable piggishness our leading men had been responsible for down at the Baths. I can't stand leading men at any price!—I have had enough of such people in my time. They are like billy-goats in a young plantation; they do mischief everywhere. They stand in a free man's way, whichever way he turns, and what I should like best would be to see them exterminated like any other vermin——.

[*Uproar.*]

PETER STOCKMANN. Mr. Chairman, can we allow such expressions to pass?

ASLAKSEN (*with his hand on his bell*). Doctor——!

DR. STOCKMANN. I cannot understand how it is that I have only now acquired a clear conception of what these gentry are, when I had almost daily before my eyes in this town such an excellent specimen of them—my brother Peter —slow-witted and hidebound in prejudice——.

[*Laughter, uproar, and hisses.* MRS. STOCKMANN *sits coughing assiduously.* ASLAKSEN *rings his bell violently.*]

THE DRUNKEN MAN (*who has got in again*). Is it me he is talking about? My name's Petersen, all right—but devil take me if I——

ANGRY VOICES. Turn out that drunken man! Turn him out.   [*He is turned out again.*]

PETER STOCKMANN. Who was that person?

FIRST CITIZEN. I don't know who he is, Mr. Mayor.

SECOND CITIZEN. He doesn't belong here.

THIRD CITIZEN. I expect he is a lumberman from over at (*the rest is inaudible.*)

ASLAKSEN. He had obviously had too much beer.—Proceed, Doctor; but please strive to be moderate in your language.

DR. STOCKMANN. Very well, gentlemen, I will say no more about our leading men. And if anyone imagines, from what I have just said, that my object is to attack these people this evening, he is wrong—absolutely wide of the mark. For I cherish the comforting conviction that these parasites —all these venerable relics of a dying school of thought— are most admirably paving the way for their own extinction; they need no doctor's help to hasten their end. Nor is it folk of that kind who constitute the most pressing danger to the community. It is not they who are most instrumental in poisoning the sources of our moral life and infecting the ground on which we stand. It is not they who are the most dangerous enemies of truth and freedom amongst us.

SHOUTS FROM ALL SIDES. Who then? Who is it? Name! Name!

DR. STOCKMANN. You may depend upon it I shall name them! That is precisely the great discovery I made yesterday. (*Raises his voice.*) The most dangerous enemy of truth and freedom amongst us is the compact majority—yes, the damned compact liberal majority—that is it! Now you know!

[*Tremendous uproar. Most of the crowd are shouting, stamping, and hissing. Some of the older men among them exchange stolen glances and seem to be enjoying themselves.* MRS. STOCKMANN *gets up, looking anxious.* EJLIF *and* MORTEN *advance threateningly upon some schoolboys who are playing pranks.* ASLAKSEN *rings his bell and begs for silence.* HOVSTAD *and* BILLING *both talk at once, but are inaudible. At last quiet is restored.*]

ASLAKSEN. As chairman, I call upon the speaker to withdraw the ill-considered expressions he has just used.

DR. STOCKMANN. Never, Mr. Aslaksen! It is the majority in our community that denies me my freedom and seeks to prevent my speaking the truth.

HOVSTAD. The majority always has right on its side.

BILLING. And truth too, by God!

DR. STOCKMANN. The majority *never* has right on its side. Never, I say! That is one of these social lies against which an independent, intelligent man must wage war. Who constitutes the majority of the population in a country? Is it the clever folk or the stupid? I don't imagine you will dispute the fact that at present the stupid people are in an absolutely overwhelming majority all the world over. But, good Lord!—you can never pretend that it is right that the stupid folk should govern the clever ones! (*Uproar and cries.*)

Oh, yes—you can shout me down, I know! but you cannot answer me. The majority has *might* on its side—unfortunately; but *right* it has *not*. I am in the right—I and a few other scattered individuals. The minority is always in the right.   [*Renewed uproar.*]

HOVSTAD. Aha!—so Dr. Stockmann has become an aristocrat since the day before yesterday!

DR. STOCKMANN. I have already said that I don't intend to waste a word on the puny, narrow-chested, short-winded crew whom we are leaving astern. Pulsating life no longer concerns itself with them. I am thinking of the few, the scattered few amongst us, who have absorbed new and vigorous truths. Such men stand, as it were, at the outposts, so far ahead that the compact majority has not yet been able to come up with them; and there they are fighting for truths that are too newly-born into the world of consciousness to have any considerable number of people on their side as yet.

HOVSTAD. So the Doctor is a revolutionary now!

DR. STOCKMANN. Good heavens—of course I am, Mr. Hovstad! I propose to raise a revolution against the lie that the majority has the monopoly of the truth. What sort of truths are they that the majority usually supports? They are truths that are of such advanced age that they are beginning to break up. And if a truth is as old as that, it is also in a fair way to become a lie, gentlemen. (*Laughter and mocking cries.*) Yes, believe me or not, as you like; but truths are by no means as long-lived as Methuselah—as some folk imagine. A normally constituted truth lives, let us say, as a rule seventeen or eighteen, or at most twenty years; seldom longer. But truths as aged as that are always worn frightfully thin, and nevertheless it is only then that the majority recognizes them and recommends them to the community as wholesome moral nourishment. There is no great nutritive value in that sort of fare, I can assure you;

and, as a doctor, I ought to know. These "majority truths" are like last year's cured meat—like rancid, tainted ham; and they are the origin of the moral scurvy that is rampant in our communities.

ASLAKSEN.   It appears to me that the speaker is wandering a long way from his subject.

PETER STOCKMANN.   I quite agree with the Chairman.

DR. STOCKMANN.   Have you gone clean out of your senses, Peter? I am sticking as closely to my subject as I can; for my subject is precisely this, that it is the masses, the majority—this infernal compact majority—that poisons the sources of our moral life and infects the ground we stand on.

HOVSTAD.   And all this because the great, broad-minded majority of the people is prudent enough to show deference only to well-ascertained and well-approved truths?

DR. STOCKMANN.   Ah, my good Mr. Hovstad, don't talk nonsense about well-ascertained truths! The truths of which the masses now approve are the very truths that the fighters at the outposts held to in the days of our grandfathers. We fighters at the outposts nowadays no longer approve of them; and I do not believe there is any other well-ascertained truth except this, that no community can live a healthy life if it is nourished only on such old marrowless truths.

HOVSTAD.   But instead of standing there using vague generalities, it would be interesting if you would tell us what these old marrowless truths are, that we are nourished on.

[*Applause from many quarters.*]

DR. STOCKMANN.   Oh, I could give you a whole string of such abominations; but to begin with I will confine myself to one well-approved truth, which at bottom is a foul lie, but upon which nevertheless Mr. Hovstad and the "People's Messenger" and all the "Messenger's" supporters are nourished.

HOVSTAD. And that is——?

DR. STOCKMANN. That is, the doctrine you have inherited from your forefathers and proclaim thoughtlessly far and wide—the doctrine that the public, the crowd, the masses are the essential part of the population—that they constitute the People—that the common folk, the ignorant and incomplete element in the community, have the same right to pronounce judgment and to approve, to direct, and to govern, as the isolated, intellectually superior personalities in it.

BILLING. Well, damn me if ever I——

HOVSTAD (*at the same time, shouting out*). Fellow-citizens, take good note of that!

A NUMBER OF VOICES (*angrily*). Oho!—we are not the People! Only the superior folks are to govern, are they?

A WORKMAN. Turn the fellow out, for talking such rubbish!

ANOTHER. Out with him!

ANOTHER (*calling out*). Blow your horn, Evensen!

[*A horn is blown loudly, amidst hisses and an angry uproar.*]

DR. STOCKMANN (*when the noise has somewhat abated*). Be reasonable! Can't you stand hearing the voice of truth for once? I don't in the least expect you to agree with me all at once; but I must say I did expect Mr. Hovstad to admit I was right, when he had recovered his composure a little. He claims to be a freethinker——

VOICES (*in murmurs of astonishment*). Freethinker, did he say? Is Hovstad a freethinker?

HOVSTAD (*shouting*). Prove it, Dr. Stockmann! When have I said so in print?

DR. STOCKMANN (*reflecting*). No, confound it, you are right!—you have never had the courage to. Well, I won't put you in a hole, Mr. Hovstad. Let us say it is I that am the freethinker, then. I am going to prove to you, scientifically, that the "People's Messenger" leads you by the nose in a shameful manner when it tells you that you—that the common people, the crowd, the masses are the real essence of the People. That is only a newspaper lie, I tell you! The common people are nothing more than the raw material of which a People is made. (*Groans, laughter and uproar.*) Well, isn't that the case? Isn't there an enormous difference between a well-bred and an ill-bred strain of animals? Take, for instance, a common barn-door hen. What sort of eating do you get from a shrivelled up old scrag of a fowl like that? Not much, do you? And what sort of eggs does it lay? A fairly good crow or a raven can lay pretty nearly as good an egg. But take a well-bred Spanish or Japanese hen, or a good pheasant or a turkey—then you will see the difference. Or take dogs, with whom we humans are on such intimate terms. Think first of an ordinary common cur—I mean one of the horrible, coarse-haired, low-bred curs that do nothing but run about the streets and befoul the walls of the houses. Compare one of these curs with a poodle whose sires for many generations have been bred in a gentleman's house, where they have had the best of food and had the opportunity of hearing soft voices and music. Do you not think that the poodle's brain is developed to quite a different degree from the cur's? Of course it is. It is puppies of well-bred poodles like that that showmen train to do incredibly clever tricks—things that a common cur could never learn to do even if it stood on its head.   [*Uproar and mocking cries.*]

A CITIZEN (*calls out*). Are you going to make out we are dogs, now?

ANOTHER CITIZEN. We are not animals, Doctor!

DR. STOCKMANN. Yes, but, bless my soul, we *are*, my friend! It is true we are the finest animals anyone could wish for; but, even amongst us, exceptionally fine animals

are rare. There is a tremendous difference between poodle-
men and cur-men. And the amusing part of it is that Mr.
Hovstad quite agrees with me as long as it is a question of
four-footed animals——

HOVSTAD. Yes, it is true enough as far as they are concerned.

DR. STOCKMANN. Very well. But as soon as I extend the
principle and apply it to two-legged animals, Mr. Hovstad
stops short. He no longer dares to think independently, or
to pursue his ideas to their logical conclusion; so he turns
the whole theory upside down and proclaims in the "People's
Messenger" that it is the barn-door hens and street curs
that are the finest specimens in the menagerie. But that
is always the way, as long as a man retains the traces of
common origin and has not worked his way up to intellectual distinction.

HOVSTAD. I lay no claim to any sort of distinction. I am
the son of humble countryfolk, and I am proud that the
stock I come from is rooted deep among the common people
he insults.

VOICES. Bravo, Hovstad! Bravo! Bravo!

DR. STOCKMANN. The kind of common people I mean are
not only to be found low down in the social scale; they crawl
and swarm all around us—even in the highest social positions. You have only to look at your own fine, distinguished
Mayor! My brother Peter is every bit as plebeian as anyone that walks in two shoes——   [Laughter and hisses.]

PETER STOCKMANN. I protest against personal allusions
of this kind.

DR. STOCKMANN (imperturbably). ——and that, not because he is, like myself, descended from some old rascal of a
pirate from Pomerania or thereabouts—because that is who
we are descended from——

PETER STOCKMANN. An absurd legend. I deny it!

DR. STOCKMANN. ——but because he thinks what his superiors think and holds the same opinions as they. People who do that are, intellectually speaking, common people; and that is why my magnificent brother Peter is in reality so very far from any distinction—and consequently also so far from being liberal-minded.

PETER STOCKMANN. Mr. Chairman——!

HOVSTAD. So it is only the distinguished men that are liberal-minded in this country? We are learning something quite new!   [*Laughter.*]

DR. STOCKMANN. Yes, that is part of my new discovery too. And another part of it is that broad-mindedness is almost precisely the same thing as morality. That is why I maintain that it is absolutely inexcusable in the "People's Messenger" to proclaim, day in and day out, the false doctrine that the masses, the crowd, the compact majority have the monopoly of broad-mindedness and morality—and that vice and corruption and every kind of intellectual depravity are the result of culture, just as all the filth that is draining into our Baths is the result of the tanneries up at Mölledal! (*Uproar and interruptions.* DR. STOCKMANN *is undisturbed, and goes on, carried away by his ardor, with a smile.*) And yet this same "People's Messenger" can go on preaching that the masses ought to be elevated to higher conditions of life! But, bless my soul, if the "Messenger's" teaching is to be depended upon, this very raising up the masses would mean nothing more or less than setting them straightway upon the paths of depravity! Happily the theory that culture demoralizes is only an old falsehood that our forefathers believed in and we have inherited. No, it is ignorance, poverty, ugly conditions of life that do the devil's work! In a house which does not get aired and swept every day—my wife Katherine maintains that the floor ought to be scrubbed as well, but that is a debatable question—in such a house, let me tell you,

people will lose within two or three years the power of thinking or acting in a moral manner. Lack of oxygen weakens
the conscience. And there must be a plentiful lack of oxygen
in very many houses in this town, I should think, judging
from the fact that the whole compact majority can be un-
conscientious enough to wish to build the town's prosperity
on a quagmire of falsehood and deceit.

ASLAKSEN. We cannot allow such a grave accusation to
be flung at a citizen community.

A CITIZEN. I move that the Chairman direct the speaker
to sit down.

VOICES (*angrily*). Hear, hear! Quite right! Make him sit
down!

DR. STOCKMANN (*losing his self-control*). Then I will go
and shout the truth at every street corner! I will write it
in other towns' newspapers! The whole country shall know
what is going on here!

HOVSTAD. It almost seems as if Dr. Stockmann's intention were to ruin the town.

DR. STOCKMANN. Yes, my native town is so dear to me
that I would rather ruin it then see it flourishing upon a
lie.

ASLAKSEN. This is really serious.

[*Uproar and cat-calls.* MRS. STOCKMANN *coughs, but to no
purpose; her husband does not listen to her any longer.*]

HOVSTAD (*shouting above the din*). A man must be a public
enemy to wish to ruin a whole community!

DR. STOCKMANN (*with growing fervor*). What does the
destruction of a community matter, if it lives on lies? It
ought to be razed to the ground, I tell you! All who live
by lies ought to be exterminated like vermin! You will end
by infecting the whole country; you will bring about such
a state of things that the whole country will deserve to be
ruined. And if things come to that pass, I shall say from

the bottom of my heart: Let the whole country perish, let all these people be exterminated!

VOICES FROM THE CROWD. That is talking like an out-and-out enemy of the people!

BILLING. There sounded the voice of the people, by all that's holy!

THE WHOLE CROWD (shouting). Yes, yes! He is an enemy of the people! He hates his country! He hates his own people!

ASLAKSEN. Both as a citizen and as an individual, I am profoundly disturbed by what we have had to listen to. Dr. Stockmann has shown himself in a light I should never have dreamed of. I am unhappily obliged to subscribe to the opinion which I have just heard my estimable fellow-citizens utter; and I propose that we should give expression to that opinion in a resolution. I propose a resolution as follows: "This meeting declares that it considers Dr. Thomas Stockmann, Medical Officer of the Baths, to be an enemy of the people."

[A storm of cheers and applause. A number of men surround the DOCTOR and hiss him. MRS. STOCKMANN and PETRA have got up from their seats. MORTEN and EJLIF are fighting the other schoolboys for hissing; some of their elders separate them.]

DR. STOCKMANN (to the men who are hissing him). Oh, you fools! I tell you that——

ASLAKSEN (ringing his bell). We cannot hear you now, Doctor. A formal vote is about to be taken; but, out of regard for personal feelings, it shall be by ballot and not verbal. Have you any clean paper, Mr. Billing?

BILLING. I have both blue and white here.

ASLAKSEN (going to him). That will do nicely; we shall get on more quickly that way. Cut it up into small strips—yes, that's it. (To the meeting.) Blue means no; white means yes. I will come round myself and collect votes.

[PETER STOCKMANN *leaves the hall.* ASLAKSEN *and one or two others go round the room with the slips of paper in their hats.*]

FIRST CITIZEN (*to* HOVSTAD). I say, what has come to the Doctor? What are we to think of it?

HOVSTAD. Oh, you know how headstrong he is.

SECOND CITIZEN (*to* BILLING). Billing, you go to their house —have you ever noticed if the fellow drinks?

BILLING. Well, I'm hanged if I know what to say. There are always spirits on the table when you go.

THIRD CITIZEN. I rather think he goes quite off his head sometimes.

FIRST CITIZEN. I wonder if there is any madness in his family?

BILLING. I shouldn't wonder if there were.

FOURTH CITIZEN. No, it is nothing more than sheer malice; he wants to get even with somebody for something or other.

BILLING. Well certainly he suggested a rise in his salary on one occasion lately, and did not get it.

THE CITIZENS (*together*). Ah!—then it is easy to understand how it is!

THE DRUNKEN MAN (*who has got amongst the audience again*). I want a blue one, I do! And I want a white one too!

VOICES. It's that drunken chap again! Turn him out!

MORTEN KIIL (*going up to* DR. STOCKMANN). Well, Stockmann, do you see what these monkey tricks of yours lead to?

DR. STOCKMANN. I have done my duty.

MORTEN KIIL. What was that you said about the tanneries at Mölledal?

DR. STOCKMANN. You heard well enough. I said they were the source of all the filth.

MORTEN KIIL. My tannery too?

DR. STOCKMANN. Unfortunately your tannery is by far the worst.

MORTEN KIIL. Are you going to put that in the papers?

DR. STOCKMANN. I shall conceal nothing.

MORTEN KIIL. That may cost you dear, Stockmann.

[Goes out.]

A STOUT MAN (*going up to* CAPTAIN HORSTER, *without taking any notice of the ladies*). Well, Captain, so you lend your house to enemies of the people?

HORSTER. I imagine I can do what I like with my own possessions, Mr. Vik.

THE STOUT MAN. Then you can have no objection to my doing the same with mine.

HORSTER. What do you mean, sir?

THE STOUT MAN. You shall hear from me in the morning.

[Turns his back on him and moves off.]

PETRA. Was that not your owner, Captain Horster?

HORSTER. Yes, that was Mr. Vik, the ship-owner.

ASLAKSEN (*with the voting-papers in his hands, gets up on to the platform and rings his bell*). Gentlemen, allow me to announce the result. By the votes of every one here except one person——

A YOUNG MAN. That is the drunk chap!

ASLAKSEN. By the votes of every one here except a tipsy man, this meeting of citizens declares Dr. Thomas Stockmann to be an enemy of the people. (*Shouts and applause.*) Three cheers for our ancient and honorable citizen community! (*Renewed applause.*) Three cheers for our able and energetic Mayor, who has so loyally suppressed the promptings of family feeling! (*Cheers.*) The meeting is dissolved.   *[Gets down.]*

BILLING. Three cheers for the Chairman!

THE WHOLE CROWD. Three cheers for Aslaksen! Hurrah!

DR. STOCKMANN. My hat and coat, Petra! Captain, have you room on your ship for passengers to the New World?

HORSTER. For you and yours we will make room, Doctor.

DR. STOCKMANN (*as* PETRA *helps him into his coat*). Good. Come, Katherine! Come, boys!

MRS. STOCKMANN (*in an undertone*). Thomas, dear, let us go out by the back way.

DR. STOCKMANN. No back ways for me, Katherine. (*Raising his voice.*) You will hear more of this enemy of the people, before he shakes the dust off his shoes upon you! I am not so forgiving as a certain Person; I do not say: "I forgive you, for ye know not what ye do."

ASLAKSEN (*shouting*). That is a blasphemous comparison, Dr. Stockmann!

BILLING. It is, by God! It's dreadful for an earnest man to listen to.

A COARSE VOICE. Threatens us now, does he?

OTHER VOICES (*excitedly*). Let's go and break his windows! Duck him in the fjord!

ANOTHER VOICE. Blow your horn, Evensen! Pip, pip!

[*Horn-blowing, hisses, and wild cries.* DR. STOCKMANN *goes out through the hall with his family,* HORSTER *elbowing a way for them.*]

THE WHOLE CROWD (*howling after them as they go*). Enemy of the People! Enemy of the People!

BILLING (*as he puts his papers together*). Well, I'm damned if I go and drink toddy with the Stockmanns tonight!

[*The crowd press towards the exit. The uproar continues outside; shouts of "Enemy of the People!" are heard from without.*]

CURTAIN

ACT FIVE

DR. STOCKMANN'S *study.   Bookcases and cabinets containing specimens line the walls.   At the back is a door leading
to the hall; in the foreground on the left, a door leading to
the sitting-room.   In the right-hand wall are two windows, of
which all the panes are broken.   The* DOCTOR'S *desk, littered
with books and papers, stands in the middle of the room, which
is in disorder.   It is morning.* [DR. STOCKMANN *in dressing-
gown, slippers, and a smoking-cap, is bending down and raking
with an umbrella under one of the cabinets.   After a little while
he rakes out a stone.*]

DR. STOCKMANN (*calling through the open sitting-room door*).
Katherine, I have found another one.

MRS. STOCKMANN (*from the sitting-room*).   Oh, you will
find a lot more yet, I expect.

DR. STOCKMANN (*adding the stone to a heap of others on the
table*).   I shall treasure these stones as relics.   Ejlif and
Morten shall look at them every day, and when they are
grown up they shall inherit them as heirlooms.   (*Rakes about
under a bookcase.*)   Hasn't—what the deuce is her name?—
the girl, you know—hasn't she been to fetch the glazier yet?

MRS. STOCKMANN (*coming in*).   Yes, but he said he didn't
know if he would be able to come today.

DR. STOCKMANN.   You will see he won't dare to come.

MRS. STOCKMANN.   Well, that is just what Randine
thought—that he didn't dare to, on account of the neigh-
bors.   (*Calls into the sitting-room.*)   What is it you want,
Randine?   Give it to me.   (*Goes in, and comes out again
directly.*)   Here is a letter for you, Thomas.

DR. STOCKMANN.   Let me see it.   (*Opens and reads it.*)
Ah!—of course.

MRS. STOCKMANN. Who is it from?

DR. STOCKMANN. From the landlord. Notice to quit.

MRS. STOCKMANN. Is it possible? Such a nice man——

DR. STOCKMANN (*looking at the letter*). Does not dare do otherwise, he says. Doesn't like doing it, but dare not do otherwise—on account of his fellow-citizens—out of regard for public opinion. Is in a dependent position—dare not offend certain influential men——

MRS. STOCKMANN. There, you see, Thomas!

DR. STOCKMANN. Yes, yes, I see well enough; the whole lot of them in the town are cowards; not a man among them dares do anything for fear of the others. (*Throws the letter onto the table.*) But it doesn't matter to us, Katherine. We are going to sail away to the New World, and——

MRS. STOCKMANN. But, Thomas, are you sure we are well advised to take this step?

DR. STOCKMANN. Are you suggesting that I should stay here, where they have pilloried me as an enemy of the people— branded me—broken my windows! And just look here, Katherine—they have torn a great rent in my black trousers too!

MRS. STOCKMANN. Oh, dear!—and they are the best pair you have got!

DR. STOCKMANN. You should never wear your best trousers when you go out to fight for freedom and truth. It is not that I care so much about the trousers, you know; you can always sew them up again for me. But that the common herd should dare to make this attack on me, as if they were my equals—that is what I cannot, for the life of me, swallow!

MRS. STOCKMANN. There is no doubt they have behaved very ill to you, Thomas; but is that sufficient reason for our leaving our native country for good and all?

DR. STOCKMANN. If we went to another town, do you suppose we should not find the common people just as inso-

lent as they are here? Depend upon it, there is not much
to choose between them. Oh, well, let the curs snap—that
is not the worst part of it. The worst is that, from one end
of this country to the other, every man is the slave of his
Party. Although, as far as that goes, I daresay it is not
much better in the free West either; the compact majority,
and liberal public opinion, and all that infernal old bag of
tricks are probably rampant there too. But there things are
done on a larger scale, you see. They may kill you, but
they won't put you to death by slow torture. They don't
squeeze a free man's soul in a vice, as they do here. And,
if need be, one can live in solitude. (*Walks up and down.*)
If only I knew where there was a virgin forest or a small
South Sea island for sale, cheap——

MRS. STOCKMANN. But think of the boys, Thomas.

DR. STOCKMANN (*standing still*). What a strange woman
you are, Katherine! Would you prefer to have the boys
grow up in a society like this? You saw for yourself last
night that half the population are out of their minds; and
if the other half have not lost their senses, it is because they
are mere brutes, with no sense to lose.

MRS. STOCKMANN. But, Thomas dear, the imprudent
things you said had something to do with it, you know.

DR. STOCKMANN. Well, isn't what I said perfectly true?
Don't they turn every idea topsy-turvy? Don't they make
a regular hotch-potch of right and wrong? Don't they say
that the things I know are true are lies? The craziest part
of it all is the fact of these "liberals," men of full age, going
about in crowds imagining that they are the broad-minded
party! Did you ever hear anything like it, Katherine?

MRS. STOCKMANN. Yes, yes, it's mad enough of them, certainly; but—— (PETRA *comes in from the sitting-room.*)
Back from school already?

PETRA. Yes. I have been given notice of dismissal.

MRS. STOCKMANN. Dismissal?

DR. STOCKMANN. You too?

PETRA. Mrs. Busk gave me my notice; so I thought it was best to go at once.

DR. STOCKMANN. You were perfectly right, too!

MRS. STOCKMANN. Who would have thought Mrs. Busk was a woman like that?

PETRA. Mrs. Busk isn't a bit like that, mother; I saw quite plainly how it hurt her to do it. But she didn't dare do otherwise, she said; and so I got my notice.

DR. STOCKMANN (*laughing and rubbing his hands*). She didn't dare do otherwise, either! It's delicious!

MRS. STOCKMANN. Well, after the dreadful scenes last night——

PETRA. It was not only that. Just listen to this, father!

DR. STOCKMANN. Well?

PETRA. Mrs. Busk showed me no less than three letters she received this morning——

DR. STOCKMANN. Anonymous, I suppose?

PETRA. Yes.

DR. STOCKMANN. Yes, because they didn't dare to risk signing their names, Katherine!

PETRA. And two of them were to the effect that a man, who has been our guest here, was declaring last night at the Club that my views on various subjects are extremely emancipated——

DR. STOCKMANN. You did not deny that, I hope?

PETRA. No, you know I wouldn't. Mrs. Busk's own views are tolerably emancipated, when we are alone together; but now that this report about me is being spread, she dare not keep me on any longer.

MRS. STOCKMANN. And some one who had been a guest of ours! That shows you the return you get for your hospitality, Thomas!

DR. STOCKMANN. We won't live in such a disgusting hole any longer. Pack up as quickly as you can, Katherine; the sooner we can get away the better.

MRS. STOCKMANN. Be quiet—I think I hear some one in the hall. See who it is, Petra.

PETRA (*opening the door*). Oh, it's you, Captain Horster! Do come in.

HORSTER (*coming in*). Good morning. I thought I would just come in and see how you were.

DR. STOCKMANN (*shaking his hand*). Thanks—that is really kind of you.

MRS. STOCKMANN. And thank you, too, for helping us through the crowd, Captain Horster.

PETRA. How did you manage to get home again?

HORSTER. Oh, somehow or other. I am fairly strong, and there is more sound than fury about these folk.

DR. STOCKMANN. Yes, isn't their swinish cowardice astonishing? Look here, I will show you something! There are all the stones they have thrown through my windows. Just look at them! I'm hanged if there are more than two decently large bits of hardstone in the whole heap; the rest are nothing but gravel—wretched little things. And yet they stood out there bawling and swearing that they would do me some violence; but as for *doing* anything—you don't see much of that in this town.

HORSTER. Just as well for you this time, Doctor!

DR. STOCKMANN. True enough. But it makes one angry all the same; because if some day it should be a question of a national fight in real earnest, you will see that public opinion will be in favor of taking to one's heels, and the compact majority will turn tail like a flock of sheep, Captain Horster. That is what is so mournful to think of; it gives me so much concern, that——. No, devil take it, it is ridiculous to care about it! They have called me an enemy of the people, so an enemy of the people let me be!

MRS. STOCKMANN. You will never be that, Thomas.

DR. STOCKMANN. Don't swear to that, Katherine. To be called an ugly name may have the same effect as a pin-scratch in the lung. And that hateful name—I can't get quit of it. It is sticking here in the pit of my stomach, eating into me like a corrosive acid. And no magnesia will remove it.

PETRA. Bah!—you should only laugh at them, father.

HORSTER. They will change their minds some day, Doctor.

MRS. STOCKMANN Yes, Thomas, as sure as you are standing here.

DR. STOCKMANN. Perhaps, when it is too late. Much good may it do them! They may wallow in their filth then and rue the day when they drove a patriot into exile. When do you sail, Captain Horster?

HORSTER. Hm!—that was just what I had come to speak about——

DR. STOCKMANN. Why, has anything gone wrong with the ship?

HORSTER. No; but what has happened is that I am not to sail in it.

PETRA. Do you mean that you have been dismissed from your command?

HORSTER (smiling). Yes, that's just it.

PETRA. You too.

MRS. STOCKMANN. There, you see, Thomas!

DR. STOCKMANN. And that for the truth's sake! Oh, if I had thought such a thing possible——

HORSTER. You mustn't take it to heart; I shall be sure to find a job with some ship-owner or other, elsewhere.

DR. STOCKMANN. And that is this man Vik—a wealthy

man, independent of every one and everything——! Shame on him!

HORSTER. He is quite an excellent fellow otherwise; he told me himself he would willingly have kept me on, if only he had dared——

DR. STOCKMANN. But he didn't dare? No, of course not.

HORSTER. It is not such an easy matter, he said, for a party man——

DR. STOCKMANN. The worthy man spoke the truth. A party is like a sausage machine; it mashes up all sorts of heads together into the same mincemeat—fatheads and blockheads, all in one mash!

MRS. STOCKMANN. Come, come, Thomas dear!

PETRA (*to* HORSTER). If only you had not come home with us, things might not have come to this pass.

HORSTER. I do not regret it.

PETRA (*holding out her hand to him*). Thank you for that!

HORSTER (*to* DR. STOCKMANN). And so what I came to say was that if you are determined to go away, I have thought of another plan——

DR. STOCKMANN. That's splendid!—if only we can get away at once.

MRS. STOCKMANN. Hush!—wasn't that some one knocking?

PETRA: That is uncle, surely.

DR. STOCKMANN. Aha! (*Calls out.*) Come in!

MRS. STOCKMANN. Dear Thomas, promise me definitely—— [PETER STOCKMANN *comes in from the hall.*]

PETER STOCKMANN. Oh, you are engaged. In that case, I will——

DR. STOCKMANN. No, no, come in.

PETER STOCKMANN. But I wanted to speak to you alone.

MRS. STOCKMANN. We will go into the sitting-room in the meanwhile.

HORSTER. And I will look in again later.

DR. STOCKMANN. No, go in there with them, Captain Horster; I want to hear more about——.

HORSTER. Very well, I will wait, then.

[*He follows* MRS. STOCKMANN *and* PETRA *into the sitting-room.*]

DR. STOCKMANN. I daresay you find it rather draughty here today. Put your hat on.

PETER STOCKMANN. Thank you, if I may. (*Does so.*) I think I caught cold last night; I stood and shivered——

DR. STOCKMANN. Really? I found it warm enough.

PETER STOCKMANN. I regret that it was not in my power to prevent those excesses last night.

DR. STOCKMANN. Have you anything particular to say to me besides that?

PETER STOCKMANN (*taking a big letter from his pocket*). I have this document for you, from the Baths Committee.

DR. STOCKMANN. My dismissal?

PETER STOCKMANN. Yes, dating from today. (*Lays the letter on the table.*) It gives us pain to do it; but, to speak frankly, we dared not do otherwise on account of public opinion.

DR. STOCKMANN (*smiling*). Dared not? I seem to have heard that word before, today.

PETER STOCKMANN. I must beg you to understand your position clearly. For the future you must not count on any practice whatever in the town.

DR. STOCKMANN. Devil take the practice! But why are you so sure of that?

PETER STOCKMANN. The Householders' Association is circulating a list from house to house. All right-minded citizens are being called upon to give up employing you; and I can assure you that not a single head of a family will risk refusing his signature. They simply dare not.

DR. STOCKMANN. No, no; I don't doubt it. But what then?

PETER STOCKMANN. If I might advise you, it would be best to leave the place for a little while——

DR. STOCKMANN. Yes, the propriety of leaving the place *has* occurred to me.

PETER STOCKMANN. Good. And then, when you have had six months to think things over, if, after mature consideration, you can persuade yourself to write a few words of regret, acknowledging your error——

DR. STOCKMANN. I might have my appointment restored to me, do you mean?

PETER STOCKMANN. Perhaps. It is not at all impossible.

DR. STOCKMANN. But what about public opinion, then? Surely you would not dare to do it on account of public feeling.

PETER STOCKMANN. Public opinion is an extremely mutable thing. And, to be quite candid with you, it is a matter of great importance to us to have some admission of that sort from you in writing.

DR. STOCKMANN. Oh, that's what you are after, is it? I will just trouble you to remember what I said to you lately about foxy tricks of that sort!

PETER STOCKMANN. Your position was quite different then. At that time you had reason to suppose you had the whole town at your back——

DR. STOCKMANN. Yes, and now I feel I have the whole town *on* my back—(*flaring up.*) I would not do it if I had the devil and his dam on my back——! Never—never, I tell you!

PETER STOCKMANN. A man with a family has no right to behave as you do. You have no right to do it, Thomas.

DR. STOCKMANN. I have no right! There is only one

single thing in the world a free man has no right to do. Do you know what that is?

PETER STOCKMANN. No.

DR. STOCKMANN. Of course you don't, but I will tell you. A free man has no right to soil himself with filth; he has no right to behave in a way that would justify his spitting in his own face.

PETER STOCKMANN. This sort of thing sounds extremely plausible, of course; and if there were no other explanation for your obstinacy——. But as it happens there is.

DR. STOCKMANN. What do you mean?

PETER STOCKMANN. You understand very well what I mean. But, as your brother and as a man of discretion, I advise you not to build too much upon expectations and prospects that may so very easily fail you.

DR. STOCKMANN. What in the world is all this about?

PETER STOCKMANN. Do you really ask me to believe that you are ignorant of the terms of Mr. Kiil's will?

DR. STOCKMANN. I know that the small amount he possesses is to go to an institution for indigent old work-people. How does that concern me?

PETER STOCKMANN. In the first place, it is by no means a small amount that is in question. Mr. Kiil is a fairly wealthy man.

DR. STOCKMANN. I had no notion of that!

PETER STOCKMANN. Hm!—hadn't you really? Then I suppose you had no notion, either, that a considerable portion of his wealth will come to your children, you and your wife having a life-income from the capital. Has he never told you so?

DR. STOCKMANN. Never, on my honor! Quite the reverse; he has consistently done nothing but fume at being so unconscionably heavily taxed. But are you perfectly certain of this, Peter?

PETER STOCKMANN. I have it from an absolutely reliable source.

DR. STOCKMANN. Then, thank God, Katherine is provided for—and the children too! I must tell her this at once—(*calls out*) Katherine, Katherine!

PETER STOCKMANN (*restraining him*). Hush, don't say a word yet!

MRS. STOCKMANN (*opening the door*). What is the matter?

DR. STOCKMANN. Oh, nothing, nothing; you can go back. (*She shuts the door.* DR. STOCKMANN *walks up and down in his excitement.*) Provided for!——Just think of it, we are all provided for! And for life! What a blessed feeling it is to know one is provided for!

PETER STOCKMANN. Yes, but that is just exactly what you are not. Mr. Kiil can alter his will any day he likes.

DR. STOCKMANN. But he won't do that, my dear Peter. The "Badger" is much too delighted at my attack on you and your wise friends.

PETER STOCKMANN (*starts and looks intently at him*). Ah, that throws a light on various things.

DR. STOCKMANN. What things?

PETER STOCKMANN. I see that the whole thing was a combined manœuvre on your part and his. These violent, reckless attacks that you have made against the leading men of the town, under the pretence that it was in the name of truth——

DR. STOCKMANN. What about them?

PETER STOCKMANN. I see that they were nothing else than the stipulated price for that vindictive old man's will.

DR. STOCKMANN (*almost speechless*). Peter—you are the most disgusting plebeian I have ever met in all my life.

PETER STOCKMANN. All is over between us. Your dismissal is irrevocable—we have a weapon against you now.

[*Goes out.*]

DR. STOCKMANN. For shame! For shame! (*Calls out.*) Katherine, you must have the floor scrubbed after him! Let—what's her name—devil take it, the girl who has always got soot on her nose——

MRS. STOCKMANN (*in the sitting-room*). Hush, Thomas, be quiet!

PETRA (*coming to the door*). Father, grandfather is here, asking if he may speak to you alone.

DR. STOCKMANN. Certainly he may. (*Going to the door.*) Come in, Mr. Kiil. (MORTEN KIIL *comes in.* DR. STOCKMANN *shuts the door after him.*) What can I do for you? Won't you sit down?

MORTEN KIIL. I won't sit. (*Looks around.*) You look very comfortable here today, Thomas.

DR. STOCKMANN. Yes, don't we?

MORTEN KIIL. Very comfortable—plenty of fresh air. I should think you have got enough today of that oxygen you were talking about yesterday. Your conscience must be in splendid order today, I should think.

DR. STOCKMANN. It is.

MORTEN KIIL. So I should think. (*Taps his chest.*) Do you know what I have got here?

DR. STOCKMANN. A good conscience, too, I hope.

MORTEN KIIL. Bah!—No, it is something better than that.

[*He takes a thick pocket-book from his breast-pocket, opens it, and displays a packet of papers.*]

DR. STOCKMANN (*looking at him in astonishment*). Shares in the Baths?

MORTEN KIIL. They were not difficult to get today.

DR. STOCKMANN. And you have been buying——?

MORTEN KIIL. As many as I could pay for.

DR. STOCKMANN. But, my dear Mr. Kiil—consider the state of the Baths' affairs!

MORTEN KIIL. If you behave like a reasonable man, you can soon set the Baths on their feet again.

DR. STOCKMANN. Well, you can see for yourself that I have done all I can, but——. They are all mad in this town!

MORTEN KIIL. You said yesterday that the worst of this pollution came from my tannery. If that is true, then my grandfather and my father before me, and I myself, for many years past, have been poisoning the town like three destroying angels. Do you think I am going to sit quiet under that reproach?

DR. STOCKMANN. Unfortunately, I am afraid you will have to.

MORTEN KIIL. No, thank you. I am jealous of my name and reputation. They call me "the Badger," I am told. A badger is a kind of pig, I believe; but I am not going to give them the right to call me that. I mean to live and die a clean man.

DR. STOCKMANN. And how are you going to set about it?

MORTEN KIIL. You shall cleanse me, Thomas.

DR. STOCKMANN. I!

MORTEN KIIL. Do you know what money I have bought these shares with? No, of course you can't know—but I will tell you. It is the money that Katherine and Petra and the boys will have when I am gone. Because I have been able to save a little bit after all, you know.

DR. STOCKMANN (*flaring up*). And you have gone and taken Katherine's money for *this!*

MORTEN KIIL. Yes, the whole of the money is invested in the Baths now. And now I just want to see whether you are quite stark, staring mad, Thomas! If you still make out that these animals and other nasty things of that sort come from my tannery, it will be exactly as if you were to flay broad strips of skin from Katherine's body, and Petra's, and the boys'; and no decent man would do that—unless he were mad.

DR. STOCKMANN (*walking up and down*). Yes, but I *am* mad; I *am* mad!

MORTEN KIIL. You cannot be so absurdly mad as all that, when it is a question of your wife and children.

DR. STOCKMANN (*standing still in front of him*). Why couldn't you consult me about it, before you went and bought all that trash?

MORTEN KIIL. What is done cannot be undone.

DR. STOCKMANN (*walks about uneasily*). If only I were not so certain about it——! But I am absolutely convinced that I am right.

MORTEN KIIL (*weighing the pocket-book in his hand*). If you stick to your mad idea, this won't be worth much, you know. (*Puts the pocket-book in his pocket.*)

DR. STOCKMANN. But, hang it all! it might be possible for science to discover some prophylactic, I should think—or some antidote of some kind——

MORTEN KIIL. To kill these animals, do you mean?

DR. STOCKMANN. Yes, or to make them innocuous.

MORTEN KIIL. Couldn't you try some rat's-bane?

DR. STOCKMANN. Don't talk nonsense! They all say it is only imagination, you know. Well, let it go at that! Let them have their own way about it! Haven't the ignorant, narrow-minded curs reviled me as an enemy of the people? —and haven't they been ready to tear the clothes off my back too?

MORTEN KIIL. And broken all your windows to pieces!

DR. STOCKMANN. And then there is my duty to my family. I must talk it over with Katherine; she is great on those things.

MORTEN KIIL. That is right; be guided by a reasonable woman's advice.

DR. STOCKMANN (*advancing towards him*). To think you could do such a preposterous thing! Risking Katherine's money in this way, and putting me in such a horribly painful dilemma! When I look at you, I think I see the devil himself——.

MORTEN KIIL. Then I had better go. But I must have an answer from you before two o'clock—yes or no. If it is no, the shares go to a charity, and that this very day.

DR. STOCKMANN. And what does Katherine get?

MORTEN KIIL. Not a halfpenny. (*The door leading to the hall opens, and* HOVSTAD *and* ASLAKSEN *make their appearance.*) Look at those two!

DR. STOCKMANN (*staring at them*). What the devil!—have *you* actually the face to come into my house?

HOVSTAD. Certainly.

ASLAKSEN. We have something to say to you, you see.

MORTEN KIIL (*in a whisper*). Yes or no—before two o'clock.

ASLAKSEN (*glancing at* HOVSTAD). Aha!

[MORTEN KIIL *goes out.*]

DR. STOCKMANN. Well, what do you want with me? Be brief.

HOVSTAD. I can quite understand that you are annoyed with us for our attitude at the meeting yesterday——

DR. STOCKMANN. Attitude, do you call it? Yes, it was a charming attitude! I call it weak, womanish—damnably shameful!

HOVSTAD. Call it what you like; we could not do otherwise.

DR. STOCKMANN. You *dared* not do otherwise—isn't that it?

HOVSTAD. Well, if you like to put it that way.

ASLAKSEN. But why did you not let us have word of it beforehand?—just a hint to Mr. Hovstad or to me?

DR. STOCKMANN. A hint? Of what?

ASLAKSEN. Of what was behind it all.

DR. STOCKMANN. I don't understand you in the least.

ASLAKSEN (*with a confidential nod*). Oh, yes, you do, Dr. Stockmann.

HOVSTAD. It is no good making a mystery of it any longer.

DR. STOCKMANN (*looking first at one of them and then at the other*). What the devil do you both mean?

ASLAKSEN. May I ask if your father-in-law is not going round the town buying up all the shares in the Baths?

DR. STOCKMANN. Yes, he has been buying Baths' shares today; but——

ASLAKSEN. It would have been more prudent to get some one else to do it—some one less nearly related to you.

HOVSTAD. And you should not have let your name appear in the affair. There was no need for anyone to know that the attack on the Baths came from you. You ought to have consulted me, Dr. Stockmann.

DR. STOCKMANN (*looks in front of him; then a light seems to dawn on him and he says in amazement:*) Are such things conceivable? Are such things possible?

ASLAKSEN (*with a smile*). Evidently they are. But it is better to use a little finesse, you know.

HOVSTAD. And it is much better to have several persons in a thing of that sort, because the responsibility of each individual is lessened, when there are others with him.

DR. STOCKMANN (*composedly*). Come to the point, gentlemen. What do you want?

ASLAKSEN. Perhaps Mr. Hovstad had better——

HOVSTAD. No, you tell him, Aslaksen.

ASLAKSEN. Well, the fact is that, now we know the bearings of the whole affair, we think we might venture to put the "People's Messenger" at your disposal.

DR. STOCKMANN. Do you dare do that now? What about

public opinion? Are you not afraid of a storm breaking upon our heads?

HOVSTAD. We will try to weather it.

ASLAKSEN. And you must be ready to go off quickly on a new tack, Doctor. As soon as your invective has done its work——

DR. STOCKMANN. Do you mean, as soon as my father-in-law and I have got hold of the shares at a low figure?

HOVSTAD. Your reasons for wishing to get the control of the Baths are mainly scientific, I take it.

DR. STOCKMANN. Of course; it was for scientific reasons that I persuaded the old "Badger" to stand in with me in the matter. So we will tinker at the conduit-pipes a little, and dig up a little bit of the shore, and it shan't cost the town a sixpence. That will be all right—eh?

HOVSTAD. I think so—if you have the "People's Messenger" behind you.

ASLAKSEN. The Press is a power in a free community, Doctor.

DR. STOCKMANN. Quite so. And so is public opinion. And you, Mr. Aslaksen—I suppose you will be answerable for the Householders' Association?

ASLAKSEN. Yes, and for the Temperance Society. You may rely on that.

DR. STOCKMANN. But, gentlemen—I really am ashamed to ask the question—but, what return do you—?

HOVSTAD. We should prefer to help you without any return whatever, believe me. But the "People's Messenger" is in rather a shaky condition; it doesn't go really well; and I should be very unwilling to suspend the paper now, when there is so much work to do here in the political way.

DR. STOCKMANN. Quite so; that would be a great trial to such a friend of the people as you are. (*Flares up.*) But I am an enemy of the people, remember! (*Walks about the room.*) Where have I put my stick? Where the devil is my stick?

HOVSTAD. What's that?

ASLAKSEN. Surely you never mean——?

DR. STOCKMANN (*standing still*). And suppose I don't give you a single penny of all I get out of it? Money is not very easy to get out of us rich folk, please to remember!

HOVSTAD. And you please to remember that this affair of the shares can be represented in two ways!

DR. STOCKMANN. Yes, and you are just the man to do it. If I don't come to the rescue of the "People's Messenger," you will certainly take an evil view of the affair; you will hunt me down, I can well imagine—pursue me—try to throttle me as a dog does a hare.

HOVSTAD. It is a natural law; every animal must fight for its own livelihood.

ASLAKSEN. And get its food where it can, you know.

DR. STOCKMANN (*walking about the room*). Then you go and look for yours in the gutter, because I am going to show you which is the strongest animal of us three! (*Finds an umbrella and brandishes it above his head.*) Ah, now——!

HOVSTAD. You are surely not going to use violence!

ASLAKSEN. Take care what you are doing with that umbrella.

DR. STOCKMANN. Out of the window with you, Mr. Hovstad!

HOVSTAD (*edging to the door*). Are you quite mad?

DR. STOCKMANN. Out of the window, Mr. Aslaksen! Jump, I tell you! You will have to do it, sooner or later.

ASLAKSEN (*running round the writing-table*). Moderation, Doctor—I am a delicate man—I can stand so little—(*calls out.*) Help, help!

[MRS. STOCKMANN, PETRA, *and* HORSTER *come in from the sitting-room.*]

MRS. STOCKMANN. Good gracious, Thomas! What is happening?

DR. STOCKMANN (*brandishing the umbrella*). Jump out, I tell you! Out into the gutter!

HOVSTAD. An assault on an unoffending man! I call you to witness, Captain Horster. [*Hurries out through the hall.*]

ASLAKSEN (*irresolutely*). If only I knew the way about here——.　　　　　　[*Steals out through the sitting-room.*]

MRS. STOCKMANN (*holding her husband back*). Control yourself, Thomas!

DR. STOCKMANN (*throwing down the umbrella*). Upon my soul, they have escaped after all.

MRS. STOCKMANN. What did they want you to do?

DR. STOCKMANN. I will tell you later on; I have something else to think about now. (*Goes to the table and writes something on a calling-card.*) Look there, Katherine; what is written there?

MRS. STOCKMANN. Three big No's; what does that mean?

DR. STOCKMANN. I will tell you that too, later on. (*Holds out the card to* PETRA.) There, Petra; tell sooty-face to run over to the "Badger's" with that, as quickly as she can. Hurry up!　　[PETRA *takes the card and goes out to the hall.*]

DR. STOCKMANN. Well, I think I have had a visit from every one of the devil's messengers today! But now I am going to sharpen my pen till they can feel its point; I shall dip it in venom and gall; I shall hurl my ink-pot at their heads!

MRS. STOCKMANN. Yes, but we are going away, you know, Thomas.　　　　　　　　　　[PETRA *comes back.*]

DR. STOCKMANN. Well?

PETRA. She has gone with it.

DR. STOCKMANN. Good.——Going away, did you say? No, I'll be hanged if we are going away! We are going to stay where we are, Katherine!

PETRA. Stay here?

MRS. STOCKMANN. Here, in the town?

DR. STOCKMANN. Yes, here. This is the field of battle—this is where the fight will be. This is where I shall triumph! As soon as I have had my trousers sewn up I shall go out and look for another house. We must have a roof over our heads for the winter.

HORSTER. That you shall have in my house.

DR. STOCKMANN. Can I?

HORSTER. Yes, quite well. I have plenty of room, and I am almost never at home.

MRS. STOCKMANN. How good of you, Captain Horster!

PETRA. Thank you!

DR. STOCKMANN (*grasping his hand*). Thank you, thank you! That is one trouble over! Now I can set to work in earnest at once. There is an endless amount of things to look through here, Katherine! Luckily I shall have all my time at my disposal, because I have been dismissed from the Baths, you know.

MRS. STOCKMANN (*with a sigh*). Oh, yes, I expected that.

DR. STOCKMANN. And they want to take my practice away from me, too. Let them! I have got the poor people to fall back upon, anyway—those that don't pay anything; and, after all, they need me most, too. But, by Jove, they will have to listen to me; I shall preach to them in season and out of season, as it says somewhere.

MRS. STOCKMANN. But, dear Thomas, I should have thought events had showed you what use it is to preach.

DR. STOCKMANN. You are really ridiculous, Katherine. Do you want me to let myself be beaten off the field by public opinion and the compact majority and all that devilry? No, thank you! And what I want to do is so simple and clear and straightforward. I only want to drum into the heads of these curs the fact that the liberals are the most insidious enemies of freedom—that party programmes strangle every young and vigorous truth—that considerations of expediency turn morality and justice upside down—and that they will end by making life here unbearable. Don't you think, Captain Horster, that I ought to be able to make people understand that?

HORSTER. Very likely; I don't know much about such things myself.

DR. STOCKMANN. Well, look here—I will explain! It is the party leaders that must be exterminated. A party leader is like a wolf, you see—like a voracious wolf. He requires a certain number of smaller victims to prey upon every year, if he is to live. Just look at Hovstad and Aslaksen! How many smaller victims have they not put an end to—or at any rate maimed and mangled until they are fit for nothing except to be householders or subscribers to the "People's Messenger"! (*Sits down on the edge of the table.*) Come here, Katherine—look how beautifully the sun shines today! And this lovely spring air I am drinking in!

MRS. STOCKMANN. Yes, if only we could live on sunshine and spring air, Thomas.

DR. STOCKMANN. Oh, you will have to pinch and save a bit—then we shall get along. That gives me very little concern. What is much worse is that I know of no one who is liberal-minded and high-minded enough to venture to take up my work after me.

PETRA. Don't think about that, father; you have plenty of time before you.——Hullo, here are the boys already!

[EJLIF *and* MORTEN *come in from the sitting-room.*]

MRS. STOCKMANN. Have you got a holiday?

MORTEN. No; but we were fighting with the other boys between lessons——

EJLIF. That isn't true; it was the other boys were fighting with us.

MORTEN. Well, and then Mr. Rörlund said we had better stay at home for a day or two.

DR. STOCKMANN (*snapping his fingers and getting up from the table*). I have it! I have it, by Jove! You shall never set foot in the school again!

THE BOYS. No more school!

MRS. STOCKMANN. But, Thomas——

DR. STOCKMANN. Never, I say. I will educate you myself; that is to say, you shan't learn a blessed thing——

MORTEN. Hooray!

DR. STOCKMANN. ——but I will make liberal-minded and high-minded men of you. You must help me with that, Petra.

PETRA. Yes, father, you may be sure I will.

DR. STOCKMANN. And my school shall be in the room where they insulted me and called me an enemy of the people. But we are too few as we are; I must have at least twelve boys to begin with.

MRS. STOCKMANN. You will certainly never get them in this town.

DR. STOCKMANN. We shall. (*To the boys.*) Don't you know any street urchins—regular ragamuffins——?

MORTEN. Yes, father, I know lots!

DR. STOCKMANN. That's capital! Bring me some specimens of them. I am going to experiment with curs, just for once; there may be some exceptional heads amongst them.

MORTEN. And what are we going to do, when you have made liberal-minded and high-minded men of us?

DR. STOCKMANN. Then you shall drive all the wolves out of the country, my boys!

[EJLIF *looks rather doubtful about it;* MORTEN *jumps about crying "Hurrah!"*]

MRS. STOCKMANN. Let us hope it won't be the wolves that will drive you out of the country, Thomas.

DR. STOCKMANN.   Are you out of your mind, Katherine? Drive me out! Now—when I am the strongest man in the town!

MRS. STOCKMANN.   The strongest—now?

DR. STOCKMANN.   Yes, and I will go so far as to say that now I am the strongest man in the whole world.

MORTEN.   I say!

DR. STOCKMANN (*lowering his voice*).   Hush! You mustn't say anything about it yet, but I have made a great discovery.

MRS. STOCKMANN.   Another one?

DR. STOCKMANN.   Yes. (*Gathers them round him, and says confidentially:*) It is this, let me tell you—that the strongest man in the world is he who stands most alone.

MRS. STOCKMANN (*smiling and shaking her head*).   Oh, Thomas, Thomas!

PETRA (*encouragingly, as she grasps her father's hands*). Father!

CURTAIN

THE WILD DUCK

[*1884*]

CHARACTERS

WERLE, *a merchant, manufacturer, etc.*

GREGERS WERLE, *his son.*

OLD EKDAL.

HIALMAR EKDAL, *his son, a photographer.*

GINA EKDAL, *Hialmar's wife.*

HEDVIG, *their daughter, a girl of fourteen.*

MRS. SÖRBY, *Werle's housekeeper.*

RELLING, *a doctor.*

MOLVIK, *student of theology.*

GRABERG, *Werle's bookkeeper.*

PETTERSEN, *Werle's servant.*

JENSEN, *a hired waiter.*

A FLABBY GENTLEMAN.

A THIN-HAIRED GENTLEMAN.

A SHORT-SIGHTED GENTLEMAN.

SIX OTHER GENTLEMEN, *guests at Werle's dinner-party.*

SEVERAL HIRED WAITERS.

The first act passes in WERLE'S *house, the remaining acts at* HIALMAR EKDAL'S.

Pronunciation of Names: GREGERS WERLE = Grayghers Verlë; HIALMAR EKDAL = Yalmar Aykdal; GINA = Cheena; GRÅBERG = Groberg; JENSEN = Yensen.

THE WILD DUCK

ACT ONE

At WERLE's *house.* *A richly and comfortably furnished study; bookcases and upholstered furniture; a writing-table, with papers and documents, in the centre of the room; lighted lamps with green shades, giving a subdued light. At the back, open folding-doors with curtains drawn back. Within is seen a large and handsome room, brilliantly lighted with lamps and branching candlesticks. In front, on the right (in the study), a small baize door leads into* WERLE's *office. On the left, in front, a fireplace with a glowing coal fire, and farther back a double door leading into the dining-room.*

[WERLE's *servant,* PETTERSEN, *in livery, and* JENSEN, *the hired waiter, in black, are putting the study in order. In the large room, two or three other hired waiters are moving about, arranging things and lighting more candles. From the dining-room, the hum of conversation and laughter of many voices are heard; a glass is tapped with a knife; silence follows, and a toast is proposed; shouts of "Bravo!" and then again a buzz of conversation.*]

PETTERSEN (*lights a lamp on the chimney-place and places a shade over it*). Hark to them, Jensen! Now the old man's on his legs holding a long palaver about Mrs. Sörby.

JENSEN (*pushing forward an armchair*). Is it true, what folks say, that they're—very good friends, eh?

PETTERSEN. Lord knows.

JENSEN. I've heard tell as he's been a lively customer in his day.

PETTERSEN. May be.

JENSEN. And he's giving this spread in honor of his son, they say.

PETTERSEN. Yes. His son came home yesterday.

JENSEN. This is the first time I ever heard as Mr. Werle had a son.

PETTERSEN. Oh, yes, he has a son, right enough. But he's a fixture, as you might say, up at the Höidal works. He's never once come to town all the years I've been in service here.

A WAITER (*in the doorway of the other room*). Pettersen, here's an old fellow wanting——

PETTERSEN (*mutters*). The devil—who's this now?

[OLD EKDAL *appears from the right, in the inner room. He is dressed in a threadbare overcoat with a high collar; he wears woollen mittens and carries in his hand a stick and a fur cap. Under his arm, a brown paper parcel. Dirty red-brown wig and small grey moustache.*]

PETTERSEN (*goes towards him*). Good Lord—what do you want here?

EKDAL (*in the doorway*). Must get into the office, Pettersen.

PETTERSEN. The office was closed an hour ago, and——

EKDAL. So they told me at the front door. But Gråberg's in there still. Let me slip in this way, Pettersen; there's a good fellow. (*Points towards the baize door.*) It's not the first time I've come this way.

PETTERSEN. Well, you may pass. (*Opens the door.*) But mind you go out again the proper way, for we've got company.

EKDAL. I know, I know—h'm! Thanks, Pettersen, good old friend! Thanks! (*Mutters softly.*) Ass!

[*He goes into the office;* PETTERSEN *shuts the door after him.*]

JENSEN. Is he one of the office people?

PETTERSEN. No he's only an outside hand that does odd jobs of copying. But he's been a tip-topper in his day, has old Ekdal.

JENSEN. You can see he's been through a lot.

PETTERSEN. Yes; he was an army officer, you know.

JENSEN. You don't say so?

PETTERSEN. No mistake about it. But then he went into the timber trade or something of the sort. They say he once played Mr. Werle a very nasty trick. They were partners in the Höidal works at the time. Oh, I know old Ekdal well, I do. Many a nip of bitters and bottle of ale we two have drunk at Madame Eriksen's.

JENSEN. He don't look as if he'd much to stand treat with.

PETTERSEN. Why, bless you, Jensen, it's me that stands treat. I always think there's no harm in being a bit civil to folks that have seen better days.

JENSEN. Did he go bankrupt, then?

PETTERSEN. Worse than that. He went to prison.

JENSEN. To prison!

PETTERSEN. Or perhaps it was the Penitentiary. (*Listens.*) Sh! They're leaving the table.

[*The dining-room door is thrown open from within by a couple of waiters.* MRS. SÖRBY *comes out conversing with two* GENTLEMEN. *Gradually the whole company follows, amongst them* WERLE. *Last come* HIALMAR EKDAL *and* GREGERS WERLE.]

MRS. SÖRBY (*in passing, to the servant*). Tell them to serve the coffee in the music-room, Pettersen.

PETTERSEN. Very well, Madam.

[*She goes with the two* GENTLEMEN *into the inner room and thence out to the right.* PETTERSEN *and* JENSEN *go out the same way.*]

A FLABBY GENTLEMAN (*to a* THIN-HAIRED GENTLEMAN). Whew! What a dinner!—It was no joke to do it justice!

THE THIN-HAIRED GENTLEMAN. Oh, with a little good-will one can get through a lot in three hours.

THE FLABBY GENTLEMAN. Yes, but afterwards, afterwards, my dear Chamberlain! *

A THIRD GENTLEMAN. I hear the coffee and maraschino are to be served in the music-room.

THE FLABBY GENTLEMAN. Bravo! Then perhaps Mrs. Sörby will play us something.

THE THIN-HAIRED GENTLEMAN (*in a low voice*). I hope Mrs. Sörby mayn't play us a tune we don't like, one of these days!

THE FLABBY GENTLEMAN. Oh, no, not she! Bertha will never turn against her old friends.

[*They laugh and pass into the inner room.*]

WERLE (*in a low voice, dejectedly*). I don't think anybody noticed it, Gregers.

GREGERS (*looks at him*). Noticed what?

WERLE. Did you not notice it either?

GREGERS. What do you mean?

WERLE. We were thirteen at table.

GREGERS. Indeed? Were there thirteen of us?

WERLE (*glances towards* HIALMAR EKDAL). Our usual party is twelve. (*To the others.*) This way, gentlemen!

[WERLE *and the others, all except* HIALMAR *and* GREGERS, *go out by the back, to the right.*]

HIALMAR (*who has overheard the conversation*). You ought not to have invited me, Gregers.

GREGERS. What! Not ask my best and only friend to a party supposed to be in my honor——?

HIALMAR. But I don't think your father likes it. You see I am quite outside his circle.

GREGERS. So I hear. But I wanted to see you and have

* "Chamberlain" was the non-hereditary honorary title conferred by the King upon men of wealth and position.

a talk with you, and I certainly shan't be staying long.—Ah, we two old schoolfellows have drifted far apart from each other. It must be sixteen or seventeen years since we met.

HIALMAR. Is it so long?

GREGERS. It is indeed. Well, how goes it with you? You look well. You have put on flesh and grown almost stout.

HIALMAR. Well, "stout" is scarcely the word; but I daresay I look a little more of a man than I used to.

GREGERS. Yes, you do; your outer man is in first-rate condition.

HIALMAR (*in a tone of gloom*). Ah, but the inner man! That is a very different matter, I can tell you! Of course you know of the terrible catastrophe that has befallen me and mine since last we met.

GREGERS (*more softly*). How are things going with your father now?

HIALMAR. Don't let us talk of it, old fellow. Of course my poor unhappy father lives with me. He hasn't another soul in the world to care for him. But you can understand that this is a miserable subject for me.—Tell me, rather, how you have been getting on up at the works.

GREGERS. I have had a delightfully lonely time of it— plenty of leisure to think and think about things. Come over here; we may as well make ourselves comfortable.

[*He seats himself in an armchair by the fire and draws* HIALMAR *down into another alongside of it.*]

HIALMAR (*sentimentally*). After all, Gregers, I thank you for inviting me to your father's table, for I take it as a sign that you have got over your feeling against me.

GREGERS (*surprised*). How could you imagine I had any feeling against you?

HIALMAR. You had at first, you know.

GREGERS. How at first?

HIALMAR.   After the great misfortune. It was natural enough that you should. Your father was within an ace of being drawn into that—well, that terrible business.

GREGERS.   Why should that give me any feeling against you? Who can have put that into your head?

HIALMAR.   I know it did, Gregers; your father told me so himself.

GREGERS (*starts*). My father! Oh, indeed. H'm.—Was that why you never let me hear from you?—not a single word.

HIALMAR.   Yes.

GREGERS.   Not even when you made up your mind to become a photographer?

HIALMAR.   Your father said I had better not write to you at all, about anything.

GREGERS (*looking straight before him*). Well, well, perhaps he was right.—But tell me now, Hialmar: are you pretty well satisfied with your present position?

HIALMAR (*with a little sigh*). Oh, yes, I am; I have really no cause to complain. At first, as you may guess, I felt it a little strange. It was such a totally new state of things for me. But of course my whole circumstances were totally changed. Father's utter, irretrievable ruin,—the shame and disgrace of it, Gregers——

GREGERS (*affected*). Yes, yes; I understand.

HIALMAR.   I couldn't think of remaining at college; there wasn't a shilling to spare; on the contrary, there were debts —mainly to your father, I believe——

GREGERS.   H'm——

HIALMAR.   In short, I thought it best to break, once for all, with my old surroundings and associations. It was your father that specially urged me to it; and since he interested himself so much in me——

GREGERS.   My father did?

HIALMAR. Yes, you surely knew that, didn't you? Where do you suppose I found the money to learn photography, and to furnish a studio and make a start? All that cost a pretty penny, I can tell you.

GREGERS. And my father provided the money?

HIALMAR. Yes, my dear fellow, didn't you know? I understood him to say he had written to you about it.

GREGERS. Not a word about his part in the business. He must have forgotten it. Our correspondence has always been purely a business one. So it was my father that——!

HIALMAR. Yes, certainly. He didn't wish it to be generally known; but he it was. And of course it was he, too, that put me in a position to marry. Don't you—don't you know about that either?

GREGERS. No, I haven't heard a word of it. (*Shakes him by the arm.*) But, my dear Hialmar, I can't tell you what pleasure all this gives me—pleasure, and self-reproach. I have perhaps done my father injustice after all—in some things. This proves that he has a heart. It shows a sort of compunction——

HIALMAR. Compunction——?

GREGERS. Yes, yes—whatever you like to call it. Oh, I can't tell you how glad I am to hear this of father.—So you are a married man, Hialmar! That is further than I shall ever get. Well, I hope you are happy in your married life?

HIALMAR. Yes, thoroughly happy. She is as good and capable a wife as any man could wish for. And she is by no means without culture.

GREGERS (*rather surprised*). No, of course not.

HIALMAR. You see, life is itself an education. Her daily intercourse with me—— And then we know one or two rather remarkable men, who come a good deal about us. I assure you, you would hardly know Gina again.

GREGERS. Gina?

HIALMAR. Yes; had you forgotten that her name was Gina?

GREGERS. Whose name? I haven't the slightest idea——

HIALMAR. Don't you remember that she used to be in service here?

GREGERS (*looks at him*). Is it Gina Hansen——?

HIALMAR. Yes, of course it is Gina Hansen.

GREGERS. ——who kept house for us during the last year of my mother's illness?

HIALMAR. Yes, exactly. But, my dear friend, I'm quite sure your father told you that I was married.

GREGERS (*who has risen*). Oh, yes, he mentioned it; but not that—— (*Walking about the room.*) Stay—perhaps he did —now that I think of it. My father always writes such short letters. (*Half seats himself on the arm of the chair.*) Now tell me, Hialmar—this is interesting—how did you come to know Gina—your wife?

HIALMAR. The simplest thing in the world. You know Gina did not stay here long; everything was so much upset at that time, owing to your mother's illness and so forth, that Gina was not equal to it all; so she gave notice and left. That was the year before your mother died—or it may have been the same year.

GREGERS. It was the same year. I was up at the works then. But afterwards——?

HIALMAR. Well, Gina lived at home with her mother, Madam Hansen, an excellent hard-working woman, who kept a little eating-house. She had a room to let, too, a very nice comfortable room.

GREGERS. And I suppose you were lucky enough to secure it?

HIALMAR. Yes; in fact, it was your father that recommended it to me. So it was there, you see, that I really came to know Gina.

GREGERS. And then you got engaged?

HIALMAR. Yes. It doesn't take young people long to fall in love——; h'm——

GREGERS (*rises and moves about a little*). Tell me: was it after your engagement—was it then that my father—I mean was it then that you began to take up photography?

HIALMAR. Yes, precisely. I wanted to make a start and to set up house as soon as possible; and your father and I agreed that this photography business was the readiest way. Gina thought so, too. Oh, and there was another thing in its favor, by-the-bye: it happened, luckily, that Gina had learnt to retouch.

GREGERS. That chimed in marvellously.

HIALMAR (*pleased, rises*). Yes, didn't it? Don't you think it was a marvellous piece of luck?

GREGERS. Oh, unquestionably. My father seems to have been almost a kind of providence for you.

HIALMAR (*with emotion*). He did not forsake his old friend's son in the hour of his need. For he has a heart, you see.

MRS. SÖRBY (*enters, arm-in-arm with* WERLE). Nonsense, my dear Mr. Werle; you mustn't stop there any longer staring at all the lights. It's very bad for you.

WERLE (*lets go her arm and passes his hand over his eyes*). I daresay you are right.

[PETTERSEN *and* JENSEN *carry round refreshment trays.*]

MRS. SÖRBY (*to the guests in the other room*). This way, if you please, gentlemen. Whoever wants a glass of punch must be so good as to come in here.

THE FLABBY GENTLEMAN (*comes up to* MRS. SÖRBY). Surely, it isn't possible that you have suspended our cherished right to smoke?

MRS. SÖRBY. Yes. No smoking here, in Mr. Werle's sanctum, Chamberlain.

THE THIN-HAIRED GENTLEMAN. When did you enact these stringent amendments on the cigar law, Mrs. Sörby?

MRS. SÖRBY. After the last dinner, Chamberlain, when certain persons permitted themselves to overstep the mark.

THE THIN-HAIRED GENTLEMAN. And may one never overstep the mark a little bit, Madame Bertha? Not the least little bit?

MRS. SÖRBY. Not in any respect whatsoever, Mr. Balle.

[*Most of the guests have assembled in the study; servants hand round glasses of punch.*]

WERLE (*to* HIALMAR, *who is standing beside a table*). What are you studying so intently, Ekdal?

HIALMAR. Only an album, Mr. Werle.

THE THIN-HAIRED GENTLEMAN (*who is wandering about*). Ah, photographs! They are quite in your line, of course.

THE FLABBY GENTLEMAN (*in an armchair*). Haven't you brought any of your own with you?

HIALMAR. No, I haven't.

THE FLABBY GENTLEMAN. You ought to have; it's very good for the digestion to sit and look at pictures.

THE THIN-HAIRED GENTLEMAN. And it contributes to the entertainment, you know.

THE SHORT-SIGHTED GENTLEMAN. And all contributions are thankfully received.

MRS. SÖRBY. The Chamberlains think that when one is invited out to dinner, one ought to exert oneself a little in return, Mr. Ekdal.

THE FLABBY GENTLEMAN. Where one dines so well, that duty becomes a pleasure.

THE THIN-HAIRED GENTLEMAN. And when it's a case of the struggle for existence, you know——

MRS. SÖRBY. I quite agree with you!

[*They continue the conversation, with laughter and joking.*]

GREGERS (*softly*). You must join in, Hialmar.

HIALMAR (*writing*). What am I to talk about?

THE FLABBY GENTLEMAN. Don't you think, Mr. Werle, that Tokay may be considered one of the more wholesome sorts of wine?

WERLE (*by the fire*). I can answer for the Tokay you had today, at any rate; it's one of the very finest seasons. Of course you would notice that.

THE FLABBY GENTLEMAN. Yes, it had a remarkably delicate flavor.

HIALMAR (*shyly*). Is there any difference between the seasons?

THE FLABBY GENTLEMAN (*laughs*). Come! That's good!

WERLE (*smiles*). It really doesn't pay to set fine wine before you.

THE THIN-HAIRED GENTLEMAN. Tokay is like photographs, Mr. Ekdal: they both need sunshine. Am I not right?

HIALMAR. Yes, light is important, no doubt.

MRS. SÖRBY. And it's exactly the same with Chamberlains—they, too, depend very much on sunshine,* as the saying is.

THE THIN-HAIRED GENTLEMAN. Oh, fie! That's a very threadbare sarcasm!

THE SHORT-SIGHTED GENTLEMAN. Mrs. Sörby is coming out——

THE FLABBY GENTLEMAN. ——and at our expense, too. (*Holds up his finger reprovingly.*) Oh, Madame Bertha, Madame Bertha!

MRS. SÖRBY. Yes, and there's not the least doubt that the seasons differ greatly. The old vintages are the finest.

THE SHORT-SIGHTED GENTLEMAN. Do you reckon me among the old vintages?

MRS. SÖRBY. Oh, far from it.

* The "sunshine" of court favor. [Trans.]

THE THIN-HAIRED GENTLEMAN. There now! But me, dear Mrs. Sörby——?

THE FLABBY GENTLEMAN. Yes, and me? What vintage should you say that we belong to?

MRS. SÖRBY. Why, to the sweet vintages, gentlemen.

[*She sips a glass of punch. The* GENTLEMEN *laugh and flirt with her.*]

WERLE. Mrs. Sörby can always find a loop-hole—when she wants to. Fill your glasses, gentlemen! Pettersen, will you see to it—! Gregers, suppose we have a glass together. (GREGERS *does not move.*) Won't you join us, Ekdal? I found no opportunity of drinking with you at table.

[GRÅBERG, *the bookkeeper, looks in at the baize door.*]

GRÅBERG. Excuse me, sir, but I can't get out.

WERLE. Have you been locked in again?

GRÅBERG. Yes, and Flakstad has carried off the keys.

WERLE. Well, you can pass out this way.

GRÅBERG. But there's some one else——

WERLE. All right; come through, both of you. Don't be afraid.   [GRÅBERG *and* OLD EKDAL *come out of the office.*]

WERLE (*involuntarily*). Ugh!

[*The laughter and talk among the guests cease.* HIALMAR *starts at the sight of his father, puts down his glass and turns towards the fireplace.*]

EKDAL (*does not look up, but makes little bows to both sides as he passes, murmuring*). Beg pardon, come the wrong way. Door locked—door locked. Beg pardon.

[*He and* GRÅBERG *go out by the back, to the right.*]

WERLE (*between his teeth*). That idiot Gråberg.

GREGERS (*open-mouthed and staring, to* HIALMAR). Why surely that wasn't——!

THE FLABBY GENTLEMAN. What's the matter? Who was it?

GREGERS. Oh, nobody; only the bookkeeper and some one with him.

THE SHORT-SIGHTED GENTLEMAN (*to* HIALMAR). Did you know that man?

HIALMAR. I don't know—I didn't notice——

THE FLABBY GENTLEMAN. What the deuce has come over every one?   [*He joins another group who are talking softly.*]

MRS. SÖRBY (*whispers to the servant*). Give him something to take with him;—something good, mind.

PETTERSEN (*nods*). I'll see to it.   [*Goes out.*]

GREGERS (*softly and with emotion, to* HIALMAR). So that was really he!

HIALMAR. Yes.

GREGERS. And you could stand there and deny that you knew him!

HIALMAR (*whispers vehemently*). But how could I——!

GREGERS. ——acknowledge your own father?

HIALMAR (*with pain*). Oh, if you were in my place——
[*The conversation amongst the guests, which has been carried on in a low tone, now swells into constrained joviality.*]

THE THIN-HAIRED GENTLEMAN (*approaching* HIALMAR *and* GREGERS *in a friendly manner*). Aha! Reviving old college memories, eh? Don't you smoke, Mr. Ekdal? May I give you a light? Oh, by-the-bye, we mustn't——

HIALMAR. No, thank you, I won't——

THE FLABBY GENTLEMAN. Haven't you a nice little poem you could recite to us, Mr. Ekdal? You used to recite so charmingly.

HIALMAR. I am sorry I can't remember anything.

THE FLABBY GENTLEMAN. Oh, that's a pity. Well, what shall we do, Balle?
[*Both* GENTLEMEN *move away and pass into the other room.*]

HIALMAR (*gloomily*). Gregers—I am going! When a man has felt the crushing hand of Fate, you see —— Say good-bye to your father for me.

GREGERS. Yes, yes. Are you going straight home?

HIALMAR. Yes. Why?

GREGERS. Oh, because I may perhaps look in on you later.

HIALMAR. No, you mustn't do that. You must not come to my home. Mine is a melancholy abode, Gregers, especially after a splendid banquet like this. We can always arrange to meet somewhere in the town.

MRS. SÖRBY (*who has quietly approached*). Are you going, Ekdal?

HIALMAR. Yes.

MRS. SÖRBY. Remember me to Gina.

HIALMAR. Thanks.

MRS SÖRBY. And say I am coming up to see her one of these days.

HIALMAR. Yes, thank you. (*To* GREGERS). Stay here; I will slip out unobserved.

[*He saunters away, then into the other room, and so out to the right.*]

MRS SÖRBY (*softly to the servant, who has come back*). Well, did you give the old man something?

PETTERSEN. Yes; I sent him off with a bottle of cognac.

MRS. SÖRBY. Oh, you might have thought of something better than that.

PETTERSEN. Oh, no, Mrs. Sörby; cognac is what he likes best in the world.

THE FLABBY GENTLEMAN (*in the doorway with a sheet of music in his hand*). Shall we play a duet, Mrs. Sörby?

MRS. SÖRBY. Yes, suppose we do.

THE GUESTS. Bravo, bravo!

[*She goes with all the guests through the back room, out to the right.* GREGERS *remains standing by the fire.* WERLE *is looking for something on the writing-table and appears to wish that* GREGERS *would go; as* GREGERS *does not move,* WERLE *goes towards the door.*]

GREGERS. Father, won't you stay a moment?

WERLE (*stops*). What is it?

GREGERS. I must have a word with you.

WERLE. Can it not wait till we are alone?

GREGERS. No, it cannot; for perhaps we shall never be alone together.

WERLE (*drawing nearer*). What do you mean by that? [*During what follows, the pianoforte is faintly heard from the distant music-room.*]

GREGERS. How has that family been allowed to go so miserably to the wall?

WERLE. You mean the Ekdals, I suppose.

GREGERS. Yes, I mean the Ekdals. Lieutenant Ekdal was once so closely associated with you.

WERLE. Much too closely; I have felt that to my cost for many a year. It is thanks to him that I—yes I—have had a kind of slur cast upon my reputation.

GREGERS (*softly*). Are you sure that he alone was to blame?

WERLE. Who else do you suppose——?

GREGERS. You and he acted together in that affair of the forests——

WERLE. But was it not Ekdal that drew the map of the tracts we had bought—that fraudulent map! It was he who felled all that timber illegally on Government ground. In fact, the whole management was in his hands. I was quite in the dark as to what Lieutenant Ekdal was doing.

GREGERS. Lieutenant Ekdal himself seems to have been very much in the dark as to what he was doing.

WERLE. That may be. But the fact remains that he was found guilty and I acquitted.

GREGERS. Yes, I know that nothing was proved against you.

WERLE. Acquittal is acquittal. Why do you rake up these old miseries that turned my hair grey before its time? Is

that the sort of thing you have been brooding over up there,
all these years? I can assure you, Gregers, here in the town
the whole story has been forgotten long ago—so far as *I* am
concerned.

GREGERS. But that unhappy Ekdal family——

WERLE. What would you have had me do for the people?
When Ekdal came out of prison he was a broken-down being,
past all help. There are people in the world who dive to
the bottom the moment they get a couple of slugs in their
body and never come to the surface again. You may take
my word for it, Gregers, I have done all I could without
positively laying myself open to all sorts of suspicion and
gossip——

GREGERS. Suspicion——? Oh, I see.

WERLE. I have given Ekdal copying to do for the office,
and I pay him far, far more for it than his work is worth——

GREGERS (*without looking at him*). H'm; that I don't
doubt.

WERLE. You laugh? Do you think I am not telling you
the truth? Well, I certainly can't refer you to my books,
for I never enter payments of that sort.

GREGERS (*smiles coldly*). No, there are certain payments
it is best to keep no account of.

WERLE (*taken aback*). What do you mean by that?

GREGERS (*mustering up courage*). Have you entered what
it cost you to have Hialmar Ekdal taught photography?

WERLE. I? How "entered" it?

GREGERS. I have learnt that it was you who paid for his
training. And I have learnt, too, that it was you who ena-
bled him to set up house so comfortably.

WERLE. Well, and yet you talk as though I had done
nothing for the Ekdals! I can assure you these people have
cost me enough in all conscience.

GREGERS. Have you entered any of these expenses in your books?

WERLE. Why do you ask?

GREGERS. Oh, I have my reasons. Now tell me: when you interested yourself so warmly in your old friend's son—it was just before his marriage, was it not?

WERLE. Why, deuce take it—after all these years, how can I——?

GREGERS. You wrote me a letter about that time—a business letter, of course; and in a postscript you mentioned—quite briefly—that Hialmar Ekdal had married a Miss Hansen.

WERLE. Yes, that was quite right. That was her name.

GREGERS. But you did not mention that this Miss Hansen was Gina Hansen—our former housekeeper.

WERLE (*with a forced laugh of derision*). No; to tell the truth, it didn't occur to me that you were so particularly interested in our former housekeeper.

GREGERS. No more I was. But (*lowers his voice.*) there were others in this house who were particularly interested in her.

WERLE. What do you mean by that? (*Flaring up.*) You are not alluding to me, I hope?

GREGERS (*softly but firmly*). Yes, I am alluding to you.

WERLE. And you dare——! You presume to——! How can that ungrateful hound—that photographer fellow—how dare he go making such insinuations!

GREGERS. Hialmar has never breathed a word about this. I don't believe he has the faintest suspicion of such a thing.

WERLE. Then where have you got it from? Who can have put such notions in your head?

GREGERS. My poor unhappy mother told me; and that the very last time I saw her.

WERLE. Your mother! I might have known as much!

You and she—you always held together. It was she who turned you against me, from the first.

GREGERS. No, it was all that she had to suffer and submit to, until she broke down and came to such a pitiful end.

WERLE. Oh, she had nothing to suffer or submit to; not more than most people, at all events. But there's no getting on with morbid, overstrained creatures—that I have learnt to my cost.—And you could go on nursing such a suspicion—burrowing into all sorts of old rumors and slanders against your own father! I must say, Gregers, I really think that at your age you might find something more useful to do.

GREGERS. Yes, it is high time.

WERLE. Then perhaps your mind would be easier than it seems to be now. What can be your object in remaining up at the works, year out and year in, drudging away like a common clerk, and not drawing a farthing more than the ordinary monthly wage? It is downright folly.

GREGERS. Ah, if I were only sure of that.

WERLE. I understand you well enough. You want to be independent; you won't be beholden to me for anything. Well, now there happens to be an opportunity for you to become independent, your own master in everything.

GREGERS. Indeed? In what way——?

WERLE. When I wrote you insisting on your coming to town at once—h'm——

GREGERS. Yes, what is it you really want of me? I have been waiting all day to know.

WERLE. I want to propose that you should enter the firm, as partner.

GREGERS. I! Join your firm? As partner?

WERLE. Yes. It would not involve our being constantly together. You could take over the business here in town, and I should move up to the works.

GREGERS. You would?

WERLE. The fact is, I am not so fit for work as I once was. I am obliged to spare my eyes, Gregers; they have begun to trouble me.

GREGERS. They have always been weak.

WERLE. Not as they are now. And, besides, circumstances might possibly make it desirable for me to live up there—for a time, at any rate.

GREGERS. That is certainly quite a new idea to me.

WERLE. Listen, Gregers: there are many things that stand between us; but we are father and son after all. We ought surely to be able to come to some sort of understanding with each other.

GREGERS. Outwardly, you mean, of course?

WERLE. Well, even that would be something. Think it over, Gregers. Don't you think it ought to be possible? Eh?

GREGERS (*looking at him coldly*). There is something behind all this.

WERLE. How so?

GREGERS. You want to make use of me in some way.

WERLE. In such a close relationship as ours, the one can always be useful to the other.

GREGERS. Yes, so people say.

WERLE. I want very much to have you at home with me for a time. I am a lonely man, Gregers; I have always felt lonely, all my life through; but most of all now that I am getting up in years. I feel the need of some one about me——

GREGERS. You have Mrs. Sörby.

WERLE. Yes, I have her; and she has become, I may say, almost indispensable to me. She is lively and even-tempered; she brightens up the house; and that is a very great thing for me.

GREGERS. Well, then, you have everything just as you wish it.

WERLE. Yes, but I am afraid it can't last. A woman so situated may easily find herself in a false position, in the eyes of the world. For that matter it does a man no good, either.

GREGERS. Oh, when a man gives such dinners as you give, he can risk a great deal.

WERLE. Yes, but how about the woman, Gregers? I fear she won't accept the situation much longer; and even if she did—even if, out of attachment to me, she were to take her chance of gossip and scandal and all that——? Do you think, Gregers—you with your strong sense of justice——

GREGERS (*interrupts him*). Tell me in one word: are you thinking of marrying her?

WERLE. Suppose I were thinking of it? What then?

GREGERS. That's what I say: what then?

WERLE. Should you be inflexibly opposed to it!

GREGERS. Not at all. Not by any means.

WERLE. I was not sure whether your devotion to your mother's memory——

GREGERS. I am not overstrained.

WERLE. Well, whatever you may or may not be, at all events you have lifted a great weight from my mind. I am extremely pleased that I can reckon on your concurrence in this matter.

GREGERS (*looking intently at him*). Now I see the use you want to put me to.

WERLE. Use to put you to? What an expression!

GREGERS. Oh, don't let us be nice in our choice of words —not when we are alone together, at any rate. (*With a short laugh.*) Well, well. So this is what made it absolutely essential that I should come to town in person. For the sake of Mrs. Sörby, we are to get up a pretence at family life in the house—a tableau of filial affection! That will be something new indeed.

WERLE. How dare you speak in that tone!

GREGERS. Was there ever any family life here? Never since I can remember. But now, forsooth, your plans demand something of the sort. No doubt it will have an excellent effect when it is reported that the son has hastened home, on the wings of filial piety, to the grey-haired father's wedding-feast. What will then remain of all the rumors as to the wrongs the poor dead mother had to submit to? Not a vestige. Her son annihilates them at one stroke.

WERLE. Gregers—I believe there is no one in the world you detest as you do me.

GREGERS (*softly*). I have seen you at too close quarters.

WERLE. You have seen me with your mother's eyes. (*Lowers his voice a little.*) But you should remember that her eyes were—clouded now and then.

GREGERS(*quivering*). I see what you are hinting at. But who was to blame for mother's unfortunate weakness? Why, you, and all those——! The last of them was this woman that you palmed off upon Hialmar Ekdal, when you were —— Ugh!

WERLE (*shrugs his shoulders*). Word for word as if it were your mother speaking!

GREGERS (*without heeding*). And there he is now, with his great, confiding, childlike mind, compassed about with all this treachery—living under the same roof with such a creature and never dreaming that what he calls his home is built upon a lie! (*Comes a step nearer.*) When I look back upon your past, I seem to see a battle-field with shattered lives on every hand.

WERLE. I begin to think the chasm that divides us is too wide.

GREGERS (*bowing, with self-command*). So I have observed; and therefore I take my hat and go.

WERLE. You are going! Out of the house?

GREGERS. Yes. For at last I see my mission in life.

WERLE. What mission?

GREGERS. You would only laugh if I told you.

WERLE. A lonely man doesn't laugh so easily, Gregers.

GREGERS (*pointing towards the background*). Look, father, —the Chamberlains are playing blind-man's-buff with Mrs. Sörby.—Good-night and good-bye.

[*He goes out by the back to the right. Sounds of laughter and merriment from the company, who are now visible in the outer room.*]

WERLE (*muttering contemptuously after* GREGERS). Ha——! Poor wretch—and he says he is not overstrained!

CURTAIN

ACT TWO

HIALMAR EKDAL'S *studio, a good-sized room, evidently in the top story of the building. On the right, a sloping roof of large panes of glass, half-covered by a blue curtain. In the right-hand corner, at the back, the entrance door; farther forward, on the same side, a door leading to the sitting-room. Two doors on the opposite side, and between them an iron stove. At the back, a wide double sliding-door. The studio is plainly but comfortably fitted up and furnished. Between the doors on the right, standing out a little from the wall, a sofa with a table and some chairs; on the table a lighted lamp with a shade; beside the stove an old arm-chair. Photographic instruments and apparatus of different kinds lying about the room. Against the back wall, to the left of the double door, stands a bookcase containing a few books, boxes, and bottles of chemicals, instruments, tools, and other objects. Photographs and small*

*articles, such as camel's-hair brushes, paper, and so forth, lie
on the table.*

[GINA EKDAL *sits on a chair by the table, sewing.* HEDVIG
*is sitting on the sofa, with her hands shading her eyes and her
thumbs in her ears, reading a book.*]

GINA (*glances once or twice at* HEDVIG, *as if with secret
anxiety; then says:*) Hedvig!   [HEDVIG *does not hear.*]

GINA (*repeats more loudly*). Hedvig!

HEDVIG (*takes away her hands and looks up*). Yes, mother?

GINA. Hedvig dear, you mustn't sit reading any longer
now.

HEDVIG. Oh, mother, mayn't I read a little more? Just
a little bit?

GINA. No, no, you must put away your book now. Father
doesn't like it; he never reads hisself in the evening.

HEDVIG (*shuts the book*). No, father doesn't care much
about reading.

GINA (*puts aside her sewing and takes up a lead pencil and
a little account-book from the table*). Can you remember how
much we paid for the butter today?

HEDVIG. It was one crown sixty-five.

GINA. That's right. (*Puts it down.*) It's terrible what a
lot of butter we get through in this house. Then there was
the smoked sausage, and the cheese—let me see—(*Writes.*)—
and the ham—(*Adds up.*) Yes, that makes just——

HEDVIG. And then the beer.

GINA. Yes, to be sure. (*Writes.*) How it do mount up!
But we can't manage with no less.

HEDVIG. And then you and I didn't need anything hot
for dinner, as father was out.

GINA. No; that was so much to the good. And then I
took eight crowns fifty for the photographs.

HEDVIG. Really! So much as that?

GINA. Exactly eight crowns fifty.

[*Silence.* GINA *takes up her sewing again;* HEDVIG *takes paper and pencil and begins to draw, shading her eyes with her left hand.*]

HEDVIG. Isn't it jolly to think that father is at Mr. Werle's big dinner-party?

GINA. You know he's not really Mr. Werle's guest. It was the son invited him. (*After a pause.*) We have nothing to do with that Mr. Werle.

HEDVIG. I'm longing for father to come home. He promised to ask Mrs. Sörby for something nice for me.

GINA. Yes, there's plenty of good things going in that house, I can tell you.

HEDVIG (*goes on drawing*). And I believe I'm a little hungry, too.

[OLD EKDAL, *with the paper parcel under his arm and another parcel in his coat pocket, comes in by the entrance door.*]

GINA. How late you are today, grandfather!

EKDAL. They had locked the office door. Had to wait in Gråberg's room. And then they let me through—h'm.

HEDVIG. Did you get some more copying to do, grand-father?

EKDAL. This whole packet. Just look.

GINA. That's capital.

HEDVIG. And you have another parcel in your pocket.

EKDAL. Eh? Oh, never mind, that's nothing. (*Puts his stick away in a corner.*) This work will keep me going a long time, Gina. (*Opens one of the sliding-doors in the back wall a little.*) Hush! (*Peeps into the room for a moment, then pushes the door carefully to again.*) Hee-hee! They're fast asleep, all the lot of them. And she's gone into the basket herself. Hee-hee!

HEDVIG. Are you sure she isn't cold in that basket, grand-father?

EKDAL. Not a bit of it! Cold? With all that straw? (*Goes towards the farther door on the left.*) There are matches in here, I suppose.

GINA. The matches is on the drawers.

[EKDAL *goes into his room.*]

HEDVIG. It's nice that grandfather has got all that copying.

GINA. Yes, poor old father; it means a bit of pocket money for him.

HEDVIG. And he won't be able to sit the whole forenoon down at that horrid Madame Eriksen's.

GINA. No more he won't.   [*Short silence.*]

HEDVIG. Do you suppose they are still at the dinner-table?

GINA. Goodness knows; as like as not.

HEDVIG. Think of all the delicious things father is having to eat! I'm certain he'll be in splendid spirits when he comes. Don't you think so, mother?

GINA. Yes; and if only we could tell him that we'd got the room let——

HEDVIG. But we don't need that this evening.

GINA. Oh, we'd be none the worst of it, I can tell you. It's no use to us as it is.

HEDVIG. I mean we don't need it this evening, for father will be in a good humor at any rate. It is best to keep the letting of the room for another time.

GINA (*looks across at her*). You like having some good news to tell father when he comes home in the evening?

HEDVIG. Yes; for then things are pleasanter somehow.

GINA (*thinking to herself*). Yes, yes, there's something in that.

[OLD EKDAL *comes in again and is going out by the foremost door to the left.*]

GINA (*half turning in her chair*).   Do you want something out of the kitchen, grandfather?

EKDAL.   Yes, yes, I do.   Don't you trouble.   [*Goes out.*]

GINA.   He's not poking away at the fire, is he?   (*Waits a moment.*)   Hedvig, go and see what he's about.

[EKDAL *comes in again with a small jug of steaming hot water.*]

HEDVIG.   Have you been getting some hot water, grandfather?

EKDAL.   Yes, hot water.   Want it for something.   Want to write, and the ink has got as thick as porridge—h'm.

GINA.   But you'd best have your supper first, grandfather.   It's laid in there.

EKDAL.   Can't be bothered with supper, Gina.   Very busy, I tell you.   No one's to come to my room.   No one —h'm.

[*He goes into his room;* GINA *and* HEDVIG *look at each other.*]

GINA (*softly*).   Can you imagine where he's got money from?

HEDVIG.   From Gråberg, perhaps.

GINA.   Not a bit of it.   Gråberg always sends the money to me.

HEDVIG.   Then he must have got a bottle on credit somewhere.

GINA.   Poor grandfather, who'd give him credit?

[HIALMAR EKDAL, *in an overcoat and grey felt hat, comes in from the right.*]

GINA (*throws down her sewing and rises*).   Why, Ekdal, is that you already?

HEDVIG (*at the same time, jumping up*).   Fancy your coming so soon, father!

HIALMAR (*taking off his hat*).   Yes, most of the people were coming away.

HEDVIG.   So early?

HIALMAR. Yes, it was a dinner-party, you know.

[*Is taking off his overcoat.*]

GINA. Let me help you.

HEDVIG. Me, too.

[*They draw off his coat;* GINA *hangs it up on the back wall.*]

HEDVIG. Were there many people there, father?

HIALMAR. Oh, no, not many. We were about twelve or fourteen at table.

GINA. And you had some talk with them all?

HIALMAR. Oh, yes, a little; but Gregers took up most of my time.

GINA. Is Gregers as ugly as ever?

HIALMAR. Well, he's not very much to look at. Hasn't the old man come home?

HEDVIG. Yes, grandfather is in his room, writing.

HIALMAR. Did he say anything?

GINA. No, what should he say?

HIALMAR. Didn't he say anything about——? I heard something about his having been with Gråberg. I'll go in and see him for a moment.

GINA. No, no, better not.

HIALMAR. Why not? Did he say he didn't want me to go in?

GINA. I don't think he wants to see nobody this evening——

HEDVIG (*making signs*). H'm—h'm!

GINA (*not noticing*). ——he has been in to fetch hot water——

HIALMAR. Aha! Then he's——

GINA. Yes, I suppose so.

HIALMAR. Oh, God! my poor old white-haired father!—— Well, well; there let him sit and get all the enjoyment he can.

[OLD EKDAL, *in an indoor coat and with a lighted pipe, comes from his room.*]

EKDAL. Got home? Thought it was you I heard talking.

HIALMAR. Yes, I have just come.

EKDAL. You didn't see me, did you?

HIALMAR. No, but they told me you had passed through —so I thought I would follow you.

EKDAL. H'm, good of you, Hialmar.—Who were they, all those fellows?

HIALMAR.—Oh, all sorts of people. There was Chamberlain Flor, and Chamberlain Balle, and Chamberlain Kaspersen and Chamberlain—this, that, and the other—I don't know who all——

EKDAL (*nodding*). Hear that, Gina! Chamberlains every one of them!

GINA. Yes, I hear as they're terrible genteel in that house nowadays.

HEDVIG. Did the Chamberlains sing, father? Or did they read aloud?

HIALMAR. No, they only talked nonsense. They wanted me to recite something for them; but I knew better than that.

EKDAL. You weren't to be persuaded, eh?

GINA. Oh, you might have done it.

HIALMAR. No; one mustn't be at everybody's beck and call. (*Walks about the room.*) That's not my way, at any rate.

EKDAL. No, no; Hialmar's not to be had for the asking, he isn't.

HIALMAR. I don't see why *I* should bother myself to entertain people on the rare occasions when I go into society. Let the others exert themselves. These fellows go from one great dinner-table to the next and gorge and guzzle day out and day in. It's for them to bestir themselves and do something in return for all the good feeding they get.

GINA. But you didn't say that?

HIALMAR (*humming*). Ho-ho-ho——; faith, I gave them a bit of my mind.

EKDAL. Not the Chamberlains?

HIALMAR. Oh, why not? (*Lightly*.) After that, we had a little discussion about Tokay.

EKDAL. Tokay! There's a fine wine for you!

HIALMAR (*comes to a standstill*). It may be a fine wine. But of course you know the vintages differ; it all depends on how much sunshine the grapes have had.

GINA. Why, you know everything, Ekdal.

EKDAL. And did they dispute that?

HIALMAR. They tried to; but they were requested to observe that it was just the same with Chamberlains— that with them, too, different batches were of different quali- ties.

GINA. What things you do think of!

EKDAL. Hee-hee! So they got that in their pipes, too?

HIALMAR. Right in their teeth.

EKDAL. Do you hear that, Gina? He said it right in the very teeth of all the Chamberlains.

GINA. Fancy——! Right in their teeth!

HIALMAR. Yes, but I don't want it talked about. One doesn't speak of such things. The whole affair passed off quite amicably of course. They were nice, genial fellows; I didn't want to wound them—not I!

EKDAL. Right in their teeth, though——!

HEDVIG (*caressingly*). How nice it is to see you in a dress- coat! It suits you so well, father.

HIALMAR. Yes, don't you think so? And this one really sits to perfection. It fits almost as if it had been made for me;—a little tight in the arm-holes perhaps;—help me, Hed- vig (*takes off the coat*). I think I'll put on my jacket. Where is my jacket, Gina?

GINA. Here it is. (*Brings the jacket and helps him.*)

HIALMAR. That's it! Don't forget to send the coat back to Molvik first thing tomorrow morning.

GINA (*laying it away*). I'll be sure and see to it.

HIALMAR (*stretching himself*). After all, there's a more homely feeling about this. A free-and-easy indoor costume suits my whole personality better. Don't you think so, Hedvig?

HEDVIG. Yes, father.

HIALMAR. When I loosen my necktie into a pair of flowing ends—like this—eh?

HEDVIG. Yes, that goes so well with your moustache and the sweep of your curls.

HIALMAR. I should not call them curls exactly; I should rather say locks.

HEDVIG. Yes, they are too big for curls.

HIALMAR. Locks describes them better.

HEDVIG (*after a pause, twitching his jacket*). Father!

HIALMAR. Well, what is it?

HEDVIG. Oh, you know very well.

HIALMAR. No, really I don't——

HEDVIG (*half laughing, half whispering*). Oh, yes, father; now don't tease me any longer!

HIALMAR. Why, what do you mean?

HEDVIG (*shaking him*). Oh, what nonsense; come, where are they, father? All the good things you promised me, you know?

HIALMAR. Oh—if I haven't forgotten all about them!

HEDVIG. Now you're only teasing me, father! Oh, it's too bad of you! Where have you put them?

HIALMAR. No, I positively forgot to get anything. But wait a little! I have something else for you, Hedvig.

[*Goes and searches in the pockets of the coat.*]

HEDVIG (*skipping and clapping her hands*). Oh, mother, mother!

GINA. There, you see; if you only give him time——

HIALMAR (*with a paper*). Look, here it is.

HEDVIG. That? Why, that's only a paper.

HIALMAR. That is the bill of fare, my dear; the whole bill of fare. Here you see: "Menu"—that means bill of fare.

HEDVIG. Haven't you anything else?

HIALMAR. I forgot the other things, I tell you. But you may take my word for it, these dainties are very unsatisfying. Sit down at the table and read the bill of fare, and then I'll describe to you how the dishes taste. Here you are, Hedvig.

HEDVIG (*gulping down her tears*). Thank you. (*She seats herself, but does not read;* GINA *makes signs to her;* HIALMAR *notices it.*)

HIALMAR (*pacing up and down the room*). It's monstrous what absurd things the father of a family is expected to think of; and if he forgets the smallest trifle, he is treated to sour faces at once. Well, well, one gets used to that, too. (*Stops near the stove, by the old man's chair.*) Have you peeped in there this evening, father?

EKDAL. Yes, to be sure I have. She's gone into the basket.

HIALMAR. Ah, she has gone into the basket. Then she's beginning to get used to it.

EKDAL. Yes; just as I prophesied. But you know there are still a few little things——

HIALMAR. A few improvements, yes.

EKDAL. They've got to be made, you know.

HIALMAR. Yes, let us have a talk about the improvements, father. Come, let us sit on the sofa.

EKDAL. All right. H'm—think I'll just fill my pipe first. Must clean it out, too. H'm.   [*He goes into his room.*]

GINA (*smiling to* HIALMAR). His pipe!

HIALMAR. Oh, yes, yes, Gina; let him alone—the poor

shipwrecked old man.—Yes, these improvements—we had better get them out of hand tomorrow.

GINA. You'll hardly have time tomorrow, Ekdal.

HEDVIG (*interposing*). Oh, yes he will, mother!

GINA. ——for remember them prints that has to be retouched; they've sent for them time after time.

HIALMAR. There now! those prints again! I shall get them finished all right! Have any new orders come in?

GINA. No, worse luck; tomorrow I have nothing but those two sittings, you know.

HIALMAR. Nothing else? Oh, no, if people won't set about things with a will——

GINA. But what more can I do? Don't I advertise in the papers as much as we can afford?

HIALMAR. Yes, the papers, the papers; you see how much good they do. And I suppose no one has been to look at the room either?

GINA. No, not yet.

HIALMAR. That was only to be expected. If people won't keep their eyes open——. Nothing can be done without a real effort, Gina!

HEDVIG (*going towards him*). Shall I fetch you the flute, father?

HIALMAR. No; no flute for me; *I* want no pleasures in this world. (*Pacing about.*) Yes, indeed I will work tomorrow; you shall see if I don't. You may be sure I shall work as long as my strength holds out.

GINA. But my dear, good Ekdal, I didn't mean it in that way.

HEDVIG. Father, mayn't I bring in a bottle of beer?

HIALMAR. No, certainly not. I require nothing, nothing—— (*Comes to a standstill.*) Beer? Was it beer you were talking about?

HEDVIG (*cheerfully*). Yes, father; beautiful, fresh beer.

HIALMAR. Well—since you insist upon it, you may bring in a bottle.

GINA. Yes, do; and we'll be nice and cosy.

[HEDVIG *runs towards the kitchen door.*]

HIALMAR (*by the stove, stops her, looks at her, puts his arm round her neck and presses her to him*). Hedvig, Hedvig!

HEDVIG (*with tears of joy*). My dear, kind father!

HIALMAR. No, don't call me that. Here have I been feasting at the rich man's table,—battening at the groaning board——! And I couldn't even——!

GINA (*sitting at the table*). Oh, nonsense, nonsense, Ekdal.

HIALMAR. It's not nonsense! And yet you mustn't be too hard upon me. You know that I love you for all that.

HEDVIG (*throwing her arms round him*). And we love you, oh, so dearly, father!

HIALMAR. And if I am unreasonable once in a while,— why then—you must remember that I am a man beset by a host of cares. There, there! (*Dries his eyes.*) No beer at such a moment as this. Give me the flute.

[HEDVIG *runs to the bookcase and fetches it.*]

HIALMAR. Thanks! That's right. With my flute in my hand and you two at my side——ah——!

[HEDVIG *seats herself at the table near* GINA; HIALMAR *paces backwards and forwards, pipes up vigorously and plays a Bohemian peasant dance, but in a slow plaintive tempo, and with sentimental expression.*]

HIALMAR (*breaking off the melody, holds out his left hand to* GINA *and says with emotion:*) Our roof may be poor and humble, Gina, but it is home. And with all my heart I say: here dwells my happiness.

[*He begins to play again; almost immediately after, a knocking is heard at the entrance door.*]

GINA (*rising*). Hush, Ekdal,—I think there's some one at the door.

HIALMAR (*laying the flute on the bookcase*). There! Again!   [GINA *goes and opens the door.*]

GREGERS WERLE (*in the passage*). Excuse me——

GINA (*starting back slightly*). Oh!

GREGERS. ——does not Mr. Ekdal, the photographer, live here?

GINA. Yes, he does.

HIALMAR (*going towards the door*). Gregers! You here after all? Well, come in then.

GREGERS (*coming in*). I told you I would come and look you up.

HIALMAR. But this evening——? Have you left the party?

GREGERS. I have left both the party and my father's house.—Good evening, Mrs. Ekdal. I don't know whether you recognize me?

GINA. Oh, yes; it's not difficult to know young Mr. Werle again.

GREGERS. No, I am like my mother; and no doubt you remember her.

HIALMAR. Left your father's house, did you say?

GREGERS. Yes, I have gone to a hotel.

HIALMAR. Indeed. Well, since you're here, take off your coat and sit down.

GREGERS. Thanks.

[*He takes off his overcoat. He is now dressed in a plain grey suit of a countrified cut.*]

HIALMAR. Here, on the sofa. Make yourself comfortable.

[GREGERS *seats himself on the sofa;* HIALMAR *takes a chair at the table.*]

GREGERS (*looking around him*). So these are your quarters, Hialmar—this is your home.

HIALMAR. This is the studio, as you see——

GINA. But it's the largest of our rooms, so we generally sit here.

HIALMAR. We used to live in a better place; but this flat has one great advantage; there are such capital outer rooms——

GINA. And we have a room on the other side of the passage that we can let.

GREGERS (*to* HIALMAR). Ah—so you have lodgers, too?

HIALMAR. No, not yet. They're not so easy to find, you see; you have to keep your eyes open. (*To* HEDVIG.) What about the beer, eh?

[HEDVIG *nods and goes out into the kitchen.*]

GREGERS. So that is your daughter?

HIALMAR. Yes, that is Hedvig.

GREGERS. And she is your only child?

HIALMAR. Yes, the only one. She is the joy of our lives, and—(*lowering his voice*)—at the same time our deepest sorrow, Gregers.

GREGERS. What do you mean?

HIALMAR. She is in serious danger of losing her eyesight.

GREGERS. Becoming blind?

HIALMAR. Yes. Only the first symptoms have appeared as yet, and she may not feel it much for some time. But the doctor has warned us. It is coming, inexorably.

GREGERS. What a terrible misfortune! How do you account for it?

HIALMAR (*sighs*). Hereditary, no doubt.

GREGERS (*starting*). Hereditary?

GINA. Ekdal's mother had weak eyes.

HIALMAR. Yes, so my father says; I can't remember her.

GREGERS. Poor child! And how does she take it?

HIALMAR. Oh, you can imagine we haven't the heart to tell her of it. She dreams of no danger. Gay and careless and chirping like a little bird, she flutters onward into a life of endless night. (*Overcome.*) Oh, it is cruelly hard on me, Gregers.

[HEDVIG *brings a tray with beer and glasses, which she sets upon the table.*]

HIALMAR (*stroking her hair*). Thanks, thanks, Hedvig.

[HEDVIG *puts her arm around his neck and whispers in his ear.*]

HIALMAR. No, no bread and butter just now. (*Looks up.*) But perhaps you would like some, Gregers.

GREGERS (*with a gesture of refusal*). No, no, thank you.

HIALMAR (*still melancholy*). Well, you can bring in a little all the same. If you have a crust, that is all I want. And plenty of butter on it, mind.

[HEDVIG *nods gaily and goes out into the kitchen again.*]

GREGERS (*who has been following her with his eyes*). She seems quite strong and healthy otherwise.

GINA. Yes. In other ways there's nothing amiss with her, thank goodness.

GREGERS. She promises to be very like you, Mrs. Ekdal. How old is she now?

GINA. Hedvig is close on fourteen; her birthday is the day after tomorrow.

GREGERS. She is pretty tall for her age, then.

GINA. Yes, she's shot up wonderful this last year.

GREGERS. It makes one realize one's own age to see these young people growing up.—How long is it now since you were married?

GINA. We've been married—let me see—just on fifteen years.

GREGERS. Is it so long as that?

GINA (*becomes attentive; looks at him*). Yes, it is indeed.

HIALMAR. Yes, so it is. Fifteen years all but a few months. (*Changing his tone.*) They must have been long years for you, up at the works, Gregers.

GREGERS. They seemed long while I was living them; now they are over, I hardly know how the time has gone.

[OLD EKDAL *comes from his room without his pipe, but with his old-fashioned uniform cap on his head; his gait is somewhat unsteady.*]

EKDAL. Come now, Hialmar, let's sit down and have a good talk about this—h'm—what was it again?

HIALMAR (*going towards him*). Father, we have a visitor here—Gregers Werle.—I don't know if you remember him.

EKDAL (*looking at* GREGERS, *who has risen*). Werle? Is that the son? What does he want with me?

HIALMAR. Nothing; it's me he has come to see.

EKDAL. Oh! Then there's nothing wrong?

HIALMAR. No, no, of course not.

EKDAL (*with a large gesture*). Not that I'm afraid, you know; but——

GREGERS (*goes over to him*). I bring you a greeting from your old hunting-grounds, Lieutenant Ekdal.

EKDAL. Hunting-grounds?

GREGERS. Yes, up in Höidal, about the works, you know.

EKDAL. Oh, up there. Yes, I knew all those places well in the old days.

GREGERS. You were a great sportsman then.

EKDAL. So I was, I don't deny it. You're looking at my uniform cap. I don't ask anybody's leave to wear it in the house. So long as I don't go out in the streets with it——

[HEDVIG *brings a plate of bread and butter, which she puts upon the table.*]

HIALMAR. Sit down, father, and have a glass of beer. Help yourself, Gregers.

[EKDAL *mutters and stumbles over to the sofa.* GREGERS *seats himself on the chair nearest to him,* HIALMAR *on the other side of* GREGERS. GINA *sits a little way from the table, sewing;* HEDVIG *stands beside her father.*]

GREGERS. Can you remember, Lieutenant Ekdal, how

Hialmar and I used to come up and visit you in the summer and at Christmas?

EKDAL. Did you? No, no, no; I don't remember it. But sure enough I've been a tidy bit of a sportsman in my day. I've shot bears, too. I've shot nine of 'em, no less.

GREGERS (*looking sympathetically at him*). And now you never get any shooting?

EKDAL. Can't just say that, sir. Get a shot now and then perhaps. Of course not in the old way. For the woods, you see—the woods, the woods——! (*Drinks.*) Are the woods fine up there now?

GREGERS. Not so fine as in your time. They have been thinned a good deal.

EKDAL. Thinned? (*More softly, and as if afraid.*) It's dangerous work that. Bad things come of it. The woods revenge themselves.

HIALMAR (*filling up his glass*). Come—a little more, father.

GREGERS. How can a man like you—such a man for the open air—live in the midst of a stuffy town, boxed within four walls?

EKDAL (*laughs quietly and glances at* HIALMAR). Oh, it's not so bad here. Not at all so bad.

GREGERS. But don't you miss all the things that used to be a part of your very being—the cool sweeping breezes, the free life in the woods and on the uplands, among beasts and birds——?

EKDAL (*smiling*). Hialmar, shall we let him see it?

HIALMAR (*hastily and a little embarrassed*). Oh, no, no, father; not this evening.

GREGERS. What does he want to show me?

HIALMAR. Oh, it's only something—you can see it another time.

GREGERS (*continues, to the old man*). You see I have been

thinking, Lieutenant Ekdal, that you should come up with me to the works; I am sure to be going back soon. No doubt you could get some copying there, too. And here, you have nothing on earth to interest you—nothing to liven you up.

EKDAL (*stares in astonishment at him*). Have *I* nothing on earth to——!

GREGERS. Of course you have Hialmar; but then he has his own family. And a man like you, who has always had such a passion for what is free and wild——

EKDAL (*thumps the table*). Hialmar, he shall see it!

HIALMAR. Oh, do you think it's worth while, father? It's all dark.

EKDAL. Nonsense; it's moonlight. (*Rises.*) He shall see it, I tell you. Let me pass! Come and help me, Hialmar.

HEDVIG. Oh, yes, do, father!

HIALMAR (*rising*). Very well then.

GREGERS (*to* GINA). What is it?

GINA. Oh, nothing so very wonderful, after all.

[EKDAL *and* HIALMAR *have gone to the back wall and are each pushing back a side of the sliding door;* HEDVIG *helps the old man;* GREGERS *remains standing by the sofa;* GINA *sits still and sews. Through the open doorway a large, deep irregular garret is seen with odd nooks and corners; a couple of stove-pipes running through it, from rooms below. There are skylights through which clear moonbeams shine in on some parts of the great room; others lie in deep shadow.*]

EKDAL (*to* GREGERS). You may come close up if you like.

GREGERS (*going over to them*). Why, what is it?

EKDAL. Look for yourself. H'm.

HIALMAR (*somewhat embarrassed*). This belongs to father, you understand.

GREGERS (*at the door, looks into the garret*). Why, you keep poultry, Lieutenant Ekdal.

EKDAL. Should think we did keep poultry. They've gone to roost now. But you should just see our fowls by daylight, sir!

HEDVIG. And there's a——

EKDAL. Sh—sh! don't say anything about it yet.

GREGERS. And you have pigeons, too, I see.

EKDAL. Oh, yes, haven't we just got pigeons! They have their nest-boxes up there under the roof-tree; for pigeons like to roost high, you see.

HIALMAR. They aren't all common pigeons.

EKDAL. Common! Should think not indeed! We have tumblers and a pair of pouters, too. But come here! Can you see that hutch down there by the wall?

GREGERS. Yes; what do you use it for?

EKDAL. That's where the rabbits sleep, sir.

GREGERS. Dear me; so you have rabbits, too?

EKDAL. Yes, you may take my word for it, we have rabbits! He wants to know if we have rabbits, Hialmar! H'm! But now comes the thing, let me tell you! Here we have it! Move away, Hedvig. Stand here; that's right,—and now look down there.—Don't you see a basket with straw in it?

GREGERS. Yes. And I can see a fowl lying in the basket.

EKDAL. H'm—"a fowl"——

GREGERS. Isn't it a duck?

EKDAL (*hurt*). Why, of course it's a duck.

HIALMAR. But what kind of duck, do you think?

HEDVIG. It's not just a common duck——

EKDAL. Sh!

GREGERS. And it's not a Muscovy duck either.

EKDAL. No, Mr.—Werle; it's not a Muscovy duck; for it's a wild duck!

GREGERS. Is it really? A wild duck?

EKDAL. Yes, that's what it is. That "fowl" as you call it—is the wild duck. It's our wild duck, sir.

HEDVIG. My wild duck. It belongs to me.

GREGERS. And can it live up here in the garret? Does it thrive?

EKDAL. Of course it has a trough of water to splash about in, you know.

HIALMAR. Fresh water every other day.

GINA (*turning towards* HIALMAR). But my dear Ekdal, it's getting icy cold here.

EKDAL. H'm, we had better shut up then. It's as well not to disturb their night's rest, too. Close up, Hedvig.

[HIALMAR *and* HEDVIG *push the garret doors together.*]

EKDAL. Another time you shall see her properly. (*Seats himself in the armchair by the stove.*) Oh, they're curious things, these wild ducks, I can tell you.

GREGERS. How did you manage to catch it, Lieutenant Ekdal?

EKDAL. *I* didn't catch it. There's a certain man in this town whom we have to thank for it.

GREGERS (*starts slightly*). That man was not my father, was he?

EKDAL. You've hit it. Your father and no one else. H'm.

HIALMAR. Strange that you should guess that, Gregers.

GREGERS. You were telling me that you owed so many things to my father; and so I thought perhaps——

GINA. But we didn't get the duck from Mr. Werle him-self——

EKDAL. It's Håkon Werle we have to thank for her, all the same, Gina. (*To* GREGERS.) He was shooting from a boat, you see, and he brought her down. But your father's sight is not very good now. H'm; she was only wounded.

GREGERS. Ah! She got a couple of slugs in her body, I suppose.

HIALMAR. Yes, two or three.

HEDVIG. She was hit under the wing, so that she couldn't fly.

GREGERS. And I suppose she dived to the bottom, eh?

EKDAL (*sleepily, in a thick voice*). Of course. Always do that, wild ducks do. They shoot to the bottom as deep as they can get, sir—and bite themselves fast in the tangle and seaweed—and all the devil's own mess that grows down there. And they never come up again.

GREGERS. But your wild duck came up again, Lieutenant Ekdal.

EKDAL. He had such an amazingly clever dog, your father had. And that dog—he dived in after the duck and fetched her up again.

GREGERS (*who has turned to* HIALMAR). And then she was sent to you here?

HIALMAR. Not at once; at first your father took her home. But she wouldn't thrive there; so Pettersen was told to put an end to her——

EKDAL (*half asleep*). H'm—yes—Pettersen—that ass——

HIALMAR (*speaking more softly*). That was how we got her, you see; for father knows Pettersen a little; and when he heard about the wild duck he got him to hand her over to us.

GREGERS. And now she thrives as well as possible in the garret there?

HIALMAR. Yes, wonderfully well. She has got fat. You see, she has lived in there so long now that she has forgotten her natural wild life; and it all depends on that.

GREGERS. You are right there, Hialmar. Be sure you never let her get a glimpse of the sky and the sea——. But I mustn't stay any longer; I think your father is asleep.

HIALMAR. Oh, as for that——

GREGERS. But, by-the-bye—you said you had a room to let—a spare room?

HIALMAR. Yes; what then? Do you know of anybody——?

GREGERS. Can *I* have that room?

HIALMAR. You?

GINA. Oh, no, Mr. Werle, you——

GREGERS. May I have the room? If so, I'll take possession first thing tomorrow morning.

HIALMAR. Yes, with the greatest pleasure——

GINA. But, Mr. Werle, I'm sure it's not at all the sort of room for you.

HIALMAR. Why, Gina! how can you say that?

GINA. Why, because the room's neither large enough nor light enough, and——

GREGERS. That really doesn't matter, Mrs. Ekdal.

HIALMAR. I call it quite a nice room, and not at all badly furnished either.

GINA. But remember the pair of them underneath.

GREGERS. What pair?

GINA. Well, there's one as has been a tutor——

HIALMAR. That's Molvik—Mr. Molvik, B.A.

GINA. And then there's a doctor, by the name of Relling.

GREGERS. Relling? I know him a little; he practised for a time up in Höidal.

GINA. They're a regular rackety pair, they are. As often as not, they're out on the loose in the evenings; and then they come home at all hours, and they're not always just——

GREGERS. One soon gets used to that sort of thing. I daresay I shall be like the wild duck——

GINA. H'm; I think you ought to sleep upon it first, anyway.

GREGERS. You seem very unwilling to have me in the house, Mrs. Ekdal.

GINA. Oh, no! What makes you think that?

HIALMAR. Well, you really behave strangely about it,

GINA. (*To* GREGERS.) Then I suppose you intend to remain in the town for the present?

GREGERS (*putting on his overcoat*). Yes, now I intend to remain here.

HIALMAR. And yet not at your father's? What do you propose to do, then?

GREGERS. Ah, if I only knew that, Hialmar, I shouldn't be so badly off! But when one has the misfortune to be called Gregers—! "Gregers"—and then "Werle" after it; did you ever hear anything so hideous?

HIALMAR. Oh, I don't think so at all.

GREGERS. Ugh! Bah! I feel I should like to spit upon the fellow that answers to such a name. But when a man is once for all doomed to be Gregers—Werle in this world, as I am——

HIALMAR (*laughs*). Ha, ha! If you weren't Gregers Werle, what would you like to be?

GREGERS. If I should choose, I should like best to be a clever dog.

GINA. A dog!

HEDVIG (*involuntarily*). Oh, no!

GREGERS. Yes, an amazingly clever dog; one that goes to the bottom after wild ducks when they dive and bite themselves fast in tangle and seaweed, down among the ooze.

HIALMAR. Upon my word now, Gregers—I don't in the least know what you're driving at.

GREGERS. Oh, well, you might not be much the wiser if you did. It's understood, then, that I move in early to-morrow morning. (*To* GINA.) I won't give you any trouble; I do everything for myself. (*To* HIALMAR.) We can talk about the rest tomorrow.—Goodnight, Mrs. Ekdal. (*Nods to* HEDVIG.) Goodnight.

GINA. Goodnight, Mr. Werle.

HEDVIG. Goodnight.

HIALMAR (*who has lighted a candle*). Wait a moment; I must show you a light; the stairs are sure to be dark.

[GREGERS *and* HIALMAR *go out by the passage door.*]

GINA (*looking straight before her, with her sewing in her lap*). Wasn't that queer-like talk about wanting to be a dog?

HEDVIG. Do you know, mother—I believe he meant something quite different by that.

GINA. Why, what should he mean?

HEDVIG. Oh, I don't know; but it seemed to me he meant something different from what he said—all the time.

GINA. Do you think so? Yes, it was sort of queer.

HIALMAR (*comes back*). The lamp was still burning. (*Puts out the candle and sets it down*). Ah, now one can get a mouthful of food at last. (*Begins to eat the bread and butter.*) Well, you see, Gina—if only you keep your eyes open——

GINA. How, keep your eyes open——?

HIALMAR. Why, haven't we at last had the luck to get the room let? And just think—to a person like Gregers—a good old friend.

GINA. Well, I don't know what to say about it.

HEDVIG. Oh, mother, you'll see; it'll be such fun!

HIALMAR. You're very strange. You were so bent upon getting the room let before; and now you don't like it.

GINA. Yes, I do, Ekdal; if it had only been to some one else—— But what do you suppose Mr. Werle will say?

HIALMAR. Old Werle? It doesn't concern him.

GINA. But surely you can see that there's something amiss between them again, or the young man wouldn't be leaving home. You know very well those two can't get on with each other.

HIALMAR. Very likely not, but——

GINA. And now Mr. Werle may fancy it's you that has egged him on——

HIALMAR. Let him fancy so, then! Mr. Werle has done a great deal for me; far be it from me to deny it. But that doesn't make me everlastingly dependent upon him.

GINA. But, my dear Ekdal, maybe grandfather'll suffer for it. He may lose the little bit of work he gets from Gråberg.

HIALMAR. I could almost say: so much the better! Is it not humiliating for a man like me to see his grey-haired father treated as a pariah? But now I believe the fulness of time is at hand. (*Takes a fresh piece of bread and butter.*) As sure as I have a mission in life, I mean to fulfil it now!

HEDVIG. Oh, yes, father, do!

GINA. Hush! Don't wake him!

HIALMAR (*more softly*). I will fulfil it, I say. The day shall come when—— And that is why I say it's a good thing we have let the room; for that makes me more independent. The man who has a mission in life must be independent. (*By the armchair, with emotion.*) Poor old white-haired father! Rely on your Hialmar. He has broad shoulders— strong shoulders, at any rate. You shall yet wake up some fine day and—— (*To* GINA.) Do you not believe it?

GINA (*rising*). Yes, of course I do; but in the meantime suppose we see about getting him to bed.

HIALMAR. Yes, come.

[*They take hold of the old man carefully.*]

CURTAIN

ACT THREE

HIALMAR EKDAL'S *studio. It is morning: the daylight shines through the large window in the slanting roof; the curtain is drawn back.*

[HIALMAR *is sitting at the table, busy retouching a photo-*

graph; several others lie before him. Presently GINA, *wearing
her hat and cloak, enters by the passage door; she has a covered
basket on her arm.*]

HIALMAR. Back already, Gina?

GINA. Oh, yes, one can't let the grass grow under one's
feet.   [*Sets her basket on a chair and takes off her things.*]

HIALMAR. Did you look in at Gregers' room?

GINA. Yes, that I did. It's a rare sight, I can tell you;
he's made a pretty mess to start off with.

HIALMAR. How so?

GINA. He was determined to do everything for himself,
he said; so he sets to work to light the stove, and what must
he do but screw down the damper till the whole room is full
of smoke. Ugh! There was a smell fit to——

HIALMAR. Well, really!

GINA. But that's not the worst of it; for then he thinks
he'll put out the fire, and goes and empties his water-jug
into the stove and so makes the whole floor one filthy pud-
dle.

HIALMAR. How annoying!

GINA. I've got the porter's wife to clear up after him, pig
that he is! But the room won't be fit to live in till the afternoon.

HIALMAR. What's he doing with himself in the meantime?

GINA. He said he was going out for a little while.

HIALMAR. I looked in upon him, too, for a moment—after
you had gone.

GINA. So I heard. You've asked him to lunch.

HIALMAR. Just to a little bit of early lunch, you know.
It's his first day—we can hardly do less. You've got something in the house, I suppose?

GINA. I shall have to find something or other.

HIALMAR. And don't cut it too fine, for I fancy Relling

and Molvik are coming up, too. I just happened to meet Relling on the stairs, you see; so I had to——

GINA. Oh, are we to have those two as well?

HIALMAR. Good Lord—couple more or less can't make any difference.

OLD EKDAL (*opens his door and looks in*). I say, Hialmar—— (*Sees* GINA.) Oh!

GINA. Do you want anything, grandfather?

EKDAL. Oh, no, it doesn't matter. H'm! [*Retires again.*]

GINA (*takes up the basket*). Be sure you see that he doesn't go out.

HIALMAR. All right, all right. And, Gina, a little herring-salad wouldn't be a bad idea; Relling and Molvik were out on the loose again last night.

GINA. If only they don't come before I'm ready for them——

HIALMAR. No, of course they won't; take your own time.

GINA. Very well; and meanwhile you can be working a bit.

HIALMAR. Well, I am working! I am working as hard as I can!

GINA. Then you'll have that job off your hands, you see.

[*She goes out to the kitchen with her basket.* HIALMAR *sits for a time penciling away at the photograph in an indolent and listless manner.*]

EKDAL (*peeps in, looks round the studio and says softly:*) Are you busy?

HIALMAR. Yes, I'm toiling at these wretched pictures——

EKDAL. Well, well, never mind,—since you're so busy—h'm! [*He goes out again; the door stands open.*]

HIALMAR (*continues for some time in silence; then he lays down his brush and goes over to the door*). Are you busy, father?

EKDAL (*in a grumbling tone, within*). If you're busy, I'm busy, too. H'm!

HIALMAR. Oh, very well, then. [*Goes to his work again.*]

EKDAL (*presently, coming to the door again*). H'm; I say, Hialmar, I'm not so very busy, you know.

HIALMAR. I thought you were writing.

EKDAL. Oh, the devil take it! can't Gråberg wait a day or two? After all, it's not a matter of life and death.

HIALMAR. No; and you're not his slave either.

EKDAL. And about that other business in there——

HIALMAR. Just what I was thinking of. Do you want to go in? Shall I open the door for you?

EKDAL. Well, it wouldn't be a bad notion.

HIALMAR (*rises*). Then we'd have that off our hands.

EKDAL. Yes, exactly. It's got to be ready first thing to-morrow. It is tomorrow, isn't it? H'm?

HIALMAR. Yes, of course it's tomorrow.

[HIALMAR *and* EKDAL *push aside each his half of the sliding door. The morning sun is shining in through the skylights; some doves are flying about; others sit cooing, upon the perches; the hens are heard clucking now and then, further back in the garret.*]

HIALMAR. There; now you can get to work, father.

EKDAL (*goes in*). Aren't you coming, too?

HIALMAR. Well, really, do you know——; I almost think—— (*Sees* GINA *at the kitchen door.*) I? No; I haven't time; I must work.—But now for our new contrivance——

[*He pulls a cord, a curtain slips down inside, the lower part consisting of a piece of old sailcloth, the upper part of a stretched fishing net. The floor of the garret is thus no longer visible.*]

HIALMAR (*goes to the table*). So! Now, perhaps I can sit in peace for a little while.

GINA. Is he rampaging in there again?

HIALMAR. Would you rather have had him slip down to

Madame Eriksen's?   (*Seats himself.*) Do you want anything?
You know you said——

GINA. I only wanted to ask if you think we can lay the
table for lunch here?

HIALMAR. Yes; we have no early appointment, I suppose?

GINA. No, I expect no one today except those two sweethearts that are to be taken together.

HIALMAR. Why the deuce couldn't they be taken together
another day?

GINA. Don't you know I told them to come in the afternoon, when you are having your nap?

HIALMAR. Oh, that's capital. Very well, let us have lunch
here then.

GINA. All right; but there's no hurry about laying the
cloth; you can have the table for a good while yet.

HIALMAR. Do you think I am not sticking at my work?
I'm at it as hard as I can!

GINA. Then you'll be free later on, you know.

[*Goes out into the kitchen again. Short pause.*]

EKDAL (*in the garret doorway, behind the net*). Hialmar!

HIALMAR. Well?

EKDAL. Afraid we shall have to move the water-trough,
after all.

HIALMAR. What else have I been saying all along?

EKDAL. H'm—h'm—h'm.

[*Goes away from the door again. HIALMAR goes on working
a little; glances towards the garret and half rises. HEDVIG
comes in from the kitchen.*]

HIALMAR (*sits down again hurriedly*). What do you want?

HEDVIG. I only wanted to come in beside you, father.

HIALMAR (*after a pause*). What makes you go prying
around like that? Perhaps you are told off to watch me?

HEDVIG. No, no.

HIALMAR. What is your mother doing out there?

HEDVIG. Oh, mother's in the middle of making the her-ring-salad. (*Goes to the table.*) Isn't there any little thing I could help you with, father?

HIALMAR. Oh, no. It is right that I should bear the whole burden—so long as my strength holds out. Set your mind at rest, Hedvig; if only your father keeps his health——

HEDVIG. Oh, no, father! You mustn't talk in that horrid way.

[*She wanders about a little, stops by the doorway and looks into the garret.*]

HIALMAR. Tell me, what is he doing?

HEDVIG. I think he's making a new path to the water-trough.

HIALMAR. He can never manage that by himself! And here am I doomed to sit——!

HEDVIG (*goes to him*). Let me take the brush, father; I can do it, quite well.

HIALMAR. Oh, nonsense; you will only hurt your eyes.

HEDVIG. Not a bit. Give me the brush.

HIALMAR (*rising*). Well, it won't take more than a minute or two.

HEDVIG. Pooh, what harm can it do then? (*Takes the brush.*) There! (*Seats herself.*) I can begin upon this one.

HIALMAR. But mind you don't hurt your eyes! Do you hear? *I* won't be answerable; you do it on your own re-sponsibility—understand that.

HEDVIG (*retouching*). Yes, yes, I understand.

HIALMAR. You are quite clever at it, Hedvig. Only a minute or two, you know.

[*He slips through by the edge of the curtain into the garret.* HEDVIG *sits at her work.* HIALMAR *and* EKDAL *are heard dis-puting inside.*]

HIALMAR (*appears behind the net*). I say, Hedvig—give me those pincers that are lying on the shelf. And the chisel.

(*Turns away inside.*) Now you shall see, father. Just let me show you first what I mean!

[HEDVIG *has fetched the required tools from the shelf and hands them to him through the net.*]

HIALMAR. Ah, thanks. I didn't come a moment too soon.

[*Goes back from the curtain again; they are heard carpentering and talking inside.* HEDVIG *stands looking in at them. A moment later there is a knock at the passage door; she does not notice it.*]

GREGERS WERLE (*bareheaded, in indoor dress, enters and stops near the door*). H'm——!

HEDVIG (*turns and goes towards him*). Good morning. Please come in.

GREGERS. Thank you. (*Looking towards the garret.*) You seem to have workpeople in the house.

HEDVIG. No, it is only father and grandfather. I'll tell them you are here.

GREGERS. No, no, don't do that; I would rather wait a little.   [*Seats himself on the sofa.*]

HEDVIG. It looks so untidy here——
                        [*Begins to clear away the photographs.*]

GREGERS. Oh, don't take them away. Are those prints that have to be finished off?

HEDVIG. Yes, they are a few I was helping father with.

GREGERS. Please don't let me disturb you.

HEDVIG. Oh, no.

[*She gathers the things to her and sits down to work;* GREGERS *looks at her, meanwhile, in silence.*]

GREGERS. Did the wild duck sleep well last night?

HEDVIG. Yes, I think so, thanks.

GREGERS (*turning towards the garret*). It looks quite different by day from what it did last night in the moonlight.

HEDVIG. Yes, it changes ever so much. It looks different

in the morning and in the afternoon; and it's different on rainy days from what it is in fine weather.

GREGERS. Have you noticed that?

HEDVIG. Yes, how could I help it?

GREGERS. Are you, too, fond of being in there with the wild duck?

HEDVIG. Yes, when I can manage it——

GREGERS. But I suppose you haven't much spare time; you go to school, no doubt.

HEDVIG. No, not now; father is afraid of my hurting my eyes.

GREGERS. Oh; then he reads with you himself?

HEDVIG. Father has promised to read with me; but he has never had time yet.

GREGERS. Then is there nobody else to give you a little help?

HEDVIG. Yes, there is Mr. Molvik; but he is not always exactly—quite——

GREGERS. Sober?

HEDVIG. Yes, I suppose that's it!

GREGERS. Why, then you must have any amount of time on your hands. And in there I suppose it is a sort of world by itself?

HEDVIG. Oh, yes, quite. And there are such lots of wonderful things.

GREGERS. Indeed?

HEDVIG. Yes, there are big cupboards full of books; and a great many of the books have pictures in them.

GREGERS. Aha!

HEDVIG. And there's an old bureau with drawers and flaps, and a big clock with figures that go out and in. But the clock isn't going now.

GREGERS. So time has come to a standstill in there—in the wild duck's domain.

HEDVIG. Yes. And then there's an old paint-box and things of that sort, and all the books.

GREGERS. And you read the books, I suppose?

HEDVIG. Oh, yes, when I get the chance. Most of them are English though, and I don't understand English. But then I look at the pictures.—There is one great big book called "Harrison's History of London."* It must be a hundred years old; and there are such heaps of pictures in it. At the beginning there is Death with an hour-glass and a woman. I think that is horrid. But then there are all the other pictures of churches, and castles, and streets, and great ships sailing on the sea.

GREGERS. But tell me, where did all those wonderful things come from?

HEDVIG. Oh, an old sea captain once lived here, and he brought them home with him. They used to call him "The Flying Dutchman." That was curious, because he wasn't a Dutchman at all.

GREGERS. Was he not?

HEDVIG. No. But at last he was drowned at sea, and so he left all those things behind him.

GREGERS. Tell me now—when you are sitting in there looking at the pictures, don't you wish you could travel and see the real world for yourself?

HEDVIG. Oh, no! I mean always to stay at home and help father and mother.

GREGERS. To retouch photographs?

HEDVIG. No, not only that. I should love above everything to learn to engrave pictures like those in the English books.

GREGERS. H'm. What does your father say to that?

HEDVIG. I don't think father likes it; father is strange about such things. Only think, he talks of my learning

---

* *A New and Universal History of the Cities of London and Westminster,* by Walter Harrison, London, 1775, folio. [Trans.]

basket-making and straw-plaiting! But I don't think that would be much good.

GREGERS. Oh, no, I don't think so either.

HEDVIG. But father was right in saying that if I had learnt basket-making I could have made the new basket for the wild duck.

GREGERS. So you could; and it was you that ought to have done it, wasn't it?

HEDVIG. Yes, for it's my wild duck.

GREGERS. Of course it is.

HEDVIG. Yes, it belongs to me. But I lend it to father and grandfather as often as they please.

GREGERS. Indeed? What do they do with it?

HEDVIG. Oh, they look after it, and build places for it, and so on.

GREGERS. I see; for no doubt the wild duck is by far the most distinguished inhabitant of the garret?

HEDVIG. Yes, indeed she is; for she is a real wild fowl, you know. And then she is so much to be pitied; she has no one to care for, poor thing.

GREGERS. She has no family, as the rabbits have——

HEDVIG. No. The hens, too, many of them, were chickens together; but she has been taken right away from all her friends. And then there is so much that is strange about the wild duck. Nobody knows her, and nobody knows where she came from either.

GREGERS. And she has been down in the depths of the sea.

HEDVIG (*with a quick glance at him, represses a smile and asks:*) Why do you say "depths of the sea"?

GREGERS. What else should I say?

HEDVIG. You could say "the bottom of the sea."*

* Gregers here uses the old-fashioned expression "havsens bund," while Hedvig would have him use the more commonplace "havets bund" or "havbunden." [Trans.]

GREGERS. Oh, mayn't I just as well say the depths of the sea?

HEDVIG. Yes; but it sounds so strange to me when other people speak of the depths of the sea.

GREGERS. Why so? Tell me why?

HEDVIG. No, I won't; it's so stupid.

GREGERS. Oh, no, I am sure it's not. Do tell me why you smiled.

HEDVIG. Well, this is the reason: whenever I come to realize suddenly—in a flash—what is in there, it always seems to me that the whole room and everything in it should be called "the depths of the sea."—But that is so stupid.

GREGERS. You mustn't say that.

HEDVIG. Oh, yes, for you know it is only a garret.

GREGERS (*looks fixedly at her*). Are you so sure of that?

HEDVIG (*astonished*). That it's a garret?

GREGERS. Are you quite certain of it?

[HEDVIG *is silent, and looks at him open-mouthed.* GINA *comes in from the kitchen with the table things.*]

GREGERS (*rising*). I have come in upon you too early.

GINA. Oh, you must be somewhere; and we're nearly ready now, anyway. Clear the table, Hedvig.

[HEDVIG *clears away her things; she and* GINA *lay the cloth during what follows.* GREGERS *seats himself in the armchair and turns over an album.*]

GREGERS. I hear you can retouch, Mrs. Ekdal.

GINA (*with a side glance*). Yes, I can.

GREGERS. That was exceedingly lucky.

GINA. How—lucky?

GREGERS. Since Ekdal took to photography, I mean.

HEDVIG. Mother can take photographs, too.

GINA. Oh, yes; I was bound to learn that.

GREGERS. So it is really you that carry on the business, I suppose?

GINA.   Yes, when Ekdal hasn't time himself——

GREGERS.   He is a great deal taken up with his old father, I daresay.

GINA.   Yes; and then you can't expect a man like Ekdal to do nothing but take pictures of Dick, Tom, and Harry.

GREGERS.   I quite agree with you; but having once gone in for the thing——

GINA.   You can surely understand, Mr. Werle, that Ekdal's not like one of your common photographers.

GREGERS.   Of course not; but still——

[*A shot is fired within the garret.*]

GREGERS (*starting up*).   What's that?

GINA.   Ugh! now they're firing again!

GREGERS.   Have they firearms in there?

HEDVIG.   They are out shooting.

GREGERS.   What! (*At the door of the garret.*) Are you shooting, Hialmar?

HIALMAR (*inside the net*).   Are you there? I didn't know; I was so taken up—— (*To* HEDVIG.) Why did you not let us know?   [*Comes into the studio.*]

GREGERS.   Do you go shooting in the garret?

HIALMAR (*showing a double-barrelled pistol*).   Oh, only with this thing.

GINA.   Yes, you and grandfather will do yourselves a mischief some day with that there pigstol.

HIALMAR (*with irritation*).   I believe I have told you that this kind of firearm is called a pistol.

GINA.   Oh, that doesn't make it much better, that I can see.

GREGERS.   So you have become a sportsman, too, Hialmar?

HIALMAR.   Only a little rabbit-shooting now and then. Mostly to please father, you understand.

GINA.   Men are strange beings; they must always have something to pervert theirselves with.

HIALMAR (*snappishly*).   Just so; we must always have something to divert ourselves with.

GINA.   Yes, that's just what I say.

HIALMAR.   H'm.   (*To* GREGERS.)   You see the garret is fortunately so situated that no one can hear us shooting. (*Lays the pistol on the top shelf of the bookcase.*)   Don't touch the pistol, Hedvig!   One of the barrels is loaded; remember that.

GREGERS (*looking through the net*).   You have a fowling-piece, too, I see.

HIALMAR.   That is father's old gun.   It's no use now; something has gone wrong with the lock.   But it's fun to have it all the same; for we can take it to pieces now and then, and clean and grease it, and screw it together again.— Of course, it's mostly father that fiddle-faddles with all that sort of thing.

HEDVIG (*beside* GREGERS).   Now you can see the wild duck properly.

GREGERS.   I was just looking at her.   One of her wings seems to me to droop a bit.

HEDVIG.   Well, no wonder; her wing was broken, you know.

GREGERS.   And she trails one foot a little.   Isn't that so?

HIALMAR.   Perhaps a very little bit.

HEDVIG.   Yes, it was by that foot the dog took hold of her.

HIALMAR.   But otherwise she hasn't the least thing the matter with her; and that is simply marvellous for a creature that has a charge of shot in her body and has been between a dog's teeth——

GREGERS (*with a glance at* HEDVIG).   ——and that has lain in the depths of the sea—so long.

HEDVIG (*smiling*).   Yes.

GINA (*laying the table*).   That blessed wild duck!   What a lot of fuss you do make over her.

HIALMAR. H'm;—will lunch soon be ready?

GINA. Yes, directly. Hedvig, you must come and help me now.   [GINA *and* HEDVIG *go out into the kitchen.*]

HIALMAR (*in a low voice*). I think you had better not stand there looking in at father; he doesn't like it. (GREGERS *moves away from the garret door.*) Besides, I may as well shut up before the others come. (*Claps his hands to drive the fowls back.*) Shh—shh, in with you! (*Draws up the curtain and pulls the doors together.*) All the contrivances are my own invention. It's really quite amusing to have things of this sort to potter with and to put to rights when they get out of order. And it's absolutely necessary, too; for Gina objects to having rabbits and fowls in the studio.

GREGERS. To be sure; and I suppose the studio is your wife's special department?

HIALMAR. As a rule, I leave the everyday details of business to her; for then I can take refuge in the parlor and give my mind to more important things.

GREGERS. What things may they be, Hialmar?

HIALMAR. I wonder you have not asked that question sooner. But perhaps you haven't heard of the invention?

GREGERS. The invention? No.

HIALMAR. Really? Have you not? Oh, no, out there in the wilds——

GREGERS. So you have invented something, have you?

HIALMAR. It is not quite completed yet; but I am working at it. You can easily imagine that when I resolved to devote myself to photography, it wasn't simply with the idea of taking likenesses of all sorts of commonplace people.

GREGERS. No; your wife was saying the same thing just now.

HIALMAR. I swore that if I consecrated my powers to this

handicraft, I would so exalt it that it should become both an art and a science. And to that end I determined to make this great invention.

GREGERS. And what is the nature of the invention? What purpose does it serve?

HIALMAR. Oh, my dear fellow, you mustn't ask for details yet. It takes time, you see. And you must not think that my motive is vanity. It is not for my own sake that I am working. Oh, no; it is my life's mission that stands before me night and day.

GREGERS. What is your life's mission?

HIALMAR. Do you forget the old man with the silver hair?

GREGERS. Your poor father? Well, but what can you do for him?

HIALMAR. I can raise up his self-respect from the dead, by restoring the name of Ekdal to honor and dignity.

GREGERS. Then that is your life's mission?

HIALMAR. Yes. I will rescue the shipwrecked man. For shipwrecked he was, by the very first blast of the storm. Even while those terrible investigations were going on, he was no longer himself. That pistol there—the one we use to shoot rabbits with—has played its part in the tragedy of the house of Ekdal.

GREGERS. The pistol? Indeed?

HIALMAR. When the sentence of imprisonment was passed —he had the pistol in his hand——

GREGERS. Had he——?

HIALMAR. Yes; but he dared not use it. His courage failed him. So broken, so demoralized was he even then! Oh, can you understand it? He, a soldier; he, who had shot nine bears, and who was descended from two lieutenant-colonels—one after the other, of course. Can you understand it, Gregers?

GREGERS. Yes, I understand it well enough.

HIALMAR. I cannot. And once more the pistol played a part in the history of our house. When he had put on the grey clothes and was under lock and key—oh, that was a terrible time for me, I can tell you. I kept the blinds drawn down over both my windows. When I peeped out, I saw the sun shining as if nothing had happened. I could not understand it. I saw people going along the street, laughing and talking about indifferent things. I could not understand it. It seemed to me that the whole of existence must be at a standstill—as if under an eclipse.

GREGERS. I felt that, too, when my mother died.

HIALMAR. It was in such an hour that Hialmar Ekdal pointed the pistol at his own breast.

GREGERS. You, too, thought of——!

HIALMAR. Yes.

GREGERS. But you did not fire?

HIALMAR. No. At the decisive moment I won the victory over myself. I remained in life. But I can assure you it takes some courage to choose life under circumstances like those.

GREGERS. Well, that depends on how you look at it.

HIALMAR. Yes, indeed, it takes courage. But I am glad I was firm: for now I shall soon perfect my invention; and Dr. Relling thinks, as I do myself, that father may be allowed to wear his uniform again. I will demand that as my sole reward.

GREGERS. So that is what he meant about his uniform ——?

HIALMAR. Yes, that is what he most yearns for. You can't think how my heart bleeds for him. Every time we celebrate any little family festival—Gina's and my wedding-day, or whatever it may be—in comes the old man in the lieutenant's uniform of happier days. But if he only hears a knock at the door—for he daren't show himself to strangers, you know—he hurries back to his room again as fast as his old legs can carry him. Oh, it's heart-rending for a son to see such things!

GREGERS. How long do you think it will take you to finish your invention?

HIALMAR. Come now, you mustn't expect me to enter into particulars like that. An invention is not a thing completely under one's own control. It depends largely on inspiration —on intuition—and it is almost impossible to predict when the inspiration may come.

GREGERS. But it's advancing?

HIALMAR. Yes, certainly, it is advancing. I turn it over in my mind every day; I am full of it. Every afternoon, when I have had my dinner, I shut myself up in the parlor, where I can ponder undisturbed. But I can't be goaded to it; it's not a bit of good; Relling says so, too.

GREGERS. And you don't think that all that business in the garret draws you off and distracts you too much?

HIALMAR. No, no, no; quite the contrary. You mustn't say that. I cannot be everlastingly absorbed in the same laborious train of thought. I must have something alongside of it to fill up the time of waiting. The inspiration, the intuition, you see—when it comes, it comes, and there's an end of it.

GREGERS. My dear Hialmar, I almost think you have something of the wild duck in you.

HIALMAR. Something of the wild duck? How do you mean?

GREGERS. You have dived down and bitten yourself fast in the undergrowth.

HIALMAR. Are you alluding to the well-nigh fatal shot that has broken my father's wing—and mine, too?

GREGERS. Not exactly to that. I don't say that your wing

has been broken; but you have strayed into a poisonous marsh, Hialmar; an insidious disease has taken hold of you, and you have sunk down to die in the dark.

HIALMAR. I? To die in the dark? Look here, Gregers, you must really leave off talking such nonsense.

GREGERS. Don't be afraid; I shall find a way to help you up again. I, too, have a mission in life now; I found it yesterday.

HIALMAR. That's all very well; but you will please leave me out of it. I can assure you that—apart from my very natural melancholy, of course—I am as contented as any one can wish to be.

GREGERS. Your contentment is an effect of the marsh poison.

HIALMAR. Now, my dear Gregers, pray do not go on about disease and poison; I am not used to that sort of talk. In my house nobody ever speaks to me about unpleasant things.

GREGERS. Ah, that I can easily believe.

HIALMAR. It's not good for me, you see. And there are no marsh poisons here, as you express it. The poor photographer's roof is lowly, I know—and my circumstances are narrow. But I am an inventor, and I am the bread-winner of a family. That exalts me above my mean surroundings.—Ah, here comes lunch!

[GINA and HEDVIG *bring bottles of ale, a decanter of brandy, glasses, etc. At the same time,* RELLING *and* MOLVIK *enter from the passage; they are both without hat or overcoat.* MOLVIK *is dressed in black.*]

GINA (*placing the things upon the table*). Ah, you two have come in the nick of time.

RELLING. Molvik got it into his head that he could smell herring-salad, and then there was no holding him.—Good morning again, Ekdal.

HIALMAR. Gregers, let me introduce you to Mr. Molvik. Doctor—— Oh, you know Relling, don't you?

GREGERS. Yes, slightly.

RELLING. Oh, Mr. Werle, junior! Yes, we two have had one or two little skirmishes up at the Höidal works. You've just moved in?

GREGERS. I moved in this morning.

RELLING. Molvik and I live right under you, so you haven't far to go for the doctor and the clergyman, if you should need anything in that line.

GREGERS. Thanks, it's not quite unlikely, for yesterday we were thirteen at table.

HIALMAR. Oh, come now, don't let us get upon unpleasant subjects again!

RELLING. You may make your mind easy, Ekdal; I'll be hanged if the finger of fate points to you.

HIALMAR. I should hope not, for the sake of my family. But let us sit down now, and eat and drink and be merry.

GREGERS. Shall we not wait for your father?

HIALMAR. No, his lunch will be taken in to him later. Come along!

[*The men seat themselves at table, and eat and drink.* GINA *and* HEDVIG *go in and out and wait upon them.*]

RELLING. Molvik was frightfully stewed yesterday, Mrs. Ekdal.

GINA. Really? Yesterday again?

RELLING. Didn't you hear him when I brought him home last night?

GINA. No, I can't say I did.

RELLING. That was a good thing, for Molvik was disgusting last night.

GINA. Is that true, Molvik?

MOLVIK. Let us draw a veil over last night's proceedings. That sort of thing is totally foreign to my better self.

RELLING (*to* GREGERS). It comes over him like a sort of possession, and then I have to go out on the loose with him. Mr. Molvik is dæmonic, you see.

GREGERS. Dæmonic?

RELLING. Molvik is dæmonic, yes.

GREGERS. H'm.

RELLING. And dæmonic natures are not made to walk straight through the world; they must meander a little now and then.—Well, so you still stick up there at those horrible grimy works?

GREGERS. I have stuck there until now.

RELLING. And did you ever manage to collect that claim you went about presenting?

GREGERS. Claim? (*Understands him.*) Ah, I see.

HIALMAR. Have you been presenting claims, Gregers?

GREGERS. Oh, nonsense.

RELLING. Faith, but he has, though! He went around to all the cottars' cabins presenting something he called "the claim of the ideal."

GREGERS. I was young then.

RELLING. You're right; you were very young. And as for the claim of the ideal—you never got it honored while *I* was up there.

GREGERS. Nor since either.

RELLING. Ah, then you've learnt to knock a little discount off, I expect.

GREGERS. Never, when I have a true man to deal with.

HIALMAR. No, I should think not, indeed. A little butter, Gina.

RELLING. And a slice of bacon for Molvik.

MOLVIK. Ugh; not bacon!   [*A knock at the garret door.*]

HIALMAR. Open the door, Hedvig; father wants to come out.

[HEDVIG *goes over and opens the door a little way;* EKDAL

enters with a fresh rabbit-skin; she closes the door after him.]

EKDAL. Good morning, gentlemen! Good sport today. Shot a big one.

HIALMAR. And you've gone and skinned it without waiting for me——!

EKDAL. Salted it, too. It's good tender meat, is rabbit; it's sweet; it tastes like sugar. Good appetite to you, gentlemen!   [*Goes into his room.*]

MOLVIK (*rising*). Excuse me——; I can't——; I must get downstairs immediately——

RELLING. Drink some soda water, man!

MOLVIK (*hurrying away*). Ugh—ugh!

[*Goes out by the passage door.*]

RELLING (*to* HIALMAR). Let us drain a glass to the old hunter.

HIALMAR (*clinks glasses with him*). To the undaunted sportsman who has looked death in the face!

RELLING. To the grey-haired—— (*Drinks.*) By-the-bye, is his hair grey or white?

HIALMAR. Something between the two, I fancy; for that matter, he has very few hairs left of any color.

RELLING. Well, well, one can get through the world with a wig. After all, you are a happy man, Ekdal; you have your noble mission to labor for——

HIALMAR. And I do labor, I can tell you.

RELLING. And then you have your excellent wife, shuffling quietly in and out in her felt slippers, and that seesaw walk of hers, and making everything cosy and comfortable about you.

HIALMAR. Yes, Gina—(*nods to her.*)—you were a good helpmate on the path of life.

GINA. Oh, don't sit there cricketizing me.

RELLING. And your Hedvig, too, Ekdal!

HIALMAR (*affected*). The child, yes! The child before everything! Hedvig, come here to me. (*Strokes her hair.*) What day is it tomorrow, eh?

HEDVIG (*shaking him*). Oh, no, you're not to say anything, father.

HIALMAR. It cuts me to the heart when I think what a poor affair it will be; only a little festivity in the garret——

HEDVIG. Oh, but that's just what I like!

RELLING. Just you wait till the wonderful invention sees the light, Hedvig!

HIALMAR. Yes, indeed—then you shall see——! Hedvig, I have resolved to make your future secure. You shall live in comfort all your days. I will demand—something or other—on your behalf. That shall be the poor inventor's sole reward.

HEDVIG (*whispering, with her arms round his neck*). Oh, you dear, kind father!

RELLING (*to* GREGERS). Come now, don't you find it pleasant, for once in a way, to sit at a well-spread table in a happy family circle?

HIALMAR. Ah, yes, I really prize these social hours.

GREGERS. For my part, I don't thrive in marsh vapors.

RELLING. Marsh vapors?

HIALMAR. Oh, don't begin with that stuff again!

GINA. Goodness knows there's no vapors in this house, Mr. Werle; I give the place a good airing every blessed day.

GREGERS (*leaves the table*). No airing you can give will drive out the taint I mean.

HIALMAR. Taint!

GINA. Yes, what do you say to that, Ekdal?

RELLING. Excuse me—may it not be you yourself that have brought the taint from those mines up there?

GREGERS. It is like you to call what I bring into this house a taint.

RELLING (*goes up to him*). Look here, Mr. Werle, junior: I have a strong suspicion that you are still carrying about that "claim of the ideal," large as life, in your coat-tail pocket.

GREGERS. I carry it in my breast.

RELLING. Well, wherever you carry it, I advise you not to come dunning us with it here, so long as *I* am on the premises.

GREGERS. And if I do so nonetheless?

RELLING. Then you'll go head-foremost down the stairs; now I've warned you.

HIALMAR (*rising*). Oh, but Relling——!

GREGERS. Yes, you may turn me out——

GINA (*interposing between them*). We can't have that, Relling. But I must say, Mr. Werle, it ill becomes you to talk about vapors and taints, after all the mess you made with your stove.   [*A knock at the passage door.*]

HEDVIG. Mother, there's somebody knocking.

HIALMAR. There now, we're going to have a whole lot of people!

GINA. I'll go—— (*Goes over and opens the door, starts, and draws back.*) Oh—oh, dear!

[WERLE, *in a fur coat, advances one step into the room.*]

WERLE. Excuse me, but I think my son is staying here.

GINA (*with a gulp*). Yes.

HIALMAR (*approaching him*). Won't you do us the honor to——?

WERLE. Thank you, I merely wish to speak to my son.

GREGERS. What is it? Here I am.

WERLE. I want a few words with you, in your room.

GREGERS. In my room? Very well——   [*About to go.*]

GINA. No, no, your room's not in a fit state——

WERLE. Well then, out in the passage here; I want to have a few words with you alone.

HIALMAR. You can have them here, sir. Come into the parlor, Relling.

[HIALMAR *and* RELLING *go off to the right.* GINA *takes* HEDVIG *with her into the kitchen.*]

GREGERS (*after a short pause*). Well, now we are alone.

WERLE. From something you let fall last evening, and from your coming to lodge with the Ekdals, I can't help inferring that you intend to make yourself unpleasant to me in one way or another.

GREGERS. I intend to open Hialmar Ekdal's eyes. He shall see his position as it really is—that is all.

WERLE. Is that the mission in life you spoke of yesterday?

GREGERS. Yes. You have left me no other.

WERLE. Is it I, then, that have crippled your mind, Gregers?

GREGERS. You have crippled my whole life. I am not thinking of all that about mother—— But it's thanks to you that I am continually haunted and harassed by a guilty conscience.

WERLE. Indeed! It is your conscience that troubles you, is it?

GREGERS. I ought to have taken a stand against you when the trap was set for Lieutenant Ekdal. I ought to have cautioned him, for I had a misgiving as to what was in the wind.

WERLE. Yes, that was the time to have spoken.

GREGERS. I did not dare to, I was so cowed and spiritless. I was mortally afraid of you—not only then, but long afterwards.

WERLE. You have got over that fear now, it appears.

GREGERS. Yes, fortunately. The wrong done to old Ekdal, both by me and by—others, can never be undone; but Hialmar I can rescue from all the falsehood and deception that are bringing him to ruin.

WERLE. Do you think that will be doing him a kindness?

GREGERS. I have not the least doubt of it.

WERLE. You think our worthy photographer is the sort of man to appreciate such friendly offices?

GREGERS. Yes, I do.

WERLE. H'm—we shall see.

GREGERS. Besides, if I am to go on living, I must try to find some cure for my sick conscience.

WERLE. It will never be sound. Your conscience has been sickly from childhood. That is a legacy from your mother, Gregers—the only one she left you.

GREGERS (*with a scornful half-smile*). Have you not yet forgiven her for the mistake you made in supposing she would bring you a fortune?

WERLE. Don't let us wander from the point.—Then you hold to your purpose of setting young Ekdal upon what you imagine to be the right scent?

GREGERS. Yes, that is my fixed resolve.

WERLE. Well, in that case I might have spared myself this visit; for, of course, it is useless to ask whether you will return home with me?

GREGERS. Quite useless.

WERLE. And I suppose you won't enter the firm either?

GREGERS. No.

WERLE. Very good. But as I am thinking of marrying again, your share in the property will fall to you at once.*

GREGERS (*quickly*). No, I do not want that.

WERLE. You don't want it?

GREGERS. No, I dare not take it, for conscience' sake.

WERLE (*after a pause*). Are you going up to the works again?

GREGERS. No; I consider myself released from your service.

---

* By Norwegian law, before a widower can marry again, a certain proportion of his property must be settled on his children by his former marriage. [Trans.]

WERLE. But what are you going to do?

GREGERS. Only to fulfil my mission; nothing more.

WERLE. Well, but afterwards? What are you going to live upon?

GREGERS. I have laid by a little out of my salary.

WERLE. How long will that last?

GREGERS. I think it will last my time.

WERLE. What do you mean?

GREGERS. I shall answer no more questions.

WERLE. Good-bye then, Gregers.

GREGERS. Good-bye.   [WERLE *goes.*]

HIALMAR (*peeping in*). He's gone, isn't he?

GREGERS. Yes.

[HIALMAR *and* RELLING *enter; also* GINA *and* HEDVIG *from the kitchen.*]

RELLING. That luncheon-party was a failure.

GREGERS. Put on your coat, Hialmar; I want you to come for a long walk with me.

HIALMAR. With pleasure. What was it your father wanted? Had it anything to do with me?

GREGERS. Come along. We must have a talk. I'll go and put on my overcoat.   [*Goes out by the passage door.*]

GINA. You shouldn't go out with him, Ekdal.

RELLING. No, don't you do it. Stay where you are.

HIALMAR (*gets his hat and overcoat*). Oh, nonsense! When a friend of my youth feels impelled to open his mind to me in private——

RELLING. But devil take it—don't you see that the fellow's mad, cracked, demented?

GINA. There, what did I tell you? His mother before him had crazy fits like that sometimes.

HIALMAR. The more need for a friend's watchful eye. (*To* GINA.) Be sure you have dinner ready in good time. Good-bye for the present.   [*Goes out by the passage door.*]

RELLING.   It's a thousand pities the fellow didn't go to hell through one of the Höidal mines.

GINA.   Good Lord! what makes you say that?

RELLING (*muttering*).   Oh, I have my own reasons.

GINA.   Do you think young Werle is really mad?

RELLING.   No, worse luck; he's no madder than most other people.   But one disease he has certainly got in his system.

GINA.   What's the matter with him?

RELLING.   Well, I'll tell you, Mrs. Ekdal.   He is suffering from an acute attack of integrity.

GINA.   Integrity?

HEDVIG.   Is that a kind of disease?

RELLING.   Yes, it's a national disease; but it only appears sporadically.   (*Nods to* GINA.)   Thanks for your hospitality.

[*He goes out by the passage door.*]

GINA (*moving restlessly to and fro*).   Ugh, that Gregers Werle—he was always a wretched creature.

HEDVIG (*standing by the table and looking searchingly at her*).   I think all this is very strange.

CURTAIN

ACT FOUR

HIALMAR EKDAL'S *studio.   A photograph has just been taken; a camera with the cloth over it, a pedestal, two chairs, a folding table, etc., are standing out in the room.   Afternoon light; the sun is going down; a little later it begins to grow dusk.*

[GINA *stands in the passage doorway, with a little box and a wet glass plate in her hand, and is speaking to somebody outside.*]

GINA.   Yes, certainly.   When I make a promise I keep it. The first dozen shall be ready on Monday.   Good afternoon.

[*Someone is heard going downstairs.* GINA *shuts the door, slips the plate into the box and puts it into the covered camera.*]

HEDVIG (*comes in from the kitchen*). Are they gone?

GINA (*tidying up*). Yes, thank goodness, I've got rid of them at last.

HEDVIG. But can you imagine why father hasn't come home yet?

GINA. Are you sure he's not down in Relling's room?

HEDVIG. No, he's not; I ran down the kitchen stair just now and asked.

GINA. And his dinner standing and getting cold, too.

HEDVIG. Yes, I can't understand it. Father's always so careful to be home to dinner!

GINA. Oh, he'll be here directly, you'll see.

HEDVIG. I wish he would come; everything seems so queer today.

GINA (*calls out*). There he is!

[HIALMAR EKDAL *comes in at the passage door.*]

HEDVIG (*going to him*). Father! Oh, what a time we've been waiting for you!

GINA (*glancing sidelong at him*). You've been out a long time, Ekdal.

HIALMAR (*without looking at her*). Rather long, yes.

[*He takes off his overcoat;* GINA *and* HEDVIG *go to help him; he motions them away.*]

GINA. Perhaps you've had dinner with Werle?

HIALMAR (*hanging up his coat*). No.

GINA (*going towards the kitchen door*). Then I'll bring some in for you.

HIALMAR. No; let the dinner alone. I want nothing to eat.

HEDVIG (*going nearer to him*). Are you not well, father?

HIALMAR. Well? Oh, yes, well enough. We have had a tiring walk, Gregers and I.

GINA. You didn't ought to have gone so far, Ekdal; you're not used to it.

HIALMAR. H'm; there's many a thing a man must get used to in this world. (*Wanders about the room.*) Has any one been here while I was out?

GINA. Nobody but the two sweethearts.

HIALMAR. No new orders?

GINA. No, not today.

HEDVIG. There will be some tomorrow, father; you'll see.

HIALMAR. I hope there will, for tomorrow I am going to set to work in real earnest.

HEDVIG. Tomorrow! Don't you remember what day it is tomorrow?

HIALMAR. Oh, yes, by-the-bye——. Well, the day after, then. Henceforth I mean to do everything myself; I shall take all the work into my own hands.

GINA. Why, what can be the good of that, Ekdal? It'll only make your life a burden to you. I can manage the photography all right, and you can go on working at your invention.

HEDVIG. And think of the wild duck, father,—and all the hens and rabbits and——!

HIALMAR. Don't talk to me of all that trash! From to-morrow I will never set foot in the garret again.

HEDVIG. Oh, but father, you promised that we should have a little party——

HIALMAR. H'm, true. Well, then, from the day after to-morrow. I should almost like to wring that cursed wild duck's neck!

HEDVIG (*shrieks*). The wild duck!

GINA. Well, I never!

HEDVIG (*shaking him*). Oh, no, father; you know it's my wild duck!

HIALMAR. That is why I don't do it. I haven't the heart

to—for your sake, Hedvig. But in my inmost soul I feel that I ought to do it. I ought not to tolerate under my roof a creature that has been through those hands.

GINA. Why, good gracious, even if grandfather did get it from that poor creature, Pettersen——

HIALMAR (*wandering about*). There are certain claims— what shall I call them?—let me say claims of the ideal— certain obligations, which a man cannot disregard without injury to his soul.

HEDVIG (*going after him*). But think of the wild duck,— the poor wild duck!

HIALMAR (*stops*). I tell you I will spare it—for your sake. Not a hair of its head shall be—I mean, it shall be spared. There are greater problems than that to be dealt with. But you should go out a little now, Hedvig, as usual; it is getting dusk enough for you now.

HEDVIG. No, I don't care about going out now.

HIALMAR. Yes, do; it seems to me your eyes are blinking a great deal; all these vapors in here are bad for you. The air is heavy under this roof.

HEDVIG. Very well, then, I'll run down the kitchen stair and go for a little walk. My cloak and hat?—oh, they're in my own room. Father—be sure you don't do the wild duck any harm while I'm out.

HIALMAR. Not a feather of its head shall be touched. (*Draws her to him.*) You and I, Hedvig—we two——! Well, go along.

[HEDVIG *nods to her parents and goes out through the kitchen.*]

HIALMAR (*walks about without looking up*). Gina.

GINA. Yes?

HIALMAR. From tomorrow—or, say, from the day after tomorrow—I should like to keep the household account-book myself.

GINA. Do you want to keep the accounts, too, now?

HIALMAR. Yes; or to check the receipts at any rate.

GINA. Lord help us! that's soon done.

HIALMAR. One would hardly think so; at any rate, you seem to make the money go a very long way. (*Stops and looks at her.*) How do you manage it?

GINA. It's because me and Hedvig, we need so little.

HIALMAR. Is it the case that father is very liberally paid for the copying he does for Mr. Werle?

GINA. I don't know as he gets anything out of the way. I don't know the rates for that sort of work.

HIALMAR. Well, what does he get, about? Let me hear!

GINA. Oh, it varies; I daresay it'll come to about as much as he costs us, with a little pocket-money over.

HIALMAR. As much as he costs us! And you have never told me this before!

GINA. No, how could I tell you? It pleased you so much to think he got everything from you.

HIALMAR. And he gets it from Mr. Werle.

GINA. Oh, well, he has plenty and to spare, he has.

HIALMAR. Light the lamp for me, please!

GINA (*lighting the lamp*). And, of course, we don't know as it's Mr. Werle himself; it may be Gråberg——

HIALMAR. Why bring in Gråberg?

GINA. I don't know; I only thought——

HIALMAR. H'm.

GINA. It wasn't me that got grandfather that copying. It was Bertha, when she used to come about us.

HIALMAR. It seems to me your voice is trembling.

GINA (*putting the lamp-shade on*). Is it?

HIALMAR. And your hands are shaking, are they not?

GINA (*firmly*). Come right out with it, Ekdal. What has he been saying about me?

HIALMAR. Is it true—can it be true that—that there was

an—an understanding between you and Mr. Werle, while you were in service there?

GINA. That's not true. Not at that time. Mr. Werle did come after me, that's a fact. And his wife thought there was something in it, and then she made such a hocus-pocus and hurly-burly, and she hustled me and bustled me about so that I left her service.

HIALMAR. But afterwards, then?

GINA. Well, then I went home. And mother—well, she wasn't the woman you took her for, Ekdal; she kept on worrying and worrying at me about one thing and another—for Mr. Werle was a widower by that time.

HIALMAR. Well, and then?

GINA. I suppose you've got to know it. He gave me no peace until he'd had his way.

HIALMAR (*striking his hands together*). And this is the mother of my child! How could you hide this from me?

GINA. Yes, it was wrong of me; I ought certainly to have told you long ago.

HIALMAR. You should have told me at the very first;—then I should have known the sort·of woman you were.

GINA. But would you have married me all the same?

HIALMAR. How can you dream that I would?

GINA. That's just why I didn't dare tell you anything, then. For I'd come to care for you so much, you see; and I couldn't go and make myself utterly miserable——

HIALMAR (*walks about*). And this is my Hedvig's mother. And to know that all I see before me—(*kicks a chair.*)—all that I call my home—I owe to a favored predecessor! Oh, that scoundrel Werle!

GINA. Do you repent of the fourteen—the fifteen years we've lived together?

HIALMAR (*placing himself in front of her*). Have you not every day, every hour, repented of the spider's-web of deceit you have spun around me? Answer me that! How could you help writhing with penitence and remorse?

GINA. Oh, my dear Ekdal, I've had all I could do to look after the house and get through the day's work——

HIALMAR. Then you never think of reviewing your past?

GINA. No; Heaven knows I'd almost forgotten those old stories.

HIALMAR. Oh, this dull, callous contentment! To me there is something revolting about it. Think of it—never so much as a twinge of remorse!

GINA. But tell me, Ekdal—what would have become of you if you hadn't had a wife like me?

HIALMAR. Like you——!

GINA. Yes; for you know I've always been a bit more practical and wide-awake than you. Of course I'm a year or two older.

HIALMAR. What would have become of me!

GINA. You'd got into all sorts of bad ways when first you met me; that you can't deny.

HIALMAR. "Bad ways" do you call them? Little do you know what a man goes through when he is in grief and despair—especially a man of my fiery temperament.

GINA. Well, well, that may be so. And I've no reason to crow over you, neither; for you turned a moral of a husband, that you did, as soon as ever you had a house and home of your own.—And now we'd got everything so nice and cosy about us; and me and Hedvig was just thinking we'd soon be able to let ourselves go a bit, in the way of both food and clothes.

HIALMAR. In the swamp of deceit, yes.

GINA. I wish to goodness that detestable thing had never set his foot inside our doors!

HIALMAR. And I, too, thought my home such a pleasant one. That was a delusion. Where shall I now find the elasticity of spirit to bring my invention into the world of reality? Perhaps it will die with me; and then it will be your past, Gina, that will have killed it.

GINA (*nearly crying*). You mustn't say such things, Ekdal. Me, that has only wanted to do the best I could for you, all my days!

HIALMAR. I ask you, what becomes of the breadwinner's dream? When I used to lie in there on the sofa and brood over my invention, I had a clear enough presentiment that it would sap my vitality to the last drop. I felt even then that the day when I held the patent in my hand—that day— would bring my—release. And then it was my dream that you should live on after me, the dead inventor's well-to-do widow.

GINA (*drying her tears*). No, you mustn't talk like that, Ekdal. May the Lord never let me see the day I am left a widow!

HIALMAR. Oh, the whole dream has vanished. It is all over now. All over!

[GREGERS WERLE *opens the passage door cautiously and looks in.*]

GREGERS. May I come in?

HIALMAR. Yes, come in.

GREGERS (*comes forward, his face beaming with satisfaction, and holds out both his hands to them*). Well, dear friends——! (*Looks from one to the other and whispers to* HIALMAR.) Have you not done it yet?

HIALMAR (*aloud*). It is done.

GREGERS. It is?

HIALMAR. I have passed through the bitterest moments of my life.

GREGERS. But also, I trust, the most ennobling.

HIALMAR. Well, at any rate, we have got through it for the present.

GINA. God forgive you, Mr. Werle.

GREGERS (*in great surprise*). But I don't understand this.

HIALMAR. What don't you understand?

GREGERS. After so great a crisis—a crisis that is to be the starting-point of an entirely new life—of a communion founded on truth, and free from all taint of deception——

HIALMAR. Yes, yes, I know; I know that quite well.

GREGERS. I confidently expected, when I entered the room, to find the light of transfiguration shining upon me from both husband and wife. And now I see nothing but dulness, oppression, gloom——

GINA. Oh, is that it?   [*Takes off the lamp-shade.*]

GREGERS. You will not understand me, Mrs. Ekdal. Ah, well, you, I suppose, need time to——. But you, Hialmar? Surely you feel a new consecration after the great crisis.

HIALMAR. Yes, of course I do. That is—in a sort of way.

GREGERS. For surely nothing in the world can compare with the joy of forgiving one who has erred and raising her up to oneself in love.

HIALMAR. Do you think a man can so easily throw off the bitter cup I have drained?

GREGERS. No, not a common man, perhaps. But a man like you——!

HIALMAR. Good God! I know that well enough. But you must keep me up to it, Gregers. It takes time, you know.

GREGERS. You have much of the wild duck in you, Hial-mar.   [RELLING *has come in at the passage door.*]

RELLING. Oho! is the wild duck to the fore again?

HIALMAR. Yes; Mr. Werle's wing-broken victim.

RELLING. Mr. Werle's——? So it's him you are talking about?

HIALMAR. Him and—ourselves.

RELLING (*in an undertone to* GREGERS).   May the devil fly away with you!

HIALMAR.   What is that you are saying?

RELLING.   Only uttering a heartfelt wish that this quack-salver would take himself off.   If he stays here, he is quite equal to making an utter mess of life, for both of you.

GREGERS.   These two will not make a mess of life, Mr. Relling.   Of course I won't speak of Hialmar—him we know. But she, too, in her innermost heart, has certainly something loyal and sincere——

GINA (*almost crying*).   You might have let me alone for what I was, then.

RELLING (*to* GREGERS).   Is it rude to ask what you really want in this house?

GREGERS.   To lay the foundations of a true marriage.

RELLING.   So you don't think Ekdal's marriage is good enough as it is?

GREGERS.   No doubt it is as good a marriage as most others, worse luck.   But a true marriage it has yet to become.

HIALMAR.   You have never had eyes for the claims of the ideal, Relling.

RELLING.   Rubbish, my boy!—but excuse me, Mr. Werle: how many—in round numbers—how many true marriages have you seen in the course of your life?

GREGERS.   Scarcely a single one.

RELLING.   Nor I either.

GREGERS.   But I have seen innumerable marriages of the opposite kind.   And it has been my fate to see at close quarters what ruin such a marriage can work in two human souls.

HIALMAR.   A man's whole moral basis may give away beneath his feet; that is the terrible part of it.

RELLING.   Well, I can't say I've ever been exactly married, so I don't pretend to speak with authority.   But this I know, that the child enters into the marriage problem. And you must leave the child in peace.

HIALMAR. Oh—Hedvig! my poor Hedvig!

RELLING. Yes, you must be good enough to keep Hedvig outside of all this. You two are grown-up people; you are free, in God's name, to make what mess and muddle you please of your life. But you must deal cautiously with Hedvig, I tell you; else you may do her a great injury.

HIALMAR. An injury!

RELLING. Yes, or she may do herself an injury—and perhaps others, too.

GINA. How can you know that, Relling?

HIALMAR. Her sight is in no immediate danger, is it?

RELLING. I am not talking about her sight. Hedvig is at a critical age. She may be getting all sorts of mischief into her head.

GINA. That's true—I've noticed it already! She's taken to carrying on with the fire, out in the kitchen. She calls it playing at house-on-fire. I'm often scared for fear she really sets fire to the house.

RELLING. You see; I thought as much.

GREGERS (to RELLING). But how do you account for that?

RELLING (sullenly). Her constitution's changing, sir.

HIALMAR. So long as the child has me——! So long as I am above ground——!   [A knock at the door.]

GINA. Hush, Ekdal; there's some one in the passage. (Calls out.) Come in!

[MRS. SÖRBY, in walking dress, comes in.]

MRS. SÖRBY. Good evening.

GINA (going towards her). Is it really you, Bertha?

MRS. SÖRBY. Yes, of course it is. But I'm disturbing you, I'm afraid?

HIALMAR. No, not at all; an emissary from that house——

MRS. SÖRBY (to GINA). To tell the truth, I hoped your

men-folk would be out at this time. I just ran up to have a little chat with you, and to say good-bye.

GINA. Good-bye? Are you going away, then?

MRS. SÖRBY. Yes, tomorrow morning,—up to Höidal. Mr. Werle started this afternoon. (*Lightly to* GREGERS.) He asked me to say good-bye for him.

GINA. Only fancy——!

HIALMAR. So Mr. Werle has gone? And now you are going after him?

MRS. SÖRBY. Yes, what do you say to that, Ekdal?

HIALMAR. I say: beware!

GREGERS. I must explain the situation. My father and Mrs. Sörby are going to be married.

HIALMAR. Going to be married!

GINA. Oh, Bertha! So it's come to that at last!

RELLING (*his voice quivering a little*). This is surely not true?

MRS. SÖRBY. Yes, my dear Relling, it's true enough.

RELLING. You are going to marry again?

MRS. SÖRBY. Yes, it looks like it. Werle has got a special licence, and we are going to be married quite quietly, up at the works.

GREGERS. Then I must wish you all happiness, like a dutiful stepson.

MRS. SÖRBY. Thank you very much—if you mean what you say. I certainly hope it will lead to happiness, both for Werle and for me.

RELLING. You have every reason to hope that. Mr. Werle never gets drunk—so far as I know; and I don't suppose he's in the habit of thrashing his wives, like the late lamented horse-doctor.

MRS. SÖRBY. Come now, let Sörby rest in peace. He had his good points, too.

RELLING. Mr. Werle has better ones, I have no doubt.

MRS. SÖRBY. He hasn't frittered away all that was good in him, at any rate. The man who does that must take the consequences.

RELLING. I shall go out with Molvik this evening.

MRS. SÖRBY. You mustn't do that, Relling. Don't do it —for my sake.

RELLING. There's nothing else for it. (*To* HIALMAR.) If you're going with us, come along.

GINA. No, thank you. Ekdal doesn't go in for that sort of dissertation.

HIALMAR (*half aloud, in vexation*). Oh, do hold your tongue!

RELLING. Good-bye, Mrs.—Werle.

[*Goes out through the passage door.*]

GREGERS (*to* MRS. SÖRBY). You seem to know Dr. Relling pretty intimately.

MRS. SÖRBY. Yes, we have known each other for many years. At one time it seemed as if things might have gone further between us.

GREGERS. It was surely lucky for you that they did not.

MRS. SÖRBY. You may well say that. But I have always been wary of acting on impulse. A woman can't afford absolutely to throw herself away.

GREGERS. Are you not in the least afraid that I may let my father know about this old friendship?

MRS SÖRBY. Why, of course, I have told him all about it myself.

GREGERS. Indeed?

MRS. SÖRBY. Your father knows every single thing that can, with any truth, be said about me. I have told him all; it was the first thing I did when I saw what was in his mind.

GREGERS. Then you have been franker than most people, I think.

MRS. SÖRBY. I have always been frank. We women find that the best policy.

HIALMAR. What do you say to that, Gina?

GINA. Oh, we're not all alike, us women aren't. Some are made one way, some another.

MRS. SÖRBY. Well, for my part, Gina, I believe it's wisest to do as I've done. And Werle has no secrets either, on his side. That's really the great bond between us, you see. Now he can talk to me as openly as a child. He has never had the chance to do that before. Fancy a man like him, full of health and vigor, passing his whole youth and the best years of his life in listening to nothing but penitential sermons! And very often the sermons had for their text the most imaginary offences—at least so I understand.

GINA. That's true enough.

GREGERS. If you ladies are going to follow up this topic, I had better withdraw.

MRS. SÖRBY. You can stay as far as that's concerned. I shan't say a word more. But I wanted you to know that I have done nothing secretly or in an underhand way. I may seem to have come in for a great piece of luck; and so I have, in a sense. But after all, I don't think I am getting any more than I am giving. I shall stand by him always, and I can tend and care for him as no one else can, now that he is getting helpless.

HIALMAR. Getting helpless?

GREGERS (to MRS. SÖRBY). Hush, don't speak of that here.

MRS. SÖRBY. There is no disguising it any longer, however much he would like to. He is going blind.

HIALMAR (starts). Going blind? That's strange. He, too, going blind!

GINA. Lots of people do.

MRS. SÖRBY. And you can imagine what that means to a

business man. Well, I shall try as well as I can to make my eyes take the place of his. But I mustn't stay any longer; I have heaps of things to do.—Oh, by-the-bye, Ekdal, I was to tell you that if there is anything Werle can do for you, you must just apply to Gråberg.

GREGERS. That offer I am sure Hialmar Ekdal will decline with thanks.

MRS. SÖRBY. Indeed? I don't think he used to be so——

GINA. No, Bertha, Ekdal doesn't need anything from Mr. Werle now.

HIALMAR (*slowly, and with emphasis*). Will you present my compliments to your future husband and say that I intend very shortly to call upon Mr. Gråberg——

GREGERS. What! You don't really mean that?

HIALMAR. To call upon Mr. Gråberg, I say, and obtain an account of the sum I owe his principal. I will pay that debt of honor—ha ha ha! a debt of honor, let us call it! In any case, I will pay the whole with five per cent interest.

GINA. But, my dear Ekdal, God knows we haven't got the money to do it.

HIALMAR. Be good enough to tell your future husband that I am working assiduously at my invention. Please tell him that what sustains me in this laborious task is the wish to free myself from a torturing burden of debt. That is my reason for proceeding with the invention. The entire profits shall be devoted to releasing me from my pecuniary obligations to your future husband.

MRS. SÖRBY. Something has happened here.

HIALMAR. Yes, you are right.

MRS. SÖRBY. Well, good-bye. I had something else to speak to you about, Gina; but it must keep till another time. Good-bye.

[HIALMAR *and* GREGERS *bow silently.* GINA *follows* MRS. SÖRBY *to the door.*]

HIALMAR.   Not beyond the threshold, Gina!

[MRS. SÖRBY *goes;* GINA *shuts the door after her.*]

HIALMAR.   There now, Gregers; I have got that burden of debt off my mind.

GREGERS.   You soon will, at all events.

HIALMAR.   I think my attitude may be called correct.

GREGERS.   You are the man I have always taken you for.

HIALMAR.   In certain cases, it is impossible to disregard the claim of the ideal.   Yet, as the breadwinner of a family, I cannot but writhe and groan under it.   I can tell you it is no joke for a man without capital to attempt the repayment of a long-standing obligation, over which, so to speak, the dust of oblivion had gathered.   But it cannot be helped: the Man in me demands his rights.

GREGERS (*laying his hand on* HIALMAR'S *shoulder*).   My dear Hialmar—was it not a good thing I came?

HIALMAR.   Yes.

GREGERS.   Are you not glad to have had your true position made clear to you?

HIALMAR (*somewhat impatiently*).   Yes, of course I am. But there is one thing that is revolting to my sense of justice.

GREGERS.   And what is that?

HIALMAR.   It is that—but I don't know whether I ought to express myself so unreservedly about your father.

GREGERS.   Say what you please, so far as I am concerned.

HIALMAR.   Well, then, is it not exasperating to think that it is not I, but he, who will realize the true marriage?

GREGERS.   How can you say such a thing?

HIALMAR.   Because it is clearly the case.   Isn't the marriage between your father and Mrs. Sörby founded upon complete confidence, upon entire and unreserved candor on both sides?   They hide nothing from each other; they keep no secrets in the background; their relation is based, if I may put it so, on mutual confession and absolution.

GREGERS. Well, what then?

HIALMAR. Well, is not that the whole thing? Did you not yourself say that this was precisely the difficulty that had to be overcome in order to found a true marriage?

GREGERS. But this is a totally different matter, Hialmar. You surely don't compare either yourself or your wife with those two——? Oh, you understand me well enough.

HIALMAR. Say what you like, there is something in all this that hurts and offends my sense of justice. It really looks as if there were no just providence to rule the world.

GINA. Oh, no, Ekdal; for God's sake don't say such things.

GREGERS. H'm; don't let us get upon those questions.

HIALMAR. And yet, after all, I cannot but recognize the guiding finger of fate. He is going blind.

GINA. Oh, you can't be sure of that.

HIALMAR. There is no doubt about it. At all events there ought not to be; for in that very fact lies the righteous retribution. He has hoodwinked a confiding fellow-creature in days gone by——

GREGERS. I fear he has hoodwinked many.

HIALMAR. And now comes inexorable, mysterious Fate and demands Werle's own eyes.

GINA. Oh, how dare you say such dreadful things! You make me quite scared.

HIALMAR. It is profitable, now and then, to plunge deep into the night side of existence.

[HEDVIG, *in her hat and cloak, comes in by the passage door. She is pleasurably excited and out of breath.*]

GINA. Are you back already?

HEDVIG. Yes, I didn't care to go any farther. It was a good thing, too; for I've just met some one at the door.

HIALMAR. It must have been that Mrs. Sörby.

HEDVIG. Yes.

HIALMAR (*walks up and down*). I hope you have seen her for the last time.

[*Silence.* HEDVIG, *discouraged, looks first at one and then at the other, trying to divine their frame of mind.*]

HEDVIG (*approaching, coaxingly*). Father.

HIALMAR. Well—what is it, Hedvig?

HEDVIG. Mrs. Sörby had something with her for me.

HIALMAR (*stops*). For you?

HEDVIG. Yes. Something for tomorrow.

GINA. Bertha has always given you some little thing on your birthday.

HIALMAR. What is it?

HEDVIG. Oh, you mustn't see it now. Mother is to give it to me tomorrow morning before I'm up.

HIALMAR. What is all this hocus-pocus that I am to be in the dark about?

HEDVIG (*quickly*). Oh, no, you may see it if you like. It's a big letter.   [*Takes the letter out of her cloak pocket.*]

HIALMAR. A letter, too?

HEDVIG. Yes, it is only a letter. The rest will come afterwards, I suppose. But fancy—a letter! I've never had a letter before. And there's "Miss" written upon it. (*Reads.*) "Miss Hedvig Ekdal." Only fancy—that's me!

HIALMAR. Let me see that letter.

HEDVIG (*hands it to him*). There it is.

HIALMAR. That is Mr. Werle's hand.

GINA. Are you sure of that, Ekdal?

HIALMAR. Look for yourself.

GINA. Oh, what do *I* know about such-like things?

HIALMAR. Hedvig, may I open the letter—and read it?

HEDVIG. Yes, of course you may, if you want to.

GINA. No, not tonight, Ekdal; it's to be kept till tomorrow.

HEDVIG (*softly*). Oh, can't you let him read it? It's sure to be something good; and then father will be glad, and everything will be nice again.

HIALMAR. I may open it, then?

HEDVIG. Yes, do, father. I'm so anxious to know what it is.

HIALMAR. Well and good. (*Opens the letter, takes out a paper, reads it through and appears bewildered.*) What is this——?

GINA. What does it say?

HEDVIG. Oh, yes, father—tell us!

HIALMAR. Be quiet. (*Reads it through again; he has turned pale, but says with self-control:*) It is a deed of gift, Hedvig.

HEDVIG. Is it? What sort of gift am I to have?

HIALMAR. Read for yourself.

[HEDVIG *goes over and reads for a time by the lamp.*]

HIALMAR (*half-aloud, clenching his hands*). The eyes! The eyes—and then that letter!

HEDVIG (*leaves off reading*). Yes, but it seems to me that it's grandfather that's to have it.

HIALMAR (*takes letter from her*). Gina—can you understand this?

GINA. I know nothing whatever about it; tell me what's the matter.

HIALMAR. Mr. Werle writes to Hedvig that her old grandfather need not trouble himself any longer with the copying, but that he can henceforth draw on the office for a hundred crowns a month——

GREGERS. Aha!

HEDVIG. A hundred crowns, mother! I read that.

GINA. What a good thing for grandfather!

HIALMAR. ——a hundred crowns a month so long as he needs it—that means, of course, so long as he lives.

GINA. Well, so he's provided for, poor dear.

HIALMAR. But there is more to come. You didn't read that, Hedvig. Afterwards this gift is to pass on to you.

HEDVIG. To me! The whole of it?

HIALMAR. He says that the same amount is assured to you for the whole of your life. Do you hear that, Gina?

GINA. Yes, I hear.

HEDVIG. Fancy—all that money for me! (*Shakes him.*) Father, father, aren't you glad——?

HIALMAR (*eluding her*). Glad! (*Walks about.*) Oh, what vistas—what perspectives open up before me! It is Hedvig, Hedvig that he showers these benefactions upon!

GINA. Yes, because it's Hedvig's birthday——

HEDVIG. And you'll get it all the same, father! You know quite well I shall give all the money to you and mother.

HIALMAR. To mother, yes! There we have it.

GREGERS. Hialmar, this is a trap he is setting for you.

HIALMAR. Do you think it's another trap?

GREGERS. When he was here this morning he said: Hialmar Ekdal is not the man you imagine him to be.

HIALMAR. Not the man——!

GREGERS. That you shall see, he said.

HIALMAR. He meant you should see that I would let myself be bought off——!

HEDVIG. Oh, mother, what does all this mean?

GINA. Go and take off your things.

[HEDVIG *goes out by the kitchen door, half-crying.*]

GREGERS. Yes, Hialmar—now is the time to show who was right, he or I.

HIALMAR (*slowly tears the paper across, lays both pieces on the table and says:*) Here is my answer.

GREGERS. Just what I expected.

HIALMAR (*goes over to* GINA, *who stands by the stove, and says in a low voice:*) Now please make a clean breast of it.

If the connection between you and him was quite over when you—came to care for me, as you call it—why did he place us in a position to marry?

GINA. I suppose he thought as he could come and go in our house.

HIALMAR. Only that? Was not he afraid of a possible contingency?

GINA. I don't know what you mean.

HIALMAR. I want to know whether—your child has the right to live under my roof.

GINA (*draws herself up; her eyes flash*). You ask that?

HIALMAR. You shall answer me this one question: Does Hedvig belong to me—or——? Well?

GINA (*looking at him with cold defiance*). I don't know.

HIALMAR (*quivering a little*). You don't know!

GINA. How should *I* know? A creature like me——

HIALMAR (*quietly turning away from her*). Then I have nothing more to do in this house.

GREGERS. Take care, Hialmar! Think what you are doing!

HIALMAR (*puts on his overcoat*). In this case, there is nothing for a man like me to think twice about.

GREGERS. Yes, indeed, there are endless things to be considered. You three must be together if you are to attain the true frame of mind for self-sacrifice and forgiveness.

HIALMAR. I don't want to attain it. Never, never! My hat! (*Takes his hat.*) My home has fallen in ruins about me. (*Bursts into tears.*) Gregers, I have no child!

HEDVIG (*who has opened the kitchen door*). What is that you're saying? (*Coming to him.*) Father, father!

GINA. There, you see!

HIALMAR. Don't come near me, Hedvig! Keep far away. I cannot bear to see you! Oh! those eyes——! Good-bye.

[*Makes for the door.*]

HEDVIG (*clinging close to him and screaming loudly*). No! no! Don't leave me!

GINA (*cries out*). Look at the child, Ekdal! Look at the child!

HIALMAR. I will not! I cannot! I must get out—away from all this!

[*He tears himself away from* HEDVIG *and goes out by the passage door.*]

HEDVIG (*with despairing eyes*). He is going away from us, mother! He is going away from us! He will never come back again!

GINA. Don't cry, Hedvig. Father's sure to come back again.

HEDVIG (*throws herself sobbing on the sofa*). No, no, he'll never come home to us any more.

GREGERS. Do you believe I meant all for the best, Mrs. Ekdal?

GINA. Yes, I daresay you did; but God forgive you, all the same.

HEDVIG (*lying on the sofa*). Oh, this will kill me! What have I done to him? Mother, you must fetch him home again!

GINA. Yes, yes, yes; only be quiet, and I'll go out and look for him. (*Puts on her outdoor things.*) Perhaps he's gone in to Relling's. But you mustn't lie there and cry. Promise me!

HEDVIG (*weeping convulsively*). Yes, I'll stop, I'll stop, if only father comes back!

GREGERS (*to* GINA, *who is going*). After all, had you not better leave him to fight out his bitter fight to the end?

GINA. Oh, he can do that afterwards. First of all, we must get the child quieted.   [*Goes out by the passage door.*]

HEDVIG (*sits up and dries her tears*). Now you must tell me what all this means. Why doesn't father want me any more?

GREGERS. You mustn't ask that till you are a big girl—quite grown-up.

HEDVIG (*sobs*). But I can't go on being as miserable as this till I'm grown-up.—I think I know what it is.—Perhaps I'm not really father's child.

GREGERS (*uneasily*). How could that be?

HEDVIG. Mother might have found me. And perhaps father has just got to know it; I've read of such things.

GREGERS. Well, but if it were so——

HEDVIG. I think he might be just as fond of me for all that. Yes, fonder almost. We got the wild duck as a present, you know, and I love it so dearly all the same.

GREGERS (*turning the conversation*). Ah, the wild duck, by-the-bye! Let us talk about the wild duck a little, Hedvig.

HEDVIG. The poor wild duck! He doesn't want to see it any more either. Only think, he wanted to wring its neck!

GREGERS. Oh, he won't do that.

HEDVIG. No; but he said he would like to. And I think it was horrid of father to say it, for I pray for the wild duck every night and ask that it may be preserved from death and all that is evil.

GREGERS (*looking at her*). Do you say your prayers every night?

HEDVIG. Yes.

GREGERS. Who taught you to do that?

HEDVIG. I myself, one time when father was very ill, and had leeches on his neck and said that death was staring him in the face.

GREGERS. Well?

HEDVIG. Then I prayed for him as I lay in bed, and since then I have always kept it up.

GREGERS. And now you pray for the wild duck, too?

HEDVIG. I thought it was best to bring in the wild duck, for she was so weak at first.

GREGERS. Do you pray in the morning, too?

HEDVIG. No, of course not.

GREGERS. Why not in the morning as well?

HEDVIG. In the morning it's light, you know, and there's nothing in particular to be afraid of.

GREGERS. And your father was going to wring the neck of the wild duck that you love so dearly?

HEDVIG. No; he said he ought to wring its neck, but he would spare it for my sake; and that was kind of father.

GREGERS (*coming a little nearer*). But suppose you were to sacrifice the wild duck of your own free will for his sake.

HEDVIG (*rising*). The wild duck!

GREGERS. Suppose you were to make a free-will offering, for his sake, of the dearest treasure you have in the world!

HEDVIG. Do you think that would do any good?

GREGERS. Try it, Hedvig.

HEDVIG (*softly, with flashing eyes*). Yes, I will try it.

GREGERS. Have you really the courage for it, do you think?

HEDVIG. I'll ask grandfather to shoot the wild duck for me.

GREGERS. Yes, do. But not a word to your mother about it.

HEDVIG. Why not?

GREGERS. She doesn't understand us.

HEDVIG. The wild duck! I'll try it tomorrow morning.

[GINA *comes in by the passage door.*]

HEDVIG (*going towards her*). Did you find him, mother?

GINA. No, but I heard as he had called and taken Relling with him.

GREGERS. Are you sure of that?

GINA. Yes, the porter's wife said so. Molvik went with them, too, she said.

GREGERS. This evening, when his mind so sorely needs to wrestle in solitude——!

GINA (*takes off her things*). Yes, men are strange creatures, so they are. The Lord only knows where Relling has dragged him to! I ran over to Madame Eriksen's, but they weren't there.

HEDVIG (*struggling to keep back her tears*). Oh, if he should never come home any more!

GREGERS. He will come home again. I shall have news to give him tomorrow; and then you shall see how he comes home. You may rely upon that, Hedvig, and sleep in peace. Good-night. [*He goes out by the passage door.*]

HEDVIG (*throws herself sobbing on* GINA'S *neck*). Mother, mother!

GINA (*pats her shoulder and sighs*). Ah, yes; Relling was right, he was. That's what comes of it when crazy creatures go about presenting the claims of the—what-you-may-call-it.

CURTAIN

ACT FIVE

HIALMAR EKDAL'S *studio. Cold, grey morning light. Wet snow lies upon the large panes of the sloping roof-window.*

[GINA *comes from the kitchen with an apron and bib on, and carrying a dusting-brush and a duster; she goes towards the sitting-room door. At the same moment* HEDVIG *comes hurriedly in from the passage.*]

GINA (*stops*). Well?

HEDVIG. Oh, mother, I almost think he's down at Relling's——

GINA. There, you see!

HEDVIG. ——because the porter's wife says she could hear that Relling had two people with him when he came home last night.

GINA. That's just what I thought.

HEDVIG. But it's no use his being there, if he won't come up to us.

GINA. I'll go down and speak to him at all events.

[OLD EKDAL, *in dressing-gown and slippers, and with a lighted pipe, appears at the door of his room.*]

EKDAL. Hialmar—— Isn't Hialmar at home?

GINA. No, he's gone out.

EKDAL. So early? And in such a tearing snowstorm? Well, well; just as he pleases; I can take my morning walk alone.

[*He slides the garret door aside;* HEDVIG *helps him; he goes in; she closes it after him.*]

HEDVIG (*in an undertone*). Only think, mother, when poor grandfather hears that father is going to leave us.

GINA. Oh, nonsense; grandfather mustn't hear anything about it. It was a heaven's mercy he wasn't at home yesterday in all that hurly-burly.

HEDVIG. Yes, but——

[GREGERS *comes in by the passage door.*]

GREGERS. Well, have you any news of him?

GINA. They say he's down at Relling's.

GREGERS. At Relling's! Has he really been out with those creatures?

GINA. Yes, like enough.

GREGERS. When he ought to have been yearning for solitude, to collect and clear his thoughts——

GINA. Yes, you may well say so.

[RELLING *enters from the passage.*]

HEDVIG (*going to him*). Is father in your room?

GINA (*at the same time*). Is he there?

RELLING. Yes, to be sure he is.

HEDVIG. And you never let us know!

RELLING. Yes, I'm a brute. But in the first place I had to look after the other brute; I mean our dæmonic friend, of course; and then I fell so dead asleep that——

GINA. What does Ekdal say today?

RELLING. He says nothing whatever.

HEDVIG. Doesn't he speak?

RELLING. Not a blessed word.

GREGERS. No, no; I can understand that very well.

GINA. But what's he doing then?

RELLING. He's lying on the sofa, snoring.

GINA. Oh, is he? Yes, Ekdal's a rare one to snore.

HEDVIG. Asleep? Can he sleep?

RELLING. Well, it certainly looks like it.

GREGERS. No wonder, after the spiritual conflict that has rent him——

GINA. And then he's never been used to gadding about out of doors at night.

HEDVIG. Perhaps it's a good thing that he's getting sleep, mother.

GINA. Of course it is; and we must take care we don't wake him up too early. Thank you, Relling. I must get the house cleaned up a bit now, and then—— Come and help me, Hedvig. [GINA and HEDVIG go into the sitting-room.]

GREGERS (turning to RELLING). What is your explanation of the spiritual tumult that is now going on in Hialmar Ekdal?

RELLING. Devil a bit of a spiritual tumult have I noticed in him.

GREGERS. What! Not at such a crisis, when his whole life has been placed on a new foundation——? How can you think that such an individuality as Hialmar's——?

RELLING. Oh, individuality—he! If he ever had any tendency to the abnormal development you call individuality, I can assure you it was rooted out of him while he was still in his teens.

GREGERS. That would be strange indeed,—considering the loving care with which he was brought up.

RELLING. By those two high-flown, hysterical maiden aunts, you mean?

GREGERS. Let me tell you that they were women who never forgot the claim of the ideal—but of course you will only jeer at me again.

RELLING. No, I'm in no humor for that. I know all about those ladies; for he has ladled out no end of rhetoric on the subject of his "two soul-mothers." But I don't think he has much to thank them for. Ekdal's misfortune is that in his own circle he has always been looked upon as a shining light——

GREGERS. Not without reason, surely. Look at the depth of his mind!

RELLING. *I* have never discovered it. That his father believed in it I don't so much wonder; the old lieutenant has been an ass all his days.

GREGERS. He has had a child-like mind all his days; that is what you cannot understand.

RELLING. Well, so be it. But then, when our dear, sweet Hialmar went to college, he at once passed for the great light of the future amongst his comrades, too! He was handsome, the rascal—red and white—a shop-girl's dream of manly beauty; and with his superficially emotional temperament, and his sympathetic voice and his talent for declaiming other people's verses and other people's thoughts——

GREGERS (*indignantly*). Is it Hialmar Ekdal you are talking about in this strain?

RELLING. Yes, with your permission; I am simply giving you an inside view of the idol you are grovelling before.

GREGERS. I should hardly have thought I was quite stone blind.

RELLING. Yes, you are—or not far from it. You are a sick man, too, you see.

GREGERS. You are right there.

RELLING. Yes. Yours is a complicated case. First of all there is that plaguy integrity-fever; and then—what's worse —you are always in a delirium of hero-worship; you must always have something to adore, outside yourself.

GREGERS. Yes, I must certainly seek it outside myself.

RELLING. But you make such shocking mistakes about every new phœnix you think you have discovered. Here again you have come to a cottar's cabin with your claim of the ideal; and the people of the house are insolvent.

GREGERS. If you don't think better than that of Hialmar Ekdal, what pleasure can you find in being everlastingly with him?

RELLING. Well, you see, I'm supposed to be a sort of doctor—save the mark! I can't but give a hand to the poor sick folk who live under the same roof with me.

GREGERS. Oh, indeed! Hialmar Ekdal is sick, too, is he?

RELLING. Most people are, worse luck.

GREGERS. And what remedy are you applying in Hialmar's case?

RELLING. My usual one. I am cultivating the life-illusion* in him.

GREGERS. Life—illusion? I didn't catch what you said.

RELLING. Yes, I said illusion. For illusion, you know, is the stimulating principle.

GREGERS. May I ask with what illusion Hialmar is inoculated?

RELLING. No, thank you; I don't betray professional secrets to quacksalvers. You would probably go and muddle his case still more than you have already. But my method

* "Livslögnen," literally "the life-lie." [Trans.]

is infallible. I have applied it to Molvik as well. I have
made him "dæmonic." That's the blister I have to put on
his neck.

GREGERS. Is he not really dæmonic, then?

RELLING. What the devil do you mean by dæmonic? It's
only a piece of gibberish I've invented to keep up a spark
of life in him. But for that, the poor harmless creature
would have succumbed to self-contempt and despair many a
long year ago. And then the old lieutenant! But he has
hit upon his own cure, you see.

GREGERS. Lieutenant Ekdal? What of him?

RELLING. Just think of the old bear-hunter shutting himself up in that dark garret to shoot rabbits! I tell you there
is not a happier sportsman in the world than that old man
pottering about in there among all that rubbish. The four
or five withered Christmas trees he has saved up are the same
to him as the whole great fresh Höidal forest; the cock and
the hens are big game-birds in the fir-tops; and the rabbits
that flop about the garret floor are the bears he has to battle
with—the mighty hunter of the mountains!

GREGERS. Poor unfortunate old man! Yes; he has indeed
had to narrow the ideals of his youth.

RELLING. While I think of it, Mr. Werle, junior—don't
use that foreign word: ideals. We have the excellent native
word: lies.

GREGERS. Do you think the two things are related?

RELLING. Yes, just about as closely as typhus and putrid
fever.

GREGERS. Dr. Relling, I shall not give up the struggle
until I have rescued Hialmar from your clutches!

RELLING. So much the worse for him. Rob the average
man of his life-illusion, and you rob him of his happiness at
the same stroke. (*To* HEDVIG, *who comes in from the sitting-
room.*) Well, little wild-duck-mother, I'm just going down

to see whether papa is still lying meditating upon that wonderful invention of his.   [*Goes out by passage door.*]

GREGERS (*approaches* HEDVIG). I can see by your face that you have not yet done it.

HEDVIG. What? Oh, that about the wild duck! No.

GREGERS. I suppose your courage failed when the time came.

HEDVIG. No, that wasn't it. But when I awoke this morning and remembered what we had been talking about, it seemed so strange.

GREGERS. Strange?

HEDVIG. Yes, I don't know—— Yesterday evening, at the moment, I thought there was something so delightful about it; but since I have slept and thought of it again, it somehow doesn't seem worth while.

GREGERS. Ah, I thought you could not have grown up quite unharmed in this house.

HEDVIG. I don't care about that, if only father would come up——

GREGERS. Oh, if only your eyes had been opened to that which gives life its value—if you possessed the true, joyous, fearless spirit of sacrifice, you would soon see how he would come up to you.—But I believe in you still, Hedvig.

[*He goes out by the passage door.* HEDVIG *wanders about the room for a time; she is on the point of going into the kitchen when a knock is heard at the garret door.* HEDVIG *goes over and opens it a little;* OLD EKDAL *comes out; she pushes the door to again.*]

EKDAL. H'm, it's not much fun to take one's morning walk alone.

HEDVIG. Wouldn't you like to go shooting, grandfather?

EKDAL. It's not the weather for it today. It's so dark there, you can scarcely see where you're going.

HEDVIG. Do you never want to shoot anything besides the rabbits?

EKDAL. Do you think the rabbits aren't good enough?

HEDVIG. Yes, but what about the wild duck?

EKDAL. Ho-ho! are you afraid I shall shoot your wild duck? Never in the world. Never.

HEDVIG. No, I suppose you couldn't; they say it's very difficult to shoot wild ducks.

EKDAL. Couldn't! Should rather think I could.

HEDVIG. How would you set about it, grandfather?—I don't mean with my wild duck, but with others?

EKDAL. I should take care to shoot them in the breast, you know; that's the surest place. And then you must shoot against the feathers, you see—not the way of the feathers.

HEDVIG. Do they die then, grandfather?

EKDAL. Yes, they die right enough—when you shoot properly. Well, I must go and brush up a bit. H'm— understand—h'm. [*Goes into his room.*]

[HEDVIG *waits a little, glances towards the sitting-room door, goes over to the book-case, stands on tip-toe, takes the double-barrelled pistol down from the shelf and looks at it.* GINA, *with brush and duster, comes from the sitting-room.* HEDVIG *hastily lays down the pistol, unobserved.*]

GINA. Don't stand raking amongst father's things, Hedvig.

HEDVIG (*goes away from the bookcase*). I was only going to tidy up a little.

GINA. You'd better go into the kitchen and see if the coffee's keeping hot; I'll take his breakfast on a tray, when I go down to him.

[HEDVIG *goes out.* GINA *begins to sweep and clean up the studio. Presently the passage door is opened with hesitation, and* HIALMAR EKDAL *looks in. He has on his overcoat, but not his hat; he is unwashed, and his hair is dishevelled and un-kempt. His eyes are dull and heavy.*]

GINA (*standing with the brush in her hand and looking at him*). Oh, there now, Ekdal—so you've come after all!

HIALMAR (*comes in and answers in a toneless voice*). I come —only to depart again immediately.

GINA. Yes, yes, I suppose so. But, Lord help us! what a sight you are!

HIALMAR. A sight?

GINA. And your nice winter coat, too! Well, that's done for.

HEDVIG (*at the kitchen door*). Mother, hadn't I better——? (*Sees* HIALMAR, *gives a loud scream of joy and runs to him.*) Oh, father, father!

HIALMAR (*turns away and makes a gesture of repulsion*). Away, away, away! (*To* GINA.) Keep her away from me, I say!

GINA (*in a low tone*). Go into the sitting-room, Hedvig.
[HEDVIG *does so without a word.*]

HIALMAR (*fussily pulls out the table-drawer*). I must have my books with me. Where are my books?

GINA. Which books?

HIALMAR. My scientific books, of course; the technical magazines I require for my invention.

GINA (*searches in the bookcase*). Is it these here paper-covered ones?

HIALMAR. Yes, of course.

GINA (*lays a heap of magazines on the table*). Shan't I get Hedvig to cut them for you?

HIALMAR. I don't require to have them cut for me.
[*Short silence.*]

GINA. Then you're still set on leaving us, Ekdal?

HIALMAR (*rummaging amongst the books*). Yes, that is a matter of course, I should think.

GINA. Well, well.

HIALMAR (*vehemently*). How can I live here, to be stabbed to the heart every hour of the day?

GINA. God forgive you for thinking such vile things of me.

HIALMAR. Prove——!

GINA. I think it's you as has got to prove.

HIALMAR. After a past like yours? There are certain claims—I may almost call them claims of the ideal——

GINA. But what about grandfather? What's to become of him, poor dear?

HIALMAR. I know my duty; my helpless father will come with me. I am going out into the town to make arrangements—— H'm—(*hesitatingly*)—has any one found my hat on the stairs?

GINA. No. Have you lost your hat?

HIALMAR. Of course I had it on when I came in last night; there's no doubt about that; but I couldn't find it this morning.

GINA. Lord help us! where have you been to with those two ne'er-do-wells?

HIALMAR. Oh, don't bother me about trifles. Do you suppose I am in the mood to remember details?

GINA. If only you haven't caught cold, Ekdal——

[*Goes out into the kitchen.*]

HIALMAR (*talks to himself in a low tone of irritation, while he empties the table-drawer*). You're a scoundrel, Relling! —You're a low fellow!—Ah, you shameless tempter!—I wish I could get some one to stick a knife into you!

[*He lays some old letters on one side, finds the torn document of yesterday, takes it up and looks at the pieces; puts it down hurriedly as* GINA *enters.*]

GINA (*sets a tray with coffee, etc., on the table*). Here's a drop of something hot, if you'd fancy it. And there's some bread and butter and a snack of salt meat.

HIALMAR (*glancing at the tray*). Salt meat? Never under this roof! It's true I have not had a mouthful of solid food for nearly twenty-four hours; but no matter.—My memoranda! The commencement of my autobiography! What has become of my diary, and all my important papers? (*Opens the sitting-room door but draws back.*) She is there, too!

GINA. Good Lord! the child must be somewhere!

HIALMAR. Come out.

[*He makes room;* HEDVIG *comes, scared, into the studio.*]

HIALMAR (*with his hand upon the door-handle, says to* GINA:) In these, the last moments I spend in my former home, I wish to be spared from interlopers——

[*Goes into the room.*]

HEDVIG (*with a bound towards her mother, asks softly, trembling*). Does that mean me?

GINA. Stay out in the kitchen, Hedvig; or, no—you'd best go into your own room. (*Speaks to* HIALMAR *as she goes in to him.*) Wait a bit, Ekdal; don't rummage so in the drawers; *I* know where everything is.

HEDVIG (*stands a moment immovable, in terror and perplexity, biting her lips to keep back the tears; then she clenches her hands convulsively and says softly:*) The wild duck.

[*She steals over and takes the pistol from the shelf, opens the garret door a little way, creeps in and draws the door to after her.* HIALMAR *and* GINA *can be heard disputing in the sitting-room.*]

HIALMAR (*comes in with some manuscript books and old loose papers, which he lays upon the table*). That portmanteau is of no use! There are a thousand and one things I must drag with me.

GINA (*following with the portmanteau*). Why not leave all the rest for the present and only take a shirt and a pair of woollen drawers with you?

HIALMAR. Whew!—all these exhausting preparations——!
[*Pulls off his overcoat and throws it upon the sofa.*]
GINA. And there's the coffee getting cold.
HIALMAR. H'm.
[*Drinks a mouthful without thinking of it and then another.*]
GINA (*dusting the backs of the chairs*). A nice job you'll have
to find such another big garret for the rabbits.
HIALMAR. What! Am I to drag all those rabbits with me,
too?
GINA. You don't suppose grandfather can get on with-
out his rabbits.
HIALMAR. He must just get used to doing without them.
Have not *I* to sacrifice very much greater things than rabbits?
GINA (*dusting the bookcase*). Shall I put the flute in the
portmanteau for you?
HIALMAR. No. No flute for me. But give me the pistol!
GINA. Do you want to take the pistol with you?
HIALMAR. Yes. My loaded pistol.
GINA (*searching for it*). It's gone. He must have taken
it in with him.
HIALMAR. Is he in the garret?
GINA. Yes, of course he's in the garret.
HIALMAR. H'm—poor lonely old man.
[*He takes a piece of bread and butter, eats it, and finishes his
cup of coffee.*]
GINA. If we hadn't have let that room, you could have
moved in there.
HIALMAR. And continued to live under the same roof
with——! Never,—never!
GINA. But couldn't you put up with the sitting-room for
a day or two? You could have it all to yourself.
HIALMAR. Never within these walls!
GINA. Well, then, down with Relling and Molvik.
HIALMAR. Don't mention those wretches' names to me!

The very thought of them almost takes away my appetite.—
Oh, no, I must go out into the storm and the snow-drift,—
go from house to house and seek shelter for my father and
myself.

GINA. But you've got no hat, Ekdal! You've been and
lost your hat, you know.

HIALMAR. Oh, those two brutes, those slaves of all the
vices! A hat must be procured. (*Takes another piece of
bread and butter.*) Some arrangements must be made. For
I have no mind to throw away my life, either.

[*Looks for something on the tray.*]

GINA. What are you looking for?

HIALMAR. Butter.

GINA. I'll get some at once.   [*Goes out into the kitchen.*]

HIALMAR (*calls after her*). Oh, it doesn't matter; dry
bread is good enough for me.

GINA (*brings a dish of butter*). Look here; this is fresh
churned.

[*She pours out another cup of coffee for him; he seats himself
on the sofa, spreads more butter on the already buttered bread
and eats and drinks awhile in silence.*]

HIALMAR. Could I, without being subject to intrusion—
intrusion of any sort—could I live in the sitting-room there
for a day or two?

GINA. Yes, to be sure you could, if you only would.

HIALMAR. For I see no possibility of getting all father's
things out in such a hurry.

GINA. And, besides, you've surely got to tell him first
as you don't mean to live with us others no more.

HIALMAR (*pushes away his coffee cup*). Yes, there is that,
too; I shall have to lay bare the whole tangled story to
him—— I must turn matters over; I must have breathing-
time; I cannot take all these burdens on my shoulders in a
single day.

GINA. No, especially in such horrible weather as it is outside.

HIALMAR (*touching* WERLE's *letter*). I see that paper is still lying about here.

GINA. Yes, *I* haven't touched it.

HIALMAR. So far as I am concerned it is mere waste paper——

GINA. Well, *I* have certainly no notion of making any use of it.

HIALMAR. ——but we had better not let it get lost all the same;—in all the upset when I move, it might easily——

GINA. I'll take good care of it, Ekdal.

HIALMAR. The donation is in the first instance made to father, and it rests with him to accept or decline it.

GINA (*sighs*). Yes, poor old father——

HIALMAR. To make quite safe—— Where shall I find some gum?

GINA (*goes to the bookcase*). Here's the gum-pot.

HIALMAR. And a brush?

GINA. The brush is here, too.   [*Brings him the things.*]

HIALMAR (*takes a pair of scissors*). Just a strip of paper at the back——(*clips and gums.*) Far be it from me to lay hands upon what is not my own—and least of all upon what belongs to a destitute old man—and to—the other as well.— There now. Let it lie there for a time; and when it is dry, take it away. I wish never to see that document again. Never!   [GREGERS WERLE *enters from the passage.*]

GREGERS (*somewhat surprised*). What,—are you sitting here, Hialmar?

HIALMAR (*rises hurriedly*). I had sunk down from fatigue.

GREGERS. You have been having breakfast, I see.

HIALMAR. The body sometimes makes its claims felt, too.

GREGERS. What have you decided to do?

HIALMAR. For a man like me, there is only one course

possible. I am just putting my most important things together. But it takes time, you know.

GINA (*with a touch of impatience*). Am I to get the room
ready for you, or am I to pack your portmanteau?

HIALMAR (*after a glance of annoyance at* GREGERS). Pack
—and get the room ready!

GINA (*takes the portmanteau*). Very well; then I'll put
in the shirt and the other things.

[*Goes into the sitting-room and draws the door to after her.*]

GREGERS (*after a short silence*). I never dreamed that this
would be the end of it. Do you really feel it a necessity to
leave house and home?

HIALMAR (*wanders about restlessly*). What would you
have me do?—I am not fitted to bear unhappiness, Gregers.
I must feel secure and at peace in my surroundings.

GREGERS. But can you not feel that here? Just try it. I
should have thought you had firm ground to build upon
now—if only you start afresh. And, remember, you have
your invention to live for.

HIALMAR. Oh, don't talk about my invention. It's perhaps still in the dim distance.

GREGERS. Indeed!

HIALMAR. Why, great heavens, what would you have me
invent? Other people have invented almost everything already. It becomes more and more difficult every day——

GREGERS. And you have devoted so much labor to it.

HIALMAR. It was that blackguard Relling that urged me
to it.

GREGERS. Relling?

HIALMAR. Yes, it was he that first made me realize my
aptitude for making some notable discovery in photography.

GREGERS. Aha—it was Relling!

HIALMAR. Oh, I have been so truly happy over it! Not
so much for the sake of the invention itself, as because

Hedvig believed in it—believed in it with a child's whole eagerness of faith.—At least, I have been fool enough to go and imagine that she believed in it.

GREGERS. Can you really think Hedvig has been false towards you?

HIALMAR. I can think anything now. It is Hedvig that stands in my way. She will blot out the sunlight from my whole life.

GREGERS. Hedvig! Is it Hedvig you are talking of? How should she blot out your sunlight?

HIALMAR (*without answering*). How unutterably I have loved that child! How unutterably happy I have felt every time I came home to my humble room, and she flew to meet me, with her sweet little blinking eyes. Oh, confiding fool that I have been! I loved her unutterably;—and I yielded myself up to the dream, the delusion, that she loved me unutterably in return.

GREGERS. Do you call that a delusion?

HIALMAR. How should I know? I can get nothing out of Gina; and besides, she is totally blind to the ideal side of these complications. But to you I feel impelled to open my mind, Gregers. I cannot shake off this frightful doubt—perhaps Hedvig has never really and honestly loved me.

GREGERS. What would you say if she were to give you a proof of her love? (*Listens.*) What's that? I thought I heard the wild duck——?

HIALMAR. It's the wild duck quacking. Father's in the garret.

GREGERS. Is he? (*His face lights up with joy.*) I say, you may yet have proof that your poor misunderstood Hedvig loves you!

HIALMAR. Oh, what proof can she give me? I dare not believe in any assurance from that quarter.

GREGERS. Hedvig does not know what deceit means.

HIALMAR. Oh, Gregers, that is just what I cannot be sure of Who knows what Gina and that Mrs. Sörby may many a time have sat here whispering and tattling about? And Hedvig usually has her ears open, I can tell you. Perhaps the deed of gift was not such a surprise to her, after all. In fact, I'm not sure but that I noticed something of the sort.

GREGERS. What spirit is this that has taken possession of you?

HIALMAR. I have had my eyes opened. Just you notice; —you'll see, the deed of gift is only a beginning. Mrs. Sörby has always been a good deal taken up with Hedvig, and now she has the power to do whatever she likes for the child. They can take her from me whenever they please.

GREGERS. Hedvig will never, never leave you.

HIALMAR. Don't be so sure of that. If only they beckon to her and throw out a golden bait——! And, oh! I have loved her so unspeakably! I would have counted it my highest happiness to take her tenderly by the hand and lead her, as one leads a timid child through a great dark empty room!—I am cruelly certain now that the poor photographer in his humble attic has never really and truly been anything to her. She has only cunningly contrived to keep on a good footing with him until the time came.

GREGERS. You don't believe that yourself, Hialmar.

HIALMAR. That is just the terrible part of it—I don't know what to believe,—I never can know it. But can you really doubt that it must be as I say? Ho-ho, you have far too much faith in the claim of the ideal, my good Gregers! If those others came, with the glamour of wealth about them, and called to the child:—"Leave him: come to us: here life awaits you——!"

GREGERS (quickly). Well, what then?

HIALMAR. If I then asked her: Hedvig, are you willing to renounce that life for me? (Laughs scornfully.) No thank you! You would soon hear what answer I should get.   [*A pistol shot is heard from within the garret.*]

GREGERS (*loudly and joyfully*). Hialmar!

HIALMAR. There now; he must needs go shooting, too.

GINA (*comes in*). Oh, Ekdal, I can hear grandfather blazing away in the garret by hisself.

HIALMAR. I'll look in——

GREGERS (*eagerly, with emotion*). Wait a moment! Do you know what that was?

HIALMAR. Yes, of course I know.

GREGERS. No, you don't know. But *I* do. That was the proof!

HIALMAR. What proof?

GREGERS. It was a child's free-will offering. She has got your father to shoot the wild duck.

HIALMAR. To shoot the wild duck!

GINA. Oh, think of that——!

HIALMAR. What was that for?

GREGERS. She wanted to sacrifice to you her most cherished possession; for then she thought you would surely come to love her again.

HIALMAR (*tenderly, with emotion*). Oh, poor child!

GINA. What things she does think of!

GREGERS. She only wanted your love again, Hialmar. She could not live without it.

GINA (*struggling with her tears*). There, you can see for yourself, Ekdal.

HIALMAR. Gina, where is she?

GINA (*sniffs*). Poor dear, she's sitting out in the kitchen, I dare say.

HIALMAR (*goes over, tears open the kitchen door and says:*) Hedvig, come, come in to me! (*Looks around.*) No, she's not here.

GINA. Then she must be in her own little room.

HIALMAR (*without*). No, she's not here either. (*Comes in.*)
She must have gone out.

GINA. Yes, you wouldn't have her anywheres in the
house.

HIALMAR. Oh, if she would only come home quickly, so
that I can tell her—— Everything will come right now,
Gregers; now I believe we can begin life afresh.

GREGERS (*quietly*). I knew it; I knew the child would
make amends.

[OLD EKDAL *appears at the door of his room; he is in full
uniform and is busy buckling on his sword.*]

HIALMAR (*astonished*). Father! Are you there?

GINA. Have you been firing in your room?

EKDAL (*resentfully, approaching*). So you go shooting
alone, do you, Hialmar?

HIALMAR (*excited and confused*). Then it wasn't you that
fired that shot in the garret?

EKDAL. Me that fired? H'm.

GREGERS (*calls out to* HIALMAR). She has shot the wild
duck herself!

HIALMAR. What can it mean? (*Hastens to the garret door,
tears it aside, looks in and calls loudly:*) Hedvig!

GINA (*runs to the door*). Good God, what's that?

HIALMAR (*goes in*). She's lying on the floor!

GREGERS. Hedvig! lying on the floor?

[*Goes in to* HIALMAR.]

GINA (*at the same time*). Hedvig! (*Inside the garret.*) No,
no, no!

EKDAL. Ho-ho! does she go shooting, too, now?

[HIALMAR, GINA, *and* GREGERS *carry* HEDVIG *into the studio;
in her dangling right hand she holds the pistol fast clasped in
her fingers.*]

HIALMAR (*distracted*). The pistol has gone off. She has
wounded herself. Call for help! Help!

GINA (*runs into the passage and calls down*). Relling! Relling! Doctor Relling; come up as quick as you can!

[HIALMAR *and* GREGERS *lay* HEDVIG *down on the sofa.*]

EKDAL (*quietly*). The woods avenge themselves.

HIALMAR (*on his knees beside* HEDVIG). She'll soon come to now. She's coming to——; yes, yes, yes.

GINA (*who has come in again*). Where has she hurt herself? I can't see anything——

[RELLING *comes hurriedly, and immediately after him* MOLVIK; *the latter without his waistcoat and necktie, and with his coat open.*]

RELLING. What's the matter here?

GINA. They say Hedvig has shot herself.

HIALMAR. Come and help us!

RELLING. Shot herself!

[*He pushes the table aside and begins to examine her.*]

HIALMAR (*kneeling and looking anxiously up at him*). It can't be dangerous? Speak, Relling! She is scarcely bleeding at all. It can't be dangerous?

RELLING. How did it happen?

HIALMAR. Oh, we don't know——

GINA. She wanted to shoot the wild duck.

RELLING. The wild duck?

HIALMAR. The pistol must have gone off.

RELLING. H'm. Indeed.

EKDAL. The woods avenge themselves. But I'm not afraid, all the same.

[*Goes into the garret and closes the door after him.*]

HIALMAR. Well, Relling,—why don't you say something?

RELLING. The ball has entered the breast.

HIALMAR. Yes, but she's coming to!

RELLING. Surely you can see that Hedvig is dead.

GINA (*bursts into tears*). Oh, my child, my child——

GREGERS (*huskily*). In the depths of the sea——

HIALMAR (*jumps up*). No, no, she must live! Oh, for God's sake, Relling—only a moment—only just till I can tell her how unspeakably I loved her all the time!

RELLING. The bullet has gone through her heart. Internal hemorrhage. Death must have been instantaneous.

HIALMAR. And I! I hunted her from me like an animal! And she crept terrified into the garret and died for love of me! (*Sobbing.*) I can never atone to her! I can never tell her——! (*Clenches his hands and cries, upwards.*) O thou above——! If thou be indeed! Why hast thou done this thing to me?

GINA. Hush, hush, you mustn't go on that awful way. We had no right to keep her, I suppose.

MOLVIK. The child is not dead, but sleepeth.

RELLING. Bosh.

HIALMAR (*becomes calm, goes over to the sofa, folds his arms and looks at* HEDVIG). There she lies so stiff and still.

RELLING (*tries to loosen the pistol*). She's holding it so tight, so tight.

GINA. No, no, Relling, don't break her fingers; let the pistol be.

HIALMAR. She shall take it with her.

GINA. Yes, let her. But the child mustn't lie here for a show. She shall go to her own room, so she shall. Help me, Ekdal. [HIALMAR *and* GINA *take* HEDVIG *between them.*]

HIALMAR (*as they are carrying her*). Oh, Gina, Gina, can you survive this?

GINA. We must help each other to bear it. For now at least she belongs to both of us.

MOLVIK (*stretches out his arms and mumbles*). Blessed be the Lord; to earth thou shalt return; to earth thou shalt return——

RELLING (*whispers*). Hold your tongue, you fool; you're drunk.

[HIALMAR *and* GINA *carry the body out through the kitchen door.* RELLING *shuts it after them.* MOLVIK *slinks out into the passage.*]

RELLING (*goes over to* GREGERS *and says:*) No one shall ever convince me that the pistol went off by accident.

GREGERS (*who has stood terrified, with convulsive twitchings*). Who can say how the dreadful thing happened?

RELLING. The powder has burnt the body of her dress. She must have pressed the pistol right against her breast and fired.

GREGERS. Hedvig has not died in vain. Did you not see how sorrow set free what is noble in him?

RELLING. Most people are ennobled by the actual presence of death. But how long do you suppose this nobility will last in him?

GREGERS. Why should it not endure and increase throughout his life?

RELLING. Before a year is over, little Hedvig will be nothing to him but a pretty theme for declamation.

GREGERS. How dare you say that of Hialmar Ekdal?

RELLING. We will talk of this again, when the grass has first withered on her grave. Then you'll hear him spouting about "the child too early torn from her father's heart;" then you'll see him steep himself in a syrup of sentiment and self-admiration and self-pity. Just you wait!

GREGERS. If you are right and I am wrong, then life is not worth living.

RELLING. Oh, life would be quite tolerable, after all, if only we could be rid of the confounded duns that keep on pestering us, in our poverty, with the claim of the ideal.

GREGERS (*looking straight before him*). In that case, I am glad that my destiny is what is.

RELLING. May I inquire,—what is your destiny?

GREGERS (*going*). To be the thirteenth at table.

RELLING. The devil it is.

CURTAIN

HEDDA GABLER

[*1 8 9 0*]

CHARACTERS

GEORGE TESMAN, *research graduate in cultural history*
HEDDA, *his wife*
MISS JULIANA TESMAN, *his aunt*
MRS. ELVSTED
JUDGE BRACK
EILERT LOEVBORG
BERTHA, *a maid*

The action takes place in TESMAN'S *villa in the fashionable quarter of town.*

HEDDA GABLER

ACT ONE

*A large drawing room, handsomely and tastefully furnished;
decorated in dark colors. In the rear wall is a broad open
doorway, with curtains drawn back to either side. It leads
to a smaller room, decorated in the same style as the drawing room. In the right-hand wall of the drawing room, a
folding door leads out to the hall. The opposite wall, on the
left, contains french windows, also with curtains drawn back
on either side. Through the glass we can see part of a ve-
randah, and trees in autumn colors. Downstage stands an
oval table, covered by a cloth and surrounded by chairs.
Downstage right, against the wall, is a broad stove tiled with
dark porcelain; in front of it stand a high-backed armchair,
a cushioned footrest, and two footstools. Upstage right, in
an alcove, is a corner sofa, with a small, round table. Downstage left, a little away from the wall, is another sofa. Upstage of the french windows, a piano. On either side of the
open doorway in the rear wall stand what-nots holding orna-
ments of terra cotta and majolica. Against the rear wall of
the smaller room can be seen a sofa, a table, and a couple
of chairs. Above this sofa hangs the portrait of a handsome
old man in general's uniform. Above the table a lamp hangs
from the ceiling, with a shade of opalescent, milky glass.
All round the drawing room bunches of flowers stand in
vases and glasses. More bunches lie on the tables. The floors
of both rooms are covered with thick carpets. Morning light.
The sun shines in through the french windows.*

[MISS JULIANA TESMAN, *wearing a hat and carrying a parasol,*
enters from the hall, followed by BERTHA, *who is carrying a*
bunch of flowers wrapped in paper. MISS TESMAN *is about*
sixty-five, of pleasant and kindly appearance. She is neatly
but simply dressed in grey outdoor clothes. BERTHA, *the maid,*
is rather simple and rustic-looking. She is getting on in years.]

MISS TESMAN (*stops just inside the door, listens and says in*
a hushed voice). No, bless my soul! They're not up yet.

BERTHA (*also in hushed tones*). What did I tell you, miss?
The boat didn't get in till midnight. And when they did
turn up—Jesus, miss, you should have seen all the things
Madam made me unpack before she'd go to bed!

MISS TESMAN. Ah, well. Let them have a good lie in. But
let's have some nice fresh air waiting for them when they do
come down. [*Goes to the french windows and throws them wide*
open.]

BERTHA (*bewildered at the table, the bunch of flowers in her*
hand). I'm blessed if there's a square inch left to put anything. I'll have to let it lie here, miss. [*Puts it on the piano.*]

MISS TESMAN. Well, Bertha dear, so now you have a new
mistress. Heaven knows it nearly broke my heart to have to
part with you.

BERTHA (*snivels*). What about me, Miss Juju? How do you
suppose I felt? After all the happy years I've spent with you
and Miss Rena?

MISS TESMAN. We must accept it bravely, Bertha. It was
the only way. George needs you to take care of him. He
could never manage without you. You've looked after him
ever since he was a tiny boy.

BERTHA. Oh, but, Miss Juju, I can't help thinking about
Miss Rena, lying there all helpless, poor dear. And that new
girl! She'll never learn the proper way to handle an invalid.

MISS TESMAN. Oh, I'll manage to train her. I'll do most of
the work myself, you know. You needn't worry about my
poor sister, Bertha dear.

BERTHA. But Miss Juju, there's another thing. I'm frightened Madam may not find me suitable.

MISS TESMAN. Oh, nonsense, Bertha. There may be one or two little things to begin with—

BERTHA. She's a real lady. Wants everything just so.

MISS TESMAN. But of course she does! General Gabler's daughter! Think of what she was accustomed to when the General was alive. You remember how we used to see her out riding with her father? In that long black skirt? With the feather in her hat?

BERTHA. Oh, yes, miss. As if I could forget! But, Lord! I never dreamed I'd live to see a match between her and Master Georgie.

MISS TESMAN. Neither did I. By the way, Bertha, from now on you must stop calling him Master Georgie. You must say: Dr. Tesman.

BERTHA. Yes, Madam said something about that too. Last night—the moment they's set foot inside the door. Is it true, then, miss?

MISS TESMAN. Indeed it is. Just imagine, Bertha, some foreigners have made him a doctor. It happened while they were away. I had no idea till he told me when they got off the boat.

BERTHA. Well, I suppose there's no limit to what he won't become. He's that clever. I never thought he'd go in for hospital work, though.

MISS TESMAN. No, he's not that kind of doctor. [*Nods impressively.*] In any case, you may soon have to address him by an even grander title.

BERTHA. You don't say! What might that be, miss?

MISS TESMAN (*smiles*). Ah! If you only knew! [*Moved.*] Dear God, if only poor dear Joachim could rise out of his grave and see what his little son has grown into! [*Looks round.*] But Bertha, why have you done this? Taken the chintz covers off all the furniture!

BERTHA. Madam said I was to. Can't stand chintz covers on chairs, she said.

MISS TESMAN. But surely they're not going to use this room as a parlor?

BERTHA. So I gathered, miss. From what Madam said. He didn't say anything. The Doctor.

[GEORGE TESMAN *comes into the rear room, from the right, humming, with an open, empty travelling bag in his hand. He is about thirty-three, of medium height and youthful appearance, rather plump, with an open, round, contented face, and fair hair and beard. He wears spectacles, and is dressed in comfortable, indoor clothes.*]

MISS TESMAN. Good morning! Good morning, George!

TESMAN (*in open doorway*). Auntie Juju! Dear Auntie Juju! [*Comes forward and shakes her hand.*] You've come all the way out here! And so early! What?

MISS TESMAN. Well, I had to make sure you'd settled in confortably.

TESMAN. But you can't have had a proper night's sleep.

MISS TESMAN. Oh, never mind that.

TESMAN. We were so sorry we couldn't give you a lift. But you saw how it was—Hedda had so much luggage—and she insisted on having it all with her.

MISS TESMAN. Yes, I've never seen so much luggage.

BERTHA, *to* TESMAN. Shall I go and ask Madam if there's anything I can lend her a hand with?

TESMAN. Er—thank you, Bertha; no, you needn't bother. She says if she wants you for anything she'll ring.

BERTHA (*over to right*). Oh. Very good.

TESMAN. Oh, Bertha—take this bag, will you?

BERTHA (*takes it*). I'll put it in the attic. [*Goes out into the hall.*]

TESMAN. Just fancy, Auntie Juju, I filled that whole bag with notes for my book. You know, it's really incredible what I've managed to find rooting through those archives.

By Jove! Wonderful old things no one even knew existed—

MISS TESMAN. I'm sure you didn't waste a single moment of your honeymoon, George dear.

TESMAN. No, I think I can truthfully claim that. But, Auntie Juju, do take your hat off. Here. Let me untie it for you. What?

MISS TESMAN (*as he does so*). Oh dear, oh dear! It's just as if you were still living at home with us.

TESMAN (*turns the hat in his hand and looks at it*). I say! What a splendid new hat!

MISS TESMAN. I bought it for Hedda's sake.

TESMAN. For Hedda's sake? What?

MISS TESMAN. So that Hedda needn't be ashamed of me, in case we ever go for a walk together.

TESMAN (*pats her cheek*). You still think of everything, don't you. Auntie Juju? [*Puts the hat down on a chair by the table.*] Come on, let's sit down here on the sofa. And have a little chat while we wait for Hedda. [*They sit. She puts her parasol in the corner of the sofa.*]

MISS TESMAN (*clasps both his hands and looks at him*). Oh, George, it's so wonderful to have you back, and be able to see you with my own eyes again! Poor dear Joachim's own son!

TESMAN. What about me! It's wonderful for me to see you again, Auntie Juju. You've been a mother to me. And a father, too.

MISS TESMAN. You'll always keep a soft spot in your heart for your old aunties, won't you, George dear?

TESMAN. I suppose Auntie Rena's no better? What?

MISS TESMAN. Alas, no. I'm afraid she'll never get better, poor dear. She's lying there just as she has for all these years. Please God I may be allowed to keep her for a little longer. If I lost her I don't know what I'd do. Especially now I haven't you to look after.

TESMAN (*pats her on the back*). There, there, there!

MISS TESMAN (*with a sudden change of mood*). Oh but George, fancy you being a married man! And to think it's you who've won Hedda Gabler! The beautiful Hedda Gabler! Fancy! She was always so surrounded by admirers.

TESMAN (*hums a little and smiles contentedly*). Yes, I suppose there are quite a few people in this town who wouldn't mind being in my shoes. What?

MISS TESMAN. And what a honeymoon! Five months! Nearly six.

TESMAN. Well, I've done a lot of work, you know. All those archives to go through. And I've had to read lots of books.

MISS TESMAN. Yes, dear, of course. [*Lowers her voice confidentially.*] But tell me, George—haven't you any—any extra little piece of news to give me?

TESMAN. You mean, arising out of the honeymoon?

MISS TESMAN. Yes.

TESMAN. No, I don't think there's anything I didn't tell you in my letters. My doctorate, of course—but I told you about that last night, didn't I?

MISS TESMAN. Yes, yes, I didn't mean that kind of thing. I was just wondering—are you—are you expecting—?

TESMAN. Expecting what?

MISS TESMAN. Oh, come on George, I'm your old aunt!

TESMAN. Well actually—yes, I am expecting something.

MISS TESMAN. I knew it!

TESMAN. You'll be happy to hear that before very long I expect to become a professor.

MISS TESMAN. Professor?

TESMAN. I think I may say that the matter has been decided. But, Auntie Juju, you know about this.

MISS TESMAN (*gives a little laugh*). Yes, of course. I'd forgotten. [*Changes her tone.*] But we were talking about your honeymoon. It must have cost a dreadful amount of money, George?

TESMAN. Oh well, you know, that big research grant I got helped a good deal.

MISS TESMAN. But how on earth did you manage to make it do for two?

TESMAN. Well, to tell the truth it was a bit tricky. What?

MISS TESMAN. Especially when one's travelling with a lady. A little bird tells me that makes things very much more expensive.

TESMAN. Well, yes, of course it does make things a little more expensive. But Hedda has to do things in style, Auntie Juju. I mean, she has to. Anything less grand wouldn't have suited her.

MISS TESMAN. No, no, I suppose not. A honeymoon abroad seems to be the vogue nowadays. But tell me, have you had time to look round the house?

TESMAN. You bet. I've been up since the crack of dawn.

MISS TESMAN. Well, what do you think of it?

TESMAN. Splendid. Absolutely splendid. I'm only wondering what we're going to do with those two empty rooms between that little one and Hedda's bedroom.

MISS TESMAN (*laughs slyly*). Ah, George dear, I'm sure you'll manage to find some use for them—in time.

TESMAN. Yes, of course, Auntie Juju, how stupid of me. You're thinking of my books. What?

MISS TESMAN. Yes, yes, dear boy. I was thinking of your books.

TESMAN. You know, I'm so happy for Hedda's sake that we've managed to get this house. Before we became engaged she often used to say this was the only house in town she felt she could really bear to live in. It used to belong to Mrs. Falk—you know, the Prime Minister's widow.

MISS TESMAN. Fancy that! And what a stroke of luck it happened to come into the market. Just as you'd left on your honeymoon.

TESMAN. Yes, Auntie Juju, we've certainly had all the luck with us. What?

MISS TESMAN. But, George dear, the expense! It's going to make a dreadful hole in your pocket, all this.

TESMAN (*a little downcast*). Yes, I—I suppose it will, won't it?

MISS TESMAN. Oh, George, really!

TESMAN. How much do you think it'll cost? Roughly, I mean? What?

MISS TESMAN. I can't possibly say till I see the bills.

TESMAN. Well, luckily Judge Brack's managed to get it on very favorable terms. He wrote and told Hedda so.

MISS TESMAN. Don't you worry, George dear. Anyway I've stood security for all the furniture and carpets.

TESMAN. Security? But dear, sweet Auntie Juju, how could you possibly stand security?

MISS TESMAN. I've arranged a mortage on our annuity.

TESMAN (*jumps up*). What? On your annuity? And— Auntie Rena's?

MISS TESMAN. Yes. Well, I couldn't think of any other way.

TESMAN (*stands in front of her*). Auntie Juju, have you gone completely out of your mind? That annuity's all you and Auntie Rena have.

MISS TESMAN. All right, there's no need to get so excited about it. It's a pure formality, you know. Judge Brack told me so. He was so kind as to arrange it all for me. A pure formality; those were his very words.

TESMAN. I dare say. All the same—

MISS TESMAN. Anyway, you'll have a salary of your own now. And, good heavens, even if we did have to fork out a little—tighten our belts for a week or two—why, we'd be happy to do so for your sake.

TESMAN. Oh, Auntie Juju! Will you never stop sacrificing yourself for me?

MISS TESMAN (*gets up and puts her hands on his shoulders*).

What else have I to live for but to smooth your road a little, my dear boy? You've never had any mother or father to turn to. And now at last we've achieved our goal. I won't deny we've had our little difficulties now and then. But now, thank the good Lord, George dear, all your worries are past.

TESMAN. Yes, it's wonderful really how everything's gone just right for me.

MISS TESMAN. Yes! And the enemies who tried to bar your way have been struck down. They have been made to bite the dust. The man who was your most dangerous rival has had the mightiest fall. And now he's lying there in the pit he dug for himself, poor misguided creature.

TESMAN. Have you heard any news of Eilert? Since I went away?

MISS TESMAN. Only that he's said to have published a new book.

TESMAN. What! Eilert Loevborg? You mean—just recently? What?

MISS TESMAN. So they say. I don't imagine it can be of any value, do you? When your new book comes out, that'll be another story. What's it going to be about?

TESMAN. The domestic industries of Brabant in the Middle Ages.

MISS TESMAN. Oh George! The things you know about!

TESMAN. Mind you, it may be some time before I actually get down to writing it. I've made these very extensive notes, and I've got to file and index them first.

MISS TESMAN. Ah, yes! Making notes; filing and indexing; you've always been wonderful at that. Poor dear Joachim was just the same.

TESMAN. I'm looking forward so much to getting down to that. Especially now I've a home of my own to work in.

MISS TESMAN. And above all, now that you have the girl you set your heart on, George dear.

TESMAN (*embraces her*). Oh, yes, Auntie Juju, yes! Hedda's the loveliest thing of all! [*Looks towards the doorway.*] I think I hear her coming. What?

[HEDDA *enters the rear room from the left, and comes into the drawing room. She is a woman of twenty-nine. Distinguished, aristocratic face and figure. Her complexion is pale and opalescent. Her eyes are steel-grey, with an expression of cold, calm serenity. Her hair is of a handsome auburn color, but is not especially abundant. She is dressed in an elegant, somewhat loose-fitting morning gown.*]

MISS TESMAN (*goes to greet her*). Good morning, Hedda dear! Good morning!

HEDDA (*holds out her hand*). Good morning, dear Miss Tesman. What an early hour to call. So kind of you.

MISS TESMAN (*seems somewhat embarrassed*). And has the young bride slept well in her new home?

HEDDA. Oh—thank you, yes. Passably well.

TESMAN (*laughs*). Passably. I say, Hedda, that's good! When I jumped out of bed, you were sleeping like a top.

HEDDA. Yes. Fortunately. One has to accustom oneself to anything new, Miss Tesman. It takes time. [*Looks left.*] Oh, that maid's left the french windows open. This room's flooded with sun.

MISS TESMAN (*goes towards the windows*). Oh—let me close them.

HEDDA. No, no, don't do that. Tesman dear, draw the curtains. This light's blinding me.

TESMAN (*at the windows*). Yes, yes, dear. There, Hedda, now you've got shade and fresh air.

HEDDA. This room needs fresh air. All these flowers—But my dear Miss Tesman, won't you take a seat?

MISS TESMAN. No, really not, thank you. I just wanted to make sure you have everything you need. I must see about getting back home. My poor dear sister will be waiting for me.

TESMAN. Be sure to give her my love, won't you? Tell her I'll run over and see her later today.

MISS TESMAN. Oh yes, I'll tell her that. Oh, George— [*Fumbles in the pocket of her skirt.*] I almost forgot. I've brought something for you.

TESMAN. What's that, Auntie Juju? What?

MISS TESMAN (*pulls out a flat package wrapped in newspaper and gives it to him*). Open and see, dear boy.

TESMAN (*opens the package*). Good heavens! Auntie Juju, you've kept them! Hedda, this is really very touching. What?

HEDDA (*by the what-not on the right*). What is it, Tesman?

TESMAN. My old shoes! My slippers, Hedda!

HEDDA. Oh, them. I remember you kept talking about them on our honeymoon.

TESMAN. Yes, I missed them dreadfully. [*Goes over to her.*] Here, Hedda, take a look.

HEDDA (*goes away towards the stove*). Thanks, I won't bother.

TESMAN (*follows her*). Fancy, Hedda, Auntie Rena's embroidered them for me. Despite her being so ill. Oh, you can't imagine what memories they have for me.

HEDDA (*by the table*). Not for me.

MISS TESMAN. No, Hedda's right there, George.

TESMAN. Yes, but I thought since she's one of the family now—

HEDDA (*interrupts*). Tesman, we really can't go on keeping this maid.

MISS TESMAN. Not keep Bertha?

TESMAN. What makes you say that, dear? What?

HEDDA (*points*). Look at that! She's left her old hat lying on the chair.

TESMAN (*appalled, drops his slippers on the floor*). But, Hedda—!

HEDDA. Suppose someone came in and saw it?

TESMAN. But Hedda—that's Auntie Juju's hat.

HEDDA. Oh?

MISS TESMAN (*picks up the hat*). Indeed it's mine. And it doesn't happen to be old, Hedda dear.

HEDDA. I didn't look at it very closely, Miss Tesman.

MISS TESMAN (*trying on the hat*). As a matter of fact, it's the first time I've worn it. As the good Lord is my witness.

TESMAN. It's very pretty, too. Really smart.

MISS TESMAN. Oh, I'm afraid it's nothing much really. [*Looks round.*] My parasol? Ah, here it is. [*Takes it.*] This is mine, too. [*Murmurs.*] Not Bertha's.

TESMAN. A new hat and a new parasol! I say, Hedda, fancy that!

HEDDA. Very pretty and charming.

TESMAN. Yes, isn't it? What? But Auntie Juju, take a good look at Hedda before you go. Isn't she pretty and charming?

MISS TESMAN. Dear boy, there's nothing new in that. Hedda's been a beauty ever since the day she was born. [*Nods and goes right.*]

TESMAN (*follows her*). Yes, but have you noticed how strong and healthy she's looking? And how she's filled out since we went away?

MISS TESMAN (*stops and turns*). Filled out?

HEDDA (*walks across the room*). Oh, can't we forget it?

TESMAN. Yes, Auntie Juju—you can't see it so clearly with that dress on. But I've good reason to know—

HEDDA (*by the french windows, impatiently*). You haven't good reason to know anything.

TESMAN. It must have been the mountain air up there in the Tyrol—

HEDDA (*curtly, interrupts him*). I'm exactly the same as when I went away.

TESMAN. You keep on saying so. But you're not. I'm right, aren't I, Auntie Juju?

MISS TESMAN (*has folded her hands and is gazing at her*). She's beautiful—beautiful. Hedda is beautiful. [*Goes over to* HEDDA, *takes her head between her hands, draws it down and kisses her hair.*] God bless and keep you, Hedda Tesman. For George's sake.

HEDDA (*frees herself politely*). Oh—let me go, please.

MISS TESMAN (*quietly, emotionally*). I shall come and see you both every day.

TESMAN. Yes, Auntie Juju, please do. What?

MISS TESMAN. Good-bye! Good-bye!

[*She goes out into the hall.* TESMAN *follows her. The door remains open.* TESMAN *is heard sending his love to* AUNT RENA *and thanking* MISS TESMAN *for his slippers. Meanwhile* HEDDA *walks up and down the room raising her arms and clenching her fists as though in desperation. Then she throws aside the curtains from the french windows and stands there, looking out. A few moments later,* TESMAN *returns and closes the door behind him.*]

TESMAN (*picks up his slippers from the floor*). What are you looking at, Hedda?

HEDDA (*calm and controlled again*). Only the leaves. They're so golden. And withered.

TESMAN (*wraps up the slippers and lays them on the table*). Well, we're in September now.

HEDDA (*restless again*). Yes. We're already into September.

TESMAN. Auntie Juju was behaving rather oddly, I thought, didn't you? Almost as though she was in church or something. I wonder what came over her. Any idea?

HEDDA. I hardly know her. Does she often act like that?

TESMAN. Not to the extent she did today.

HEDDA (*goes away from the french windows*). Do you think she was hurt by what I said about the hat?

TESMAN. Oh, I don't think so. A little at first, perhaps—

HEDDA. But what a thing to do, throw her hat down in someone's drawing room. People don't do such things.

TESMAN. I'm sure Auntie Juju doesn't do it very often.

HEDDA. Oh well, I'll make it up with her.

TESMAN. Oh Hedda, would you?

HEDDA. When you see them this afternoon invite her to come out here this evening.

TESMAN. You bet I will! I say, there's another thing which would please her enormously.

HEDDA. Oh?

TESMAN. If you could bring yourself to call her Auntie Juju. For my sake, Hedda? What?

HEDDA. Oh no, really Tesman, you mustn't ask me to do that. I've told you so once before. I'll try to call her Aunt Juliana. That's as far as I'll go.

TESMAN (*after a moment*). I say, Hedda, is anything wrong? What?

HEDDA. I'm just looking at my old piano. It doesn't really go with all this.

TESMAN. As soon as I start getting my salary we'll see about changing it.

HEDDA. No, no, don't let's change it. I don't want to part with it. We can move it into that little room and get another one to put in here.

TESMAN (*a little downcast*). Yes, we—might do that.

HEDDA (*picks up the bunch of flowers from the piano*). These flowers weren't here when we arrived last night.

TESMAN. I expect Auntie Juju brought them.

HEDDA. Here's a card. [*Takes it out and reads.*] "Will come back later today." Guess who it's from?

TESMAN. No idea. Who? What?

HEDDA. It says: "Mrs. Elvsted."

TESMAN. No, really? Mrs. Elvsted! She used to be Miss Rysing, didn't she?

HEDDA. Yes, She was the one with that irritating hair she was always showing off. I hear she used to be an old flame of yours.

TESMAN (*laughs*). That didn't last long. Anyway, that was before I got to know you, Hedda. By Jove, fancy her being in town!

HEDDA. Strange she should call. I only knew her at school.

TESMAN. Yes, I haven't seen her for—oh, heaven knows how long. I don't know how she manages to stick it out up there in the north. What?

HEDDA (*thinks for a moment, then says suddenly*). Tell me, Tesman, doesn't he live somewhere up in those parts? You know—Eilert Loevborg?

TESMAN. Yes, that's right. So he does.

[BERTHA *enters from the hall.*]

BERTHA. She's here again, madam. The lady who came and left the flowers. [*Points.*] The ones you're holding.

HEDDA. Oh, is she? Well, show her in.

[BERTHA *opens the door for* MRS. ELVSTED *and goes out.* MRS. ELVSTED *is a delicately built woman with gentle, attractive features. Her eyes are light blue, large, and somewhat prominent, with a frightened, questioning expression. Her hair is extremely fair, almost flaxen, and is exceptionally wavy and abundant. She is two or three years younger than* HEDDA. *She is wearing a dark visiting dress, in good taste but not quite in the latest fashion.*]

HEDDA (*goes cordially to greet her*). Dear Mrs. Elvsted, good morning. How delightful to see you again after all this time.

MRS. ELVSTED (*nervously, trying to control herself*). Yes, it's many years since we met.

TESMAN. And since *we* met. What?

HEDDA. Thank you for your lovely flowers.

MRS. ELVSTED. Oh, please—I wanted to come yesterday afternoon. But they told me you were away—

TESMAN. You've only just arrived in town, then? What?

MRS. ELVSTED. I got here yesterday, around midday. Oh, I became almost desperate when I heard you weren't here.

HEDDA. Desperate? Why?

TESMAN. My dear Mrs. Rysing—Elvsted—

HEDDA. There's nothing wrong, I hope?

MRS. ELVSTED. Yes, there is. And I don't know anyone else here whom I can turn to.

HEDDA (*puts the flowers down on the table*). Come and sit with me on the sofa—

MRS. ELVSTED. Oh, I feel too restless to sit down.

HEDDA. You must. Come along, now. [*She pulls* MRS. ELVSTED *down on to the sofa and sits beside her.*]

TESMAN. Well? Tell us, Mrs.—er—

HEDDA. Has something happened at home?

MRS. ELVSTED. Yes—that is, yes and no. Oh, I do hope you won't misunderstand me—

HEDDA. Then you'd better tell us the whole story, Mrs. Elvsted.

TESMAN. That's why you've come. What?

MRS. ELVSTED. Yes—yes, it is. Well, then—in case you don't already know—Eilert Loevborg is in town.

HEDDA. Loevborg here?

TESMAN. Eilert back in town? By Jove, Hedda, did you hear that?

HEDDA. Yes, of course I heard.

MRS. ELVSTED. He's been here a week. A whole week! In this city. Alone. With all those dreadful people—

HEDDA. But my dear Mrs. Elvsted, what concern is he of yours?

MRS. ELVSTED (*gives her a frightened look and says quickly*). He's been tutoring the children.

HEDDA. Your children?

MRS. ELVSTED. My husband's. I have none.

HEDDA. Oh, you mean your stepchildren.

MRS. ELVSTED. Yes.

TESMAN (*gropingly*). But was he sufficiently—I don't know how to put it—sufficiently regular in his habits to be suited to such a post? What?

MRS. ELVSTED. For the past two to three years he has been living irreproachably.

TESMAN. You don't say! By Jove, Hedda, hear that?

HEDDA. I hear.

MRS. ELVSTED. Quite irreproachably, I assure you. In every respect. All the same—in this big city—with money in his pockets—I'm so dreadfully frightened something may happen to him.

TESMAN. But why didn't he stay up there with you and your husband?

MRS. ELVSTED. Once his book had come out, he became restless.

TESMAN. Oh, yes—Auntie Juju said he'd brought out a new book.

MRS. ELVSTED. Yes, a big new book about the history of civilisation. A kind of general survey. It came out a fortnight ago. Everyone's been buying it and reading it—it's created a tremendous stir—

TESMAN. Has it really? It must be something he's dug up, then.

MRS. ELVSTED. You mean from the old days?

TESMAN. Yes.

MRS. ELVSTED. No, he's written it all since he came to live with us.

TESMAN. Well, that's splendid news, Hedda. Fancy that!

MRS. ELVSTED. Oh, yes! If only he can go on like this!

HEDDA. Have you met him since you came here?

MRS. ELVSTED. No, not yet. I had such dreadful difficulty

finding his address. But this morning I managed to track him down at last.

HEDDA (*looks searchingly at her*). I must say I find it a little strange that your husband—hm—

MRS. ELVSTED (*starts nervously*). My husband! What do you mean?

HEDDA. That he should send you all the way here on an errand of this kind. I'm surprised he didn't come himself to keep an eye on his friend.

MRS. ELVSTED. Oh, no, no—my husband hasn't the time. Besides, I—er—wanted to do some shopping here.

HEDDA (*with a slight smile*). Ah. Well, that's different.

MRS. ELVSTED (*gets up quickly, restlessly*). Please, Mr. Tesman, I beg you—be kind to Eilert Loevborg if he comes here. I'm sure he will. I mean, you used to be such good friends in the old days. And you're both studying the same subject, as far as I can understand. You're in the same field, aren't you?

TESMAN. Well, we used to be, anyway.

MRS. ELVSTED. Yes—so I beg you earnestly, do please, please, keep an eye on him. Oh, Mr. Tesman, do promise me you will.

TESMAN. I shall be only too happy to do so, Mrs. Rysing.

HEDDA. Elvsted.

TESMAN. I'll do everything for Eilert that lies in my power. You can rely on that.

MRS. ELVSTED. Oh, how good and kind you are! [*Presses his hands.*] Thank you, thank you, thank you. [*Frightened.*] My husband's so fond of him, you see.

HEDDA (*gets up*). You'd better send him a note, Tesman. He may not come to you of his own accord.

TESMAN. Yes, that'd probably be the best plan, Hedda. What?

HEDDA. The sooner the better. Why not do it now?

MRS. ELVSTED (*pleadingly*). Oh yes, if only you would!

TESMAN. I'll do it this very moment. Do you have his address, Mrs.—er—Elvsted?

MRS. ELVSTED. Yes. [*Takes a small piece of paper from her pocket and gives it to him.*]

TESMAN. Good, good. Right, well I'll go inside and— [*Looks round.*] Where are my slippers? Oh yes, here. [*Picks up the package and is about to go.*]

HEDDA. Try to sound friendly. Make it a nice long letter.

TESMAN. Right, I will.

MRS. ELVSTED. Please don't say anthing about my having seen you.

TESMAN. Good heavens no, of course not. What? [*Goes out through the rear room to the right.*]

HEDDA (*goes over to* MRS. ELVSTED, *smiles, and says softly*). Well! Now we've killed two birds with one stone.

MRS. ELVSTED. What do you mean?

HEDDA. Didn't you realise I wanted to get him out of the room?

MRS. ELVSTED. So that he could write the letter?

HEDDA. And so that I could talk to you alone.

MRS. ELVSTED (*confused*). About this?

HEDDA. Yes, about this.

MRS. ELVSTED (*in alarm*). But there's nothing more to tell, Mrs. Tesman. Really there isn't.

HEDDA. Oh, yes there is. There's a lot more. I can see that. Come along, let's sit down and have a little chat. [*She pushes* MRS. ELVSTED *down into the armchair by the stove and seats herself on one of the footstools.*]

MRS. ELVSTED (*looks anxiously at her watch*). Really, Mrs. Tesman, I think I ought to be going now.

HEDDA. There's no hurry. Well? How are things at home?

MRS. ELVSTED. I'd rather not speak about that.

HEDDA. But my dear, you can tell me. Good heavens, we were at school together.

MRS. ELVSTED. Yes, but you were a year senior to me. Oh, I used to be terribly frightened of you in those days.

HEDDA. Frightened of me?

MRS. ELVSTED. Yes, terribly frightened. Whenever you met me on the staircase you used to pull my hair.

HEDDA. No, did I?

MRS. ELVSTED. Yes. And once you said you'd burn it all off.

HEDDA. Oh, that was only in fun.

MRS. ELVSTED. Yes, but I was so silly in those days. And then afterwards—I mean, we've drifted so far apart. Our backgrounds were so different.

HEDDA. Well, now we must try to drift together again. Now listen. When we were at school we used to call each other by our Christian names—

MRS. ELVSTED. No, I'm sure you're mistaken.

HEDDA. I'm sure I'm not. I remember it quite clearly. Let's tell each other our secrets, as we used to in the old days. [*Moves closer on her footstool.*] There, now. [*Kisses her on the cheek.*] You must call me Hedda.

MRS. ELVSTED (*squeezes her hands and pats them*). Oh, you're so kind. I'm not used to people being so nice to me.

HEDDA. Now, now, now. And I shall call you Tora, the way I used to.

MRS. ELVSTED. My name is Thea.

HEDDA. Yes, of course. Of course. I meant Thea. [*Looks at her sympathetically.*] So you're not used to kindness, Thea? In your own home?

MRS. ELVSTED. Oh, if only I had a home! But I haven't. I've never had one.

HEDDA (*looks at her for a moment*). I thought that was it.

MRS. ELVSTED (*stares blankly and helplessly*). Yes—yes—yes.

HEDDA. I can't remember exactly now, but didn't you first go to Mr. Elvsted as a housekeeper?

MRS. ELVSTED. Governess, actually. But his wife—at the time, I mean—she was an invalid, and had to spend most of her time in bed. So I had to look after the house too.

HEDDA. But in the end, you became mistress of the house.

MRS. ELVSTED (*sadly*). Yes, I did.

HEDDA. Let me see. Roughly, how long ago was that?

MRS. ELVSTED. When I got married, you mean?

HEDDA. Yes.

MRS. ELVSTED. About five years.

HEDDA. Yes; it must be about that.

MRS. ELVSTED. Oh, those five years! Especially the last two or three. Oh, Mrs. Tesman, if you only knew—!

HEDDA (*slaps her hand gently*). Mrs. Tesman? Oh, Thea!

MRS. ELVSTED. I'm sorry, I'll try to remember. Yes—if you had any idea—

HEDDA (*casually*). Eilert Loevborg's been up there too, for about three years, hasn't he?

MRS. ELVSTED (*looks at her uncertainly*). Eilert Loevborg? Yes, he has.

HEDDA. Did you know him before? When you were here?

MRS. ELVSTED. No, not really. That is—I knew him by name, of course.

HEDDA. But up there, he used to visit you?

MRS. ELVSTED. Yes, he used to come and see us every day. To give the children lessons. I found I couldn't do that as well as manage the house.

HEDDA. I'm sure you couldn't. And your husband—? I suppose being a magistrate he has to be away from home a good deal?

MRS. ELVSTED. Yes. You see, Mrs.—you see, Hedda, he has to cover the whole district.

HEDDA (*leans against the arm of* MRS. ELVSTED'S *chair*).

Poor, pretty little Thea! Now you must tell me the whole
story. From beginning to end.

MRS. ELVSTED. Well—what do you want to know?

HEDDA. What kind of man is your husband, Thea? I
mean, as a person. Is he kind to you?

MRS. ELVSTED (*evasively*). I'm sure he does his best to be.

HEDDA. I only wonder if he isn't too old for you. There's
more than twenty years between you, isn't there?

MRS. ELVSTED (*irritably*). Yes, there's that too. Oh, there
are so many things. We're different in every way. We've
nothing in common. Nothing whatever.

HEDDA. But he loves you, surely? In his own way?

MRS. ELVSTED. Oh, I don't know. I think he just finds me
useful. And then I don't cost much to keep. I'm cheap.

HEDDA. Now you're being stupid.

MRS. ELVSTED (*shakes her head*). It can't be any different.
With him. He doesn't love anyone except himself. And
perhaps the children—a little.

HEDDA. He must be fond of Eilert Loevborg, Thea.

MRS. ELVSTED (*looks at her*). Eilert Loevborg? What makes
you think that?

HEDDA. Well, if he sends you all the way down here to look
for him— [*Smiles almost imperceptibly.*] Besides, you said so
yourself to Tesman.

MRS. ELVSTED (*with a nervous twitch*). Did I? Oh yes, I
suppose I did. [*Impulsively, but keeping her voice low.*] Well,
I might as well tell you the whole story. It's bound to come
out sooner or later.

HEDDA. But my dear Thea—?

MRS. ELVSTED. My husband had no idea I was coming here.

HEDDA. What? Your husband didn't know?

MRS. ELVSTED. No, of course not. As a matter of fact, he
wasn't even there. He was away at the assizes. Oh, I couldn't
stand it any longer, Hedda! I just couldn't. I'd be so
dreadfully lonely up there now.

HEDDA. Go on.

MRS. ELVSTED. So I packed a few things. Secretly. And went.

HEDDA. Without telling anyone?

MRS. ELVSTED. Yes. I caught the train and came straight here.

HEDDA. But my dear Thea! How brave of you!

MRS. ELVSTED (*gets up and walks across the room*). Well, what else could I do?

HEDDA. But what do you suppose your husband will say when you get back?

MRS. ELVSTED (*by the table, looks at her*). Back there? To him?

HEDDA. Yes. Surely—?

MRS. ELVSTED. I shall never go back to him.

HEDDA (*gets up and goes closer*). You mean you've left your home for good?

MRS. ELVSTED. Yes. I didn't see what else I could do.

HEDDA. But to do it so openly!

MRS. ELVSTED. Oh, it's no use trying to keep a thing like that secret.

HEDDA. But what do you suppose people will say?

MRS. ELVSTED. They can say what they like. [*Sits sadly, wearily on the sofa.*] I had to do it.

HEDDA (*after a short silence*). What do you intend to do now? How are you going to live?

MRS. ELVSTED. I don't know. I only know that I must live wherever Eilert Loevborg is. If I am to go on living.

HEDDA (*moves a chair from the table, sits on it near MRS. ELVSTED and strokes her hands*). Tell me, Thea, how did this —friendship between you and Eilert Loevborg begin?

MRS. ELVSTED. Oh, it came about gradually. I developed a kind of—power over him.

HEDDA. Oh?

MRS. ELVSTED. He gave up his old habits. Not because I

asked him to. I'd never have dared to do that. I suppose he just noticed I didn't like that kind of thing. So he gave it up.

HEDDA (*hides a smile*). So you've made a new man of him. Clever little Thea!

MRS. ELVSTED. Yes—anyway, he says I have. And he's made a—sort of—real person of me. Taught me to think— and to understand all kinds of things.

HEDDA. Did he give you lessons too?

MRS. ELVSTED. Not exactly lessons. But he talked to me. About—oh, you've no idea—so many things! And then he let me work with him. Oh, it was wonderful. I was so happy to be allowed to help him.

HEDDA. Did he allow you to help him!

MRS. ELVSTED. Yes. Whenever he wrote anything we always—did it together.

HEDDA. Like good pals?

MRS. ELVSTED (*eagerly*). Pals! Yes—why, Hedda, that's exactly the word he used! Oh, I ought to feel so happy. But I can't. I don't know if it will last.

HEDDA. You don't seem very sure of him

MRS. ELVSTED (*sadly*). Something stands between Eilert Loevborg and me. The shadow of another woman.

HEDDA. Who can that be?

MRS. ELVSTED. I don't know. Someone he used to be friendly with in—in the old days. Someone he's never been able to forget.

HEDDA. What has he told you about her?

MRS. ELVSTED. Oh, he only mentioned her once, casually.

HEDDA. Well! What did he say?

MRS. ELVSTED. He said when he left her she tried to shoot him with a pistol.

HEDDA (*cold, controlled*). What nonsense. People don't do such things. The kind of people we know.

MRS. ELVSTED. No. I think it must have been that red-haired singer he used to—

HEDDA. Ah yes, very probably.

MRS. ELVSTED. I remember they used to say she always carried a loaded pistol.

HEDDA. Well then, it must be her.

MRS. ELVSTED. But Hedda, I hear she's come back, and is living here. Oh, I'm so desperate—!

HEDDA (*glances towards the rear room*). Ssh! Tesman's coming. [*Gets up and whispers.*] Thea, we mustn't breathe a word about this to anyone.

MRS. ELVSTED (*jumps up*). Oh, no, no! Please don't!

[GEORGE TESMAN *appears from the right in the rear room with a letter in his hand, and comes into the drawing room.*]

TESMAN. Well, here's my little epistle all signed and sealed.

HEDDA. Good. I think Mrs. Elvsted wants to go now. Wait a moment—I'll see you as far as the garden gate.

TESMAN. Er—Hedda, do you think Bertha could deal with this?

HEDDA (*takes the letter*). I'll give her instructions.

[BERTHA *enters from the hall.*]

BERTHA. Judge Brack is here and asks if he may pay his respects to Madam and the Doctor.

HEDDA. Yes, ask him to be so good as to come in. And—wait a moment—drop this letter in the post box.

BERTHA (*takes the letter*). Very good, madam.

[*She opens the door for* JUDGE BRACK, *and goes out.* JUDGE BRACK *is forty-five; rather short, but well-built, and elastic in his movements. He has a roundish face with an aristocratic profile. His hair, cut short, is still almost black, and is carefully barbered. Eyes lively and humorous. Thick eyebrows. His moustache is also thick, and is trimmed square at the ends. He is wearing outdoor clothes which are elegant but a*

*little too youthful for him. He has a monocle in one eye; now
and then he lets it drop.*]

BRACK (*hat in hand, bows*). May one presume to call so
early?

HEDDA. One may presume.

TESMAN (*shakes his hand*). You're welcome here any time.
Judge Brack—Mrs. Rysing. [HEDDA *sighs.*]

BRACK (*bows*). Ah—charmed—

HEDDA (*looks at him and laughs*). What fun to be able to
see you by daylight for once, Judge.

BRACK. Do I look—different?

HEDDA. Yes. A little younger, I think.

BRACK. Obliged.

TESMAN. Well, what do you think of Hedda? What?
Doesn't she look well? Hasn't she filled out—?

HEDDA. Oh, do stop it. You ought to be thanking Judge
Brack for all the inconvenience he's put himself to—

BRACK. Nonsense, it was a pleasure—

HEDDA. You're a loyal friend. But my other friend is
pining to get away. Au revoir, Judge. I won't be a minute.

[*Mutual salutations.* MRS. ELVSTED *and* HEDDA *go out
through the hall.*]

BRACK. Well, is your wife satisfied with everything?

TESMAN. Yes, we can't thank you enough. That is—we
may have to shift one or two things around, she tells me.
And we're short of one or two little items we'll have to
purchase.

BRACK. Oh? Really?

TESMAN. But you mustn't worry your head about that.
Hedda says she'll get what's needed. I say, why don't we sit
down? What?

BRACK. Thanks, just for a moment. [*Sits at the table.*]
There's something I'd like to talk to you about, my dear
Tesman.

TESMAN. Oh? Ah yes, of course. [*Sits.*] After the feast comes the reckoning. What?

BRACK. Oh, never mind about the financial side—there's no hurry about that. Though I could wish we'd arranged things a little less palatially.

TESMAN. Good heavens, that'd never have done. Think of Hedda, my dear chap. You know her. I couldn't possibly ask her to live like a suburban housewife.

BRACK. No, no—that's just the problem.

TESMAN. Anyway, it can't be long now before my nomination comes through.

BRACK. Well, you know, these things often take time.

TESMAN. Have you heard any more news? What?

BRACK. Nothing definite. [*Changing the subject.*] Oh, by the way, I have one piece of news for you.

TESMAN. What?

BRACK. Your old friend Eilert Loevborg is back in town.

TESMAN. I know that already.

BRACK. Oh? How did you hear that?

TESMAN. She told me. That lady who went out with Hedda.

BRACK. I see. What was her name? I didn't catch it.

TESMAN. Mrs. Elvsted.

BRACK. Oh, the magistrate's wife. Yes, Loevborg's been living up near them, hasn't he?

TESMAN. I'm delighted to hear he's become a decent human being again.

BRACK. Yes, so they say.

TESMAN. I gather he's published a new book, too. What?

BRACK. Indeed he has.

TESMAN. I hear it's created rather a stir.

BRACK. Quite an unusual stir.

TESMAN. I say, isn't that splendid news! He's such a gifted chap—and I was afraid he'd gone to the dogs for good.

BRACK. Most people thought he had.

TESMAN. But I can't think what he'll do now. How on earth will he manage to make ends meet? What?

[*As he speaks his last words,* HEDDA *enters from the hall.*]

HEDDA (*to* BRACK, *laughs slightly scornfully*). Tesman is always worrying about making ends meet.

TESMAN. We were talking about poor Eilert Loevborg, Hedda dear.

HEDDA (*gives him a quick look*). Oh, were you? [*Sits in the armchair by the stove and asks casually.*] Is he in trouble?

TESMAN. Well, he must have run through his inheritance long ago by now. And he can't write a new book every year. What? So I'm wondering what's going to become of him.

BRACK. I may be able to enlighten you there.

TESMAN. Oh?

BRACK. You mustn't forget he has relatives who wield a good deal of influence.

TESMAN. Relatives? Oh, they've quite washed their hands of him, I'm afraid.

BRACK. They used to regard him as the hope of the family.

TESMAN. Used to, yes. But he's put an end to that.

HEDDA. Who knows? [*With a little smile.*] I hear the Elvsteds have made a new man of him.

BRACK. And then this book he's just published—

TESMAN. Well, let's hope they find something for him. I've just written him a note. Oh, by the way, Hedda, I asked him to come over and see us this evening.

BRACK. But my dear chap, you're coming to me this evening. My bachelor party. You promised me last night when I met you at the boat.

HEDDA. Had you forgotten, Tesman?

TESMAN. Good heavens, yes, I'd quite forgotten.

BRACK. Anyway, you can be quite sure he won't turn up here.

TESMAN. Why do you think that? What?

BRACK (*a little unwillingly, gets up and rests his hands on the back of his chair*). My dear Tesman—and you, too, Mrs. Tesman—there's something I feel you ought to know.

TESMAN. Concerning Eilert?

BRACK. Concerning him and you.

TESMAN. Well, my dear Judge, tell us, please!

BRACK. You must be prepared for your nomination not to come through quite as quickly as you hope and expect.

TESMAN (*jumps up uneasily*). Is anything wrong? What?

BRACK. There's a possibility that the appointment may be decided by competition—

TESMAN. Competition! By Jove, Hedda, fancy that!

HEDDA (*leans further back in her chair*). Ah! How interesting!

TESMAN. But who else—? I say, you don't mean—?

BRACK. Exactly. By competition with Eilert Loevborg.

TESMAN (*clasps his hands in alarm*). No, no, but this is inconceivable! It's absolutely impossible! What?

BRACK. Hm. We may find it'll happen, all the same.

TESMAN. No, but—Judge Brack, they couldn't be so inconsiderate towards me! [*Waves his arms.*] I mean, by Jove, I—I'm a married man! It was on the strength of this that Hedda and I *got* married! We ran up some pretty hefty debts. And borrowed money from Auntie Juju! I mean, good heavens, they practically promised me the appointment. What?

BRACK. Well, well, I'm sure you'll get it. But you'll have to go through a competition.

HEDDA (*motionless in her armchair*). How exciting, Tesman. It'll be a kind of duel, by Jove.

TESMAN. My dear Hedda, how can you take it so lightly?

HEDDA (*as before*). I'm not. I can't wait to see who's going to win.

BRACK. In any case, Mrs. Tesman, it's best you should know how things stand. I mean before you commit yourself to these little items I hear you're threatening to purchase.

HEDDA. I can't allow this to alter my plans.

BRACK. Indeed? Well, that's your business. Good-bye. [*To* TESMAN.] I'll come and collect you on the way home from my afternoon walk.

TESMAN. Oh, yes, yes. I'm sorry, I'm all upside down just now.

HEDDA (*lying in her chair, holds out her hand*). Good-bye, Judge. See you this afternoon.

BRACK. Thank you. Good-bye, good-bye.

TESMAN (*sees him to the door*). Good-bye, my dear Judge. You will excuse me, won't you?

[JUDGE BRACK *goes out throuah the hall.*]

TESMAN (*pacing up and down*). Oh, Hedda! One oughtn't to go plunging off on wild adventures. What?

HEDDA (*looks at him and smiles*). Like you're doing?

TESMAN. Yes. I mean, there's no denying it, it was a pretty big adventure to go off and get married and set up house merely on expectation.

HEDDA. Perhaps you're right.

TESMAN. Well, anyway, we have our home, Hedda. By Jove, yes. The home we dreamed of. And set our hearts on. What?

HEDDA (*gets up slowly, wearily*). You agreed that we should enter society. And keep open house. That was the bargain.

TESMAN. Yes. Good heavens, I was looking forward to it all so much. To seeing you play hostess to a select circle! By Jove! What? Ah, well, for the time being we shall have to make do with each other's company, Hedda. Perhaps have Auntie Juju in now and then. Oh dear, this wasn't at all what you had in mind—

HEDDA. I won't be able to have a liveried footman. For a start.

TESMAN. Oh no, we couldn't possibly afford a footman.

HEDDA. And that thoroughbred horse you promised me—

TESMAN (*fearfully*). Thoroughbred horse!

HEDDA. I mustn't even think of that now.

TESMAN. Heaven forbid!

HEDDA (*walks across the room*). Ah, well. I still have one thing left to amuse myself with.

TESMAN (*joyfully*). Thank goodness for that. What's that, Hedda? What?

HEDDA (*in the open doorway, looks at him with concealed scorn*). My pistols, George darling.

TESMAN (*alarmed*). Pistols!

HEDDA (*her eyes cold*). General Gabler's pistols. [*She goes into the rear room and disappears.*]

TESMAN (*runs to the doorway and calls after her*). For heaven's sake, Hedda dear, don't touch those things. They're dangerous. Hedda—please—for my sake! What?

CURTAIN

ACT TWO

The same as in Act One, except that the piano has been removed and an elegant little writing table, with a bookcase, stands in its place. By the sofa on the left a smaller table has been placed. Most of the flowers have been removed. MRS. ELVSTED'S *bouquet stands on the larger table, downstage. It is afternoon.*

[HEDDA, *dressed to receive callers, is alone in the room. She is standing by the open french windows, loading a revolver. The pair to it is lying in an open pistol case on the writing table.*]

HEDDA (*looks down into the garden and calls*). Good afternoon, Judge.

BRACK (*in the distance, below*). Afternoon, Mrs. Tesman.

HEDDA (*raises the pistol and takes aim*). I'm going to shoot you, Judge Brack.

BRACK (*shouts from below*). No, no, no! Don't aim that thing at me!

HEDDA. This'll teach you to enter houses by the back door. [*Fires.*]

BRACK (*below*). Have you gone completely out of your mind?

HEDDA. Oh dear! Did I hit you?

BRACK (*still outside*). Stop playing these silly tricks.

HEDDA. All right, Judge. Come along in.

[JUDGE BRACK, *dressed for a bachelor party, enters through the french windows. He has a light overcoat on his arm.*]

BRACK. For God's sake! Haven't you stopped fooling around with those things yet? What are you trying to hit?

HEDDA. Oh, I was just shooting at the sky.

BRACK (*takes the pistol gently from her hand*). By your leave, ma'am. [*Looks at it.*] Ah, yes—I know this old friend well. [*Looks around.*] Where's the case? Oh, yes. [*Puts the pistol in the case and closes it.*] That's enough of that little game for today.

HEDDA. Well, what on earth *am* I to do?

BRACK. You haven't had any visitors?

HEDDA (*closes the french windows*). Not one. I suppose the best people are all still in the country.

BRACK. Your husband isn't home yet?

HEDDA (*locks the pistol away in a drawer of the writing table*). No. The moment he'd finished eating he ran off to his aunties. He wasn't expecting you so early.

BRACK. Ah, why didn't I think of that? How stupid of me.

HEDDA (*turns her head and looks at him*). Why stupid?

BRACK. I'd have come a little sooner.

HEDDA (*walks across the room*). There'd have been no one to receive you. I've been in my room since lunch, dressing.

BRACK. You haven't a tiny crack in the door through which we might have negotiated?

HEDDA. You forgot to arrange one.

BRACK. Another stupidity.

HEDDA. Well, we'll have to sit down here. And wait. Tesman won't be back for some time.

BRACK. Sad. Well, I'll be patient.

[HEDDA *sits on the corner of the sofa.* BRACK *puts his coat over the back of the nearest chair and seats himself, keeping his hat in his hand. Short pause. They look at each other.*]

HEDDA. Well?

BRACK (*in the same tone of voice*). Well?

HEDDA. I asked first.

BRACK (*leans forward slightly*). Yes, well, now we can enjoy a nice, cosy little chat—Mrs. Hedda.

HEDDA (*leans further back in her chair*). It seems such ages since we had a talk. I don't count last night or this morning.

BRACK. You mean: *à deux?*

HEDDA. Mm—yes. That's roughly what I meant.

BRACK. I've been longing so much for you to come home.

HEDDA. So have I.

BRACK. You? Really, Mrs. Hedda? And I thought you were having such a wonderful honeymoon.

HEDDA. Oh, yes. Wonderful!

BRACK. But your husband wrote such ecstatic letters.

HEDDA. He! Oh, yes! He thinks life has nothing better to offer than rooting around in libraries and copying old pieces of parchment, or whatever it is he does.

BRACK (*a little maliciously*). Well, that *is* his life. Most of it, anyway.

HEDDA. Yes, I know. Well, it's all right for him. But for me! Oh no, my dear Judge. I've been bored to death.

BRACK (*sympathetically*). Do you mean that? Seriously?

HEDDA. Yes. Can you imagine? Six whole months without ever meeting a single person who was one of us, and to whom I could talk about the kind of things we talk about.

BRACK. Yes, I can understand. I'd miss that, too.

HEDDA. That wasn't the worst, though.

BRACK. What was?

HEDDA. Having to spend every minute of one's life with— with the same person.

BRACK (*nods*). Yes. What a thought! Morning; noon; and—

HEDDA (*coldly*). As I said: every minute of one's life.

BRACK. I stand corrected. But dear Tesman is such a clever fellow, I should have thought one ought to be able—

HEDDA. Tesman is only interested in one thing, my dear Judge. His special subject.

BRACK. True.

HEDDA. And people who are only interested in one thing don't make the most amusing company. Not for long, anyway.

BRACK. Not even when they happen to be the person one loves?

HEDDA. Oh, don't use that sickly, stupid word.

BRACK (*starts*). But. Mrs. Hedda—!

HEDDA (*half laughing, half annoyed*). You just try it, Judge. Listening to the history of civilisation morning, noon and—

BRACK (*corrects her*). Every minute of one's life.

HEDDA. All right. Oh, and those domestic industries of Brabant in the Middle Ages! That really is beyond the limit.

BRACK (*looks at her searchingly*). But, tell me—if you feel like this why on earth did you—? Ha—

HEDDA. Why on earth did I marry George Tesman?

BRACK. If you like to put it that way.

HEDDA. Do you think it so very strange?

BRACK. Yes—and no, Mrs. Hedda.

HEDDA. I'd danced myself tired, Judge. I felt my time was up— [*Gives a slight shudder.*] No, I mustn't say that. Or even think it.

BRACK. You've no rational cause to think it.

HEDDA. Oh—cause, cause— [*Looks searchingly at him.*] After all, George Tesman—well, I mean, he's a very respectable man.

BRACK. Very respectable, sound as a rock. No denying that.

HEDDA. And there's nothing exactly ridiculous about him. Is there?

BRACK. Ridiculous? N-no, I wouldn't say that.

HEDDA. Mm. He's very clever at collecting material and all that, isn't he? I mean, he may go quite far in time.

BRACK (*looks at her a little uncertainly*). I thought you believed, like everyone else, that he would become a very prominent man.

HEDDA (*looks tired*). Yes, I did. And when he came and

begged me on his bended knees to be allowed to love and to cherish me, I didn't see why I shouldn't let him.

BRACK. No, well—if one looks at it like that—

HEDDA. It was more than my other admirers were prepared to do, Judge dear.

BRACK (*laughs*). Well, I can't answer for the others. As far as I myself am concerned, you know I've always had a considerable respect for the institution of marriage. As an institution.

HEDDA (*lightly*). Oh, I've never entertained any hopes of you.

BRACK. All I want is to have a circle of friends whom I can trust, whom I can help with advice or—or by any other means, and into whose houses I may come and go as a—trusted friend.

HEDDA. Of the husband?

BRACK (*bows*). Preferably, to be frank, of the wife. And of the husband too, of course. Yes, you know, this kind of—triangle is a delightful arrangement for all parties concerned.

HEDDA. Yes, I often longed for a third person while I was away. Oh, those hours we spent alone in railway compartments—.

BRACK. Fortunately your honeymoon is now over.

HEDDA (*shakes her head*). There's a long, long way still to go. I've only reached a stop on the line.

BRACK. Why not jump out and stretch your legs a little, Mrs. Hedda?

HEDDA. I'm not the jumping sort.

BRACK. Aren't you?

HEDDA. No. There's always someone around who—

BRACK (*laughs*). Who looks at one's legs?

HEDDA. Yes. Exactly.

BRACK. Well, but surely—

HEDDA (*with a gesture of rejection*). I don't like it. I'd

rather stay where I am. Sitting in the compartment. *À deux.*

BRACK. But suppose a third person were to step into the compartment?

HEDDA. That would be different.

BRACK. A trusted friend—someone who understood—

HEDDA. And was lively and amusing—

BRACK. And interested in—more subjects than one—

HEDDA (*sighs audibly*). Yes, that'd be a relief.

BRACK (*hears the front door open and shut*). The triangle is completed.

HEDDA (*half under breath*). And the train goes on.

[GEORGE TESMAN, *in grey walking dress with a soft felt hat, enters from the hall. He has a number of paper-covered books under his arm and in his pockets.*]

TESMAN (*goes over to the table by the corner sofa*). Phew! It's too hot to be lugging all this around. [*Puts the books down.*] I'm positively sweating, Hedda. Why, hullo, hullo! You here already, Judge? What? Bertha didn't tell me.

BRACK (*get up*). I came in through the garden.

HEDDA. What are all those books you've got there?

TESMAN (*stands glancing through them*). Oh, some new publications dealing with my special subject. I had to buy them.

HEDDA. Your special subject?

BRACK. His special subject, Mrs. Tesman. [BRACK *and* HEDDA *exchange a smile.*]

HEDDA. Haven't you collected enough material on your special subject?

TESMAN. My dear Hedda, one can never have too much. One must keep abreast of what other people are writing.

HEDDA. Yes. Of course.

TESMAN (*rooting among the books*). Look—I bought a copy of Eilert Loevborg's new book, too. [*Holds it out to her.*] Perhaps you'd like to have a look at it, Hedda? What?

HEDDA. No, thank you. Er—yes, perhaps I will, later.

TESMAN. I glanced through it on my way home.

BRACK. What's your opinion—as a specialist on the subject?

TESMAN. I'm amazed how sound and balanced it is. He never used to write like that. [*Gathers his books together.*] Well, I must get down to these at once. I can hardly wait to cut the pages. Oh, I've got to change, too. [*To* BRACK.] We don't have to be off just yet, do we? What?

BRACK. Heavens, no. We've plenty of time yet.

TESMAN. Good, I needn't hurry, then. [*Goes with his books, but stops and turns in the doorway.*] Oh, by the way, Hedda, Auntie Juju won't be coming to see you this evening.

HEDDA. Won't she? Oh—the hat, I suppose.

TESMAN. Good heavens, no. How could you think such a thing of Auntie Juju? Fancy—! No, Auntie Rena's very ill.

HEDDA. She always is.

TESMAN. Yes, but today she's been taken really bad.

HEDDA. Oh, then it's quite understandable that the other one should want to stay with her. Well, I shall have to swallow my disappointment.

TESMAN. You can't imagine how happy Auntie Juju was in spite of everything. At your looking so well after the honeymoon!

HEDDA (*half benearth her breath, as she rises*). Oh, these everlasting aunts!

TESMAN. What?

HEDDA (*goes over to the french windoes*). Nothing.

TESMAN. Oh. All right. [*Goes into the rear room and out of sight.*]

BRACK. What was that about the hat?

HEDDA. Oh, something that happened with Miss Tesman this morning. She'd put her hat down on a chair. [*Looks at him and smiles.*] And I pretended to think it was the servant's.

BRACK (*shakes his head*). But my dear Mrs. Hedda, how could you do such a thing? To that poor old lady?

HEDDA (*nervously, walking across the room*). Sometimes a mood like that hits me. And I can't stop myself. [*Throws herself down in the armchair by the stove.*] Oh, I don't know how to explain it.

BRACK (*behind her chair*). You're not really happy. That's the answer.

HEDDA (*stares ahead of her*). Why on earth should I be happy? Can you give me a reason?

BRACK. Yes. For one thing you've got the home you always wanted.

HEDDA (*looks at him*). You really believe that story?

BRACK. You mean it isn't true?

HEDDA. Oh, yes, it's partly true.

BRACK. Well?

HEDDA. It's true I got Tesman to see me home from parties last summer—

BRACK. It was a pity my home lay in another direction.

HEDDA. Yes. Your interests lay in another direction, too.

BRACK (*laughs*). That's naughty of you, Mrs. Hedda. But to return to you and Tesman—

HEDDA. Well, we walked past this house one evening. And poor Tesman was fidgeting in his boots trying to find something to talk about. I felt sorry for the great scholar—

BRACK (*smiles incredulously*). Did you? Hm.

HEDDA. Yes, honestly I did. Well, to help him out of his misery, I happened to say quite frivolously how much I'd love to live in this house.

BRACK. Was that all?

HEDDA. That evening, yes.

BRACK. But—afterwards?

HEDDA. Yes. My little frivolity had its consequences, my dear Judge.

BRACK. Our little frivolities do. Much too often, unfortunately.

HEDDA. Thank you. Well, it was our mutual admiration for the late Prime Minister's house that brought George Tesman and me together on common ground. So we got engaged, and we got married, and we went on our honeymoon, and—Ah well, Judge, I've—made my bed and I must lie in it, I was about to say.

BRACK. How utterly fantastic! And you didn't really care in the least about the house?

HEDDA. God knows I didn't.

BRACK. Yes, but now that we've furnished it so beautifully for you?

HEDDA. Ugh—all the rooms smell of lavender and dried roses. But perhaps Auntie Juju brought that in.

BRACK (*laughs*). More likely the Prime Minister's widow, rest her soul.

HEDDA. Yes, it's got the odour of death about it. It reminds me of the flowers one has worn at a ball—the morning after. [*Clasps her hands behind her neck, leans back in the chair and looks up at him.*] Oh, my dear Judge, you've no idea how hideously bored I'm going to be out here.

BRACK. Couldn't you find some kind of occupation, Mrs. Hedda? Like your husband?

HEDDA. Occupation? That'd interest me?

BRACK. Well—preferably.

HEDDA. God knows what. I've often thought— [*Breaks off.*] No, that wouldn't work either.

BRACK. Who knows? Tell me about it.

HEDDA. I was thinking—if I could persuade Tesman to go into politics, for example.

BRACKS (*laughs*). Tesman! No, honestly, I don't think he's quite cut out to be a politician.

HEDDA. Perhaps not. But if I could persuade him to have a go at it?

BRACK. What satisfaction would that give you? If he turned out to be no good? Why do you want to make him do that?

HEDDA. Because I'm bored. [*After a moment.*] You feel there's absolutely no possibility of Tesman becoming Prime Minister, then?

BRACK. Well, you know, Mrs. Hedda, for one thing he'd have to be pretty well off before he could become that.

HEDDA (*gets up impatiently*). There you are! [*Walks across the room.*] It's this wretched poverty that makes life so hateful. And ludicrous. Well, it is!

BRACK. I don't think that's the real cause.

HEDDA. What is, then?

BRACK. Nothing really exciting has ever happened to you.

HEDDA. Nothing serious, you mean?

BRACK. Call it that if you like. But now perhaps it may.

HEDDA (*tosses her head*). Oh, you're thinking of this competition for that wretched professorship? That's Tesman's affair. I'm not going to waste my time worrying about that.

BRACK. Very well, let's forget about that then. But suppose you were to find yourself faced with what people call—to use the conventional phrase—the most solemn of human responsibilities? [*Smiles.*] A new responsibility, little Mrs. Hedda.

HEDDA (*angrily*). Be quiet! Nothing like that's going to happen.

BRACK (*warily*). We'll talk about it again in a year's time. If not earlier.

HEDDA (*curtly*). I've no leanings in that direction, Judge. I don't want any—responsibilities.

BRACK. But surely you must feel some inclination to make use of that—natural talent which every woman—

HEDDA (*over by the french windows*). Oh, be quiet, I say! I often think there's only one thing for which I have any natural talent.

BRACK (*goes closer*). And what is that, if I may be so bold as to ask?

HEDDA (*stands looking out*). For boring myself to death. Now you know. [*Turns, looks toward the rear room and laughs.*] Talking of boring, here comes the Professor.

BRACK (*quietly, warningly*). Now, now, now, Mrs. Hedda!

[GEORGE TESMAN, *in evening dress, with gloves and hat in his hand, enters through the rear room from the right.*]

TESMAN. Hedda, hasn't any message come from Eilert? What?

HEDDA. No.

TESMAN. Ah, then we'll have him here presently. You wait and see.

BRACK. You really think he'll come?

TESMAN. Yes, I'm almost sure he will. What you were saying about him this morning is just gossip.

BRACK. Oh?

TESMAN. Yes. Auntie Juju said she didn't believe he'd ever dare to stand in my way again. Fancy that!

BRACK. Then everything in the garden's lovely.

TESMAN (*puts his hat, with his gloves in it, on a chair, right*). Yes, but you really must let me wait for him as long as possible.

BRACK. We've plenty of time. No one'll be turning up at my place before seven or half past.

TESMAN. Ah, then we can keep Hedda company a little longer. And see if he turns up. What?

HEDDA (*picks up* BRACK'S *coat and hat and carries them over to the corner sofa*). And if the worst comes to the worst, Mr. Loevborg can sit here and talk to me.

BRACK (*offering to take his things from her*). No, please. What do you mean by "if the worst comes to the worst"?

HEDDA. If he doesn't want to go with you and Tesman.

TESMAN (*looks doubtfully at her*). I say, Hedda, do you think it'll be all right for him to stay here with you? What? Remember Auntie Juju isn't coming.

HEDDA. Yes, but Mrs. Elvsted is. The three of us can have a cup of tea together.

TESMAN. Ah, that'll be all right then.

BRACK (*smiles*). It's probably the safest solution as far as he's concerned.

HEDDA. Why?

BRACK. My dear Mrs. Tesman, you always say of my little bachelor parties that they should be attended only by men of the strongest principles.

HEDDA. But Mr. Loevborg is a man of principle now. You know what they say about a reformed sinner—

[BERTHA *enters from the hall.*]

BERTHA. Madam, there's a gentleman here who wants to see you—

HEDDA. Ask him to come in.

TESMAN (*quietly*). I'm sure it's him. By Jove. Fancy that!

[EILERT LOEVBORG *enters from the hall. He is slim and lean, of the same age as* TESMAN, *but looks older and somewhat haggard. His hair and beard are of a blackish-brown; his face is long and pale, but with a couple of reddish patches on his cheekbones. He is dressed in an elegant and fairly new black suit, and carries black gloves and a top hat in his hand. He stops just inside the door and bows abruptly. He seems somewhat embarrassed.*]

TESMAN (*goes over and shakes his hand*). My dear Eilert! How grand to see you again after all these years!

EILERT LOEVBORG (*speaks softly*). It was good of you to

write, George. [*Goes nearer to* HEDDA.] May I shake hands with you, too, Mrs. Tesman?

HEDDA (*accepts his hand*). Delighted to see you, Mr. Loevborg. [*With a gesture.*] I don't know if you two gentlemen—

LOEVBORG (*bows slightly*). Judge Brack, I believe.

BRACK (*also with a slight bow*). Correct. We—met some years ago—

TESMAN (*puts his hands on* LOEVBORG'S *shoulders*). Now you're to treat this house just as though it were your own home, Eilert. Isn't that right, Hedda? I hear you've decided to settle here again? What?

LOEVBORG. Yes. I have.

TESMAN. Quite understandable. Oh, by the bye—I've just bought your new book. Though to tell the truth I haven't found time to read it yet.

LOEVBORG. You needn't bother.

TESMAN. Oh? Why?

LOEVBORG. There's nothing much in it.

TESMAN. By Jove, fancy hearing that from you!

BRACK. But everyone's praising it.

LOEVBORG. That was exactly what I wanted to happen. So I only wrote what I knew everyone would agree with.

BRACK. Very sensible.

TESMAN. Yes, but my dear Eilert—

LOEVBORG. I want to try to re-establish myself. To begin again—from the beginning.

TESMAN (*a little embarrassed*). Yes, I—er—suppose you do. What?

LOEVBORG (*smiles, puts down his hat and takes a package wrapped in paper from his coat pocket*). But when this gets published—George Tesman—read it. This is my real book. The one in which I have spoken with my own voice.

TESMAN. Oh, really? What's it about?

LOEVBORG. It's the sequel.

TESMAN. Sequel? To what?

LOEVBORG. To the other book.

TESMAN. The one that's just come out?

LOEVBORG. Yes.

TESMAN. But my dear Eilert, that covers the subject right up to the present day.

LOEVBORG. It does. But this is about the future.

TESMAN. The future! But, I say, we don't know anything about that.

LOEVBORG. No. But there are one or two things that need to be said about it. [*Opens the package.*] Here, have a look.

TESMAN. Surely that's not your handwriting?

LOEVBORG. I dictated it. [*Turns the pages.*] It's in two parts. The first deals with the forces that will shape our civilisation. [*Turns further on towards the end.*] And the second indicates the direction in which that civilisation may develop.

TESMAN. Amazing! I'd never think of writing about anything like that.

HEDDA (*by the french windows, drumming on the pane*). No. You wouldn't.

LOEVBORG (*puts the pages back into their cover and lays the package on the table*). I brought it because I thought I might possibly read you a few pages this evening.

TESMAN. I say, what a kind idea! Oh, but this evening—? [*Glances at* BRACK.] I'm not quite sure whether—

LOEVBORG. Well, some other time, then. There's no hurry.

BRACK. The truth is, Mr. Loevborg, I'm giving a little dinner this evening. In Tesman's honor, you know.

LOEVBORG (*looks round for his hat*). Oh—then I mustn't—

BRACK. No wait a minute. Won't you do me the honor of joining us?

LOEVBORG (*curtly, with decision*). No I can't. Thank you so much.

BRACK. Oh, nonsense. Do—please. There'll only be a few of us. And I can promise you we shall have some good sport, as Mrs. Hed—as Mrs. Tesman puts it.

LOEVBORG. I've no doubt. Nevertheless—

BRACK. You could bring your manuscript along. and read it to Tesman at my place. I could lend you a room.

TESMAN. By Jove, Eilert, that's an idea. What?

HEDDA (*interposes*). But Tesman, Mr. Loevborg doesn't want to go. I'm sure Mr. Loevborg would much rather sit here and have supper with me.

LOEVBORG (*looks at her*). With you, Mrs. Tesman?

HEDDA. And Mrs. Elvsted.

LOEVBORG. Oh. [*Casually.*] I ran into her this afternoon.

HEDDA. Did you? Well, she's coming here this evening. So you really must stay, Mr. Loevborg. Otherwise she'll have no one to see her home.

LOEVBORG. That's true. Well—thank you, Mrs. Tesman, I'll stay then.

HEDDA. I'll just tell the servant. [*She goes to the door which leads into the hall, and rings.* BERTHA *enters.* HEDDA *talks softly to her and points towards the rear room.* BERTHA *nods and goes out.*]

TESMAN (*to* LOEVBORG, *as* HEDDA *does this*). I say, Eilert. This new subject of yours—the—er—future—is that the one you're going to lecture about?

LOEVBORG. Yes.

TESMAN. They told me down at the bookshop that you're going to hold a series of lectures here during the autumn.

LOEVBORG. Yes, I am. I—hope you don't mind, Tesman.

TESMAN. Good heavens, no! But—?

LOEVBORG. I can quite understand it might queer your pitch a little.

TESMAN (*dejectedly*). Oh well, I can't expect you to put them off for my sake.

LOEVBORG. I'll wait till your appointment's been announced.

TESMAN. You'll wait! But—but—aren't you going to compete with me for the post? What?

LOEVBORG. No. I only want to defeat you in the eyes of the world.

TESMAN. Good heavens! Then Auntie Juju was right after all! Oh, I knew it, I knew it! Hear that, Hedda? Fancy! Eilert *doesn't* want to stand in our way.

HEDDA (*curtly*). Our? Leave me out of it, please. [*She goes towards the rear room, where* BERTHA *is setting a tray with decanters and glasses on the table.* HEDDA *nods approval, and comes back into the drawing room.* BERTHA *goes out.*]

TESMAN (*while this is happening*). Judge Brack, what do you think about all this? What?

BRACK. Oh, I think honor and victory can be very splendid things—

TESMAN. Of course they can. Still—

HEDDA (*looks at* TESMAN *with a cold smile*). You look as if you'd been hit by a thunderbolt.

TESMAN. Yes, I feel rather like it.

BRACK. There was a black cloud looming up, Mrs. Tesman. But it seems to have passed over.

HEDDA (*points towards the rear room*). Well, gentlemen, won't you go in and take a glass of cold punch?

BRACK (*glances at his watch*). A stirrup cup? Yes, why not?

TESMAN. An admirable suggestion, Hedda. Admirable! Oh, I feel so relieved!

HEDDA. Won't you have one, too, Mr. Loevborg?

LOEVBORG. No, thank you. I'd rather not.

BRACK. Great heavens, man, cold punch isn't poison. Take my word for it.

LOEVBORG. Not for everyone, perhaps.

HEDDA. I'll keep Mr. Loevborg company while you drink.

TESMAN. Yes, Hedda dear, would you?

[*He and* BRACK *go into the rear room, sit down, drink punch, smoke cigarettes and talk cheerfully during the following scene.* EILERT LOEVBORG *remains standing by the stove.* HEDDA *goes to the writing table.*]

HEDDA (*raising her voice slightly*). I've some photographs I'd like to show you, if you'd care to see them. Tesman and I visted the Tyrol on our way home.

[*She comes back with an album, places it on the table by the sofa and sits in the upstage corner of the sofa.* EILERT LOEVBORG *comes towards her, stops and looks at her. Then he takes a chair and sits down on her left, with his back towards the rear room.*]

HEDDA (*opens the album*). You see these mountains, Mr. Loevborg? That's the Ortler group. Tesman has written the name underneath. You see: "The Ortler Group near Meran."

LOEVBORG (*has not taken his eyes from her; says softly, slowly*). Hedda—Gabler!

HEDDA (*gives him a quick glance*). Ssh!

LOEVBORG (*repeats softly*). Hedda Gabler!

HEDDA (*looks at the album*). Yes, that used to be my name. When we first knew each other.

LOEVBORG. And from now on—for the rest of my life—I must teach myself never to say: Hedda Gabler.

HEDDA (*still turning the pages*). Yes, you must. You'd better start getting into practice. The sooner the better.

LOEVBORG (*bitterly*). Hedda Gabler married? And to George Tesman?

HEDDA. Yes. Well—that's life.

LOEVBORG. Oh, Hedda, Hedda! How could you throw yourself away like that?

HEDDA (*looks sharply at him*). Stop it.

LOEVBORG. What do you mean?

[TESMAN *comes in and goes towards the sofa.*]

HEDDA (*hears him coming and says casually*). And this,

Mr. Loevborg, is the view from the Ampezzo valley. Look at those mountains. [*Glances affectionately up at* TESMAN.] What did you say those curious mountains were called, dear?

TESMAN. Let me have a look. Oh, those are the Dolomites.

HEDDA. Of course. Those are the Dolomites, Mr. Loevborg.

TESMAN. Hedda, I just wanted to ask you, can't we bring some punch in here? A glass for you, anyway. What?

HEDDA. Thank you, yes. And a biscuit or two, perhaps.

TESMAN. You wouldn't like a cigarette?

HEDDA. No.

TESMAN. Right. [*He goes into the rear room and over to the right.* BRACK *is sitting there, glancing occasionally at* HEDDA *and* LOEVBORG.]

LOEVBORG (*softly, as before*). Answer me, Hedda. How could you do it?

HEDDA (*apparently absorbed in the album*). If you go on calling me Hedda I won't talk to you any more.

LOEVBORG. Mayn't I even when we're alone?

HEDDA. No. You can think it. But you mustn't say it.

LOEVBORG. Oh, I see. Because you love George Tesman.

HEDDA (*glances at him and smiles*). Love? Don't be funny.

LOEVBORG. You don't love him?

HEDDA. I don't intend to be unfaithful to him. That's not what I want.

LOEVBORG. Hedda—just tell me one thing—

HEDDA. Ssh!

[TESMAN *enters from the rear room, carrying a tray.*]

TESMAN. Here we are! Here come the goodies! [*Puts the tray down on the table.*]

HEDDA. Why didn't you ask the servant to bring it in?

TESMAN (*fills the glasses*). I like waiting on you, Hedda.

HEDDA. But you've filled both glasses. Mr. Loevborg doesn't want to drink.

TESMAN. Yes, but Mrs. Elvsted'll be here soon.

HEDDA. Oh yes, that's true. Mrs. Elvsted—

TESMAN. Had you forgotten her? What?

HEDDA. We're so absorbed with these photographs. [*Shows him one.*] You remember this little village?

TESMAN. Oh, that one down by the Brenner Pass. We spent a night there—

HEDDA. Yes, and met all those amusing people.

TESMAN. Oh yes, it was there, wasn't it? By Jove, if only we could have had you with us, Eilert! Ah, well. [*Goes back into the other room and sits down with* BRACK.]

LOEVBORG. Tell me one thing, Hedda.

HEDDA. Yes?

LOEVBORG. Didn't you love me either? Not—just a little?

HEDDA. Well now, I wonder? No, I think we were just good pals— Really good pals who could tell each other anything. [*Smiles.*] You certainly poured your heart out to me.

LOEVBORG. You begged me to.

HEDDA. Looking back on it, there was something beautiful and fascinating—and brave—about the way we told each other everything. That secret friendship no one else knew about.

LOEVBORG. Yes, Hedda, yes! Do you remember? How I used to come up to your father's house in the afternoon—and the General sat by the window and read his newspapers—with his back towards us—

HEDDA. And we sat on the sofa in the corner—

LOEVBORG. Always reading the same illustrated magazine—

HEDDA. We hadn't any photograph album.

LOEVBORG. Yes, Hedda. I regarded you as a kind of confessor. Told you things about myself which no one else knew about—then. Those days and nights of drinking and— Oh, Hedda, what power did you have to make me confess such things?

HEDDA. Power? You think I had some power over you?

LOEVBORG. Yes—I don't know how else to explain it. And all those—oblique questions you asked me—

HEDDA. You knew what they meant.

LOEVBORG. But that you could sit there and ask me such questions! So unashamedly—

HEDDA. I thought you said they were oblique.

LOEVBORG. Yes, but you asked them so unashamedly. That you could question me about—about that kind of thing!

HEDDA. You answered willingly enough.

LOEVBORG. Yes—that's what I can't understand—looking back on it. But tell me, Hedda—what you felt for me—wasn't that—love? When you asked me those questions and made me confess my sins to you, wasn't it because you wanted to wash me clean?

HEDDA. No, not exactly.

LOEVBORG. Why did you do it, then?

HEDDA. Do you find it so incredible that a young girl, given the chance to do so without anyone knowing, should want to be allowed a glimpse into a forbidden world of whose existence she is supposed to be ignorant?

LOEVBORG. So that was it?

HEDDA. One reason. One reason—I think.

LOEVBORG. You didn't love me, then. You just wanted—knowledge. But if that was so, why did you break it off?

HEDDA. That was your fault.

LOEVBORG. It was you who put an end to it.

HEDDA. Yes, when I realised that our friendship was threatening to develop into something—something else. Shame on you, Eilert Loevborg! How could you abuse the trust of your dearest friend?

LOEVBORG (*clenches his fists*). Oh, why didn't you do it? Why didn't you shoot me dead? As you threatened to?

HEDDA. I was afraid. Of the scandal.

LOEVBORG. Yes, Hedda. You're a coward at heart.

HEDDA. A dreadful coward. [*Changes her tone.*] Luckily for you. Well, now you've found consolation with the Elvsteds.

LOEVBORG. I know what Thea's been telling you.

HEDDA. I dare say you told her about us.

LOEVBORG. Not a word. She's too silly to understand that kind of thing.

HEDDA. Silly?

LOEVBORG. She's silly about that kind of thing.

HEDDA. And I am a coward. [*Leans closer to him, without looking him in the eyes, and says quietly.*] But let me tell you something. Something you don't know. ·

LOEVBORG (*tensely*). Yes?

HEDDA. My failure to shoot you wasn't my worst act of cowardice that evening.

LOEVBORG (*looks at her for a moment, realises her meaning and whispers passionately*). Oh, Hedda! Hedda Gabler! Now I see what was behind those questions. Yes! It wasn't knowledge you wanted! It was life!

HEDDA (*flashes a look at him and says quietly*). Take care! Don't you delude yourself!

[*It has begun to grow dark.* BERTHA, *from outside, opens the door leading into the hall.*]

HEDDA (*closes the album with a snap and cries, smiling*). Ah, at last! Come in, Thea dear!

[MRS. ELVSTED *enters from the hall, in evening dress. The door is closed behind her.*]

HEDDA (*on the sofa, stretches out her arms towards her*). Thea darling, I thought you were never coming!

[MRS. ELVSTED *makes a slight bow to the gentlemen in the rear room as she passes the open doorway, and they to her. Then she goes to the table and holds out her hand to* HEDDA.

EILERT LOEVBORG *has risen from his chair. He and* MRS. ELVSTED *nod silently to each other.*]

MRS. ELVSTED. Perhaps I ought to go in and say a few words to your husband?

HEDDA. Oh, there's no need. They're happy by themselves. They'll be going soon.

MRS. ELVSTED. Going?

HEDDA. Yes, they're off on a spree this evening.

MRS. ELVSTED (*quickly, to* LOEVBORG). You're not going with them?

LOEVBORG. No.

HEDDA. Mr. Loevborg is staying here with us.

MRS. ELVSTED (*takes a chair and is about to sit down beside him*). Oh, how nice it is to be here!

HEDDA. No, Thea darling, not there. Come over here and sit beside me. I want to be in the middle.

MRS. ELVSTED. Yes, just as you wish. [*She goes round the table and sits on the sofa, on* HEDDA'S *right.* LOEVBORG *sits down again in his chair.*]

LOEVBORG (*after a short pause, to* HEDDA). Isn't she lovely to look at?

HEDDA (*strokes her hair gently*). Only to look at?

LOEVBORG. Yes. We're just good pals. We trust each other implicitly. We can talk to each other quite unashamedly.

HEDDA. No need to be oblique?

MRS. ELVSTED (*nestles close to* HEDDA *and says quietly*). Oh, Hedda I'm so happy. Imagine—he says I've inspired him!

HEDDA (*looks at her with a smile*). Dear Thea! Does he really?

LOEVBORG. She has the courage of her convictions, Mrs. Tesman.

MRS. ELVSTED. I? Courage?

LOEVBORG. Absolute courage. Where friendship is concerned.

HEDDA. Yes. Courage. Yes. If only one had that—

LOEVBORG. Yes?

HEDDA. One might be able to live. In spite of everything. [*Changes her tone suddenly.*] Well, Thea darling, now you're going to drink a nice glass of cold punch.

MRS. ELVSTED. No, thank you. I never drink anything like that.

HEDDA. Oh. You, Mr. Loevborg?

LOEVBORG. Thank you, I don't either.

MRS. ELVSTED. No, he doesn't either.

HEDDA (*looks into his eyes*). But if I want you to?

LOEVBORG. That doesn't make any difference.

HEDDA (*laughs*). Have I no power over you at all? Poor me!

LOEVBORG. Not where this is concerned.

HEDDA. Seriously, I think you should. For your own sake.

MRS. ELVSTED. Hedda!

LOEVBORG. Why?

HEDDA. Or perhaps I should say for other people's sake.

LOEVBORG. What do you mean?

HEDDA. People might think you didn't feel absolutely and unashamedly sure of yourself. In your heart of hearts.

MRS. ELVSTED (*quietly*). Oh, Hedda, no!

LOEVBORG. People can think what they like. For the present.

MRS. ELVSTED (*happily*). Yes, that's true.

HEDDA. I saw it so clearly in Judge Brack a few minutes ago.

LOEVBORG. Oh. What did you see?

HEDDA. He smiled so scornfully when he saw you were afraid to go in there and drink with them.

LOEVBORG. Afraid! I wanted to stay here and talk to you.

MRS. ELVSTED. That was only natural, Hedda.

HEDDA. But the Judge wasn't to know that. I saw him

wink at Tesman when you showed you didn't dare to join their wretched little party.

LOEVBORG. Didn't dare! Are you saying I didn't dare?

HEDDA. I'm not saying so. But that was what Judge Brack thought.

LOEVBORG. Well, let him.

HEDDA. You're not going, then?

LOEVBORG. I'm staying here with you and Thea.

MRS. ELVSTED. Yes, Hedda, of course he is.

HEDDA (*smiles, and nods approvingly to* LOEVBORG). Firm as a rock! A man of principle! That's how a man should be! [*Turns to* MRS. ELVSTED *and strokes her cheek.*] Didn't I tell you so this morning when you came here in such a panic—

LOEVBORG (*starts*). Panic?

MRS. ELVSTED (*frightened*). Hedda! But—Hedda!

HEDDA. Well, now you can see for yourself. There's no earthly need for you to get scared to death just because— [*Stops.*] Well! Let's all three cheer up and enjoy ourselves.

LOEVBORG. Mrs. Tesman, would you mind explaining to me what this is all about?

MRS. ELVSTED. Oh, my God, my God, Hedda, what are you saying? What are you doing?

HEDDA. Keep calm. That horrid Judge has his eye on you?

LOEVBORG. Scared to death, were you? For my sake?

MRS. ELVSTED (*quietly, trembling*). Oh, Hedda! You've made me so unhappy!

LOEVBORG (*looks coldly at her for a moment. His face is distorted*). So that was how much you trusted me.

MRS. ELVSTED. Eilert dear, please listen to me—

LOEVBORG (*takes one of the glasses of punch, raises it and says quietly, hoarsely*). Skoal, Thea! [*Empties the glass, puts it down and picks up one of the others.*]

MRS. ELVSTED (*quietly*). Hedda, Hedda! Why did you want this to happen?

HEDDA. I—want it? Are you mad?

LOEVBORG. Skoal to you too, Mrs. Tesman. Thanks for telling me the truth. Here's to the truth! [*Empties his glass and refills it.*]

HEDDA (*puts her hand on his arm*). Steady. That's enough for now. Don't forget the party.

MRS. ELVSTED. No, no, no!

HEDDA. Ssh! They're looking at you.

LOEVBORG (*puts down his glass*). Thea, tell me the truth—

MRS. ELVSTED. Yes!

LOEVBORG. Did your husband know you were following me?

MRS. ELVSTED. Oh, Hedda!

LOEVBORG. Did you and he have an agreement that you should come here and keep an eye on me? Perhaps he gave you the idea? After all, he's a magistrate. I suppose he needed me back in his office. Or did he miss my companionship at the card table?

MRS. ELVSTED (*quietly, sobbing*). Eilert, Eilert!

LOEVBORG (*seizes a glass and is about to fill it*). Let's drink to him, too.

HEDDA. No more now. Remember you're going to read your book to Tesman.

LOEVBORG (*calm again, puts down his glass*). That was silly of me, Thea. To take it like that, I mean. Don't be angry with me, my dear. You'll see—yes, and they'll see, too—that though I fell, I—I have raised myself up again. With your help, Thea.

MRS. ELVSTED (*happily*). Oh, thank God!

[BRACK *has meanwhile glanced at his watch. He and* TESMAN *get up and come into the drawing room.*]

BRACK (*takes his hat and overcoat*). Well, Mrs. Tesman, it's time for us to go.

HEDDA. Yes, I suppose it must be.

LOEVBORG (*gets up*). Time for me too, Judge.

MRS. ELVSTED (*quietly, pleadingly*). Eilert, please don't!

HEDDA (*pinches her arm*). They can hear you.

MRS. ELVSTED (*gives a little cry*). Oh!

LOEVBORG (*to* BRACK). You were kind enough to ask me to join you.

BRACK. Are you coming?

LOEVBORG. If I may.

BRACK. Delighted.

LOEVBORG (*puts the paper package in his pocket and says to* TESMAN). I'd like to show you one or two things before I send it off to the printer.

TESMAN. I say, that'll be fun. Fancy—! Oh, but Hedda, how'll Mrs. Elvsted get home? What?

HEDDA. Oh, we'll manage somehow.

LOEVBORG (*glances over towards the ladies*). Mrs. Elvsted? I shall come back and collect her, naturally. [*Goes closer.*] About ten o'clock, Mrs. Tesman? Will that suit you?

HEDDA. Yes. That'll suit me admirably.

TESMAN. Good, that's settled. But you mustn't expect me back so early, Hedda.

HEDDA. Stay as long as you c— as long as you like, dear.

MRS. ELVSTED (*trying to hide her anxiety*). Well then, Mr. Loevborg, I'll wait here till you come.

LOEVBORG (*his hat in his hand*). Pray do, Mrs. Elvsted.

BRACK. Well, gentlemen, now the party begins. I trust that, in the words of a certain fair lady, we shall enjoy good sport.

HEDDA. What a pity the fair lady can't be there, invisible.

BRACK. Why invisible?

HEDDA. So as to be able to hear some of your uncensored witticisms, your honor.

BRACK (*laughs*). Oh, I shouldn't advise the fair lady to do that.

TESMAN (*laughs too*). I say, Hedda, that's good. By Jove!
Fancy that!

BRACK. Well, good night, ladies, good night!

LOEVBORG (*bows farewell*). About ten o'clock, then.

[BRACK, LOEVBORG, *and* TESMAN *go out through the hall. As
they do so,* BERTHA *enters from the rear room with a lighted
lamp. She puts it on the drawing-room table, then goes out
the way she came.*]

MRS. ELVSTED (*has got up and is walking uneasily to and
fro*). Oh Hedda, Hedda! How is all this going to end?

HEDDA. At ten o'clock, then. He'll be here. I can see him.
With a crown of vine-leaves in his hair. Burning and
unashamed!

MRS. ELVSTED. Oh, I do hope so!

HEDDA. Can't you see? Then he'll be himself again! He'll
be a free man for the rest of his days!

MRS. ELVSTED. Please God you're right.

HEDDA. That's how he'll come! [*Gets up and goes closer.*]
You can doubt him as much as you like. I believe in him!
Now we'll see which of us—

MRS. ELVSTED. You're after something, Hedda.

HEDDA. Yes, I am. For once in my life I want to have the
power to shape a man's destiny.

MRS. ELVSTED. Haven't you that power already?

HEDDA. No, I haven't. I've never had it.

MRS. ELVSTED. What about your husband?

HEDDA. Him! Oh, if you could only understand how poor I
am. And you're allowed to be so rich, so rich! [*Clasps her
passionately.*] I think I'll burn your hair off after all!

MRS. ELVSTED. Let me go! Let me go! You frighten me,
Hedda!

BERTHA (*in the open doorway*). I've laid tea in the dining
room, madam.

HEDDA. Good, we're coming.

MRS. ELVSTED. No, no, no! I'd rather go home alone! Now—at once!

HEDDA. Rubbish! First you're going to have some tea, you little idiot. And then—at ten o'clock—Eilert Loevborg will come. With a crown of vine-leaves in his hair!

[*She drags* MRS. ELVSTED *almost forcibly towards the open doorway.*]

CURTAIN

ACT THREE

The same. The curtains are drawn across the open door-way, and also across the french windows. The lamp, half turned down, with a shade over it, is burning on the table. In the stove, the door of which is open, a fire has been burning, but it is now almost out.

[MRS. ELVSTED, *wrappd in a large shawl and with her feet resting on a footstool, is sitting near the stove, huddled in the armchair.* HEDDA *is lying asleep on the sofa, fully dressed, with a blanket over her.*]

MRS. ELVSTED (*after a pause, suddenly sits up in her chair and listens tensely. Then she sinks wearily back again and sighs*). Not back yet! Oh, God! Oh, God! Not back yet!

[BERTHA *tiptoes cautiously in from the hall. She has a letter in her hand.*]

MRS. ELVSTED (*turns and whispers*). What is it? Has some-one come?

BERTHA (*quietly*). Yes, a servant's just called with this letter.

MRS. ELVSTED (*quickly, holding out her hand*). A letter! Give it to me!

BERTHA. But it's for the Doctor, madam.

MRS. ELVSTED. Oh. I see.

BERTHA. Miss Tesman's maid brought it. I'll leave it here on the table.

MRS. ELVSTED. Yes, do.

BERTHA (*puts down the letter*). I'd better put the lamp out. It's starting to smoke.

MRS. ELVSTED. Yes, put it out. It'll soon be daylight.

BERTHA (*puts out the lamp*). It's daylight already, madam.

MRS. ELVSTED. Yes. Broad day. And not home yet.

BERTHA. Oh dear, I was afraid this would happen.

MRS. ELVSTED. Were you?

BERTHA. Yes. When I heard that a certain gentleman had returned to town, and saw him go off with them. I've heard all about him.

MRS. ELVSTED. Don't talk so loud. You'll wake your mistress.

BERTHA (*looks at the sofa and sighs*). Yes. Let her go on sleeping, poor dear. Shall I put some more wood on the fire?

MRS. ELVSTED. Thank you, don't bother on my account.

BERTHA. Very good. [*Goes quietly out through the hall.*]

HEDDA (*wakes as the door closes and looks up*). What's that?

MRS. ELVSTED. It was only the maid.

HEDDA (*looks round*). What am I doing here? Oh, now I remember. [*Sits up on the sofa, stretches herself and rubs her eyes.*] What time is it, Thea?

MRS. ELVSTED. It's gone seven.

HEDDA. When did Tesman get back?

MRS. ELVSTED. He's not back yet.

HEDDA. Not home yet?

MRS. ELVSTED (*gets up*). No one's come.

HEDDA. And we sat up waiting for them till four o'clock.

MRS. ELVSTED. How I waited for him!

HEDDA (*yawns and says with her hand in front of her mouth*). Oh, dear. We might have saved ourselves the trouble.

MRS. ELVSTED. Did you manage to sleep?

HEDDA. Oh, yes. Quite well, I think. Didn't you get any?

MRS. ELVSTED. Not a wink, I couldn't, Hedda. I just couldn't.

HEDDA (*gets up and comes over to her*). Now, now, now. There's nothing to worry about. I know what's happened.

MRS. ELVSTED. What? Please tell me.

HEDDA. Well, obviously the party went on very late—

MRS. ELVSTED. Oh dear, I suppose it must have. But—

HEDDA. And Tesman didn't want to come home and wake

us all up in the middle of the night. [*Laughs.*] Probably wasn't too keen to show his face either, after a spree like that.

MRS. ELVSTED. But where could he have gone?

HEDDA. I should think he's probably slept at his aunts'. They keep his old room for him.

MRS. ELVSTED. No, he can't be with them. A letter came for him just now from Miss Tesman. It's over there.

HEDDA. Oh? [*Looks at the envelope.*] Yes, it's Auntie Juju's handwriting. Well, he must still be at Judge Brack's then. And Eilert Loevborg is sitting there, reading to him. With a crown of vine-leaves in his hair.

MRS. ELVSTED. Hedda, you're only saying that. You don't believe it.

HEDDA. Thea, you really are a little fool.

MRS. ELVSTED. Perhaps I am.

HEDDA. You look tired to death.

MRS. ELVSTED. Yes. I am tired to death.

HEDDA. Go to my room and lie down for a little. Do as I say, now; don't argue.

MRS. ELVSTED. No, no. I couldn't possibly sleep.

HEDDA. Of course you can.

MRS. ELVSTED. But your husband'll be home soon. And I must know at once—

HEDDA. I'll tell you when he comes.

MRS. ELVSTED. Promise me, Hedda?

HEDDA. Yes, don't worry. Go and get some sleep.

MRS. ELVSTED. Thank you. All right, I'll try.

[*She goes out through the rear room.* HEDDA *goes to the french windows and draws the curtains. Broad daylight floods into the room. She goes to the writing table, takes a small hand mirror from it and arranges her hair. Then she goes to the door leading into the hall and presses the bell. After a few moments,* BERTHA *enters.*]

BERTHA. Did you want anything, madam?

HEDDA. Yes, put some more wood on the fire. I'm freezing.

BERTHA. Bless you, I'll soon have this room warmed up. [*She rakes the embers together and puts a fresh piece of wood on them. Suddenly she stops and listens.*] There's someone at the front door, madam.

HEDDA. Well, go and open it. I'll see to the fire.

BERTHA. It'll burn up in a moment.

[*She goes out through the hall.* HEDDA *kneels on the footstool and puts more wood in the stove. After a few seconds,* GEORGE TESMAN *enters from the hall. He looks tired, and rather worried. He tiptoes towards the open doorway and is about to slip through the curtains.*]

HEDDA (*at the stove, without looking up*). Good morning.

TESMAN (*turns*). Hedda! [*Comes nearer.*] Good heavens, are you up already? What?

HEDDA. Yes, I got up very early this morning.

TESMAN. I was sure you'd still be sleeping. Fancy that!

HEDDA. Don't talk so loud. Mrs. Elvsted's asleep in my room.

TESMAN. Mrs. Elvsted? Has she stayed the night here?

HEDDA. Yes. No one came to escort her home.

TESMAN. Oh. No, I suppose not.

HEDDA (*closes the door of the stove and gets up*). Well. Was it fun?

TESMAN. Have you been anxious about me? What?

HEDDA. Not in the least. I asked if you'd had fun.

TESMAN. Oh yes, rather! Well, I thought, for once in a while— The first part was the best; when Eilert read his book to me. We arrived over an hour too early—what about that, eh? By Jove! Brack had a lot of things to see to, so Eilert read to me.

HEDDA (*sits at the right-hand side of the table*). Well? Tell me about it.

TESMAN (*sits on a footstool by the stove*). Honestly, Hedda, you've no idea what a book that's going to be. It's really one of the most remarkable things that's ever been written. By Jove!

HEDDA. Oh, never mind about the book—

TESMAN. I'm going to make a confession to you, Hedda. When he'd finished reading a sort of beastly feeling came over me.

HEDDA. Beastly feeling?

TESMAN. I found myself envying Eilert for being able to write like that. Imagine that, Hedda!

HEDDA. Yes. I can imagine.

TESMAN. What a tragedy that with all those gifts he should be so incorrigible.

HEDDA. You mean he's less afraid of life than most men?

TESMAN. Good heavens, no. He just doesn't know the meaning of the word moderation.

HEDDA. What happened afterwards?

TESMAN. Well, looking back on it I suppose you might almost call it an orgy, Hedda.

HEDDA. Had he vine-leaves in his hair?

TESMAN. Vine-leaves? No, I didn't see any of them. He made a long, rambling oration in honor of the woman who'd inspired him to write this book. Yes, those were the words he used.

HEDDA. Did he name her?

TESMAN. No. But I suppose it must be Mrs. Elvsted. You wait and see!

HEDDA. Where did you leave him?

TESMAN. On the way home. We left in a bunch—the last of us, that is—and Brack came with us to get a little fresh air. Well, then, you see, we agreed we ought to see Eilert home. He'd had a drop too much.

HEDDA. You don't say?

TESMAN. But now comes the funny part, Hedda. Or I should really say the tragic part. Oh, I'm almost ashamed to tell you. For Eilert's sake, I mean—

HEDDA. Why, what happened?

TESMAN. Well, you see, as we were walking towards town I happened to drop behind for a minute. Only for a minute —er—you understand—

HEDDA. Yes, yes—?

TESMAN. Well then, when I ran on to catch them up, what do you think I found by the roadside. What?

HEDDA. How on earth should I know?

TESMAN. You mustn't tell anyone, Hedda. What? Promise me that—for Eilert's sake. [*Takes a package wrapped in paper from his coat pocket.*] Just fancy! I found this.

HEDDA. Isn't this the one he brought here yesterday?

TESMAN. Yes! The whole of that precious, irreplaceable manuscript! And he went and lost it! Didn't even notice! What about that? By Jove! Tragic.

HEDDA. But why didn't you give it back to him?

TESMAN. I didn't dare to, in the state he was in.

HEDDA. Didn't you tell any of the others?

TESMAN. Good heavens, no. I didn't want to do that. For Eilert's sake, you understand.

HEDDA. Then no one else knows you have his manuscript?

TESMAN. No. And no one must be allowed to know.

HEDDA. Didn't it come up in the conversation later?

TESMAN. I didn't get a chance to talk to him any more. As soon as we got into the outskirts of town, he and one or two of the others gave us the slip. Disappeared, by Jove!

HEDDA. Oh? I suppose they took him home.

TESMAN. Yes, I imagine that was the idea. Brack left us, too.

HEDDA. And what have you been up to since then?

TESMAN. Well, I and one or two of the others—awfully

jolly chaps, they were—went back to where one of them lived, and had a cup of morning coffee. Morning-after coffee—what? Ah, well. I'll just lie down for a bit and give Eilert time to sleep it off, poor chap, then I'll run over and give this back to him.

HEDDA (*holds out her hand for the package*). No, don't do that. Not just yet. Let me read it first.

TESMAN. Oh no, really, Hedda dear, honestly, I daren't do that.

HEDDA. Daren't?

TESMAN. No—imagine how desperate he'll be when he wakes up and finds his manuscript's missing. He hasn't any copy, you see. He told me so himself.

HEDDA. Can't a thing like that be rewritten?

TESMAN. Oh no, not possibly, I shouldn't think. I mean, the inspiration, you know—

HEDDA. Oh, yes. I'd forgotten that. [*Casually.*] By the way, there's a letter for you.

TESMAN. Is there? Fancy that!

HEDDA (*holds it out to him*). It came early this morning.

TESMAN. I say, it's from Auntie Juju! What on earth can it be? [*Puts the package on the other footstool, opens the letter, reads it and jumps up.*] Oh, Hedda! She says poor Auntie Rena's dying.

HEDDA. Well, we've been expecting that.

TESMAN. She says if I want to see her I must go quickly. I'll run over at once.

HEDDA (*hides a smile*). Run?

TESMAN. Hedda dear, I suppose you wouldn't like to come with me? What about that, eh?

HEDDA (*gets up and says wearily and with repulsion*). No, no, don't ask me to do anything like that. I can't bear illness or death. I loathe anything ugly.

TESMAN. Yes, yes. Of course. [*In a dither.*] My hat? My

overcoat? Oh yes, in the hall. I do hope I won't get there too late, Hedda? What?

HEDDA. You'll be all right if you run.

[BERTHA *enters from the hall.*]

BERTHA. Judge Brack's outside and wants to know if he can come in.

TESMAN. At this hour? No, I can't possibly receive him now.

HEDDA. I can. [*To* BERTHA.] Ask his honor to come in. [BERTHA *goes.*]

HEDDA (*whispers quickly*). The manuscript, Tesman. [*She snatches it from the footstool.*]

TESMAN. Yes, give it to me.

HEDDA. No, I'll look after it for now.

[*She goes over to the writing table and puts it in the book-case.* TESMAN *stands dithering, unable to get his gloves on.* JUDGE BRACK *enters from the hall.*]

HEDDA (*nods to him*). Well, you're an early bird.

BRACK. Yes, aren't I? [*To* TESMAN.] Are you up and about, too?

TESMAN. Yes, I've got to go and see my aunts. Poor Auntie Rena's dying.

BRACK. Oh dear, is she? Then you mustn't let me detain you. At so tragic a—

TESMAN. Yes, I really must run. Good-bye! Good-bye! [*Runs out through the hall.*]

HEDDA (*goes nearer*). You seem to have had excellent sport last night—Judge.

BRACK. Indeed yes, Mrs. Hedda. I haven't even had time to take my clothes off.

HEDDA. You haven't either?

BRACK. As you see. What's Tesman told you about last night's escapades?

HEDDA. Oh, only some boring story about having gone and drunk coffee somewhere.

BRACK. Yes, I've heard about that coffee party. Eilert Loevborg wasn't with them, I gather?

HEDDA. No, they took him home first.

BRACK. Did Tesman go with him?

HEDDA. No, one or two of the others, he said.

BRACK (*smiles*). George Tesman is a credulous man, Mrs. Hedda.

HEDDA. God knows. But—has something happened?

BRACK. Well, yes, I'm afraid it has.

HEDDA. I see. Sit down and tell me.

[*She sits on the left of the table,* BRACK *at the long side of it, near her.*]

HEDDA. Well?

BRACK. I had a special reason for keeping track of my guests last night. Or perhaps I should say some of my guests.

HEDDA. Including Eilert Loevberg?

BRACK. I must confess—yes.

HEDDA. You're beginning to make me curious.

BRACK. Do you know where he and some of my other guests spent the latter half of last night, Mrs. Hedda?

HEDDA. Tell me. If it won't shock me.

BRACK. Oh, I don't think it'll shock you. They found themselves participating in an exceedingly animated *soirée*.

HEDDA. Of a sporting character?

BRACK. Of a highly sporting character.

HEDDA. Tell me more.

BRACK. Loevborg had received an invitation in advance— as had the others. I knew all about that. But he had refused. As you know, he's become a new man.

HEDDA. Up at the Elvsteds', yes. But he went?

BRACK. Well, you see, Mrs. Hedda, last night at my house, unhappily, the spirit moved him.

HEDDA. Yes, I hear he became inspired.

BRACK. Somewhat violently inspired. And as a result, I

suppose, his thoughts strayed. We men, alas, don't always stick to our principles as firmly as we should.

HEDDA. I'm sure you're an exception, Judge Brack. But go on about Loevborg.

BRACK. Well, to cut a long story short, he ended up in the establishment of a certain Mademoiselle Danielle.

HEDDA. Mademoiselle Danielle?

BRACK. She was holding the *soirée*. For a selected circle of friends and admirers.

HEDDA. Has she got red hair?

BRACK. She has.

HEDDA. A singer of some kind?

BRACK. Yes—among other accomplishments. She's also a celebrated huntress—of men, Mrs. Hedda. I'm sure you've heard about her. Eilert Loevborg used to be one of her most ardent patrons. In his salad days.

HEDDA. And how did all this end?

BRACK. Not entirely amicably, from all accounts. Mademoiselle Danielle began by receiving him with the utmost tenderness and ended by resorting to her fists.

HEDDA. Against Loevborg?

BRACK. Yes. He accused her, or her friends, of having robbed him. He claimed his pocketbook had been stolen. Among other things. In short, he seems to have made a bloodthirsty scene.

HEDDA. And what did this lead to?

BRACK. It led to a general free-for-all, in which both sexes participated. Fortunately, in the end the police arrived.

HEDDA. The police too?

BRACK. Yes. I'm afraid it may turn out to be rather an expensive joke for Master Eilert. Crazy fool!

HEDDA. Oh?

BRACK. Apparently he put up a very violent resistance.

Hit one of the constables on the ear and tore his uniform.
He had to accompany them to the police station.

HEDDA. Where did you learn all this?

BRACK. From the police.

HEDDA (*to herself*). So that's what happened. He didn't
have a crown of vine-leaves in his hair.

BRACK. Vine-leaves, Mrs. Hedda?

HEDDA (*in her normal voice again*). But, tell me, Judge,
why do you take such a close interest in Eilert Loevborg?

BRACK. For one thing it'll hardly be a matter of complete
indifference to me if it's revealed in court that he came there
straight from my house.

HEDDA. Will it come to court?

BRACK. Of course. Well, I don't regard that as particularly
serious. Still, I thought it my duty, as a friend of the family,
to give you and your husband a full account of his nocturnal
adventures.

HEDDA. Why?

BRACK. Because I've a shrewd suspicion that he's hoping
to use you as a kind of screen.

HEDDA. What makes you think that?

BRACK. Oh, for heaven's sake, Mrs. Hedda, we're not
blind. You wait and see. This Mrs. Elvsted won't be going
back to her husband just yet.

HEDDA. Well, if there were anything between those two
there are plenty of other places where they could meet.

BRACK. Not in anyone's home. From now on every respectable house will once again be closed to Eilert Loevborg.

HEDDA. And mine should be too, you mean?

BRACK. Yes. I confess I should find it more than irksome if
this gentleman were to be granted unrestricted access to
this house. If he were superfluously to intrude into—

HEDDA. The triangle?

BRACK. Precisely. For me it would be like losing a home.

HEDDA (*looks at him and smiles*). I see. You want to be the cock of the walk.

BRACK (*nods slowly and lowers his voice*). Yes, that is my aim. And I shall fight for it with—every weapon at my disposal.

HEDDA (*as her smile fades*). You're a dangerous man, aren't you? When you really want something.

BRACK. You think so?

HEDDA. Yes, I'm beginning to think so. I'm deeply thankful you haven't any kind of hold over me.

BRACK (*laughs equivocally*). Well, well, Mrs. Hedda— perhaps you're right. If I had, who knows what I might not think up?

HEDDA. Come, Judge Brack. That sounds almost like a threat.

BRACK (*gets up*). Heaven forbid! In the creation of a triangle—and its continuance—the question of compulsion should never arise.

HEDDA. Exactly what I was thinking.

BRACK. Well, I've said what I came to say. I must be getting back. Good-bye, Mrs. Hedda. [*Goes towards the french windows.*]

HEDDA (*gets up*). Are you going out through the garden?

BRACK. Yes, it's shorter.

HEDDA. Yes. And it's the back door, isn't it?

BRACK. I've nothing against back doors. They can be quite intriguing—sometimes.

HEDDA. When people fire pistols out of them, for example?

BRACK (*in the doorway, laughs*). Oh, people don't shoot tame cocks.

HEDDA (*laughs too*). I suppose not. When they've only got one.

[*They nod good-bye, laughing. He goes. She closes the french windows behind him, and stands for a moment, looking out pensively. Then she walks across the room and glances through the curtains in the open doorway. Goes to the writing table, takes* LOEVBORG'S *package from the bookcase and is about to leaf through the pages when* BERTHA *is heard remonstrating loudly in the hall.* HEDDA *turns and listens. She hastily puts the package back in the drawer, locks it and puts the key on the inkstand.* EILERT LOEVBORG, *with his overcoat on and his hat in his hand, throws the door open. He looks somewhat confused and excited.*]

LOEVBORG (*shouts as he enters*). I must come in, I tell you! Let me pass! [*He closes the door, turns, sees* HEDDA, *controls himself immediately and bows.*]

HEDDA (*at the writing table*). Well, Mr. Loevborg, this is rather a late hour to be collecting Thea.

LOEVBORG. And an early hour to call on you. Please forgive me.

HEDDA. How do you know she's still here?

LOEVBORG. They told me at her lodgings that she has been out all night.

HEDDA (*goes to the table*). Did you notice anything about their behavior when they told you?

LOEVBORG (*looks at her, puzzled*). Notice anything?

HEDDA. Did they sound as if they thought it—strange?

LOEVBORG (*suddenly understands*). Oh, I see what you mean. I'm dragging her down with me. No, as a matter of fact I didn't notice anything. I suppose Tesman isn't up yet?

HEDDA. No, I don't think so.

LOEVBORG. When did he get home?

HEDDA. Very late.

LOEVBORG. Did he tell you anything?

HEDDA. Yes. I gather you had a merry party at Judge Brack's last night.

LOEVBORG. He didn't tell you anything else?

HEDDA. I don't think so. I was so terribly sleepy—

[MRS. ELVSTED *comes through the curtains in the open doorway.*]

MRS. ELVSTED (*runs towards him*). Oh, Eilert! At last!

LOEVBORG. Yes—at last. And too late.

MRS. ELVSTED. What is too late?

LOEVBORG. Everything—now. I'm finished, Thea.

MRS. ELVSTED. Oh, no, no! Don't say that!

LOEVBORG. You'll say it yourself, when you've heard what I—

MRS. ELVSTED. I don't want to hear anything!

HEDDA. Perhaps you'd rather speak to her alone? I'd better go.

LOEVBORG. No, stay.

MRS. ELVSTED. But I don't want to hear anything, I tell you!

LOEVBORG. It's not about last night.

MRS. ELVSTED. Then what—?

LOEVBORG. I want to tell you that from now on we must stop seeing each other.

MRS. ELVSTED. Stop seeing each other!

HEDDA (*involuntarily*). I knew it!

LOEVBORG. I have no further use for you, Thea.

MRS. ELVSTED. You can stand there and say that! No further use for me! Surely I can go on helping you? We'll go on working together, won't we?

LOEVBORG. I don't intend to do any more work from now on.

MRS. ELVSTED (*desperately*). Then what use have I for my life?

LOEVBORG. You must try to live as if you had never known me.

MRS. ELVSTED. But I can't!

LOEVBORG. Try to, Thea. Go back home—

MRS. ELVSTED. Never! I want to be wherever you are! I

won't let myself be driven away like this! I want to stay here—and be with you when the book comes out.

HEDDA (*whispers*). Ah, yes! The book!

LOEVBORG (*looks at her*). Our book; Thea's and mine. It belongs to both of us.

MRS. ELVSTED. Oh yes! I feel that too! And I've a right to be with you when it comes into the world. I want to see people respect and honor you again. And the joy! The joy! I want to share it with you!

LOEVBORG. Thea—our book will never come into the world.

HEDDA. Ah!

MRS. ELVSTED. Not—?

LOEVBORG. It cannot. Ever.

MRS. ELVSTED. Eilert—what have you done with the manuscript? Where is it?

LOEVBORG. Oh Thea, please don't ask me that!

MRS. ELVSTED. Yes, yes—I must know. I've a right to know. Now!

LOEVBORG. The manuscript. I've torn it up.

MRS. ELVSTED (*screams*). No, no!

HEDDA (*involuntarily*). But that's not—!

LOEVBORG (*looks at her*). Not true, you think?

HEDDA (*controls herself*). Why—yes, of course it is, if you say so. It just sounded so incredible—

LOEVBORG. It's true, nevertheless.

MRS. ELVSTED. Oh, my God, my God, Hedda—he's destroyed his own book!

LOEVBORG. I have destroyed my life. Why not my life's work, too?

MRS. ELVSTED. And you—did this last night?

LOEVBORG. Yes, Thea. I tore it into a thousand pieces. And scattered them out across the fjord. It's good, clean, salt water. Let it carry them away; let them drift in the

current and the wind. And in a little while, they will sink.
Deeper and deeper. As I shall, Thea.

MRS. ELVSTED. Do you know, Eilert—this book—all my
life I shall feel as though you'd killed a little child?

LOEVBORG. You're right. It is like killing a child.

MRS. ELVSTED. But how could you? It was my child, too!

HEDDA (*almost inaudibly*). Oh—the child—!

MRS. ELVSTED (*breathes heavily*). It's all over, then. Well—
I'll go now, Hedda.

HEDDA. You're not leaving town?

MRS. ELVSTED. I don't know what I'm going to do. I can't
see anything except—darkness. [*She goes out through the hall.*]

HEDDA (*waits a moment*). Aren't you going to escort her
home, Mr. Loevborg?

LOEVBORG. I? Through the streets? Do you want me to
let people see her with me?

HEDDA. Of course I don't know what else may have
happened last night. But is it so utterly beyond redress?

LOEVBORG. It isn't just last night. It'll go on happening. I
know it. But the curse of it is, I don't want to live that kind
of life. I don't want to start all that again. She's broken my
courage. I can't spit in the eyes of the world any longer.

HEDDA (*as though to herself*). That pretty little fool's been
trying to shape a man's destiny. [*Looks at him.*] But how
could you be so heartless towards her?

LOEVBORG. Don't call me heartless!

HEDDA. To go and destroy the one thing that's made her
life worth living? You don't call that heartless?

LOEVBORG. Do you want to know the truth, Hedda?

HEDDA. The truth?

LOEVBORG. Promise me first—give me your word—that
you'll never let Thea know about this.

HEDDA. I give you my word.

LOEVBORG. Good. Well; what I told her just now was a lie.

HEDDA. About the manuscript?

LOEVBORG. Yes. I didn't tear it up. Or throw it in the fjord.

HEDDA. You didn't? But where is it, then?

LOEVBORG. I destroyed it, all the same. I destroyed it, Hedda!

HEDDA. I don't understand.

LOEVBORG. Thea said that what I had done was like killing a child.

HEDDA. Yes. That's what she said.

LOEVBORG. But to kill a child isn't the worst thing a father can do to it.

HEDDA. What could be worse than that?

LOEVBORG. Hedda—suppose a man came home one morning, after a night of debauchery, and said to the mother of his child: "Look here. I've been wandering round all night. I've been to—such-and-such a place and such-and-such a place. And I had our child with me. I took him to—these places. And I've lost him. Just—lost him. God knows where he is or whose hands he's fallen into."

HEDDA. I see. But when all's said and done, this was only a book—

LOEVBORG. Thea's heart and soul were in that book. It was her whole life.

HEDDA. Yes. I understand.

LOEVBORG. Well, then you must also understand that she and I cannot possibly ever see each other again.

HEDDA. Where will you go?

LOEVBORG. Nowhere. I just want to put an end to it all. As soon as possible.

HEDDA (takes a step towards him). Eilert Loevborg, listen to me. Do it—beautifully!

LOEVBORG. Beautifully? [Smiles.] With a crown of vine-leaves in my hair? The way you used to dream of me—in the old days?

HEDDA. No. I don't believe in that crown any longer. But—do it beautifully, all the same. Just this once. Goodbye. You must go now. And don't come back.

LOEVBORG. Adieu, madam. Give my love to George Tesman. [*Turns to go.*]

HEDDA. Wait. I want to give you a souvenir to take with you.

[*She goes over to the writing table, opens the drawer and the pistol-case, and comes back to* LOEVBORG *with one of the pistols.*]

LOEVBORG (*looks at her*). This? Is this the souvenir?

HEDDA (*nods slowly*). You recognise it? You looked down its barrel once.

LOEVBORG. You should have used it then.

HEDDA. Here! Use it now!

LOEVBORG (*puts the pistol in his breast pocket*). Thank you.

HEDDA. Do it beautifully, Eilert Loevborg. Only promise me that!

LOEVBORG. Good-bye, Hedda Gabler.

[*He goes out through the hall.* HEDDA *stands by the door for a moment, listening. Then she goes over to the writing table, takes out the package containing the manuscript, glances inside it, pulls some of the pages half out and looks at them. Then she takes it to the armchair by the stove and sits down with the package in her lap. After a moment, she opens the door of the stove; then she opens the packet.*]

HEDDA (*throws one of the pages into the stove and whispers to herself*). I'm burning your child, Thea! You with your beautiful wavy hair! [*She throws a few more pages into the stove.*] The child Eilert Loevborg gave you. [*Throws the rest of the manuscript in.*] I'm burning it! I'm burning your child!

CURTAIN

ACT FOUR

The same. It is evening. The drawing room is in darkness.
The small room is illuminated by the hanging lamp over the
table. The curtains are drawn across the french windows.
[HEDDA, dressed in black, is walking up and down in the
darkened room. Then she goes into the small room and crosses
to the left. A few chords are heard from the piano. She comes
back into the drawing room. BERTHA comes through the small
room from the right with a lighted lamp, which she places on the
table in front of the corner sofa in the drawing-room. Her eyes
are red with crying, and she has black ribbons on her cap.
She goes quietly out, right. HEDDA goes over to the french
windows, draws the curtains slightly to one side and looks out
into the darkness. A few moments later, MISS TESMAN enters
from the hall. She is dressed in mourning, with a black hat and
veil. HEDDA goes to meet her and holds out her hand.]

MISS TESMAN. Well, Hedda, here I am in the weeds of
sorrow. My poor sister has ended her struggles at last.

HEDDA. I've already heard. Tesman sent me a card.

MISS TESMAN. Yes, he promised me he would. But I
thought, no, I must go and break the news of death to Hedda
myself—here, in the house of life.

HEDDA. It's very kind of you.

MISS TESMAN. Ah, Rena shouldn't have chosen a time like
this to pass away. This is no moment for Hedda's house to
be a place of mourning.

HEDDA (*changing the subject*). She died peacefully, Miss
Tesman?

MISS TESMAN. Oh, it was quite beautiful! The end came so
calmly. And she was so happy at being able to see George
once again. And say good-bye to him. Hasn't he come home
yet?

HEDDA. No. He wrote that I mustn't expect him too soon. But please sit down.

MISS TESMAN. No, thank you, Hedda dear—bless you. I'd like to. But I've so little time. I must dress her and lay her out as well as I can. She shall go to her grave looking really beautiful.

HEDDA. Can't I help with anything?

MISS TESMAN. Why, you mustn't think of such a thing! Hedda Tesman mustn't let her hands be soiled by contact with death. Or her thoughts. Not at this time.

HEDDA. One can't always control one's thoughts.

MISS TESMAN (*continues*). Ah, well, that's life. Now we must start to sew poor Rena's shroud. There'll be sewing to be done in this house too before long, I shouldn't wonder. But not for a shroud, praise God.

[GEORGE TESMAN *enters from the hall.*]

HEDDA. You've come at last! Thank heavens!

TESMAN. Are you here, Auntie Juju? With Hedda? Fancy that!

MISS TESMAN. I was just on the point of leaving, dear boy. Well, have you done everything you promised me?

TESMAN. No, I'm afraid I forgot half of it. I'll have to run over again tomorrow. My head's in a complete whirl today. I can't collect my thoughts.

MISS TESMAN. But George dear, you mustn't take it like this.

TESMAN. Oh? Well—er—how should I?

MISS TESMAN. You must be happy in your grief. Happy for what's happened. As I am.

TESMAN. Oh, yes, yes. You're thinking of Aunt Rena.

HEDDA. It'll be lonely for you now, Miss Tesman.

MISS TESMAN. For the first few days, yes. But it won't last long, I hope. Poor dear Rena's little room isn't going to stay empty.

TESMAN. Oh? Whom are you going to move in there? What?

MISS TESMAN. Oh, there's always some poor invalid who needs care and attention.

HEDDA. Do you really want another cross like that to bear?

MISS TESMAN. Cross! God forgive you, child. It's been no cross for me.

HEDDA. But now—if a complete stranger comes to live with you—?

MISS TESMAN. Oh, one soon makes friends with invalids. And I need so much to have someone to live for. Like you, my dear. Well, I expect there'll soon be work in this house too for an old aunt, praise God!

HEDDA. Oh—please!

TESMAN. By Jove, yes! What a splendid time the three of us could have together if—

HEDDA. If?

TESMAN (*uneasily*). Oh, never mind. It'll all work out. Let's hope so—what?

MISS TESMAN. Yes, yes. Well, I'm sure you two would like to be alone. [*Smiles.*] Perhaps Hedda may have something to tell you, George. Good-bye. I must go home to Rena. [*Turns to the door.*] Dear God, how strange! Now Rena is with me and with poor dear Joachim.

TESMAN. Fancy that. Yes, Auntie Juju! What?

[MISS TESMAN *goes out through the hall.*]

HEDDA (*follows* TESMAN *coldly and searchingly with her eyes*). I really believe this death distresses you more than it does her.

TESMAN. Oh, it isn't just Auntie Rena. It's Eilert I'm so worried about.

HEDDA (*quickly*). Is there any news of him?

TESMAN. I ran over to see him this afternoon. I wanted to tell him his manuscript was in safe hands.

HEDDA. Oh? You didn't find him?

TESMAN. No. He wasn't at home. But later I met Mrs. Elvsted and she told me he'd been here early this morning.

HEDDA. Yes, just after you'd left.

TESMAN. It seems he said he'd torn the manuscript up. What?

HEDDA. Yes, he claimed to have done so.

TESMAN. You told him we had it, of course?

HEDDA. No. [*Quickly*]. Did you tell Mrs. Elvsted?

TESMAN. No, I didn't like to. But you ought to have told him. Think if he should go home and do something desperate! Give me the manuscript, Hedda. I'll run over to him with it right away. Where did you put it?

HEDDA (*cold and motionless, leaning against the armchair*). I haven't got it any longer.

TESMAN. Haven't got it? What on earth do you mean?

HEDDA. I've burned it.

TESMAN (*starts, terrified*). Burned it! Burned Eilert's manuscript!

HEDDA. Don't shout. The servant will hear you.

TESMAN. Burned it! But in heaven's name—! Oh, no, no, no! This is impossible!

HEDDA. Well, it's true.

TESMAN. But Hedda, do you realise what you've done? That's appropriating lost property! It's against the law! By Jove! You ask Judge Brack and see if I'm not right.

HEDDA. You'd be well advised not to talk about it to Judge Brack or anyone else.

TESMAN. But how could you go and do such a dreadful thing? What on earth put the idea into your head? What came over you? Answer me! What?

HEDDA (*represses an almost imperceptible smile*). I did it for your sake, George.

TESMAN. For my sake?

HEDDA. When you come home this morning and described how he'd read his book to you—

TESMAN. Yes, yes?

HEDDA. You admitted you were jealous of him.

TESMAN. But, good heavens, I didn't mean it literally!

HEDDA. No matter. I couldn't bear the thought that any-one else should push you into the background.

TESMAN (*torn between doubt and joy*). Hedda—is this true? But—but—but I never realized you loved me like that! Fancy—

HEDDA. Well, I suppose you'd better know. I'm going to have— [*Breaks off and says violently.*] No, no—you'd better ask your Auntie Juju. She'll tell you.

TESMAN. Hedda! I think I understand what you mean. [*Clasps his hands.*] Good heavens, can it really be true! What?

HEDDA. Don't shout. The servant will hear you.

TESMAN (*laughing with joy*). The servant! I say, that's good! The servant! Why, that's Bertha! I'll run out and tell her at once!

HEDDA (*clenches her hands in despair*). Oh, it's destroying me, all this—it's destroying me!

TESMAN. I say, Hedda, what's up? What?

HEDDA (*cold, controlled*). Oh, it's all so—absurd—George.

TESMAN. Absurd? That I'm so happy? But surely—? Ah, well—perhaps I won't say anything to Bertha.

HEDDA. No, do. She might as well know too.

TESMAN. No, no, I won't tell her yet. But Auntie Juju—I must let her know! And you—you called me George! For the first time! Fancy that! Oh, it'll make Auntie Juju so happy, all this! So very happy!

HEDDA. Will she be happy when she hears I've burned Eilert Loevborg's manuscript—for your sake?

TESMAN. No, I'd forgotten about that. Of course no one

must be allowed to know about the manuscript. But that you're burning with love for me, Hedda, I must certainly let Auntie Juju know that. I say, I wonder if young wives often feel like that towards their husbands? What?

HEDDA. You might ask Auntie Juju about that too.

TESMAN. I will, as soon as I get the chance. [*Looks uneasy and thoughtful again.*] But I say, you know, that manuscript. Dreadful business. Poor Eilert!

[MRS. ELVSTED, *dressed as on her first visit, with hat and overcoat, enters from the hall.*]

MRS. ELVSTED (*greets them hastily and tremulously*). Oh, Hedda dear, do please forgive me for coming here again.

HEDDA. Why, Thea, what's happened?

TESMAN. Is it anything to do with Eilert Loevborg? What?

MRS. ELVSTED. Yes—I'm so dreadfully afraid he may have met with an accident.

HEDDA (*grips her arm*). You think so?

TESMAN. But, good heavens, Mrs. Elvsted, what makes you think that?

MRS. ELVSTED. I heard them talking about him at the boarding-house, as I went in. Oh, there are the most terrible rumors being spread about him in town today.

TESMAN. Fancy. Yes, I heard about them too. But I can testify that he went straight home to bed. Fancy that!

HEDDA. Well—what did they say in the boarding-house?

MRS. ELVSTED. Oh, I couldn't find out anything. Either they didn't know, or else— They stopped talking when they saw me. And I didn't dare to ask.

TESMAN (*fidgets uneasily*). We must hope—we must hope you misheard them, Mrs. Elvsted.

MRS. ELVSTED. No, no, I'm sure it was he they were talking about. I heard them say something about a hospital—

TESMAN. Hospital!

HEDDA. Oh no, surely that's impossible!

MRS. ELVSTED. Oh, I became so afraid. So I went up to his rooms and asked to see him.

HEDDA. Do you think that was wise, Thea?

MRS. ELVSTED. Well, what else could I do? I couldn't bear the uncertainty any longer.

TESMAN. But *you* didn't manage to find him either? What?

MRS. ELVSTED. No. And they had no idea where he was. They said he hadn't been home since yesterday afternoon.

TESMAN. Since yesterday? Fancy that!

MRS. ELVSTED. I'm sure he must have met with an accident.

TESMAN. Hedda, I wonder if I ought to go into town and make one or two enquiries?

HEDDA. No, no, don't you get mixed up in this.

[JUDGE BRACK *enters from the hall, hat in hand.* BERTHA, *who has opened the door for him, closes it. He looks serious and greets them silently.*]

TESMAN. Hullo, my dear Judge. Fancy seeing you!

BRACK. I had to come and talk to you.

TESMAN. I can see Auntie Juju's told you the news.

BRACK. Yes, I've heard about that too.

TESMAN. Tragic, isn't it?

BRACK. Well, my dear chap, that depends how you look at it.

TESMAN (*looks uncertainly at him*). Has something else happened?

BRACK. Yes.

HEDDA. Another tragedy?

BRACK. That also depends on how you look at it, Mrs. Tesman.

MRS. ELVSTED. Oh, it's something to do with Eilert Loevborg!

BRACK (*looks at her for a moment*). How did you guess? Perhaps you've heard already—?

MRS. ELVSTED (*confused*). No, no, not at all—I—

TESMAN. For heaven's sake, tell us!

BRACK (*shrugs his shoulders*). Well, I'm afraid they've taken him to the hospital. He's dying.

MRS. ELVSTED (*screams*). Oh God, God!

TESMAN. The hospital! Dying!

HEDDA (*involuntarily*). So quickly!

MRS. ELVSTED (*weeping*). Oh, Hedda! And we parted enemies!

HEDDA (*whispers*). Thea—Thea!

MRS. ELVSTED (*ignoring her*). I must see him! I must see him before he dies!

BRACK. It's no use, Mrs. Elvsted. No one's allowed to see him now.

MRS. ELVSTED. But what's happened to him? You must tell me!

TESMAN. He hasn't tried to do anything to himself? What?

HEDDA. Yes, he has. I'm sure of it.

TESMAN. Hedda, how can you—?

BRACK (*who has not taken his eyes from her*). I'm afraid you've guessed correctly, Mrs. Tesman.

MRS. ELVSTED. How dreadful!

TESMAN. Attempted suicide! Fancy that!

HEDDA. Shot himself!

BRACK. Right again, Mrs. Tesman.

MRS. ELVSTED (*tries to compose herself*). When did this happen, Judge Brack?

BRACK. This afternoon. Between three and four.

TESMAN. But, good heavens—where? What?

BRACK (*a little hesitantly*). Where? Why, my dear chap, in his rooms of course.

MRS. ELVSTED. No, that's impossible. I was there soon after six.

BRACK. Well, it must have been somewhere else, then. I

don't know exactly. I only know that they found him. He'd shot himself—through the breast.

MRS. ELVSTED. Oh, how horrible! That he should end like that!

HEDDA (*to* BRACK). Through the breast, you said?

BRACK. That is what I said.

HEDDA. Not through the head?

BRACK. Through the breast, Mrs. Tesman.

HEDDA. The breast. Yes; yes. That's good, too.

BRACK. Why, Mrs. Tesman?

HEDDA. Oh—no, I didn't mean anything.

TESMAN. And the wound's dangerous, you say? What?

BRACK. Mortal. He's probably already dead.

MRS. ELVSTED. Yes, yes—I feel it! It's all over. All over. Oh Hedda—!

TESMAN. But, tell me, how did you manage to learn all this?

BRACK (*curtly*). From the police. I spoke to one of them.

HEDDA (*loudly, clearly*). At last! Oh, thank God!

TESMAN (*appalled*). For God's sake, Hedda, what are you saying?

HEDDA. I am saying there's beauty in what he has done.

BRACK. Hm—Mrs. Tesman—

TESMAN. Beauty! Oh, but I say!

MRS. ELVSTED. Hedda, how can you talk of beauty in connection with a thing like this?

HEDDA. Eilert Loevborg has settled his account with life. He's had the courage to do what—what he had to do.

MRS. ELVSTED. No, that's not why it happened. He did it because he was mad.

TESMAN. He did it because he was desperate.

HEDDA. You're wrong! I know!

MRS. ELVSTED. He must have been mad. The same as when he tore up the manuscript.

BRACK (*starts*). Manuscript? Did he tear it up?

MRS. ELVSTED. Yes. Last night.

TESMAN (*whispers*). Oh, Hedda, we shall never be able to escape from this.

BRACK. Hm. Strange.

TESMAN (*wanders round the room*). To think of Eilert dying like that. And not leaving behind him the thing that would have made his name endure.

MRS. ELVSTED. If only it could be pieced together again!

TESMAN. Yes, fancy! If only it could! I'd give anything—

MRS. ELVSTED. Perhaps it can, Mr. Tesman.

TESMAN. What do you mean?

MRS. ELVSTED (*searches in the pocket of her dress*). Look! I kept the notes he dictated it from.

HEDDA (*takes a step nearer*). Ah!

TESMAN. You kept them, Mrs. Elvsted! What?

MRS. ELVSTED. Yes, here they are. I brought them with me when I left home. They've been in my pocket ever since.

TESMAN. Let me have a look.

MRS. ELVSTED (*hands him a wad of small sheets of paper*). They're in a terrible muddle. All mixed up.

TESMAN. I say, just fancy if we can sort them out! Perhaps if we work on them together—?

MRS. ELVSTED. Oh, yes! Let's try, anyway!

TESMAN. We'll manage it. We must! I shall dedicate my life to this.

HEDDA. *You*, George? Your life?

TESMAN. Yes—well, all the time I can spare. My book'll have to wait. Hedda, you do understand? What? I owe it to Eilert's memory.

HEDDA. Perhaps.

TESMAN. Well, my dear Mrs. Elvsted, you and I'll have to pool our brains. No use crying over spilt milk, what? We must try to approach this matter calmly.

MRS. ELVSTED. Yes, yes, Mr. Tesman. I'll do my best.

TESMAN. Well, come over here and let's start looking at these notes right away. Where shall we sit? Here? No, the other room. You'll excuse us, won't you, Judge? Come along with me, Mrs. Elvsted.

MRS. ELVSTED. Oh, God! If only we can manage to do it!

[TESMAN *and* MRS. ELVSTED *go into the rear room. He takes off his hat and overcoat. They sit at the table beneath the hanging lamp and absorb themselves in the notes.* HEDDA *walks across to the stove and sits in the armchair. After a moment,* BRACK *goes over to her.*]

HEDDA (*half aloud*). Oh, Judge! This act of Eilert Loevborg's—doesn't it give one a sense of release!

BRACK. Release, Mrs. Hedda? Well, it's a release for him, of course—

HEDDA. Oh, I don't mean him—I mean me! The release of knowing that someone can do something really brave! Something beautiful!

BRACK (*smiles*). Hm—my dear Mrs. Hedda—

HEDDA. Oh, I know what you're going to say. You're a bourgeois at heart too, just like—ah, well!

BRACK (*looks at her*). Eilert Loevborg has meant more to you than you're willing to admit to yourself. Or am I wrong?

HEDDA. I'm not answering questions like that from you. I only know that Eilert Loevborg has had the courage to live according to his own principles. And now, at last, he's done something big! Something beautiful! To have the courage and the will to rise from the feast of life so early!

BRACK. It distresses me deeply, Mrs. Hedda, but I'm afraid I must rob you of that charming illusion.

HEDDA. Illusion?

BRACK. You wouldn't have been allowed to keep it for long, anyway.

HEDDA. What do you mean?

BRACK. He didn't shoot himself on purpose.

HEDDA. Not on purpose?

BRACK. No. It didn't happen quite the way I told you.

HEDDA. Have you been hiding something? What is it?

BRACK. In order to spare poor Mrs. Elvsted's feelings, I permitted myself one or two small—equivocations.

HEDDA. What?

BRACK. To begin with, he is already dead.

HEDDA. He died at the hospital?

BRACK. Yes. Without regaining consciousness.

HEDDA. What else haven't you told us?

BRACK. The incident didn't take place at his lodgings.

HEDDA. Well, that's utterly unimportant.

BRACK. Not utterly. The fact is, you see, that Eilert Loevborg was found shot in Mademoiselle Danielle's boudoir.

HEDDA (*almost jumps up, but instead sinks back in her chair*). That's impossible. He can't have been there today.

BRACK. He was there this afternoon. He went to ask for something he claimed they'd taken from him. Talked some crazy nonsense about a child which had got lost—

HEDDA. Oh! So that was the reason!

BRACK. I thought at first he might have been referring to his manuscript. But I hear he destroyed that himself. So he must have meant his pocketbook—I suppose.

HEDDA. Yes, I suppose so. So they found him there?

BRACK. Yes; there. With a discharged pistol in his breast pocket. The shot had wounded him mortally.

HEDDA. Yes. In the breast.

BRACK. No. In the—hm—stomach. The—lower part—

HEDDA (*looks at him with an expression of repulsion*). That too! Oh, why does everything I touch become mean and ludicrous? It's like a curse!

BRACK. There's something else, Mrs. Hedda. It's rather disagreeable, too.

HEDDA. What?

BRACK. The pistol he had on him—

HEDDA. Yes? What about it?

BRACK. He must have stolen it.

HEDDA (*jumps up*). Stolen it! That isn't true! He didn't!

BRACK. It's the only explanation. He must have stolen it. Ssh!

[TESMAN *and* MRS. ELVSTED *have got up from the table in the rear room and come into the drawing-room.*]

TESMAN (*his hands full of papers*). Hedda, I can't see properly under that lamp. Think!

HEDDA. I am thinking.

TESMAN. Do you think we could possible use your writing table for a little? What?

HEDDA. Yes, of course. [*Quickly.*] No, wait! Let me tidy it up first.

TESMAN. Oh, don't you trouble about that. There's plenty of room.

HEDDA. No, no, let me tidy it up first, I say. I'll take these in and put them on the piano. Here.

[*She pulls an object, covered with sheets of music, out from under the bookcase, puts some more sheets on top and carries it all into the rear room and away to the left.* TESMAN *puts his papers on the writing table and moves the lamp over from the corner table. He and* MRS. ELVSTED *sit down and begin working again.* HEDDA *comes back.*]

HEDDA (*behind* MRS. ELVSTED'S *chair, ruffles her hair gently*). Well, my pretty Thea! And how is work progressing on Eilert Loevborg's memorial?

MRS. ELVSTED (*looks up at her, dejectedly*). Oh, it's going to be terribly difficult to get these into any order.

TESMAN. We've got to do it. We must! After all, putting other people's papers into order is rather my speciality, what?

[HEDDA *goes over to the stove and sits on one of the footstools.* BRACK *stands over her, leaning against the armchair.*]

HEDDA (*whispers*). What was that you were saying about the pistol?

BRACK (*softly*). I said he must have stolen it.

HEDDA. Why do you think that?

BRACK. Because any other explanation is unthinkable, Mrs. Hedda, or ought to be.

HEDDA. I see.

BRACK (*looks at her for a moment*). Eilert Loevborg was here this morning. Wasn't he?

HEDDA. Yes.

BRACK. Were you alone with him?

HEDDA. For a few moments.

BRACK. You didn't leave the room while he was here?

HEDDA. No.

BRACK. Think again. Are you sure you didn't go out for a moment?

HEDDA. Oh—yes, I might have gone into the hall. Just for a few seconds.

BRACK. And where was your pistol-case during this time?

HEDDA. I'd locked it in that—

BRACK. Er—Mrs. Hedda?

HEDDA. It was lying over there on my writing table.

BRACK. Have you looked to see if both the pistols are still there?

HEDDA. No.

BRACK. You needn't bother. I saw the pistol Loevborg had when they found him. I recognised it at once. From yesterday. And other occasions.

HEDDA. Have you got it?

BRACK. No. The police have it.

HEDDA. What will the police do with this pistol?

BRACK. Try to trace the owner.

HEDDA. Do you think they'll succeed?

BRACK (*leans down and whispers*). No, Hedda Gabler. Not as long as I hold my tongue.

HEDDA (*looks nervously at him*). And if you don't?

BRACK (*shrugs his shoulders*). You could always say he'd stolen it.

HEDDA. I'd rather die!

BRACK (*smiles*). People say that. They never do it.

HEDDA (*not replying*). And suppose the pistol wasn't stolen? And they trace the owner? What then?

BRACK. There'll be a scandal, Hedda.

HEDDA. A scandal!

BRACK. Yes, a scandal. The thing you're so frightened of. You'll have to appear in court. Together with Mademoiselle Danielle. She'll have to explain how it all happened. Was it an accident, or was it—homicide? Was he about to take the pistol from his pocket to threaten her? And did it go off? Or did she snatch the pistol from his hand, shoot him and then put it back in his pocket? She might quite easily have done it. She's a resourceful lady, is Mademoiselle Danielle.

HEDDA. But I had nothing to do with this repulsive business.

BRACK. No. But you'll have to answer one question. Why did you give Eilert Loevborg this pistol? And what conclusions will people draw when it is proved you did give it to him?

HEDDA (*bows her head*). That's true. I hadn't thought of that.

BRACK. Well, luckily there's no danger as long as I hold my tongue.

HEDDA (*looks up at him*). In other words, I'm in your power, Judge. From now on, you've got your hold over me.

BRACK (*whispers, more slowly*). Hedda, my dearest—believe me—I will not abuse my position.

HEDDA. Nevertheless, I'm in your power. Dependent on your will, and your demands. Not free. Still not free! [*Rises passionately.*] No. I couldn't bear that. No.

BRACK (*looks half-derisively at her*). Most people resign themselves to the inevitable, sooner or later.

HEDDA (*returns his gaze*). Possibly they do. [*She goes across to the writing table, represses an involuntary smile and says in* TESMAN'S *voice.*] Well, George. Think you'll be able to manage? What?

TESMAN. Heaven knows, dear. This is going to take months and months.

HEDDA (*in the same tone as before*). Fancy that, by Jove! [*Runs her hands gently through* MRS. ELVSTED'S *hair.*] Doesn't it feel strange, Thea? Here you are working away with Tesman just the way you used to work with Eilert Loevborg.

MRS. ELVSTED. Oh—if only I can inspire your husband too!

HEDDA. Oh, it'll come. In time.

TESMAN. Yes—do you know, Hedda, I really think I'm beginning to feel a bit—well—that way. But you go back and talk to Judge Brack.

HEDDA. Can't I be of use to you two in any way?

TESMAN. No, none at all. [*Turns his head.*] You'll have to keep Hedda company from now on, Judge, and see she doesn't get bored. If you don't mind.

BRACK (*glances at* HEDDA). It'll be a pleasure.

HEDDA. Thank you. But I'm tired this evening. I think I'll lie down on the sofa in there for a little while.

TESMAN. Yes, dear—do. What?

[HEDDA *goes into the rear room and draws the curtains behind her. Short pause. Suddenly she begins to play a frenzied dance melody on the piano.*]

MRS. ELVSTED (*starts up from her chair*). Oh, what's that?

TESMAN (*runs to the doorway*). Hedda dear, please! Don't play dance music tonight! Think of Auntie Rena. And Eilert.

HEDDA (*puts her head out through the curtains*). And Auntie

Juju. And all the rest of them. From now on I'll be quiet. [*Closes the curtains behind her.*]

TESMAN (*at the writing table*). It distresses her to watch us doing this. I say, Mrs. Elvsted, I've an idea. Why don't you move in with Auntie Juju? I'll run over each evening, and we can sit and work there. What?

MRS. ELVSTED. Yes, that might be the best plan.

HEDDA (*from the rear room*). I can her what you're saying, Tesman. But how shall I spend the evenings out here?

TESMAN (*looking through his papers*). Oh, I'm sure Judge Brack'll be kind enough to come over and keep you company. You won't mind my not being here, Judge?

BRACK (*in the armchair, calls gaily*). I'll be delighted, Mrs. Tesman. I'll be here every evening. We'll have great fun together, you and I.

HEDDA (*loud and clear*). Yes, that'll suit you, won't it, Judge? The only cock on the dunghill—!

[*A shot is heard from the rear room.* TESMAN, MRS. ELVSTED *and* JUDGE BRACK *start from their chairs.*]

TESMAN. Oh, she's playing with those pistols again.

[*He pulls the curtains aside and runs in.* MRS. ELVSTED *follows him.* HEDDA *is lying dead on the sofa. Confusion and shouting.* BERTHA *enters in alarm from the right.*]

TESMAN (*screams to* BRACK). She's shot herself! Shot herself in the head! By Jove! Fancy that!

BRACK (*half paralysed in the armchair*). But, good God! People don't do such things!

CURTAIN

INDEX OF ILLUSTRATIONS

Ibsen did not invent but certainly developed the method of describing the stage and the movement of actors about it used by careful dramatists since, when they prepare their text for readers. Clearly, as he wrote, Ibsen visualized stage setting and actors moving about it and tried hard to convey that vision to his readers. Readers, however, usually have to train themselves with serious effort to recreate Ibsen's vision in their imaginations. Illustrations such as those located here will help them do it. Reference to them will enrich the reading of the play and provide the closest possible equivalent to performance.

Illustrations in books are listed first, followed by those in yearbooks and encyclopedias, and those in periodicals. When illustrations are grouped without page number in a source, a letter is alphabetically assigned following a hyphen and the last numbered page, as opp. 86-D means the fourth picture-page after page 86.

ABBREVIATIONS:

ed(s). — editor(s), edition
front. — frontispiece
n.d. — no date
no. — number
n.s. — new series
opp. — facing
rev. — revised
supp. — supplement
— plate number

GHOSTS
(Gengangere)

Altman, George, *et al.*, *Theater Pictorial*, #296.
Bablet, Denis, *Esthétique générale du decor du Théâtre de 1870 à 1914*, #58.
Biedrzynski, Richard, *Schauspieler; Regisseure; Intendanten*, #46.
Binns, Archie, *Mrs. Fiske and the American Theatre*, opp. 278–AC.
Block, Haskell M., and Shedd, Robert G., eds., *Masters of the Modern Drama*, front.–B.
Blum, Daniel, *Great Stars of the American Stage*, #54.
———, *A Pictorial History of the American Theatre, 1900–1950;* ———, *1900–1956*, 27, 178, 220.
———, *A Pictorial History of the American Theatre, 100 Years, 1860–1960*, 5.
———, *A Pictorial History of the Silent Screen*, 88.
Borelius, Hilma, *Die nordische literaturen*, 114.
Cinquanta Anni di teatro in Italia, #18.
Corson, Richard, *Stage Makeup*, 77.

Bühne und Welt, I(March 15, 1899), 553; III(March 1, 1901), 447; IV(Nov. 1, 1901), 118; VII(Aug. 1, 1905), opp. 884; XI(April 15, 1909), 598.

Drama, n.s., no. 52(Spring 1959), 24.

Drama Magazine (Chicago), XVI(March 1926), 221; XXI(May 1931), 27.

The Graphic, XCV(June 30, 1917), 804.

The Illustrated London News, CXC(Nov. 20, 1937), 906; CCXXXIII(Nov. 29, 1958), 958; CCXLVI(April 24, 1965), 26.

Illustrirte Zeitung, CXXVIII(June 20, 1907), 1086.

Piccola Illustrazione Italiana (Jan. 1948), 6.

Play Pictorial, LXVII(Oct. 1935), 22; LXXII(Feb. 1938), 15.

Plays and Players, VI(Dec. 1958), 18, 19 (Jan. 1959), 5.

Stage, XIII(Jan. 1936), 4 (Feb. 1936), 28, 47.

Teatr (Russ. translit.), no vol. no. (Sept. 1954), 95, 97, 99; Aug. 1956, opp. 73; Dec. 1957, 128, 129.

Theatre Arts, XIX(Sept. 1935), 653; XX(Feb. 1936), 117 (July 1936), 528 (Dec. 1936), 952; XXII(Jan. 1938), 26; XXX(July 1946), 413; XXXVIII(Oct. 1954), 63; XLII(Aug. 1958), 51.

Theatre Guild Magazine, VII(Jan. 1930), 18.

Theatre Magazine, III(April 1903), 100; VI(Sept. 1906), 239; XXV(June 1917), 340; XXXI(May 1920), 419; XXXVII(June 1923), 21; XL(June 1924), 19.

Theatre World, LV(Jan. 1959), 24, 25 (April 1959), 6.

World Theatre, III–4(Autumn 1954), 75; V–2(Spring 1956), 141; VI–1(Spring 1957), 16; XII–4(Winter 1963–1964), 334.

AN ENEMY OF THE PEOPLE
(En Folkefiende)

Blum, Daniel, *Great Stars of the American Stage,* #61.

———, *A Pictorial History of the American Theatre,* 185, 284.

d'Amico, Silvio, *Storia del teatro drammatico*, III, 270.

Durham, Willard Higley, and Dodds, John W., eds., *British and American Plays*, opp. 100.

Koht, Halvdan, *The Life of Ibsen*, tr. McMahon and Larsen, II, 172.

Lambourne, Norah, *Staging the Play*, 49.

Mander, Raymond, and Mitchenson, Joe, *A Pictorial History of the British Theatre*, #437.

Mather, Charles C., and others, *Behind the Footlights*, 47.

McCleery, Albert, and Glick, Carl, *Curtains Going Up*, opp. 148–G.

Moscow Art Theatre, Illustrations and Documents (Russian translated title), 98.

Moscow Art Theatre, 1898–1917 (Russian translated title), 74, 75.

Pitoeff, Aniouta, *Ludmilla, ma mère*, 240.

Williamson, Audrey, *Old Vic Drama*, #40.

Daniel Blum's Theatre World, VII(1950–1951), 63; XV (1958–1959), 159.

Enciclopedia dello Spettacolo, VI, #63.

"*The Stage*" *Year Book*, 1910, opp. 60–B; 1914, opp. 42–B.

Bühne und Welt, III(Feb. 1901), 405; IV(Nov. 1901), 116; (July 1902), 825.

Drama, n.s., no. 37(Summer 1955), 49.

Illustrirte Zeitung, CXCV(Nov. 28, 1940), 456.

Play Pictorial, LXXIII(Mar. 1939), 2.

Theatre Arts, XI(Dec. 1927), 884, 891, 892; XVIII(July 1934), 524; XXXV(Mar. 1951), 15, 25; XXXVI(Jan. 1952), 16; XL(Oct. 1956), 20; XLIII(July 1959), 19; XLIV(Aug. 1960), 19.

Theatre Magazine, XXXVI(Sept. 1922), 141; XLVI(Dec. 1927), 84.

HEDDA GABLER

Rinehart Editions